The Woman in Green Was the First.

Her picture was behind the bar: an oil painting of a lady in green. Now she was a lanky crumple on the scuffed oak floor. There was yellow chalk outlining her body and a dime-size blot of red at her throat. Her slim dead legs were encased in the kind of hosiery women used to wear, with garters and seams running up the backs.

On the bar there was an ashtray with Chesterfield butts in it, next to Celia's patent-leather pocketbook. And also her saucer and cup, which was maybe a quarter-way full of milk streaked with Scotch. A forensic cop was dusting things with fingerprint powder for whatever good it could do. Logue, from Central Homicide, went straight to it: "The proprietor says you, Hockaday, were one of the last persons besides the killer who talked to the deceased. . . . "

THOMAS ADCOCK

POCKET BOOKS

New York   London   Toronto   Sydney   Tokyo   Singapore

This book is a work of fiction. Names, characters, places and
incidents are either products of the author's imagination or are
used fictitiously. Any resemblance to actual events or locales or
persons, living or dead, is entirely coincidental.

An *Original* Publication of POCKET BOOKS

POCKET BOOKS, a division of Simon & Schuster Inc.
1230 Avenue of the Americas, New York, NY 10020

ISBN 978-1-4516-4681-8

This Pocket Books paperback printing May 2004

10 9 8 7 6 5 4 3 2

POCKET and colophon are registered trademarks of
Simon & Schuster Inc.

Cover design and art by Tom McKevney

Printed in the U.S.A.

For my brother, Dale

It is of no use to criticize humanity. Like all creations, it survives its critics. The only interesting thing is to try to understand it or, at least, appreciate. Perhaps Coney Island is the most human thing that God ever made, or permitted the Devil to make.

—Richard LeGallienne,
1905

DARK MAZE

PROLOGUE

Wide gateways that once were filled by wooden chutes and screams of dumb fear, now sealed with cement and cinder block; ten stout floors in all, windows shuttered over in tin; and the big terra-cotta busts of ring-muzzled hogs and lambs and steers set high along the old, red-brick walls. And all of it coated gray from the perpetual swirl of exhaust grime that comes from the Lincoln Tunnel traffic.

There was a steel trash bin set against the limestone base of the rear wall. I pushed past it to find the opening, a small triangular gap punched between two sections of crumbled brick. I bent, flashed light inside, and startled a rat. Then I hunched my shoulders and exhaled, and squeezed my way into the black insides.

I stood in heavy darkness and waited for my eyes to adjust, and my ears.

Now came fading echoes. And furtive scratchings from interior walls alive with vermin. I drew out my big piece, the .44 Charter Arms Bulldog in my shoulder holster. This I held in my right hand. With my left, I swept my surroundings with the flashlight beam.

I had entered a wide corridor beneath an iron staircase. Down the corridor and beyond the stairs was a line of tall hollow spaces, each the size of a large door. A bank of elevators must have been there years ago.

I directed the flashlight beam up along the staircase rails and disturbed a nest of bats clinging upside-down to an asbestos-covered pipe. The animals dropped through the dank air in frenzied loops. I covered my head and moved forward, and headed up the stairs.

Near the top of the first flight, a rusted step gave way. My leg sank into a hole and pain filled my knee. From that point on, I tested each riser before putting down my full weight. And I walked along the edges of the steps, close against the wall, the way a good burglar will quietly stalk through an unfamiliar room.

At the fourth floor, there was the strong odor of cats—male cats who had sprayed urine to mark their territories. Anybody living in this place was sure to have cats about to control rodents.

I went up one more floor where the cat odor was strongest. Then I moved toward the north side of the building, through a hallway where there once might have been offices full of people with work to do. Emptiness and stillness now, with all the doors gone but one.

The single remaining door was closed. On it was written:

HOME IS WHERE
THE HATRED IS

I knocked. There was no answer. I kicked the door, and it fell open stiffly.

At least a dozen cats were in the big room beyond the

door—backs arched, yellow-green eyes wide, fangs bared, throats hissing and growling.

Then, something cold and hard poked at my neck.

And a ragged whisper: "Hang onto your rosary beads and say good-bye!"

ONE

"**C**op, ain't you?"

There was a funny edge to his voice. Funny as in tragic. Out of politeness I ignored this first impression and told myself, here is just some guy in the park curious to know if he has me rightly pegged.

He was short and moonfaced, somewhere past sixty years and too heavy by about twenty pounds. His eyes were brown and magnified by thick spectacles in round, wire frames. His pale pink face was arranged in a careful blank, his chin napped with a goatee that was a mix of red and gray. He wore a shapeless pair of twill pants, worn-out suede shoes, a thrift-shop sport coat over a faded denim shirt, and a navy woolen beret on top of what I guessed was a bald head.

He perspired despite the cool April air. Two thin lines of sweat trickled down from someplace up under his beret, down over the front of his ears and then forward along the edges of his jaw until droplets vanished in his whiskers.

Fifteen minutes ago, when I walked into the park with my *Times* and a buttered roll and coffee from the deli, I had casually noticed this guy and how it was just the two of us there in the little park in the middle of a weekday morning. I had my own concerns. He certainly had his.

I had sat down on one of the only two functional benches left in the park. This was the bench in the sun. He was already settled on the other one, across a walkway filled with broken brick and glass, in the faint shade of city trees sprouting new leaves. I noted that he had one of those supermarket tabloids spread open across his knees.

A couple of times when I turned a page or took a sip of coffee, I happened to glance over his way. And I had caught him looking at me instead of at the paper in his lap.

And now, here he was on his feet in front of me, close enough so I could hear his raspy breathing. Here he was, curious in a funny way. As in not funny, actually.

I looked at my wristwatch: half-past ten. I also looked at the block-letter streamer on the cover of his tabloid: STATUE OF ELVIS FOUND ON MARS. And I told myself, All right, so here is this neighborhood geezer who has innocently come outdoors for the nice fresh air; so what of it?

Finally I answered him with a question of my own: "How do you know I'm a cop?"

He turned to somebody standing beside him. Only there was nobody there, of course. "This one, he says, *'How'd y'know?'* Can you beat it?" he said to Nobody.

Then to me he said, "Friendly, if you want, I can take you to the beach and if there's a cop there I can pick him out, easy's pie. Even if he was wearing one of them bathing suits with little sailboats on the bum, I could make him as a cop from everybody else laying around in the sand half bare-assed. How is this? Because of the fact that I have a very great power of observation is how, okay?"

"Okay."

He smiled. "Haw! If you could just get a load of your own puss right now, you'd see cop written all over it, same as I see."

"How so?"

"Well, for one thing, you'd see yourself looking me over like some high-flying buzzard looks for blood down on the snow. The way you're looking at me now, you got to be either a dopey little kid or a cop. And it's kind of hard for me to figure you were ever cute enough to have been a little kid."

"I see . . ."

"There's another thing that tells me you're a cop. You're listening close. A cop, he'll listen to anybody no matter if he's nothing but a slobbering drunk or a strung-out junkie or a Jesus-jumping loon."

"We're supposed to listen."

"I ain't saying you're not. I am only saying this is what I have observed, okay?"

"Okay."

"Also I observed by your hands how you're a cop."

"My hands?"

"Don't take this wrong, friendly, but even somebody who does not have my power of observation can see that you're a guy who is the lunch-bucket type. But, you have got no callouses on your hands, which from experience says to me you're a cop, since cops are guys who gravitate into the department because they are mainly lunch-bucket types such as yourself who don't want to actually do any manual labor on the job. Now, ain't that right?"

"Maybe," I said. Too true, I thought. I said, "So it's nothing for you to make any cop in town?"

"It's relatively pretty much of a snap, yeah. Except for your lady cops. They're trickier since they're females. But give me the time and I can mostly make them, too."

"I see . . ."

"Of course you do. Like I said, I got a great power. Besides which, I have been watching you in case you didn't know . . ."

Watching me? "No, I didn't know that."

"So now you know." He shrugged. "Anyhow, I made you for a cop from day one. And you are now telling me how right I was. Ain't that right?"

He did not wait for my answer. Instead, he turned to Nobody next to him, and said, "Damn straight I'm right."

Then he folded the tabloid that dangled from his hand. He stuffed the paper into the side pocket of this thrift-shop jacket, which was a cream-colored linen number that might have been good in its day. He fished out a lacquer-paper packet of skinny cheroots from the other pocket and put one of them between his lips and offered me one, too. We lit up, then we both turned our heads to watch the Tenth Avenue traffic roll along uptown. Neither of us said a word for about a minute. He had his thoughts, I had mine.

In a city unsubtle in all other moods, this geezer here talking to me and to Nobody was one of the true heralds of spring in New York. In most other places during the month of April, you can suddenly see lots of ladies in housedresses hanging out laundry in the sweet new winds, and robins digging up fat worms from wet grass and fragrant mud. In New York, you can be certain that winter has died when you see girls in schoolyards jumping rope double Dutch; when you see how every third guy in a business suit is wearing a yellow necktie; when clusters of people with apprehension in their fair-skinned faces are walking around midtown Manhattan with street maps growing out of their back pockets; and when neighborhood parks see the return of old coots who sit in wait of someone to talk to after the long and lonesome winter indoors. It is spring when they will tell strangers—even cop strangers—the disquieting stories of their lives, and what they have spent the winter thinking about. . . .

* * *

8

"So I was wondering, by the by," he said, exhaling pungent blue smoke, "if you dress like that all the time or else if this here's your day off, or what?"

"You might say both."

I was wearing chinos with holes in the knees and about ten years' worth of paint stains, a green tee-shirt from a Hoboken exterminating company that had a picture of a dead cockroach on the chest, a poplin jacket without much collar or cuffs left to it, a Yankees baseball cap, and black high-top P-F Flyer sneakers I have owned since about the last of the Miss Rheingolds.

"Oh, I get it," he said. "You're plainclothes. Like maybe an undercover detective, hey? I like detective stories. Maybe I seen something about you in the newspapers?"

I said, "Not in that paper in your jacket pocket."

He poked an elbow into Nobody's ribs and said to him, "Here we have an officer with a sense of humor, hey? I like that in a cop. When cops can crack a smile, the city's less jumpy. Ain't I right? Damn straight I am."

Then to me, "Well, I read all types of papers, friendly. All the way from your *New York Times* down to this bugle in my pocket, which I can tell you is very often no weirder than stories they put in your polite press. This is on account of the fact that I have observed how everybody is pretty much equally depraved nowadays."

He stuck out a soft pink hand and added, with a neighborly sort of smile, "Well, anyhow, I am pleased to finally meet up with you."

We shook and he said, "I bet you don't know who I am."

I said he would win that wager.

"Well, don't worry, it ain't your fault you don't know me," he said. "I ain't made much of a mark in this life."

He finished his cheroot and tossed the butt down into the walkway where it would eventually burn out. I thought about telling him how it has been my observation that a lot of people in the world wind up tossed to the ground as casually as he had just dropped his cheroot. But I kept my own thoughts quiet in order to concentrate on his, which he had already observed is the obvious nature of a cop like me.

He sat down next to me on the bench and took a handkerchief from his coat pocket and, slipping off his beret, mopped sweat off a full head of skin. *I knew he was bald!* He asked, "Care to know my name?"

I shrugged an assent.

"Everybody who knows me, or thinks he knows me, calls me Picasso. Care to know how come?"

I naturally answered, "Because you're a painter?"

Which was exactly what he had anticipated my saying, and which was why he sneered at me right as the words slid stupidly from my mouth. After which he turned to Nobody, who had presumably joined us on the bench, and said, "This one, he says, *'Because you're a painter?'* Can you beat it?"

He put his beret back on his head and pocketed the dampened handkerchief. Then he lit up another one of his skinny cheroots, but did not offer me one this time. He sat puffing silently, and gazing out toward the avenue. Then he said, "Come on over with me, you'll see something about me and the art world."

I followed him up from the bench, leaving behind my *Times* and my half-eaten roll and most of my coffee. We walked to the bus stop sign on the avenue. He pointed to the other side and said, "See over there across the way in the bodega window where it says 'special today, pork two-nineteen a pound' and there's a picture of a big fat pig that looks scared out of his gourd?"

I saw it, I said.

"Well you're looking at a genuine Picasso. I bet you never knew that Picasso dabbled in the medium of calcimine paint, hey?" He laughed hard at this. It was one of the sorriest, nastiest laughs I had ever heard.

"I paint up the Puerto Rican's windows over there

regular," he explained, "in return for which instead of putting out actual money he keeps me in these good smokes and wine that ain't good at all, and sandwiches. And this is mainly how I now have the artistic thrill of being a painter these days.

"You know, I wish you would cross over there to the bodega sometime before next week's special—so you can see up close how I captured the essential terror of the doomed pig. Like I said, I am a great one for studying the essence of things. You know, like I have been studying you all these months—"

Traffic noise interrupted. Picasso stopped talking and stared at the bodega window through the passing cars and trucks and vans and taxicabs. A Mercury convertible with Jersey plates and front and back seats full of raucous teenage girls out cutting classes waved at the ill-clad guys standing around a bus stop, which is one of the main activities of teenage motorists from Jersey.

I looked at Picasso looking at his rendering of the doomed pig and I said to myself, You can let all this wormy stuff go; you have all sorts of other things to do; it is the first day of your well-earned furlough; you recently made the acquaintance of one Ruby Flagg, and she is very gorgeous, and it is the spring of the year.

Instead, as if I cannot get enough of this sort of thing, I waited for the traffic to break and asked him some more about himself: "What do you do for actual money?"

"As little as possible since I am saving myself for my art!" He laughed another one of his malignant laughs. "Lucky for me, though, I am a resourceful old bastard and get by."

"How?"

"Sometimes I will return bottles and cans for deposit. Sometimes passing out palm cards for this topless joint over on Seventh Avenue, the Horny Poodle. Sometimes this and sometimes that. You know how it goes in this fine service economy of ours."

"Do you live around here?"

He waved an arm, taking in a large part of the neighborhood. "Around here, around there. You know."

"What about medical?"

He sneered again and said, "By that, your meaning is what? I'm ready for the drooling academy? People call me Picasso and so you go figuring that I need my head shrunk, is that it?"

"What I mean is . . ."

"Aw, save it! Let me tell you this: you're sent to the puzzle house nowadays on account of one basic reason, which is you went and did something so bad that it ain't acceptably nuts, it's barking nuts—if you see the difference. Then one day . . ."

He stopped and took in a deep, rasping breath. Then he went on. "One day, they just suddenly put you out and wish you all the best. That's all they know how to do once they finally admit they ain't got the answers, only questions. The streets are full of us. You think maybe I'm wrong?"

"I think you're right," I said. When another clump of noisy traffic had passed, I asked, "How come you've been shadowing me? And how come you want to tell me all this that you're telling me?"

He said to Nobody, "Now he wants to know *'how come?'!* This one's maybe the last bleeding heart left in a bloody old heartless city, hey? Can you beat it?"

He looked down the avenue. The M-11 bus was idling down at the light over Forty-second Street. It would be up at the park stop in a few minutes. He dug around in his pants pockets for coins.

Then he turned to me and calmly inquired, "You know from extenuating circumstances, am I right?"

I said he was.

"Of course you do. You're a cop. So maybe I wanted somebody to know about me and my 'extenuating circumstances.' Which even a nutso has got. And I am a genuine regulation nutso since I have been checking in and out of Bellevue since somewheres during Ike's second term, okay?"

"Okay."

"But Bellevue, see, it's no use to me. The doctors are right guys and all, but they're still only ignorant doctors who can only see maybe two sides to a story. Real stories with real people in them have got lots more than two sides, you ever notice?"

"I have noticed that real stories are full of extenuating circumstances," I said.

He smiled and said, "Yah" because my remark pleased him. For a change, the smile was pleasant. And then he became hurried and counted out coins in his hand, enough for bus fare. The M-11 was now a block away.

"So since you're interested," he said, "I will tell you that once-upon-a-time I was another kind of regulation guy, with a wife and a kid. But as a husband and a papa, I was a lousy flop. The family wasn't so much better. The wife, she went rotten; the kid went Christian.

"Oh, but hell, family life and all that apple pie, it ain't my game. When I figured this out, I took off to New York. Which is where us odd socks belong. In a manner of speaking, I ran away to join the circus."

He laughed at this. One of his joyless barks it was. "Yah, that's rich!" he said. "The circus!"

"Did you ever get to paint what you wanted to paint? I mean, did you ever paint seriously?"

He said to Nobody, "Ho, ho, did I paint or did I paint? Was I serious or was I serious? And, *how come* did I paint what I painted?"

To me, he said, *"Serious* paintings? Them I got loads of hanging around town. Here and there, like me; not so anybody should notice, also like me. Which is how come it's such a big goddamn joke they call me Picasso, hey?"

He added, "Matter of fact, friendly, guess where I got one painting hanging as we speak?"

13

"Where?"

"In a bar where you yourself hang out regular . . ."

The bus groaned to a stop in front of us, killing my last chance to ask Picasso exactly how long he had been watching me. And exactly why.

Picasso stepped aboard.

Then—just before the pleated doors closed behind him, before he walked to the rear of the bus and sat down, and laughed and laughed at me through the broad back window as I stood there on Tenth Avenue staring at him like a dopey cop—he said:

"Yah—and since you're interested—maybe you want to know that I am very sick to death of all the *how comes* of my busted-up life. Which is how come I am working a plan, a plan to kill what's been responsible for making me fall so far and spectacular as you seen I have fell . . ."

TWO

In the city that I sometimes love and sometimes hate, I have been assaulted many scores of times by fists, bottles, sticks, metal pipes and miscellaneous blunt objects. I have also been spat on, stoned and shot at (by bullets in all such cases, save for the time I chased through Central Park in unsuccessful pursuit of a perpetrator with a bow and quiver of arrows). And then, of course, there are the unsolicited homicidal sentiments from the likes of "Picasso."

Such events come with the territory of Manhattan, whether or not you are a cop. Which, of course, I am.

I am Detective Neil Hockaday and I carry the gold shield of the New York Police Department, which has assigned me to a special squad known as the SCUM Patrol, which very fittingly stands for Street Crimes Unit, Manhattan.

To most, I am just plain Hock. And mostly I am out doing my job in the streets every day, dressed like a plain ordinary vagrant so that you would not likely have reason or desire to look my way.

But if you did, you might reasonably believe that you see in me a man sadder but wiser for all the times he has dealt with life's ruder angels. At least that is how I see myself; at least, I try to keep in mind the only clear fact of life in the kind of place I live: New York, where everybody mutinies and nobody deserts.

The clear fact is that my city is an incubator for crazies. Every day of every year there are maybe a thousand budding crazies who hit town. All of them are dead sure they have found the Emerald City, and that very soon they will swing on stars. One or two of them will be right, or lucky. And by such crazy odds, we know that New York is not Kansas.

I know, I know.

And I know the others—the ones who discover that travel is not necessarily broadening, and that New York offers few tender embraces for its immigrants.

Some of these will return home to make of that what they can. Some settle into lives in New York that are remarkably similar to life in Kansas.

Some get mean. Their lives grow as rough and cracked as plowed cement. Then finally they become the dark, unseen essence of the Emerald City—falling men finding their shelter in crazy shadows—and the bailiwick of the SCUM Patrol.

There is precious little we can do to protect ourselves against the perils of falling men. Is that not so?

And all I am is one mere cop, born into the world where I live and work. Like all others here, I am sometimes persuaded that life in New York is a constant struggle to die of natural causes.

So there stood I on that April day, staring dumbly at the wire-frame spectacles and the red-gray goatee and the bouncing beret in the back window of a disappearing bus. I told myself, Okay, so remember this, pal: you're at liberty, you're not obliged to get involved. Besides which, nothing happened.

Is that not so?

DARK MAZE

Now I no longer wished to think. Tomorrow would be soon enough for that. Now I wanted a drink.

I had never studied it before, though it had been there all this time. Odd how I had scarcely even noticed the thing. Well, but maybe this was because it was so unassuming and predictable in a pub. But now with Picasso so inescapably on my mind, I studied what could only be his work. High on the wall behind the brass-railed mahogany bar at the front of Angelo's Ebb Tide, there it had hung for so long: an oil painting of the owner himself, Angelo Cifelli, and a lone customer perched on a stool.

The customer in the painting is a lady in a smart green dress. There is a coffee cup in a saucer, set down in front of her. She is wearing a hat, which is something women used to do. Her legs are interestingly crossed and she is talking to the barman's wide round back. Which belongs to Angelo, in his black silk vest and his white shirt rolled at the sleeves and his fringe of black hair and the unmistakable profile of his great Roman nose. He is bent to the task of rinsing glasses in a sink full of hot water.

Now, as I stepped into the Ebb Tide, muzzy from my recent unsettling encounter in the park, I studied not only the painting overhead but the almost identical real-life scene.

A lady in a dark green dress drank coffee and chatted at Angelo as he rinsed glasses. She wore a hat with a feather. Sunlight floated in through Venetian blinds and shone kindly on her face. From where I stood at the door, she looked nearly young and beautiful and high-spirited; she seemed to be telling Angelo a story from a time when she was young and beautiful and high-spirited.

She would have continued, but when Angelo spotted me he gave me a very big and noisy hello. The lady stopped talking, turned my way, and smiled.

I sat down on a stool a few over from hers. I inspected her, of course—she and her twin in the painting. I had come to the Ebb Tide all decided on having only a Molson ale since it was not quite noon. But now that things were even more off-balance than they were before I arrived, I told Angelo with some embarrassment in my voice that I would like my regular. Which is a shot of Johnnie Walker red, followed by the Molson.

"Don't worry about it," Angelo said. "You've had earlier starts at it than this." He set me up and then, by way of friendly bartenderish introductions, he said to his only two customers, "Hock, Celia. Celia, Hock."

I started by telling Celia that I was sorry for interrupting her story. Angelo told her quickly, "You ought to know that Hock here is a cop, but he's all right."

Celia did not say anything. The little feather on the side of her hat began shaking happily, then she tipped her head back aways and laughed. Her voice was scratchy from whiskey and cigarettes and at close range the light on her face no longer flattered. I noticed a fresh packet of Chesterfields tucked inside her pocketbook, which was unclasped and lying on the bar next to her cup and saucer. Also I noticed it was not coffee in the cup, it was milk.

She said to Angelo, "Oh, don't worry, baby. You know I've been out of circulation about a hundred years, way past the statute of limitations anyway." Then she turned my way and said, "Look here, Officer Hock, I only dropped by to see my longtime pal Angelo. And so here we are just talking over the old days when I made a good dishonest living, and how what's happened to me since is a crime."

I smiled and said nothing.

She crossed her legs and smiled back and it was an easy thing to see how she had once been young and beautiful. She picked open her Chesterfields and Angelo lit her. She smoked while her hazel eyes combed through me. Her green dress was made out of something smooth and yielding, and so was her hat with the delicate feather. The ensemble did a fine job of softening Celia's hardening edges.

I asked if I could buy her another cup of milk.

She declined. Then by way of enlightening me, she said tonelessly, "Ulcers. About five o'clock, though, I usually pep it up with Scotch. As I have told my doctor, ulcers is a daytime sickness."

"Does the doctor buy that?"

"He says to me, 'Celia, if that's the way you feel, then why not forget the milk altogether and just drink your booze from morning to night and blow up your guts and be done with it?' "

Angelo said, "Maybe under certain circumstances that's good medical advice. I mean, waiting around for some merciful god to do it to you natural is unfair as hell."

He returned to his glasses. I asked Celia, "You mentioned something about a crime?"

"Oh, you want to hear about that, really?"

"Sure," I said. And I heard a funny echo from someplace. . . . *"A cop, he'll listen to anybody."*

Celia said, "One rainy day there's this little man at my door. He's wearing cheap corduroy and he's carrying a portable adding machine and says he's from the IRS. I ring up my lawyer. For all the money he's making off me, my lawyer says I have no choice about seeing the little man— who doesn't *look* so scary, but who it turns out is a guy who eats his young."

"Well," I said, "it's their nature."

"You're telling me!" There was a sad catch in Celia's voice. She turned from me and looked straight ahead at the mirror on the other side of the bar.

I asked Angelo for another red and ale. He brought this, and also set down a fresh cup of milk for Celia and took away what had been there. Celia only ignored him. She stubbed out her Chesterfield, lit up another, and continued to stare at her reflected image.

And then I looked at her face in the mirror, too. And saw the tears and how her makeup was melting down her cheeks, how her face began to resemble a cake caught outdoors in the rain.

Celia searched through her pocketbook, found a cosmetics case and became intensely busy with it. Nobody said anything. The only noise now was Angelo clinking his glasses and, way back in the rear dining room, waiters setting up tables.

And then the Ebb Tide started filling with the first wave of the luncheon trade. Some neighborhood sorts passed through the bar on their way to the dining room—the guy who runs my delicatessen, along with somebody who was not his wife; my dry cleaner; a couple of the barbers from the shop across the way called Three Aces.

I looked up at Picasso's painting again, remembering how I wanted to ask about it. But Angelo was now occupied with some customers down at the far end of the bar and Celia was daubing at her eyes, so I got off my barstool and walked over to Angelo and said, "I'll be back later."

"Okay," Angelo said. "Only do yourself a favor and come after seven, you know? We get the bad crowd from five until about then."

"What bad crowd?"

"The type who during the day market software and leverage buyouts and who want to be twelve-year-olds at night."

So I told Angelo I would skip happy hour. And I said to the feather in Celia's hat, "Maybe I'll see you around again, and I'm sorry for your troubles. . . ."

"Yeah, later," she said. But she did not look up.

On my walk home from the Ebb Tide, I did a couple of errands. I picked up shirts from my Chinese laundry, because there are some occasions in my life when I wear something with starch and a necktie. I also picked up a fresh copy of the *Times* since I left one back in the park. And I also wrote out a check to my liquor store for some Perrier-Jouët in the flowered bottle since I do not carry around a lot of cash in neighborhoods like mine and since I wanted something nice on ice, in hopes of my dinner date that evening with Ruby Flagg extending on to dessert and so forth at my place.

When I got home, I listened to jazz on WBGO-FM while I did some things around the place to see if it might make a difference in appearance, which mostly it did not. I ate a sandwich. This and the housework made me drowsy and so I stretched out on the couch under the parlor window and fell asleep with a dustrag in my hand.

For quite a while, I was gone. I woke once to use the toilet and then I dozed some more on the couch, convinced that my energies would be more productively spent on beauty sleep than in any further efforts to tidy up my poor old apartment.

Then somewhere around five o'clock, when the twelve-year-olds would be flocking into the Ebb Tide, there was a lot of noise outside from all the Jersey-bound motorists honking themselves silly on their way to the Lincoln Tunnel.

Then the telephone call, and Angelo's summons.

That was about half-past five.

I ran all the way to the Ebb Tide, six blocks from my place on West Forty-third Street and Tenth Avenue (as in *Slaughter on . . .*).

THREE

When I saw Celia lying there with a bullet in her neck, I was sadly unsurprised. And from the expression on her face, I would guess that Celia felt about the same the last time she felt anything.

She was a lanky crumple of green against the scuffed oak floor. There was yellow chalk outlining her body and a dime-size blot of red at her throat. Her slim dead legs were encased in the kind of hosiery women used to wear, with garters, and seams running up the backs.

On the bar there was an ashtray with Chesterfield butts in it, next to Celia's patent-leather pocketbook. And also her saucer and cup, which was maybe a quarter-way full of milk streaked with Scotch. A forensic cop was dusting things with fingerprint powder for whatever good it could do.

The twelve-year-olds had been herded back into the dining room. From the way some of them were sprawled in the banquettes, they had either fainted or thought murder was the floor show. The others were squawking as to how this would ruin all their plans for the evening. Nevertheless, nobody was leaving for the time being and that included even the ones with their wristwatch alarms going off.

Over near the phone booth in front was a bulky redheaded detective of my slight acquaintance—Logue, from Central Homicide. I could not think of his first name, nor he mine as it turned out. He wore a square, brown suit and a brown tie and he held a pad of yellow paper in his puffy hand. He was asking Angelo questions—until he noticed me and waved me over.

Logue came straight to it: "The proprietor, here, he tells me some of the things I need to know. Also he says, you, Hockaday, were one of the last persons besides the killer who talked to the deceased . . ."

I looked at Angelo. He was all right, except for his damp forehead and the fact that his skin had gone the color of Elmer's glue.

"He tells me you're on furlough, Detective Hockaday. But since you're living right in the neighborhood, I asked him to give you a call over. As a professional consideration. So, you want to tell me anything?"

"Yeah, I want to. But I can't. I knew the lady only a couple of minutes, long enough to see how there was a long story to her. But I never heard it."

Logue sucked his teeth. I asked him, "What can you tell me?"

He put the yellow pad back in his pocket and shook his fleshy head sideways. We shook hands since we had not done that yet. And then he disagreed with me some.

"Oh, I don't think there's so much to say about her, or about the way she checked out," Logue said. "Except you don't have to be no Einstein to see it was personal."

"You think so?"

"Sure I do. For one thing, where's the signs of any struggles?"

There were none. It appeared that Celia had simply slid

23

off her barstool after getting herself quietly shot in a five o'clock crowd. Any cop would reasonably surmise that the shooter had been well acquainted with the victim, since any good cop will read a dead face the same as he would a live one. Also, any cop would assume the shooter was a professional; the job was done up-close and personal, neatly executed with a small-bore pistol so as not to make too much noise. Then the shooter had simply walked away in the crowd and commotion of happy hour, leaving Celia to fall down like an axed tree.

I asked Angelo, "What was she doing here all through the afternoon? And who came to join her recently?"

Angelo thought for a few seconds, wanting to be careful and correct. He finally answered, slowly, "Celia and I talked about the old days. When she was a player—a gambler. Years ago she used to come here sometimes when we had some penny-ante stuff in the back room. Dice, mostly. Dice was her favorite.

"Small chat like that, Hock. She had lunch at the bar, the fish-and-chips special. I gave her a lot of change for phone calls . . ."

"Calls from the booth in here?" I asked.

"Yeah. She was on the phone a whole lot when she wasn't sitting at the bar, right where you met her earlier. I honestly don't remember anybody coming in here asking to see her. And I don't remember noticing that she talked to anybody, except on the phone.

"Hock, if I could help, I would."

I turned to Logue and asked him, "You already got that about the phone calls?

Logue said he had, that he was on top of it; he had already put in the police request for the New York Telephone Company to conduct a computer search of its coin-op logs for all outgoing calls from the booth at the Ebb Tide, between the hours of noon and half-past five. Logue added with a shrug, "For what it's worth."

I asked what he meant by that crack.

"You know, Hock. This job's just a nine-to-five, no overtime."

I wanted to say "Maybe to you, Logue." But I said nothing.

Logue said wearily, "From what I seen and have been told so far, all we got here is the well-done cancellation of one . . ."

He took the pad from his pocket and flipped through yellow pages. "One . . . Celia Furman, according to papers in her bag. Now also, according to the proprietor of the crime scene who knows her from bygone days, I am told that the late Ms. Furman was once-upon-a-time connected."

"Connected how?" I asked.

Logue shrugged and so Angelo gave me the answer. "Gaming, that's all, Hock. She started out in Detroit, as a cigarette girl in the sawdust houses. Remember them?"

I remembered. Back before a lot of people in my own neighborhood lost their jobs to the onslaught of legal gambling in the OTB parlors, and the state lotteries, and down in Atlantic City, there were colorful places all up and down the West Side where you could have drinks and a little music and shoot craps at the same time. Or play some tonk, or twenty-one. Some joints came equipped with wire rooms for playing the horses, or the national sports betting line. Every place had runners for the incidentals the clientele needed, like tip sheets for the races at Aqueduct or takeout Chinese or a fresh deck of cards. I remember all that because as a kid new to long pants, I myself was sometimes employed as a runner.

Now Angelo looked down at the body in the green dress with the good legs sticking out. "It's hard for me to figure Celia ever doing anything so bad to somebody that she had to wind up this way. Now I see I didn't know her so well as I thought."

"How well do we ever know anybody?" I said.

"That's very true."

Then Logue said, "I'll tell you what I make of all this. I think we have got here a case of somebody being out of circulation so long she was off-balance about her prospects for longevity. Now, ain't that evident—and ain't you seen it play that way before, Detective Hockaday?"

"You mean so off-balance that she forgot how you're never out of the rackets, even when you're not in the action?" I said, thinking out loud. "Maybe."

"Maybe nothing, that's it," Logue said. "Whatever she done and whoever she done it to, it all goes way back into something too murky for any of us to see. So that's why I don't get too excited about this being no more than a routine mop-up, even though it was a lady who got it."

From Logue's point of view, I could see that. Even so, I told him, "Celia told me how she once had tax trouble, and how it wrecked her life. There should be something in the way of leads there."

"Maybe," Logue said. "So I might get a few lines, so what?"

I asked Angelo again if he had seen her talking to anyone in particular. He shook his head and told me what he had already told Logue. "Honest, Hock. I'm so busy with this bad crowd that comes in nowadays, I just didn't pay her any attention since about five."

Logue stepped away from us, to speak to the police photographer who had just arrived. I told Angelo he should stop sweating so much. Then I joined Logue.

The photographer stepped over and around the corpse in order to take pictures from every possible angle of what to him was just another lump. I heard somebody from the back dining room say, "Oh, ish!"

I looked at Celia's face, white from the loss of blood and now whiter still in the strobe light. The corners of her lips were turned up slightly, as if she had been sneering at somebody she knew well enough to despise. I saw that her hair was short and black and cut like women cut their hair back in the '20s, like Louise Brooks in her bob. I had not noticed her hair before; she had been wearing a hat with a feather, but now it was nowhere around.

A spurt of blood escaped from one of her nostrils. I have seen enough of this sort of thing through the years to know that a tiny bullet was lodged in bone somewhere in Celia's neck or head, and that her dead body was hemorrhaging. Soon every visible orifice would be leaking. The photographer knew this, too, which is why he was being quick about his role in the mop-up.

"From the look of her," I said to Logue, "I think the lady received unpleasant news."

"That's putting it mild," he said.

"I would also say that poor Celia Furman somehow half expected what happened was going to happen."

Logue agreed. "Yeah, well, she don't look shocked like most stiffs do. So how do you figure it played?"

"I think she took some kind of bait to get set up like she was. That might come from being off-balance, like you said; in the rackets, you have to be figuring what awful thing can be done to you that is even worse than some awful thing you're doing—or have done—to somebody else."

"Makes sense."

"Sense, I don't know."

I wanted a drink very badly right then. But I thought about meeting Ruby for dinner in a few hours and so instead I asked Angelo for a seltzer with lime.

Then I asked Logue if he or the forensics officers had come across the shell casing to the bullet that was still somewhere inside Celia. He said no. "So what kind of piece did the shooter use, do you think?"

"I'd bet on a .25 automatic with blowback action," Logue

said. "Notice how you don't see no burns on her neck there, just the clean hole. An automatic's quiet, too, and in a crowd it ain't no trick to squeeze one off with nobody the wiser until they see somebody fall down on their face . . ."

"Which, in a bar, happens."

"Happens, yeah." Logue yawned and looked at his watch again.

Logue and I stood there silently, watching the forensics team pick up bar napkins with tweezers and dust things with sticky black powder and rummage through Celia's pocketbook. Angelo rinsed out glasses behind the bar.

The paramedics arrived and wrapped Celia head to toe in canvas, which happened also to be green. Then they took her away to the morgue in an ambulance, but they did not bother with the flashing light or the siren.

Logue asked Angelo for change of a dollar. He muttered, "I got to call up the wife."

I asked the forensics cop now finished with Celia's pocketbook if he had come across anything interesting. He recited the usual list of a lady's gear, which is considerable. Then he showed me what he was about to slip into a plastic evidence bag—an old, curling, black-and-white snapshot, about two inches by three.

The details were hard to make out because of all the rips and creases in the photo paper, but there was no doubt about the main subject—a young, beautiful, high-spirited girl in a bathing suit, Celia on a boardwalk, in a frozen moment of her carefree past. Behind her was a Ferris wheel, and people walking by in shorts and straw hats. Along one crinkled margin of the snapshot was some writing in blue fountain-pen ink: *Coney I., summer '54.*

The bathing beauty stood on the boardwalk between two men, each with an arm clasped around her slender waist. One of them was Celia's height, or slightly taller. The other was shorter by at least two inches, and thickset.

DARK MAZE

I noticed the shorter man's bearded chin. And his glasses, and his beret.

Logue had finished talking to his wife and was standing beside me again, telling me how he was going to call it a day and how he did not see much percentage in the usual business of closing and sealing the scene himself. And that if I thought of anything useful to the cause, then maybe I ought to ring him at Central Homicide, ". . . for what it's worth."

For what it was worth, I decided to sleep on my thoughts at least one night. At the same time, I told myself again, *You can let all this wormy stuff go now . . .*

But of course, I could not. I asked Logue, "Did anybody find a green hat with a feather, a hat Celia's size?"

"Hat? She wore a hat?"

I said yes. Logue said no, nobody found a hat.

I said, "Maybe I'll drop by to see you sometime in the next day or two."

Logue yawned and left.

Then I asked Angelo about the painting.

"That I got back in the early '60s, sometime when you were up studying at City College, Hock. Now I don't think I want it hanging here anymore."

"Because it's her in the picture—Celia?"

"It's her, please God."

Angelo turned to the back bar and picked up a bottle of Johnnie Walker red. He offered me a jar on the house, which I reluctantly declined in the interest of my dinner plans. He poured one for himself, though, and stared sadly at the thick amber. In the back room, where Celia threw craps once-upon-a-time, the uniforms were nearly finished with the happy hour types. I heard one of them complain, "But, Officer—this is, like, so inconvenient!" Angelo tipped his glass, spilling a few drops of Scotch out of respect for his circle of absent friends, now increased by one.

He put back the whiskey, then raised the empty glass to toast the painting of Celia and himself. I asked who the artist was.

"That would be Celia's long-lost husband, Charlie Furman."

"If Charlie had come in here today," I asked, "would Celia have recognized him? Would you?"

"Charlie Furman, in here?" Angelo shook his head. "I don't think so."

"Did you know him, too?"

"Well, I met him a few times if that's what you mean. I only talked to him about what he wanted in the way of a drink, though."

"But, here at the bar, that's where you met him?"

"Yeah, a long time back when he would sometimes come by with Celia. She'd go in the back and shoot craps and he'd sit up here drinking and watching the scenery. Man, the guy was quite the watcher."

"Why do you call him Celia's 'long-lost' husband?"

"Celia and Charlie, they had lots of problems. First, Celia's line is not conducive to long marriages; second, Charlie was an artist and artists are mostly nuts. He drifted off someplace and when he went Celia also cleared out the paintings the guy never sold, which in my case is what you see hanging over the bar."

"There's a street character here in the neighborhood who calls himself Picasso," I said. There was no recognition in Angelo's face. "Know him?"

Angelo thought and said, "No."

I told myself, You've gone as far as you can . . . call up Logue tomorrow and tell him what you know; it's his case, and besides, you're on furlough!

I started to leave. The happy hour crowd was given its liberty; the front bar started filling up.

Angelo said, "Funny, isn't it?"

"How do you mean?"

"Funny how she wore green in the painting and how she wore green today."

"The lady liked green?"

"She almost always wore green. She said it was her lucky color."

FOUR

There sat I, at a small table in a warm room, looking into the candlelit face of Ruby Flagg with her chocolate eyes and almond skin and black, black hair and her full lips touched with maroon and her smooth slim neck flowing from the top of a white lace blouse. She raised a slender hand to her neck, pinched the edge of her blouse and fluttered the fabric to cool herself. And damn me! Damn me with my thoughts all crowded by images of Picasso and his crazed threats . . . and Celia and the unsurprised way her face had greeted death.

Ruby was talking. I had asked her to tell me more about herself, since this was only our second date, if we counted the night we met at a party in Soho and she had come with a foolish man who was indifferent to our spending most of the evening together in a far corner of the loft. I asked her to tell me about setting off for New York from her hometown, which was New Orleans; I asked her if she believed in the Emerald City. And my thoughts were crowded as she answered.

". . . Oh, I knew it was going to be rough and tough," she

was saying. "And I had no end of relations back home who had never been outside Louisiana in their lives, but who knew all about New York City anyhow and how it was no place for me; how I'd come dragging my sorrowful tail back down South soon enough, hopefully in one piece."

There was a five-piece band in Princess Pamela's Little Kitchen, which is a lot of music for a place with only an eight-foot bar and a dozen tables for dinner. But this did not overpower our conversation. The musicians were five old fellows with five old instruments and no one had much wind. The band played a soft set of Bix Beiderbecke tunes—"Fidgety Feet," "Flock o' Blues," and "Prince of Wails" among them. Behind the band was a curtained doorway, behind which would be the Princess herself, tending the fried chicken you can smell all over the Lower East Side.

But neither the music nor Ruby's pretty face and voice nor the aroma from Princess Pamela's stove drove away my thoughts of Celia and Charlie Furman and the many questions their lives had raised all of a sudden. What had Picasso meant by saying to me, *"I been watching you for months in case you didn't know"*? What had he meant by saying, *"I will take you into my confidence"*? And why had he steered me to the Ebb Tide, where his painting hung in obscurity, where life had imitated art, until it died?

". . . I remember being scared by all the sweet, loving lies the family told me about New York," Ruby was saying. "But I was so much more frightened by the thought of staying home and marrying young and growing old fast, and having to make up lies of my own to keep young people from leaving me.

"Besides, I wasn't right in the head. I wanted to go into the theatre."

Artists, they're mostly nuts.

Ruby laughed. "Well, I got on stage my very first year here, how about that? This was a theatre down on Bond

33

Street, in a cellar. In my first role, I played a cannibal in an unfunny comedy about Amway distributors who open new sales territories in the African bush."

"In my time I have been trapped into witnessing plays like that," I told her.

And I thought, If Celia had sat at the Ebb Tide all day making telephone calls, she was obviously waiting for someone to come meet her; she could make calls from anywhere. Did her familiar killer finally stop by, knowing the bar would be crowded at five o'clock? Was it Picasso—Charlie Furman—who stopped by? But wouldn't Angelo have noticed him?

Ruby laughed again. "So when the offers for bigger and better parts did not rain down upon me, I did some more plays like the one at Bond Street. Which, as you know, does not pay the rent. And which, if you keep up this glorious art, will make you poor, which happened."

"And then?"

"Then I decided I didn't like poor. So, through a friend of mine, I wound up with a job on Madison Avenue with a pretty good agency that thought it was hip to advance me up the executive ladder—me being female and black, but not *too* black to their minds."

"You're speaking here of minds that are easily read?"

She smiled at me. "And so for more years than I want to confess, Detective Hockaday, I was your regulation advertising hotshot. I wore all the correct female business suits and I spent many hours lunching at Table 89 in the Pool Room at the Four Seasons so that every other advertising hotshot in town could get a load of me in my executive splendor."

"Well, you made money at least."

"I made loads. I won't say 'earned.' Enough money so I could buy a place up on East Seventy-fourth off Fifth Avenue, with a big wrap-around terrace overlooking Central

Park. I would hire a piano player for parties on summer nights and he'd play Gershwin and Porter, and I would try to believe I loved my career and that I was successful in New York and that all the people drinking my liquor were my dear, close friends.

"But I didn't and I wasn't and they weren't. I didn't have anything truly important . . ."

Princess Pamela joined us. She carried big plates full of smothered chicken in her ample arms, and smaller plates laden with Creole potato salad and cornbread and string beans. She set these down on our table, then drew up a chair for herself without asking and settled her two hundred pounds in it. She poked the red-blonde wig on her head and called to the bartender, "Darlin', give us a Bud over here." Then she indulged in the house custom of free advice and counsel to her customers, based on her eavesdropping.

"Let me tell you what's important, my darlin's," Princess said. "You got to know crap from Christmas. Let's say you get invited to a lawn party someplace nice out in the country. Now, you can play croquet—or you can head for the card table in the shade where there's some good sun tea and a hot game of whist. Crap from Christmas."

The bartender brought Princess her can of Budweiser. She popped the tab and drank, looking carefully at me. Then she said, "Hock, I ain't seen you come by with a decent-lookin' woman in I-don't-know-when. Now here you are and you ain't but half-listenin' to Pretty. What's troublin' your mind, darlin'?"

I told Princess—and Ruby—about Celia's death. And also a little bit about Picasso. And about Logue, and how I knew he had a crowded desk at Central Homicide and that he would put Celia's file over toward the edge in hopes it might fall into the wastepaper basket. And I apologized for being distracted, especially since it was my first day of a well-deserved furlough and all.

When I finished, Princess turned and said to Ruby, "Pretty, if you want this man then you got to come 'round to understandin' he is a poor fool who can't help but bein' this all-day cop in a twenty-four-hour town. No more than he can help bein' the only cop who knows how every life's maybe not valuable, but how every life's a big deal. My friend Hock—well, he ain't a easy man, Pretty."

Princess stood up. "Y'all be good," she said. Then she belched daintily and moved her ministry along to the next table.

Ruby said, "I like her, Hock. She talks like Hemingway said a writer ought to write. Which is know everything there is to know about your subject, then toss it all out except for the essentials. Hemingway called it resonance. Princess would call it soul."

Then Ruby folded her hands and tucked them under her chin and leaned forward. I leaned forward, too, and kissed her. And the Little Kitchen band played "Old Devil Moon," and I believe that was the exact moment when I knew that Ruby Flagg and I were slow-dancing together.

"You haven't told me yet if you believe in the Emerald City," I said.

"No, but I believe in the Yellow Brick Road," Ruby said.

"Along which, the advertising dodge was, what, a pit stop?"

"You might say. The trick was to get back on the road after the stop."

"And how did you do that?"

"One day, I just got up from my big desk in my corner office with the view of the East River clear down to the Williamsburg Bridge. I walked out and never returned. Not even for my final paycheck . . ."

Damn me! Damn my thoughts for drifting back to Charlie and Celia! What about Charlie Furman's failures as a husband and father? *The wife, she went rotten. The kid went Christian.* What about the taller man in the snapshot from a happy day at Coney Island back in the summer of '54?

". . . So now, as you know, I am living over the shop. Over my very own little theatre. Only we do real plays there, written by real playwrights. My apartment upstairs is smaller than my old office uptown, and I draw less than ten percent of what I used to make."

I said, "Made, not earned."

"That's right."

"And I suppose you would tell me that you have never been happier."

"Are you accusing me of having a mind that's easy to read?"

I laughed. Then I kissed her again.

And then we just ate our supper and ordered sweet-potato pie and coffee for dessert. Then Ruby asked, in all innocence, "What's it like being a cop?"

Which is the perfect question to ask a cop when you want to be entertained because there are things that happen in the life of a cop that nobody who writes books and movies about cops could ever dream up.

For instance, there was the perfectly usual morning a few years ago when I stopped in at my usual neighborhood spoon and ordered my usual eggs over easy with sausages and rye toast and black coffee. And when I had finished the mess, I left the usual dollar tip. Thus fortified with usualness, I hit the street. And then the street hit me, in a manner of speaking.

"Outta my way, bub!"

This was shrieked at me by an agitated heavy-hipped curly-haired crone in a straw bonnet and pink dress with cabbage roses all over it. She looked like the wallpaper in the parlor of the Hell's Kitchen apartment where I grew up, which is not so far from my Hell's Kitchen apartment today.

Anyway, the crone backed up her words with a right straight-arm to my Adam's apple, which just about decked me. So I stepped out of harm's way to see what her rush was all about.

What she was trying to do, it appeared, was catch up with a skinny punk sauntering down the street with the handbag he had recently snatched off her shoulder. The crone was making plenty of good squawk, but nobody on the street besides me seemed to care about it, which did not make it much of a sporting proposition. The poor old thing with the mean right had too many years on her and too much ballast. Well down the street now, the punk turned around and laughed at us both.

I went over and asked her what was up. She had stopped, and was catching her breath. "Honest t'God," she said, "would you look at that little snot down there? He swiped my purse and my rent money inside of it and my keys and my last bottle of Kaopectate. And it ain't nothing but a joke to him. He's thinking he'll get clean away with it. He's prob'ly one of them crack junkies. Where's a goddamn cop when you need one?"

I did not have the chance right then to introduce myself professionally because just then the punk started coming back toward us. I suppose he was a crackhead; dopers do very crazy things, like right away returning to the scene of a crime.

"Now's my chance!" the old lady said.

She waited until he was about a half-block away, then she did something as amazing and exciting and dead-on gorgeous as anything I have seen speeding off Phil Niekro's knuckles back when he was on the mound up at Yankee Stadium in the bottom of the ninth with two away and Niekro has got only one pitch on a full count to shut out a Red Sox designated hitter in order to hang onto the Yanks' one run lead.

Only the crone did not use a baseball.

Instead, she plucked a glass eye from the left side of her

head, went into something approximating a windup, and burned one-quarter pound of blue iris crystal straight on down the street, scoring a bull's-eye dead square on the laughing punk's nose. Which then burst into red like it was an exploding paint can. The punk was not laughing when he went down.

"C'mon, bub! Give a helpless old lady a hand, why don't you?"

Adrenalin got the helpless old lady to the punk about the same time I got there myself to make a nice, sweet collar on aggravated robbery. I was reaching into my back pocket for the bracelets when the crone took a joyful hop into the air and pounced on the punk's chest, just like I have seen wrestlers do on television. "I'll sit here on the crumb-bum while you go call up the cops, okay?"

She had recovered her purse and was bashing it into the squashed punk's face. The glass eye rolled off the curb into a grating and disappeared into a sticky dark bog of tired-out chewing gum, cigarette butts, spittle and latex mementos of curbside revels. "Hell!" she crowed. "The insurance's paid up and I been wanting a new one anyways."

Ruby had been laughing steadily since *"C'mon, bub, give a helpless old lady a hand . . ."*

She said, "If that's not an Irishman's fable, I've never heard one."

"Irish I am," I answered. "I would steal from you, but I would never lie."

"Tell me why you became a cop, Irish."

"I can never say for sure. But I like to imagine that a cop, if he's good, is somebody who wants to make some sense of the world."

"Oh, then it's true what they say about Detective Neil Hockaday; you're not an easy man."

"What is an easy man?"

"He's somebody who wouldn't think twice about trying to

make sense of things because he already knows that if the world made any sense at all, it would be the men riding sidesaddle."

I laughed for what seemed a long time, and it felt good. "Can there be any Irish in Ruby Flagg?"

"It could happen," she said.

Ruby fixed me with her chocolate eyes. Then she folded her hands again, long fingers with clear, polished nails touched the tiny cleft in her chin.

I thought about the champagne on ice at home.

And I almost forgot about Charlie and Celia, almost.

This is happening so soon. Sooner than I ever expected!

Oh, but it was a good one, hey? And brother, did she have it coming—the rotten! Didn't she, didn't she?

I got to get ready!

My paints, my canvasses . . . my camera.

Where in holy hell'd she put them?

Holy hell! That's rich, ain't it?

Oh God, I wished I seen it for myself.

Ho, ho, what a sight that must of been. Ain't that right? Damn straight!

The rotten . . . !

Well, there you are. She went and got herself blind-sided late in the game, boy. That's it. Can you beat it?

D'you suppose she ever once figured the sweet irony? I mean, after a lifetime of craps—and mostly on the house side of the table—the dice went and turned against her. Hah!

She had her streak, sure. I give her that.

But every streak comes to an end. This I have observed many times.

And nobody beats the odds. Not even those that make them.

FIVE

Either I am the world's most dedicated cop, or I am the world's most ungrateful fool. These I figured to be my choices on the morning I woke up with company for a change, yet with a head running almost entirely to thoughts of collaring Charlie Furman, the desperate Picasso.

There beside me in my ordinarily lonesome bed was the still-slumbering Ruby Flagg, her smooth bare shoulders rising and falling as she breathed. I touched her warm skin and felt sorry for her, and for all the other unfortunate women who have to go falling for New York cops.

I had first laid eyes on Ruby Flagg at that party in Soho. That night, I experienced a minor philosophical miracle; it hit me all of a sudden how it was the human race had managed to survive itself. Because—as cynical as I can get about life in general and women in particular, given a marriage that so far as it ran was a triumph of habit over hate—I was just plain knocked loopy by the sight of her. Ruby Flagg and her kind and pretty face, her soft, slim shape, those devastating legs, those eyes.

41

That was one night two weeks ago in a crowded room, leading to last night in my small apartment and the elemental time we made of it. Just the two of us.

Back at the restaurant, during the last bites of sweet-potato pie, she had said to me, "The way you're looking at me, buster, you'd better mean it."

I said I meant it. She said she wanted to see where I lived.

Then there was I, sitting in my green-fringed chair from the Salvation Army that looks as if it might have been cast out of some long-ago whorehouse parlor, and her on the couch by the window slipping off her shoes, she said, "Tell me the story of your life, Hock."

I said, "It's long and mostly untrue."

"I'll learn it, by-and-by."

And then we drank the Perrier-Jouët, all of it. I played a treasured LP on the stereo, ballads by the late Leslie Hutchinson, including my favorite rendition of "A Nightingale Sang in Berkeley Square." Also I entertained Ruby with a confession of my detective work since the Soho affair; how I had nosed around about her dopey escort and discovered he was a theatrical casting agent who wore a gold locket around his neck that contained a tiny heart-shaped photograph of somebody named Vito; how I reasoned, therefore, that it would not be wasting my time and energies to ring up the lady for a date.

She laughed at me and said, "You're a dope, Hock. But you're my kind of dope."

Now there was I, my finger tracing Ruby's smooth shoulder, about to be a real dope.

Quietly as I could, I rose from the bed and showered and dressed and made coffee. And one telephone call.

Then Ruby, wrapped alluringly in my shirt and standing in front of me as I hung up the telephone, asked, "Who was that?"

"A man I have to go see."

"About a job." The way she said it, she knew.

"Yes."

"Okay, but remember, buster—I'm waiting for you."

"How do you think I got here where I am, Hock?" This was Inspector Tomassino Neglio's first reaction to my account of meeting Picasso; being called to view the remains of his wife the same day he had issued murder threats; my concerns that Celia Furman's untimely death would not likely make it to the top of Logue's agenda. A very rotten thing of me to be doing, talking this way behind another cop's back. *"How do you think I got here where I am?"*

I would want to think carefully about an answer. My boss is fond of elliptic questions. Straight responses under such conversational circumstances can easily put me in the position of being idiot nephew to his world-wise uncle. This is the natural result of two different kinds of cops seated on opposite sides of a desk over which something of a delicate nature is under discussion. A regular cop like me in chinos and a baseball jacket tends to ask blunt questions to find out what a person knows; a man of the bureau, like Neglio—a cop with suits tailor-made in Chinatown, a cop who rarely carries his piece anymore—tends to ask loaded questions in order to find out what a person does not know. Any New York detective who fails to see the difference is about as effective as a tap dancer on carpet.

"You slept with somebody, sir?" I have found by experience that cracking wise is often the best course with Neglio. He generally ignores me, which was the case that morning.

"I came to recognize the danger of this here little item, Hock." Neglio pointed to the telephone on his desk. He saw the idiot glint in my eyes, smiled a satisfied smile and explained patiently, "Every time this thing rings, it's trouble."

Neglio stood up from his desk. He locked his manicured fingers behind his back, turned and stepped to the window. His view from an upper floor of One Police Plaza was New

York Harbor—Ellis and Governors Islands, the Statue of Liberty, the ferry boats gliding out to gray Staten Island—and I thought to myself how it was sort of pathetic that a man with such a great view and such great suits up here in this great office was afraid of his telephone. I shook my head sadly, as he could not see me. Then I recognized that by this action, secret though it was, I had betrayed a reasonably good cop, man of the bureau or not.

He turned and stared at me hard. "I got smart and learned to be cautious, Hock. About everything. Even cautious about answering the phone. Which you can now see is smart of me, since I took your call this morning and look where it's got us."

"There's no trouble as I see it, Inspector. I am only going by the book here . . ."

"Covering your ass, you mean."

"Being cautious."

Neglio sat down and sighed. "I am only trying to give you good advice, Hock. You don't have to answer every call. Understand?"

"I appreciate that, and I understand."

"You're entitled to your furlough."

"Don't I know it."

"But, instead . . ."

"Inspector, you know where the job's going to be going under Logue."

"I know, I know," Neglio admitted. "Logue's on the precipice of pension, so he's strictly nine-to-five until he's settled down in Florida somewheres. You go telling anybody I said that about him and I'll call you a goddamn liar, okay? But, yeah, I see your point."

"Thanks. The book says when I have some compelling reason for poaching on a cop's job, I should tell the boss. So I'm telling you, so you can make a record of it in case I need it. Off the record, well, it's personal reasons."

"Oh for Christ's sake, Hock! That's blowing rule number

one. You don't make this business personal; it's hard enough dealing with strangers."

I said nothing since he was right.

"When are you going to learn? All we happen to be is cops; we didn't make the world, and we aren't responsible for anybody else making the world."

I tried to think of some answer, but could not. Once more, Neglio found what I did not know—even about myself. I shook my head sadly again, recognizing how this game was getting easier and easier for my boss to play.

Impatient with the silence, Neglio added, "All right, so I give you this, Hock: it's not Logue's kind of a story, it's got you written all over it."

He motioned me to get the hell out of his office and leave him alone. But before I got out the door, he stopped me with, "I maybe can see how you take this personal, even if you don't see yourself. Know what I mean?"

I answered with a meek, "No."

"I know from all the times over all the years when I have sprung for drinks late at night, when you're all on about growing up alone with your mother, God bless her soul. That and how your old man was lost in the war, and how you never knew him, and how your mother never talked of him—and the mysteries of it all. You're a real sucker for a certain kind of a story, Hock. That's what I mean."

"What kind of story?"

"Most cops—myself included, I suppose—would be perfectly satisfied to collar a guy who, one fine day after twenty-five years of marriage, takes a cleaver to his missus and makes a bloody mess of her all over the kitchen floor. Case closed.

"But not you, Hock. You, you Irish snoop—you want to trespass into the mystery of it all."

"What mystery?"

"The mystery of how a guy loved a woman so much twenty-five years ago that he married her; then how one day he hated her so bad that he diced her. You're the kind of trespassing cop who wants to know the story of what happened during those twenty-five years.

"Now, if you want to say that makes you a good cop, Hock, I will agree with you. But when I say that trespassing brings a lot of trouble, too—well, I would like it if you could try seeing how I'm right."

I only touched the doorknob and said, "So this is, what, your blessing?"

Neglio sighed. "Yeah, go on, Hock. If it comes to it, I'll square things with Logue."

"Thanks, sir."

"Don't thank me. And don't forget two things."

"What?"

"One, there's lots of questions in the world that are best left unanswered. And two, you're on your own damn clock on this."

Two hours later, I was riding the Lexington Avenue local from the City Hall Station up to East Thirty-third Street. Then I walked to First Avenue where, behind black-iron gates sits a hulking cluster of dirty, red-brick buildings known collectively as Bellevue Hospital Center. This was the only place that might have something in the way of a record on Charlie Furman, a/k/a Picasso.

While still downtown I had checked some of the usual places where I can sometimes get a start on tracking down a man—the State Unemployment Compensation Bureau, the Human Resources Administration where a marginal artist might have filed for welfare, the Social Security Office at Federal Plaza. All I learned from this was that Charlie Furman's life was completely off the books. Not surprisingly, telephone information was no help to me, and neither was the guy a voter.

I followed signs at the gate of the main entrance to Bellevue and found the psychiatric ward, where I remember

Picasso telling me he had been an outpatient for quite a long while. There was a herd of patients in wheelchairs sitting at one end of the lobby in an area marked off by purple tape on the floor. They were full of Thorazine and there were straps across their laps to keep them from pitching out of their chairs.

I showed my gold shield to the duty nurse and said I wanted to speak to somebody who could help me with the medical file on Charlie Furman. And while she punched this name into a buzzing desk computer, I asked her for good measure if she had ever heard of a patient called Picasso.

"Oh, sure, the painter gentleman," she said. "He used to come by pretty regular, a real cutey. But I don't know, we ain't seen him in I-don't-know-when."

This would be the first time I heard a nurse say "ain't." She stared at her computer screen, chewed gum and hiked up her undergarments. "I got nothing here showing on no Furman, Charlie. Or Charles, neither."

"Well," I asked her, "when Picasso used to come by, did he have any regular doctor?"

"Sure," she said, giving her eyes a roll. "That'd be Dr. Reiser. Ronald Reiser. He's up in the Zoo—and if you ask me, it's rubbed off on him. Um, you know the Zoo?"

I knew, I said. Though I had not been to the top floor of the Bellevue psych ward in a lot of years, I could not imagine that much had changed. A sprawling open floor, full of heavily sedated patients lying on their backs in beds secured to the floor with electromagnetic locks, nylon restraining belts around their stomachs, wrists and ankles secured to bedposts with leather lashes. There were no windows anywhere. Several doctors in long white coats streamed from bed to bed, murmuring their sweet nothings: "We're all here to help you . . . this is all for your own good . . ."

I spoke to the head nurse, who in turn showed me to a huge-jawed security guard posted outside a hallway door with a sign that read TO ROOF. I was told that Dr. Reiser could be found tending his garden. And so I took the stairs, walked out along the graveled rooftop and spotted a collection of wooden planting tubs, at the center of which was a short man in a polo shirt with a frizz of black hair blowing up over a round sunburned head.

"Dr. Ronald Reiser?"

He turned and said, suspiciously, "Who wants to know?"

I showed him my shield. "I need to talk to you about a patient of yours who calls himself Picasso. His real name is Furman, Charlie Furman."

"So that's his name, hey?"

"Yes, sir."

"Do you like tomatoes, Officer?"

"Actually, it's Detective Hockaday, Hock, if you want."

"Sure, Detective. You like tomatoes?"

"Actually, yes. I'm a big chili maker."

"Oh, that's good. You'd be surprised how hard it is for me to give away good tomatoes like I grow up here on top of this nut house. Come back around the middle of August, you'll see my beauties."

"I'll do that, maybe. About Furman . . . Picasso . . ."

"Oh, yeah. How's the patient?"

"That's what I want you to tell me."

Reiser muttered something and went back to digging around with a trowel in the new soil of his planting tubs. "Four, five years I have been seeing this guy, which I am not supposed to be doing since he won't come clean with a name or anything. I am wasting the taxpayers' money four, five years—and everybody else around here the same before me. Nobody gets nothing out of this guy but his observations on this and that, this and that. Nothing that adds up to anything whole, though."

"Do you know where he lives?"

"He's in police trouble?"

"Do you have an address?"

"I don't know where the guy lives, no."

"Did you know his wife, Celia?"

"Not by name. I figured he was married once. He used to talk about his rotten crooked wife who was a gambler. Hey! Did he give his wife the business?"

"I just want him for questioning."

Reiser slapped his crimson forehead. "So this is very serious? Why else would a cop be standing out on a roof with a shrink?"

"It's serious, yes."

"Let's go down to my office, what do you say?"

"You're the doctor."

"I am, I am."

I followed Reiser down the staircase back out into the Zoo hallway where the guard with the jaw was still loyally on duty. Reiser greeted him with a friendly wave of his garden trowel and a "Hi ya', how are ya?" in the manner of the late Governor Rockefeller. He said the same to a gaggle of nurses and fellow shrinks. And then we wound our way through one hall, down another, then another, all the while Reiser leading the way with friendly waves of his trowel and the "Hi ya" treatment to a small army of oversize security guards. Finally we reached a row of office doors with steel plates on them, one of which bore Reiser's name and title: DR. RONALD REISER, SUPERVISING PSYCHIATRIST.

The office was not much. I have seen better accommodations at some precinct station houses, even up in the Bronx. There was a big brown desk at the center of the room, overflowing with newspapers and telephone message slips and food crumbs and dried-up styrofoam coffee cups. To the side sat a brown leather couch you could not sit on because of all the stacks of medical magazines; and in the corner a brown file cabinet, which Reiser started pawing through.

I sat down on a steel chair with cracked vinyl pads and scanned a wall of bookshelves. There were a lot of medical volumes mostly, but I spotted a couple of Robertson Davies novels and this told me that Reiser was probably all right.

Two of the bookends on his shelves were human skulls that looked to be the real goods.

On the edge of his desk there were pens and pencils standing up in a ceramic mug with the message, "You toucha my cup, I breaka you face" on its side. On the wall behind the desk was a framed photograph of Sigmund Freud.

Reiser found what he was looking for in the brown cabinet and sat down with it at his desk. He opened a manila folder and riffled through years of notes inked on pale-blue lined paper. He made a few clucking sounds, then asked, "Would you be interested in knowing the very first words that our friend Picasso said to me?"

I said I was interested.

"This was at our first session, on the seventeenth of November, 1984. I wrote it down I was so impressed." Reiser removed a piece of blue paper from his file. "He was sitting where you're sitting now, and he looked up at the picture on the wall in back of me and he said, 'I want to make one brief statement about psychoanalysis: Fuck Dr. Freud.'"

"Picasso is not your hesitant conversationalist."

Reiser clucked again. "I respectfully disagree with that, Detective Hockaday. The way he operates, Picasso always starts by putting you way off-balance . . ."

In between that and the rest of what Reiser told me, I kept hearing Logue's words from the other day as we stood over Celia Furman's leaking body: *We have got here a case of somebody being out of circulation so long she was off-balance about her prospects for longevity. Now, ain't that evident— and ain't you seen it play that way before, Detective Hockaday?"*

". . . and then in this way, he forces you to listen to what he calls his 'observations,' which are quite important to him; and then when he's finished with you, he puts you off-balance again and you can't quite get this bird out of your mind.

"And the thing that really keeps you off-balance is that you never know anything about this guy. Well, not very much that adds up, let's say. And he's not about to tell you much, either. When he does give you something in the way of a fact, it may or may not be true; more than likely, he'll toss you a riddle, then it's up to you to reason it out.

"Speaking as Picasso's psychiatrist, and as a man of science, I would say our poor Charlie is wacko."

That was pretty straightforward for a doctor, I thought. "The other doctors here, before you took him on, did they think Charlie was wacko, too?" I asked.

"Oh, I don't think anybody ever diagnosed him in any serious way. Nobody kept notes like I do; nobody ever found time or had the motive to work out the riddles. Ah yes, the riddles . . ."

Reiser opened a desk drawer and removed a box of cigars, good ones. We both lit up.

"You see," Reiser continued, "the way Picasso usually came in here was with a couple of cops who would find him howling in the street, usually outside some art gallery somewhere. They didn't bother making it official since he never hurt anybody. They'd just run him in here, and the staff shrinks would go through the motions because they had enough hard cases to report on . . ."

I interrupted with, "Why didn't anybody ever take the man seriously?"

"Aha! Well that *is* the question, isn't it?"

"What's the answer?"

"Practically speaking, we have this guy who apparently has no fixed address and who goes around calling himself Picasso and whose only offense against the peace of our tranquil city is once in a while hollering outside some gallery. So who wants to mess with paper work? Besides which, Picasso isn't telling anybody his name or address or anything, and we're not allowed to beat it out of him, right? So what have we really got but this, this unofficial man?

"Funny thing, Hock. One night a couple years ago, the cops brought him in here as usual for hollering outside a downtown gallery. The owner of this gallery, he tells the cops how he *likes* having Picasso shrieking outside his place; he says it's 'performance art.' Picasso is so disgusted with this character, he has never hollered outside that place again."

We had a laugh, and we puffed our cigars. "So all right, I see the practicality of keeping Picasso unofficial. But, do you have any other ideas?"

"Oh, yes, I do. I have a theory: if you're a real genuine New York wacko, then you're smart enough to know how not to get yourself caught up in the system we have invented for keeping tabs on our New York wackos. The way it works in Picasso's case is, he comes in here making himself too much and too little trouble to be papered, if you follow me; then he puts us all off-balance, which has its strange charms; and Picasso winds up taking away with him whatever he decides might be useful, by which I mean something that one of us charmed and obliging croakers might possibly say that he might possibly find soothing to a troubled head."

"He must love you, Doc."

Reiser clucked. He shut the manila folder on his desk and said, "Well we have our pleasant moments, sometimes. I know *I* like *him*. Oh, I know what you're thinking. When a shrink says he 'likes' a patient, the truth is he just pities the poor dumb fruitcake. But I am saying that I honestly enjoy this guy's company. Picasso's a fruitcake, but he's got a first-class brain."

By now, I was thinking that if and when I crack I want Ronald Reiser for my shrink. I was not crazy about the clucking, but I liked smoking his brand and I liked what I heard. Maybe I could have a special medic-alert card printed up for my wallet.

"He didn't mention you, Doc," I said, thinking back to my chat with Picasso in the park. "But he mentioned shrinks and, as I recall, he does not hold your fraternity in his highest regard."

"As a fraternity, neither do I. So that's why I get such a kick out of his trying to get a rise out of me with his observations on the trade. One time, he said to me, 'You know, Reiser, your hero up there on the wall, Dr. Freud, he used to smoke cigars, too. And his pal, Carl Jung, would steal them from him. Ponder the meaning of that sometime.'"

We had another good laugh.

The doctor went on, "He used to say to me all the time, 'Reiser, you high-classed lunatic, I got only one observation about psychotherapy: it has conned millions of simple people into believing they're complex.' I really miss the old wacko."

"That's what I heard, that Picasso's been missing from around here," I said. "When was the last time he dropped by?"

"Six, seven months ago, thereabouts. And now here we sit, you and me—the shrink in his life and the cop in his life. I just went and violated my patient's privacy all to hell. But you, you're not telling me dick, Dick. Tell me what in hell Picasso did, and how in hell you found out his real name?"

"I don't know for sure that he did anything . . ."

I was going to be evasive, but I changed my mind. Instead, I gave Reiser the outline of what had happened from the first moment in the park, to see what he made of it. "So," I said, finishing up, "he eventually tells me that he's been shadowing me for a long time; he tells me he wants me to know the 'extenuating circumstances' of his failed life; then he winds up this lovely chin with a few threats."

"Threats?"

"He says, and I am pretty much quoting, 'I am working up a plan—a plan to kill what's been responsible for making me fall so far and spectacular as you have seen I have fell.'"

I waited for some kind of reaction from Reiser, but there was none. "Doc, in my business you hear lots of threats. I wouldn't be bothering you about this one unless there was something behind it, which maybe there is."

Again, no reaction.

"In the park, Picasso is telling me . . . well, he and his imaginary friend are telling me . . ."

"Oh that," Reiser said. "Yes, I've seen his alter-ego routine."

I continued. "Picasso tells me he's called Picasso because he's a painter. When I ask him if he's got anything serious in the way of work I could see, he tells me one of his paintings is hanging right in a bar in the neighborhood where I happen to do my drinking."

"A painting?" And now Reiser's eyebrows arched, so high that his face looked like the letter M.

"So," I said, "I go to the bar and there it is—something I never much noticed, a picture of a lady in green sitting at the bar talking to the bartender. There is nothing special about the painting. Well, I am no art expert, but I don't think we'll be seeing this thing mounted up at the Met, you know?

"However, there is something special right below Picasso's painting. It's another lady in green. I mean, a lady in the flesh, wearing green and sitting at the bar talking to my friend Angelo, the owner. It's a real-life pose out of the painting up on the wall."

Reiser said, "Oh, God." He said this quietly, almost as if he knew what might be coming.

"The lady ID's as one Celia Furman. I chat with her for a while, long enough to know that she, too, has got some hard-luck story in her. But I leave before I get much of it.

Then later that same day, I am called back to the bar by Angelo, on account of how Celia Furman has been murdered."

Reiser said, "Oh, God," again. And his face conveyed that same kind of unsurprised mood that I saw in Celia's dead face.

I said, "I found an old snapshot in Celia's pocketbook that was interesting—a picture of Celia and two guys. One looks like a young Picasso, right down to the whiskers and beret. The three of them are strolling along the boardwalk, a long time ago, out in Brooklyn—Coney Island."

The eyebrows went up again, then back down. Then, without expression, "Oh, God—Astroland."

I continued. "It seems Celia stopped in at the bar yesterday to visit her old pal, Angelo, who she has not seen in a very long time. From Angelo I get that Celia used to be a very big-shot gambler once married to a small-time painter who was such a nut job she had to put him away somewhere. Charlie was the husband's name."

"I see how you naturally connected Picasso to Charlie Furman," Reiser said.

"Naturally."

"So, Picasso killed his wife in the bar and somehow got away?"

"That I don't know, Doc. Celia was shot with a small-caliber pistol at close range in a crowded bar, and nobody saw anything. Which for once is the truth. And Angelo says he definitely would have remembered seeing Charlie Furman in the place—which he did not."

"So naturally, you want Picasso for questioning."

"Naturally."

Reiser's sunburned face did not look so sunburned anymore. He said, "He wants to be questioned, Hock. He wants to be found, but he sure isn't going to make it easy for you."

"What do you know, Doc? Help me."

Reiser put down his cigar like it was suddenly making him sick. Weakly, he said, "I mentioned how we had our pleasant moments, Picasso and me?"

"You did."

"Well, we also had a major falling-out. That was the last day I saw the man, which as I said before was six or seven months back."

"And . . .?"

"And that's when I presented him with my grand theory, which did not got over so well. . . .

"You see, we always had this same exasperating talk about art whenever he'd come here. Which would be following one of his episodes."

"By which you mean the hollering sessions?"

"Right. Always the same pattern. The cops would find him standing outside a gallery yelling at the top of his lungs, 'Philistines!' Over and over, to the point where he was scaring off customers. So, of course, I asked him why he was doing that.

"He said, 'Because they're a bunch of numbnuts in there, why else d'you think they're selling them lousy pictures by them no-talent painters?' To which I would say, 'You could do better?' Then he would say, 'I done plenty better!'"

I said, "I'm no medical expert, but that doesn't sound like any sort of a path to progress."

"Not directly, it isn't. But at least it got us onto the subject of art sometimes, the only thing personal that Picasso would ever discuss. Otherwise, it was all about his 'observations' or his reliably dim view of life, or that damn alter-ego routine.

"But, Hock, you met him, you know what an intriguing bastard the guy is. You just want to solve the riddles of the guy, you know? Do you?"

I did not answer right away, thinking back to what Neglio had told me, by way of warning me about myself. Eventually, though, I managed, "Yeah, I guess so."

"Sure, you know how it is, Hock. I mean, I've talked with

cops before. You're the first one I've met with a measurable attention span."

I shrugged.

Reiser went on. "Anyway, there were two main things I could never get out of Picasso like you did—his real name, and a look at one of his paintings. So finally, one bright day it dawns on me what this guy's pathology is. However, I am not bright enough to keep the revelation to myself; I have to go blabbing my grand theory to Picasso.

"I told him on that last day of ours, 'Picasso, my pixilated friend, what makes you the loon you are is that you're the worst kind of artist there is, the kind that gets ignored.'

"To which Picasso says, 'The way I see it, when a tree falls down in the forest and nobody's around to hear it, you better believe it still makes a big noise! You're calling that crazy, Doc, are you?'"

Reiser laughed. It was an unfunny series of snorts, really, and no doubt inherited from Picasso. "Guess what he does next?" Reiser asks.

I gave up.

"Picasso says, 'Okay, I had just about enough of this bug house!' Then he stands up from the chair where you're sitting now, and he coldcocks me. Knocks me clear off my chair, the wacko! Then I was down on the floor, rolling around with a dislocated jaw. And Picasso is standing over me with his eyes rolling and his fists waving and he's hollering, 'Philistine!'

"I am in such agony, all I see is Picasso's wild blurry head chasing around in circles with Freud's head behind him, from the picture up on the wall. And I can't tell which one of them is yelling at me, 'You ignorant shrink! Open your eyeballs and see!'"

I said, "And that's the last you saw of him?"

"Yeah. He knocked me down, then a couple of the security goons came in here and jacketed him. We doped him out for a couple of days. I didn't make an issue of it. I mean, what could I do anyway? We'd been carrying this guy off the record for decades, right? He wasn't cooperating, and we kept taking him back. What do you expect?

"Besides," Reiser added, "the day we let him go, he dropped by my office and told me I was fired as his doctor. How do you like that?"

Reiser opened the manila folder again. He removed an item and handed it to me—a white business-size envelope, the cheap kind that comes from Lamston's in hundred-count boxes. It had been mailed to Dr. Ronald Reiser, in care of Bellevue. But there was no return address. The postmark was Brooklyn. The cancelled stamp was a flag issue, pasted upside-down in the upper right corner of the envelope.

"That thing," Reiser explained, "came about one week after he coldcocked me. Just get a load of what's inside of it."

I pulled out a Polaroid photograph, about four inches square. The image was overexposed and muddy, as Polaroids sometimes are. I made out the picture of a large building, neither an apartment house nor a shop, but something else—full of colors, mostly reds and yellows. And a small building in the foreground, a sort of shed with a sign on it that read: TICKETS.

Around the edges of the photo were neatly printed letters, all in black ballpoint capitals: BEHOLD, MY MASTERPIECE—LOVE & KISSES, PICASSO.

"What is it?"

Reiser said, "In the trade, they call it a *dark maze.* You'll find it out in Coney Island."

SIX

There is always the singular moment when I know for certain that I am about to be wedded to a case, for better or for worse, until death do us part. Walking out of Dr. Ronald Reiser's office in the Zoo wing of Bellevue was that grim moment.

Feeling the way I did, I figured it in the best interests of family harmony to make a straightforward, diplomatic call to Detective Logue at Central Homicide. Better he should hear it from me now, instead of from Inspector Neglio later.

"Listen, go right ahead and be my guest," Logue said after I spent a couple of minutes telling him about the wedding. "Like I told you before—what am I going to do with overtime?"

That settled, I asked, "Any progress yet?"

"There's Celia's rap. Which is a good place to start if you got the time and interest, which I see you got. Hold on, I got notes here someplace." Logue shuffled papers on his desk. "Okay, it turns out the G really did a number on the lady, back during one of those times that happen once in a while when everybody down in Washington's got a hard-on for the mob, right?"

"And Celia Furman was in the wrong place at the time?"

"Right. She was what's known as a "big whale" in the casinos, meaning she was good for a fifty-grand credit line anywhere's in Vegas, and in the European and Caribbean joints, too. Also she was a lady who made a habit of being a real pal to the right kinds of useful men . . ."

"Of which some were connected?"

"Right again," Logue said. "It's how she got started making her pile. Useful guys backed her when she started taking over sawdust houses in Detroit and gradually worked her way up to running a string of class joints all the way around the lakeshore from Detroit to Cleveland. Good square houses, so they say; always dice the specialty."

"But the government doesn't care about any of that."

"Naw, they're after some of Celia's boyfriends. Since Celia's very probably a key to lots of things these characters do not wish to confide to Uncle. Well, you heard this drill before, Hockaday."

"So they leaned hard on Celia."

"Right. And for the best kind of leaning there is, they sent the IRS around. They know she can't stand up to no unrelenting income-tax audit."

"Then they haul her into Federal Tax Court?"

"Not before they cleaned her out, but good. One by one, they shut down her string of houses, leaving her no more gold mine to stake for the serious money on the big whale circuit. Which is the only way she's got of making good on everything she never forked over on her Form 1040s from all those earnings she shouldn't have earned. This is kind of screwy, but remember we're talking government here."

"All part of the drill," I said. "So, next they offered her the testimony deal?"

"I guess they tried. They hauled her in front of grand

juries all over the country. Detroit, Chicago, L.A., New Orleans, Boston, here in New York. You name the town, Celia's been in its grand jury room."

"Did she talk?"

"My friend who is telling me this," Logue said, "he doesn't think so."

"Who's your friend?"

"Oh, this guy my own age. We came up through the ranks together in the department, then one year he gets sense enough to go work for the feds. He's doing records now at Justice, down in D.C., in an office with his own telephone and a parking space and an air conditioner in the window that's got a view of the Lincoln Memorial. . . .

"Anyway, my friend says to me, 'Your subject spent lots of time in front of grand juries that never delivered up indictments that meant much, so by that I would conclude that the lady was no canary.'"

Logue added to this, with his sincerest disgust, "For what honor that was worth."

I asked what he meant.

"Here was this class-A lady, the way I see it," he answered. "She never ratted out nobody, but everybody she ever knew in the business assumed she must've spilled something once every so often just to break the monotony of flying from one grand jury to the other. So they went and cut her off! Jesus, it was pathetic when you think about it. The only dice left to her was on Monopoly boards.

"Just to tell you how heartbreaking it was, Hock, my friend says the last thing on his records about Celia Furman is that she was so broke some assistant D.A. took pity on her and helped her file for Social Security. What a freaking shame, hey?"

"That it is, my friend," I said. "She was death before she got dead for real."

I was anxious to get off the telephone with Logue, anxious

to speak to Inspector Neglio about putting out an APB on Charlie Furman a/k/a Picasso, anxious to put money on the street in hopes one or two of my snitches could sell me a lead to his whereabouts, and anxious to get home, where Ruby Flagg was waiting.

Then I remembered about the phone logs.

"Before she was shot," I said to Logue, "Celia made several calls from the booth at the Ebb Tide, remember? You were going to get the phone logs. Anything interesting show up?"

"Oh that, yeah." I heard Logue shuffle papers some more. "Okay, lots of these entries on the log we can probably discount pretty quick once we check them all out. We got calls to a neighborhood bookie, for instance; I know the number myself, see? Then we got two calls to this street pay phone that we know is a drug line. Also we have some calls to guys' apartments where Celia probably don't figure, and some calls to this answering service that's probably for pross . . ."

"Give it to me efficient, Logue. Are you showing anything that relates at all to Celia Furman?"

"Well, I don't know how in hell it would relate, but there's nine calls to the same number in the logs. So I figure, maybe that's her calls, on account of they were so long-winded she had to put in extra coins."

I heard papers shuffled again. Then Logue said, "The nine calls, they list to a public phone at another bar, a joint called the Neptune, out in Brooklyn."

"Brooklyn," I said flatly. "As in Coney Island."

"Yeah. . . . Hey, what do you know?"

"I know I'm taking a trip out to Coney Island, for the first time since I was a kid."

Off and on through the day, I had certain thrilling ideas about being back at my place with Ruby. She said she would wait, did she not? I did not want to spoil these thoughts by calling up my place even once to see if she was still there. This is the pathology of a man who has been cut off at the knees once in his life, which is a lot like being divorced.

Back when I was married, I would miss my wife Judy during the day—and sometimes at night—and I would call home and she was usually not there. And when I came to find out some of the reasons she was never there, I stopped calling home altogether.

You would think that a man as bright as I enjoy believing I am would know the difference between one woman and another, especially when the women are as highly contrasting as Judy and Ruby. But no. Along with all those thrilling angles I had considered during the course of the day, there was a sour note: the lasting memory of being sandbagged by wounded vanity.

So I had not telephoned.

And now I was sliding the key into the lock, opening the door, taking the chance, again.

And there was Ruby Flagg, sitting on my couch under the window, one leg curled up beneath her hips, a book open in her lap and a teapot and cup on the side table along with a glass full of flowers she must have bought at the Korean greengrocer on the corner. She wore spectacles I had never seen, spectacles that betrayed her as very nearsighted. She yanked them off.

"I don't like you seeing me in these," she said. "They make me look funny, like a bug."

I said, lamely, "You're still here."

"Like I said—I mean it, buster."

Outside, it started raining the sort of soft rain that comes late in the afternoon on April days, the sort of rain that takes away all the shrillness of the city. I could hear foghorns out on the Hudson River, and cops on horseback down in the street.

"When you say, *'I mean it'*, you mean? . . ."

"Both of us have been around the block. And we both have probably been run over a few times. We are both slightly past the prime of youth. Do you know what I'm saying?"

I said I was not at all sure, even though maybe I was.

"I'm saying you and I are at the age when we should take it easy, but we should take it."

Then Ruby got up off the couch and walked to me and put her arms up around my neck and pulled my head down to hers and kissed me on the lips. Afterwards, she said, "Now this is what I call throwing my whole self at you, buster. For better or for worse. How about paying me some attention?"

"Maybe we could go for drinks and talk, then go to dinner someplace nice," I said.

"We're having dinner someplace nice," Ruby said. "Right here. Drinks, too."

She sat me down and poured from the bottle of Johnnie Walker on the sideboard. One for me, then one for herself, mixed with water. Then she read my mind.

"You took that murder case, didn't you?"

I said yes. And I told her all about my talk with Neglio, my futile checks on Charlie Furman, my talk with Dr. Reiser and the call to Logue.

And one other thing. Which was my developing hunch that Charlie Furman, if he killed his wife, had only just begun.

"Have you ever been to Coney Island?" I asked.

"No. But I'll bet it can wait until tomorrow."

That settled, I gave Ruby my fullest attention for the balance of an evening's long, slow dance.

Morning was bright-skied and cool.

We made an early start of it, with eggs and bagels down at the spoon I see out my window—Pete Pitsikoulis' All-Night

Eats & World's Best Coffee. Then a brisk walk over to the F train at Sixth Avenue and Forty-second. We both mostly dozed during the long trip out to the farthest reaches of Brooklyn.

A curly-headed young woman was opening up the first shop you encounter when emerging from the Stillwell Avenue station of the IND subway—the Philips Salt Water Taffee and Ka-Ra-Me-La stand. Before the day was out, even though it was April and school was still in session, she would sell a few hundred pounds of licorice whips, pistachios, gumdrops, chocolate turtles with cashews, nonpareils, peanut-butter fudge, and cheese popcorn. Coney Islanders do not cut svelte figures on the beach.

Across Stillwell Avenue was another familiar stand, where starting about mid-June there would be sweet corn for sale. The stand was empty now, but in my mind there was the smell of dozens and dozens of bright yellow ears of cooked corn, soaked in sugar and dripping with melted butter. I could hear summertime sounds—big-bellied men with thick arms and straw hats and red noses full of broken veins hawking their games of skill and their confections and all the newest kitchen gadgets; a million small boys chasing after a million small girls; my mother's leather thongs making slapping sounds on the boardwalk as we walked hand in hand, surveying the beach for the best spot to pitch our blanket and umbrella for the day.

I turned to where there once was a busy newsstand, where people would buy things to read on the beach, back before transistor radios, back when people still read. The newsstand was gone.

I said to Ruby, "They used to sell the *Brooklyn Eagle* right about here. And the *Daily Mirror.* And all those movie magazines, and *Boy's Life* and the comics and *Popular Detective.* That was all about a hundred years ago."

Ruby looked as if she felt sorry for me. Sorry for all the

things lost from the present and sorry that anything remaining from the past was so badly worn.

I looked up into the windows of the Seashore Hotel across from the subway station. When I was a kid, I had not seen old fellows sitting in those windows in their undershirts staring dumbly at television sets. Now I did.

I held Ruby's hand as we crossed Surf Avenue and walked toward the rambling green-and-yellow Nathan's Famous for coffee. I was relieved to see that Nathan's was still pretty much the same: still open all day and night, every day of the year, with the fragrant steam of frankfurters and French-fried potatoes still pouring into the street and out toward the boardwalk from the cookstoves.

The long wooden open-air counters of Nathan's were speckled with customers. We stood a few feet away from a man with tattoos on his arms busy with a big plate of oysters daubed with horseradish and hot sauce.

"Look at his oysters," I said to Ruby. She looked at the tattooed man's plate. "See how they're all gray? Mother Nature made oysters pink, which is how I remember eating them when I was a kid. The oil industry went and made them gray."

Ruby groaned. "We came all the way out here today so you could reminisce about the poor old pink oysters?"

"Okay, forget oysters," I said. Then I filled her in about the photograph that Picasso had sent to Dr. Reiser at Bellevue, the picture of his "masterpiece." And how Reiser had explained that Picasso had painted the outside illustrations of a boardwalk attraction, how that was what we had come all the way out to Coney Island to find.

"So exactly where will we find it?" Ruby asked.

"Somewhere in Astroland."

"Astroland?"

"It's what they call the amusement park here at Coney Island, like the midway at a carnival. We're looking for a dark maze attraction here; that's carnival lingo for a spook house. Ours is called 'Fire and Brimstone.' "

"Oh, good. They had a spook house at City Park in New Orleans, when I was a kid. God, I used to love it! Big and dark inside and full of twisty little hallways, with mirrors to confuse you and creepy noises and sudden drafts. Skeletons and witches would be jumping out from everyplace."

Ruby clasped her elbows in her hands and rocked herself, remembering. "It scared me real good, every time." Her eyes were wide, and as radiant as whitecaps out on the sunlit Atlantic.

"I wish we'd been kids together," I said.

"You were one of those boys who just loved to get a girl all screaming and silly with a spider or a toad, weren't you, Hock?"

"I might have tried that on you."

"For you, I might have screamed."

Back in the city this could have been a lovely moment that could have had us hurrying back to my place to draw the curtains. I hate Brooklyn.

We finished our coffee and rounded the back of Nathan's to Bowery Avenue, which cuts through Astroland on the way to the boardwalk and the beach. We passed by the Eldorado Arcade, Sportland, Faber's Fascination, the Silver Ski, and Treasure Island. And a few dozen booths where the red-nosed carnies challenged me to knock down milk bottles with beanbags, or toss rings around spindles or fire pellets at moving lines of tin ducks. *"Hey, rubberneck! How's about taking a chance to win a nice prize for tootsie? C'mon, show us you're a big guy."*

By this enticement, I could only recollect those unpleasant times I have been plucked by Astroland sharpies hollering at me from booths, when I was a skinny young curly-headed Harp singing soprano in the boys' choir at Holy Cross Church; times when these sharpies gave thanks to the heavenly saints as they saw me coming. Even today, now that I am a wised-up cop, I am sore about those times. So it was not difficult for me to blow off anybody calling me a rubberneck.

I just turned my back on them and I turned Ruby around, too. I pointed west from Bowery Avenue while the sharpies hollered at somebody else and I said to Ruby, "Over there is the king of roller coasters, the Thunderbolt. It's that half-broken-down thing you can see is dead now. Which is a crime since Coney Island is where they invented the roller coaster."

Ruby squeezed my arm. "Nobody should see it that way. There should be more respect for a king."

And right then and there is when I should have told Ruby for the first time that I loved her. Maybe we would have forgotten all about the Fire and Brimstone and gone back to Manhattan—or at least gone down to the beach, where maybe I could have scooped up some wriggling thing from the sand or the sea and made Ruby scream. Maybe.

We heard a voice from somewhere.

"Enjoying the sun and the salt air with your girly there, are you, buddy?"

I had to look down to see where the words were coming from. And there stood a dwarf, a baby-faced man about fifty and four feet high at the highest. He had a cigarette in his mouth and wore a white jumpsuit and white sailor cap and he had a newspaper carrier's canvas bag slung over one shoulder.

He laid the bag down and said, "So, you two live around here?"

"No," Ruby answered for us both. "We're just out for the day, looking over memories."

The dwarf sniffed. "Memories ain't what they used to be."

Then he reached into his bag and pulled out two hand-bills. He gave one to me and one to Ruby. They read:

DARK MAZE

HOW SWEET IT WAS!
WE CAN BRING IT ALL BACK!
LEGALIZE CASINOS!
IT'S OUR BOARDWALK!
LET'S GET INVOLVED!

Running beneath the exclamatories was small type that spelled out: Concerned Citizens for Coney Island, followed by a Manhattan postal box and a Manhattan telephone number.

When I had finished reading, I looked at the dwarf and started to say something. But he interrupted with, "Pass the good word, okay, buddy?"

"What's the good word?" I asked.

"Gambling," he said.

"I see."

I had for years heard of one ad hoc group after another formed to lobby the legislature up in Albany for a local-option gambling bill, on the order of what they did over in New Jersey to bring about the dubious salvation of Atlantic City. One by one, the efforts sputtered out in New York, largely due to oppositionists trotting out the abused citizens of Atlantic City for their sorry testimonies.

"So, you're from around here?" Ruby asked the dwarf.

"Sure as hell I am, good-looking."

"Can you tell us where the Fire and Brimstone is? The spook house?"

"Well, of course I can," he said. "I worked every attraction in this place one time or the other. But hell, what's a nice couple of folks like you want with a place like that on a nice bright day like it is?"

Ruby smiled. "Just tell us, darling. Okay?"

The dwarf shrugged. "You go around to the right there, past the Tilt-a-Whirl," he said. "Then cut yourself another right, go down the lane and you'll find your dark maze right over by the Unicef Pavilion. You can't miss it."

We thanked him and he said, "You know, that attraction's all closed up nowadays."

I folded the handbill and put it in my back pocket. Then Ruby and I took a right, and another right to the lane just past the Tilt-a-Whirl.

The dwarf was right. We could not miss it.

Ruby covered her mouth with both hands and said, "Oh, Hock. Oh, my God."

SEVEN

Well, sure I sent it. Said I would, didn't I? Don't I always do like I say? Damn straight I do.

Sent it the day before yesterday, so he's either got it, or he gets it today. Ho, ho, will he get it!

Ought to get his attention real good, boy. Ought to scare him damn good, too. Haw! Scare him so bad he'll wet his pants. Yeah—and try ignoring that!

When murder is a lifetime in the creation, the killer is more fatally wounded than his victim. The dearly despatched may—or may not—be mourned before he is forgotten. But the survivor left holding the smoking gun or blooded knife or throat-warmed rope has already suffered a long delirium of rage and sorrow. Now he knows only the additional regret that nothing, really, has been settled after all.

Was this, after all, why Celia Furman's dead face registered no surprise?

The finer, nastier meanings behind so much of the business of homicide are not found in the mere facts of a newspaper story or a detective's report. Journalists are no more qualified to trouble themselves with the mess of the whole and lengthy truth of life and death than are their readers. And it pains me to say that while cops may be a suspicious lot, precious few are cursed with strong curiosity. Which is why there is poetry and theatre and literature—and painting—to help us consider the unthinkable, if we must.

Which I could hardly fail to consider on that Coney Island morning, standing beside poor, pretty, horrified Ruby; the two of us there, face-to-face with Picasso's self-proclaimed masterpiece—the great obscure work of an artist with a cancer on his heart.

And was his masterpiece, after all, the mark of a wounded killer?

Dr. Reiser had been shrewd to leave unspoken the shock and sickness he must have felt on seeing this work. He had recognized me as a rarely cursed cop, had he not? He had tipped me to the Fire and Brimstone, figuring I was the type who could not resist a visit to Brooklyn to see it for myself. Right he was.

Picasso had painted a mural the size of a small barn. His canvas was a two-storey, sectioned steel facade surrounding the dark, narrow doorway of Fire and Brimstone. There was a theme to the work, I discovered, as I viewed downward from the top right and left-hand sides of the ugly thing.

First, there was a satanic figure with a face like a tree stump and a great lashing split tongue who was feeding epsom salts in solution from a bottle to cringing nude men seated on overflowing toilet commodes. Below this, naked frightened women in chains drank from curling tubes connected to the commodes above. They, in turn, were seated on toilets that drained into a brown river clogged with gagging men, women and children and whole rafts of dead bodies.

DARK MAZE

Opposite the first satanic figure was another, this one playing a piano from sheet music whose title read, "Andante Shake & Hammer Blow Struck." Rising from the top of the piano were two gnarled hands controlling chains that were shackled to the bleeding arms and legs of hugely pregnant women.

At the center of the carnage, seemingly presiding over it all, was a white-haired demon with four arms and four hands, steam billowing out from manhole-size nostrils. He used two hands to toss fireballs into the already flaming and defoliated scenery; with the other two, he twisted a thick, hairy tail that snaked down between long legs. A buxom she-devil was sprawled at his feet, stroking the pointed tip of his tail; lesser endowed she-devils crowded about her, sinking their impressive fangs into her bare back and buttocks.

Ruby, meanwhile, dug her fingers into my arm the way panicky types maul their seatmates on airplane takeoffs. "It's the middle of a sunny morning and I'm standing next to an armed cop, and this *thing* I'm looking at is giving me the shaking creeps!"

From the nearby Unicef Pavilion came carillon music playing "It's a Small World After All."

I tried to be reassuring, but if I were Ruby I am not sure I would have bought the performance. "Well, that's the whole idea," I said. "Besides, I thought you liked being scared. This ought to be *fun* for you today."

She took a breath. "No, it's not. I guess it's hitting me all of a sudden why we're here, and how this is not your average Coney Island date. We're out here looking at an artist's so-called masterpiece because the other day he walked up to you in a park and talked about killing people, then he told you about a painting at a bar and you went to take a look at it and met his wife, then the next thing you know, she winds up with a bullet in her neck. And now this . . . this painting, this diseased *thing!*"

I swept my eyes over Picasso's masterpiece again and this time it took me back to all the times I had been to Astroland as a kid and had seen just this kind of horrific carny artwork—well, maybe not *this* horrific—and how I was so strangely drawn to it; how everybody else was, too, the kids and grown-ups alike. But we never looked close, as I recall. A glimpse of someone else's nightmare, and then a round of brave laughs—that was all we needed to slip into the proper spook-house mood. What reason had we to wonder about an artist's mind?

Here and there in the immense mural, paint was chipped and dulled from the winter. Panels were missing. Then I noticed the little fenced compound off to the side of Fire and Brimstone, where the weather-damaged panels were stacked and covered in gray-white primer paint, ready to be retouched for the upcoming summer season of thrills and chills. Two German shepherds guarded the art inside the fence, which was topped out in razor wire. A masterpiece deserved protection. Picasso must have been pleased.

Ruby was still jumpy. "I really do wonder what troubled old Charlie when he painted this one," she said.

"So, you think there's a message here?"

"If there is, I guess it's that we're poor dumb creatures feeding on the waste of our cruelties."

I nodded.

Ruby's eyes remained fixed on the mural. But soon she stepped away, to where she could see through the carnival booths and buildings out to the blue sea and the beach dotted with April's early sunbathers. I walked over to her.

"We spend way too much time ignoring warnings that people like Charlie Furman are always giving us," she said, "until it's too late. I know that's not very original, Hock."

"The world is unoriginal, which is why we mostly ignore each other. Forget what you might have heard—there's never been an age of reason. Life in the human race is pretty much spent in a dark maze, where we keep getting surprised by the same old things."

"Where did you learn that pretty lesson?"

"The street."

"Somebody should put it in a book."

"That would only keep people off the streets."

Ruby kissed me.

"Had enough?" she asked.

"Of this, yes," I said. And as we made our way toward the pleasant ocean vista, I told Ruby how Picasso had asked of his invisible friend and myself, *"Ho, ho, and how come I painted what I painted?"*

It was not yet noon. But here again was a day when I wanted to start drinking early. Besides which, now that I had beheld Picasso's masterpiece, was I not also at Coney Island for the purpose of visiting a certain boardwalk dive? The Neptune it was the place Celia Furman had spent the last afternoon of her life ringing up on the public telephone.

And as we walked, Ruby said, "You want to know what I sometimes think about New York, especially right now? If New York City was a movie, nobody under eighteen would be allowed in."

The Neptune did not have its actual establishment name on the sign over the door. The sign just said BAR. Being that it was the only bar left on Coney Island's boardwalk, which was crammed full of gin mills and beer gardens when I was a kid, I assumed that BAR meant Neptune.

A big rectangular place, it had a long bar with a railing along one wall. Tables and chairs were strewn around, all of them unoccupied when we walked in. The toilets were in the back, with one door marked Gents and the other Ladies and cardboard signs hung over the doorknobs that read No Changing—This Means You.

At the bar was an assortment of matted-down middle-aged men whose lives had in one way or another been twisted and pounded into fierce shapes of survival. The survivor nearest the door sat with a brown bottle of beer in a right hand nearly twice the size of the left; his buddy on the next stool had a crease in the side of his head where an ear should have been. Down aways from these two, beyond the long row of others nursing dollar drafts and unfiltered cigarettes, there was an old doll in a blonde Woolworth's wig and a gash of maroon on her lips picking at a scab on her neck. Our friend the dwarf was in animated conversation with the bartender down at the far end.

Our entrance did nothing to disturb the essential somber peace of the place. People looked up, then they looked back into their amber glasses. We were none of their business. Ruby thought we should settle down near our short friend from Bowery Avenue.

"Hi ya there, buddy," the dwarf said to me, breaking it off with the bartender. He winked at Ruby. The bartender's face was flushed and full of twitching veins, like he had been arguing strenuously. The dwarf asked us sweetly, "You two been out spreading the good word like I as't?"

I said, "Sure."

The bartender snorted. Then he asked what we would like. Ruby said club soda and I said I liked the idea of a red and a Molson. Ruby did not approve, judging by the look she shot me, but at least she kept quiet about it.

When the bartender brought our drinks and set them down, he tipped his head toward the dwarf and said, "Don't pay no attention to the little pisser. Big Stuff, we call him. He's trying to rile them up around here with his casino crapola."

Big Stuff protested, "It's the casinos that'll save our ass!"

The bartender waved a clenched fist at the dwarf and Big Stuff feinted. Then the bartender said to me, "There's other ways of bringing Coney Island back to life."

"Like hell!" Big Stuff hollered.

"Keep quiet, you nasty little shit," the bartender warned him. He pointed at us. "These here are friendly folks who dropped by for a friendly drink, which means none of your goddamn politics. So zip it. Or go peddle your handbills someplace they'll tolerate your crapola."

A few survivors took lazy note of this contention, not that they were prepared to expend any energy taking sides. But most kept drinking, or staring at drinks. The old doll kept picking her scab.

The bartender stuck out his hand. "Haven't seen you two in here before. My name's Johnny, Johnny Halo. I own the joint."

I shook his hand and then Ruby did. "I'm Neil Hockaday," I said. "May I present Ruby Flagg?"

"Nice to have newcomers," Halo said. He crossed his arms and waited for one of us to say something by way of explaining ourselves. But we kept our mouths shut, which forced Halo to put it to us bluntly: "What's your business out here today?"

"Christ on a stick," Big Stuff said. "Can't you let the nice folks have their drinks in peace?"

"It's all right," I said. "Actually, I came by to use the telephone. You have one on the premises?"

"Right over by the men's can," Halo said.

I left Ruby for a minute and went to the telephone and confirmed the number as the one Logue had given me from the phone company logs. This was the Neptune, all right. I put in a call to Logue at Central Homicide and when he answered I cupped the receiver with my hand to ask if anybody had picked up Picasso yet on the APB. No such luck, he said.

Everybody watched me as I walked back to the bar. Everybody had made me. Halo, Big Stuff, the survivors—all of them.

I sat down next to Ruby, and she right away sensed my

predicament and changed the focus neatly by asking Halo, "So how long have you been here in Coney Island?"

"I was born here, before Coney had a hospital. I never left here but once, which was the day they came and took me out of this sand and dressed me up in a uniform and sent me over to the sand in Africa with the 800 Regiment of the U.S. Army Engineers."

"All that sand," Ruby said. "It must have kept you from being homesick."

"No way," Halo said. "All the time I was gone, I couldn't wait to get back to Coney. Because this here is God's country . . ."

Big Stuff interrupted: "For which now He won't do nothing!"

Halo glared at him.

Then he asked Ruby, "You want to know how Coney I am? I'm going to tell you. I remember when a guy named Archibald Leach wore a sandwich board and walked around Surf Avenue on stilts advertising the Steeplechase; then years later you would see in the movies that he'd changed that pansy name of his to Cary Grant. Okay?

"Also I seen Abie Relis when he got tossed out a window of the Half-Moon Hotel by the goons from Murder Incorporated when he was supposed to be stashed out here in Coney for police protection. Hah! That was hilarious."

Halo glared at me.

"I seen the neighborhood change a lot," he said. "And I changed lots. But the ocean, it ain't changed. Out there, it's still blue."

A couple of reflective seconds passed and then I asked, "So you know just about everybody who ever came through Coney?"

Halo did not care much for this turn of the conversation, let alone the fact that I had entered it. He answered warily. "I guess so, just about. You're a cop, ain't that right?"

Picasso's voice again. *"Cop, ain't you?"*

I took the gold shield from my pocket and put it on the bar. "Detective Hockaday. You can call me Hock."

"She a cop, too?" Halo asked, a hammy thumb directed at Ruby.

"No, she isn't," Ruby said. "I'm just along to learn about the street."

Then Big Stuff got excited. He rose from his stumpy legs, which he had folded up beneath him on the barstool, and said to Halo, "Johnny, him and the woman, they as't about Fire and Brimstone."

"Shut up!" Halo snarled.

"Do you know a man named Charlie Furman who sometimes calls himself Picasso?" I asked him.

"Never heard of him."

Big Stuff also shook his head. A bodyguard of lies was spread all over their faces.

I asked Halo, "How about Celia Furman?"

"Likewise," Halo said.

"Nope," Big Stuff said.

I decided the conversation needed stimulation. "Celia Furman was murdered two days ago, in the city. Before she got it, she made a lot of telephone calls—to that phone over there by the gents'."

Halo's eyes flickered disagreeably. He said, "Too bad about the lady."

"According to telephone company logs," I said, "she pretty much tied up your telephone over there for the afternoon. I think you'd notice that."

"What day was it again?" Halo said.

"Two days ago. In the afternoon."

"Oh, yeah, I remember now. That's the day we got real, real busy in here."

I looked down the bar. Everybody stared at drinks. This was none of their business. "So busy you never noticed all the phone calls?"

"Afraid not."

This could have gone on for hours. Which only tells you how badly I handled it. I would have to come back once I figured out why Johnny Halo was lying, and once I remembered rule number one of being a detective: know most of the answers to most of your questions before you ask.

We finished our drinks and left, then walked back to where we had started, the taffy stand just outside the subway station. Ruby said, "So the day shouldn't be a complete waste, Hock, why don't you spring for some cotton candy? I haven't had cotton candy since I was a kid in plaits and mama-jama dresses."

I gave a couple of dollars to the curly-headed young woman running the stand, and she obliged with a fat wad of feathery pink cotton candy. I said she should keep the change and she said, "God bless."

Then Ruby and I rode the F train back to Manhattan.

I suggested lunch at Angelo's Ebb Tide, which Ruby thought was a good idea since she could then study another of Picasso's paintings. And then after a good long lunch, we made plans for a night downtown at Ruby's place. But first we would stop by my apartment because Ruby had some telephone calls to make and I wanted to collect my toothbrush and read my mail.

Good plans are sometimes unkept, even by the most well intentioned. In our case, this was because of the mail.

Specifically because of a plain white business-size envelope addressed to me, with a city postmark. It was the cheap kind of envelope that comes a hundred to the box at any Lamston's store. There was a flag stamp on the envelope, upside down.

And inside, a Polaroid photograph.

It was the picture of a painting hung on a bare wall. The artist had rendered the figure of a man with a frizz of black hair. The man lay on his belly on a rooftop garden, with a knife plunged into his back.

EIGHT

I telephoned Logue, who of course had called it a day. Then I rang Neglio, who of course had done the same. And then I made the mistake of dialing Bellevue.

"Admissions, may I help you?"

"I want to speak to Dr. Ronald Reiser."

"Dr. Pfizer retired. Last year or maybe the year before."

"No, Reiser. Not Pfizer, *Reiser.*"

"You don't want Dr. Pfizer?"

"No, I want Reiser."

"This Dr. Kaiser, he's with Bellevue Hospital?"

"I don't want Kaiser, I want *Reiser.*"

"Young man, is this some kind of game?"

"What?"

"You guys in the barrooms, you think you're pretty funny, hey?"

"Look, lady. I'm a cop and I want to talk to Dr. Ronald Reiser."

"Well I don't have any way of knowing who I'm talking to, and besides I don't know anybody here named Rice."

"What the hell is your name, lady?"

"That is certainly none of your business!"

I counted to ten fast and said, "Let's start all over. My name is Detective Hockaday . . ."

"Oh, and a detective yet."

"Please, I would like to speak to Dr. Ronald Reiser. That's spelled R-E-I-S-E-R."

"You think I don't know how to spell?"

"I think you don't know how to answer a telephone."

"Don't tell me how to do my job!"

"Transfer this call to the Zoo for Christ's sake!"

"So we're familiar with the name Zoo? I thought as much."

"Transfer the freaking call!"

I waited. The line clicked. A woman with at least a double load of chewing gum came on.

"Psych services."

"Dr. Ronald Reiser please."

"Usually he's gone out of here by this time. He supposed to be on tonight?"

"I don't know. You tell me."

"Got no time for games, man."

"Me neither. So I'm going to say this once: My name is Neil Hockaday, I'm a detective with the New York City Police Department, and I want to talk to Dr. Ronald Reiser, if that's all right with you."

"Whoa, man!"

She connected me to a line that rang a dozen times, then she cut back in. "Told you. He's gone." She giggled.

"But he's not always in his private office. He might be walking around the ward. You want to page him, darling?"

"Whoa, man!" The pace of her chewing quickened. Then she covered the telephone speaker and I heard her muffled call to someone, "Hey, Freddy, check out Doc Reiser, see if he ain't gone home yet."

The phone slammed down on a desk, which I took as my cue to stand by while Freddy searched the Zoo floor. I waited. I listened to gum popping, patients mumbling and shuffling along in felt slippers, the occasional scream. Meanwhile, Ruby sat across from me on the couch under the window and examined the Polaroid of the grisly painting and declared, "No doubt about it, this is Charlie Furman's style." Then I heard Freddy (presumably) say, "Well I went and looked pretty much everyplace. I guess he's gone checked out."

And then, "Hey man, you still there?"

I put on my shoulder holster and a tweed jacket. Ruby put on a pout.

"What am I supposed to do while you're gone?"

"Don't be like that, Ruby."

"How sweet. Our first argument."

"Come off it. The inmates are running the asylum. You know I have to go."

"Sure, go. And leave me here again."

In two and a half turns of her head, Ruby took a disapproving inventory of my sorry little apartment: lumpy couch, green fringed chair next to table with an old wooden radio and a rotary telephone, non-working fireplace, books crammed onto a wall of shelves, the kitchen alcove blighted with a sink full of dishes and a crusted chili pot on the stove, door to the untidy bath, unmade bed through the archway to the other room, the sideboard with Johnnie Walker in the cupboard and a black-and-white Philco on top.

"You could watch television."

"Oh, swell suggestion, Hock."

"It passes the time."

"Yes, and it's so educational. The minute somebody turns on television, I go and read a book."

"That's my girl," I laughed. "I hate to say it, but don't wait up."

Ruby did not laugh. "I hate to hear it. But I suppose I'll have to get used to it."

"Do you?"

She got up from the couch and came to me. She ran her almond fingers over my coat buttons and smoothed the sleeves and folded her arms around my waist, grazing me with her hips. She slipped one of her knees between mine. If I ever got out the door and downstairs to the street, I thought, I would possess the strength of ten men.

Her voice was low, like a lady disc jockey's on an overnight jazz show. "Got your guns now, Detective Hockaday?"

"Yes, ma'am."

"Your badge, and that nasty picture?"

"Yes."

"That's my boy."

And then I had to leave, ready or not.

I walked over toward the Midtown North Precinct, which is luckily only a block from my apartment. Lucky because I was wobbly in the knees, exactly the way I had been one fateful May evening when the world was young and I had to pin a gardenia onto a spaghetti strap of Judy McKelvey's prom dress. I wound up married to Judy McKelvey, but it was not a heaven-made match and we divorced. After all that, I was now merely a big wobbly cop suddenly hit by the warm fact that somebody was waiting for me at home again, and right in the middle of a case of murder, too. As a regular person, at least, I was making progress.

The desk sergeant obliged my request for a driver by assigning me an auxiliary cop named Liz. Liz was like lots of other female auxiliary cops I have seen: hair done up in a ruthless bun, breasts weirdly flattened by her uniform, plenty of makeup, eager to the point of twitching. It could have been worse; the desk sergeant could have found me a Chuck.

"Oh, Detective Hockaday!" Liz chirped. "I've heard about you."

"I didn't know that."

"Well, I have. I've heard all about you!" She stared at me like I was some jock come to life off a baseball card. "Where're we going tonight? Should I wear a vest?"

"I guess vests are okay, so far as they go," I said. "But nowadays, you know, the bad guys are mostly shooting headers at cops."

Eagerness faded from Liz's lips. "I never actually realized that."

"Not too many people do. And there's practically no way of protecting yourself against headers, especially now with the bad guys just shoving their semiautomatics right in your face and squeezing off a clip. You never know. But we might be safe for tonight. I only want a lift across town, all right?"

"Oh. Right. I'll bring a car around."

"That would be nice."

Liz did not care to chat with me anymore, which was the idea. So I enjoyed a nice conversation-free ride in her auxiliary patrol car over to the East Side. I used the quiet time to contemplate how somebody would have to conduct himself to elude Bellevue's crack security staff if he got it into his head to kill his psychiatrist. Which, unless Ronald Reiser was at home in shorts watching television or something—in my haste and dread, I had not bothered to check out—was maybe what recently happened.

But wait. The last time Picasso showed his face at Bellevue, he assaulted Reiser and they tossed the net over him. Why return now? Because he painted a murderscape? Because he sent me a Polaroid picture of this handiwork in the mail? Did I really expect I would, ipso facto, find death imitating art? Was this line of thinking nuts, or what?

Or what. I had Liz drop me off three blocks from the Bellevue gate so I could walk in unannounced as a cop. Along the way, I bought a big spray of daisies from a florist shop.

In the lobby of the psychiatric ward were a few of the

same zoned-out patients in wheelchairs I had seen the other day. But instead of a duty nurse, there was a badly undernourished clerk manning an access control desk. He had one pair of horn-rimmed spectacles propped up on top of his bony head and he used another, smaller pair to pore over a crossword puzzle magazine.

"Say is that the newest issue?" I asked him.

He jumped and his top pair of glasses slid off. "Huh? Yup, bought it this morning."

"I do all the crosswords myself," I said, which was partly a lie since I only do the puzzles in the *Times* and the *Daily News* but never on Sundays.

"Y'do?"

"Sure, sure. What's Q-U-O-C-N-G-U, brother?"

He slapped the thin blue-white skin of his forehead and said, "Wait a minute now . . . I know that one. Ah— *quocngu* . . . the Vietnamese alphabet!"

I stuck out a hand. "Put her there, pal. You're a real tack."

We shook. I tried not to pull off his arm. He waited for me to state my business. And waited. I have found by long experience in the police business that, if I keep my mouth shut when all about me the world is noisy and overly talkative, people I am dealing with become nervous and awkward, and that when they are in such a state it is not so difficult for me to persuade them to do what I want done. Lying also helps.

"Ah, you're here to what, visit somebody or something?" he finally asked. "Visiting hours don't start 'til after they finish the feeding time, you know."

I paused, looked at my flowers and grinned at him. "Oh, you mean these."

"Yeah. You taking them up to a patient?"

I grinned.

"Please, mister, you got to tell me what you want."

I grinned some more, stalling for time to improvise a

response. "Oh, I'm not here to see a patient. Well, not exactly."

"What then?"

"Didn't they tell you about me?"

"Who?"

"Say now, you weren't so wrapped up doing those crossword puzzles you didn't get the word, were you?"

His face flushed deep red. He stammered, "Hell, I been doing my job here like I'm supposed to."

"Say no more, brother. I understand how it gets down here. A man's got to do something to relax. You got the public to deal with, you got doctors to deal with. Us doctors, we're the worst. Am I right?"

"Well, yeah . . ."

"God bless you. What's your name?"

"Stanley." He was suddenly worried. "Hey, you ain't going to say I been cooping!"

"You got no problem with me, so don't worry. I'm Dr. Neil, from up in White Plains. Anybody asks me, I'll tell them you knew that. Have you got a cigarette, Stanley?"

He fumbled in his pants pockets and one hand came up with a pack of Kools. "You can't smoke except for in the special lounges."

"Hey, I know that. We got the same rules up in White Plains. It's for later."

"Oh, yeah. Sorry, Dr. Neil."

"You like these flowers?"

"They're okay."

"You think my wife's going to like them?"

"Yup."

"Good. It's our anniversary and she's waiting for me up there in Westchester and here I am stuck in the city on a consultation up in the Zoo. You think they've got a vase and water up in the Zoo, Stanley?"

"I don't know about that."

"Gosh, I sure hope so. I want to keep these fresh for the missus. You know."

"Yup."

I grinned at Stanley for a second or two. And he waited for me to say something. And waited. "I'd better get up there now, don't you think, Stanley? What do I need from you, a pass or something?"

"Oh—a'course."

Stanley could not move fast enough to tage me with a badge that said VISITING PHYSICIAN. I said, "Thanks a lot, Stanley—from one *blinkard* to another, right?"

His face brightened, and as I started moving toward the elevator restricted for doctors only I heard him saying, *"Blinkard*—one with bad eyes, a stupid or obtuse person, someone who ignores or avoids something."

Up on the Zoo floor, I followed my ears to the sound of gum-chewing at the receptionist's station and beheld the woman I had spoken to earlier on the telephone. This one was plump and cross-eyed and her name tag said she was Desiree. I stood there with my flowers looking at her.

Desiree read my VISITING PHYSICIAN badge and stared at my flowers and waited. I finally said, "Dr. Neil, to see Dr. Ronald Reiser."

"Well, um, he's gone."

"That's odd. He's expecting me."

"We just been looking for him ourselves. 'Bout a half hour ago, maybe forty-five minutes. We couldn't find him no-where."

I gave her the flowers. "He said you liked daisies."

"What you talking 'bout Doc Reiser say I like daisies?"

I shrugged.

"What time you supposed to see Doc Reiser anyhow?"

I looked at my wristwatch. "Oh, I'm a little early."

"Oh, so he must be coming in tonight."

"That must be it. I guess he didn't tell you? Us doctors, we'd forget everything if it wasn't for the staff, am I right?"

"That's the truth." She found a vase in a cabinet under the reception desk and started arranging the daisies in it. "You want to take a seat?"

"Well, actually, Dr. Reiser told me he might be a little late and that I should ask for Freddy to show me right on into his office."

"Okay. I'll get him."

She hollered for Freddy and in about five minutes I found myself inside Reiser's private office, thanks to the accommodating Freddy and his special keys to the double electromagnetic locks on the psychiatrists' office doors.

"You want any coffee, or a sandwich with it? Or anything?" Freddy asked.

I took a look around Reiser's cluttered little office, with the picture of Freud on the wall and the you-toucha-my-cup, I-breaka-you-face mug on his desk. It was a quick look, but long enough so I could see that nothing violent had happened in there. The mug could have used a rinsing. I grinned at Freddy standing in the doorway, waiting for me to say something. Freddy grinned back.

I pulled Stanley's cigarette out from my shirt pocket. "I wouldn't want to stink up Ron's office."

"Naw, I wouldn't neither. People're pretty snorty about that these days." Freddy jangled the impressive batch of keys clamped to his belt. "You gotta come with me and I'll take you down t'the staff smokers' lounge."

As we walked down a corridor, I asked, "You keep the smoking lounge locked up, too?"

"Hell, yes, Doc. We're tighter'n a drum around here. Gotta be. In case you ain't noticed, this floor's crawlin' with loons who'd kill you if they got half the chance."

"Nothing gets by you security guys, right, Freddy?"

"Very little, my friend."

I stopped when I spotted the sign that read TO ROOF. And I said to Freddy, "It's such a nice night, maybe I should go up there to have my smoke."

"Sure, go on. That door's open."

"It is?"

Freddy sighed. "Yeah, Doc Reiser, he's forever goin' up there to his tomatoes and he can't never remember to use the right key, so one day when he's usin' the wrong one he goes and breaks it off in the slot and t'make a long story short we hadda bust off the whole damn lock to make the door open up and shut normal and we ain't fixed the situation yet."

"How long has the lock been broken on this door?"

"I guess a month, thereabouts."

"A month and you can't get a locksmith up here?"

"Hey, Doc, this is New York. You get a maintenance man inside of a year, it's a rush job."

"I see what you mean." I put my hand on the broken lock. "Earlier tonight, I hear you were looking for Dr. Reiser. Did you look up on the roof?"

Freddy's face was quizzical, like he was an infant on the verge of soiling his diaper. "No, man. I didn't think of that."

"Let's go take a look now, Freddy."

Sure, I told her plenty of times. Plenty! Damn straight I did.

I even told her what it says right there in the Holy goddamn Bible, black on white, where it says, "I will betroth thee unto me forever; yea, I will betroth thee unto me in righteousness, and in judgement, and in loving kindness, and in mercies."

Women—haw! Oh, they really got their hooks into every goddamn thing there is, don't they? Ain't I telling the truth?

Did you know there's more women than anything else on Earth, except insects?

Damn straight.

I know that sounds buggy. Well, all right. I'm a crazy freaking bedbug and I ain't never claimed otherwise. That's how come I seen all them headshrinkers for so long, okay?

But, hey, no more of that!

You think I ever got a ounce of sympathy from that crowd?

DARK MAZE

Even when I told them about her? Even when I showed how you can't count on the Holy goddamn Bible no more? Haw!

This one shrinker, though . . . he listened to me hard. Hard like a cop listens. This one, he was sneaky like that.

He thinks he's so funny. This one, he thinks laughing's going to do me good. Once he says to me, "Life's a zoo inside of a jungle."

How about that? Well, that I got to laugh at.

But laughing, what good's that going to do for us crazy freaking bedbugs?

That's what I'm telling you about shrinkers: they ought to know better and they say they know better. But they don't. Not even when it comes to laughs.

Laugh and the world laughs with you. Cry, and they really start laughing.

NINE

$\mathbf{F}$reddy had to be sick.

I asked him if he could wait until I had the chance to take him back downstairs. But instead of answering he covered up his mouth with both hands and ballooned his cheeks and flapped his elbows and hopped up and down, which made all the keys on his belt jangle.

I told him to please go toss it over by the steam generators and vents on the opposite end of the roof. Otherwise, he would seriously contaminate the crime scene where Dr. Reiser reposed, gut side down among his prize tomato vines, with a foot-long butcher knife sunk nearly all the way into his back along the middle seam of his blood-streaked lab coat.

Strictly by the book, a cop who happens on a murdered corpse is supposed to right away call out a forensics squad and enough uniforms to rope off the general vicinity and discourage a crowd of lawyers and gawkers from gathering; then Central Homicide, which is supposed to contact the D.A.'s office, which in turn is supposed to ring up the Medical Examiner at the morgue, which in the borough of

DARK MAZE

Manhattan is next door to Bellevue Hospital. But in this case, I did not see the need of standing on ceremony. I wanted a few minutes alone in the moonlight with the remains of Ronald Reiser before the rest of the world learned that somebody could bluff his way into Bellevue fairly easily and kill a psychiatrist if he wanted. Besides, I could not in very good conscience go downstairs and put in my calls while Freddy stayed up on the roof woozing and heaving and jangling.

Poor Freddy. All the way up the stairs from the Zoo to the rooftop he kept apologizing for the oversight in his search for Reiser. I knew what he was thinking: *This floor's crawlin' with loons . . .*

The atmosphere on the roof did nothing to help Freddy's sweat glands. It was still and black up there, the way Ruby once told me it gets down in Louisiana just before a hurricane blows up from the Gulf of Mexico; the air felt wet and dead. We walked the three hundred or so feet from the door to Reiser's garden, where his big wooden planters were arranged six in a circle with a seventh one at the center. The sound of our feet moving over the close-packed gravel was muffled by the roaring hum of air-conditioning pumps and incinerator chimneys.

Then we noticed the pigeons.

Maybe thirty to forty pigeons were clustered around a single tub in the garden, the middle one. They were pecking furiously at something, silent but for the rustling of wings. Another step closer and we were hit by the sharp, sickening odor of blood, urine and feces. Which was when Freddy took ill.

As Freddy loped off, I shooed away the scavenging pigeons. Then I stepped into an inky shaft of light wafting from the fluorescent stairwell of an adjacent building and fished out the Polaroid that Picasso had mailed from a jacket pocket. I squinted and studied the photograph in this poor light. The painting in the photo showed Reiser from the rear, flopped over the edge of one of his planter tubs with the knife sticking up about where his belt loops would be. Then I stepped back to Reiser's body, to compare compositions.

The knife as it actually appeared in Reiser was considerably higher up the back than in Picasso's painting. In the painting, the blade would have been piercing through Reiser's kidneys en route to his lower abdomen. In real death, however, one or both of Reiser's lungs had been sliced open, judging from the knife's final position, and by the huge pool of blood beneath his head. Where Reiser's face lay smashed in the planter tub, the soil glistened. A knife-ripped lung quickly fills with blood, which then gushes up through the windpipe and pours out of the body through the mouth and nostrils; almost always, the victim of a back-stabbing such as Reiser's gags to death on his own blood before the lung ceases its respiratory function.

The heavy expulsion of bodily wastes told me that Reiser had been completely at ease before the surprise assault, that his back was undoubtedly turned on his killer and that he never knew what hit him. Consequently, his bladder and bowels never clenched tight, as they do when a man takes on his assailant face-to-face.

By now, the odor was overwhelming me. And the handkerchief that I had bunched up to cover my nose and mouth no longer worked. There was not much more that I could learn by my preliminary examination.

A garden trowel lay about ten feet from the tub that held Reiser's lifeless body; it must have flown from his hand the first time he was struck. I touched the blood caked on Reiser's lab coat; it was still somewhat tacky, but turning dusty the way blood does after exposure to the air for a few hours. The autopsy report would pinpoint the time of his death, but for right now I guessed that Reiser got it right about when the Bellevue medical staff was changing from day to evening shift and anybody might reasonably assume

1e had left for home. He probably got it when Ruby and I were eating a late luncheon of fish and chips at Angelo's Ebb Tide.

I was halfway across the roof toward Freddy when it struck me: in Picasso's painting, Dr. Reiser was not wearing a lab coat. I made a mental note to write this down later.

Freddy had nothing left inside him but coughs and whimpers. I held him by the shoulders. He looked at me gratefully as I steered him back downstairs.

Central Homicide was having a slow night. It was closing n on ten o'clock and during the whole day I had turned up he only murder in all five boroughs of New York City. Early April is a relatively nonviolent time of the year in New York, but the city's killing pace grows brisker as income-tax deadlines near and then we get up to a fine breakneck speed by August's dog days. Right then, though, sullen detectives n bad suits and unflattering light were mostly idled. They typed up hated case-load status reports or otherwise chuffed through hated indoor tasks, or else they ate doughnuts and drank coffee.

I myself had engaged in the latter activity for the past thirty-five minutes, practically ever since arriving from Bellevue. I had dutifully made my initial calls from the hospital. Then, when the rooftop party was in full attendance and I could gracefully slip away, I decided to have one of the uniforms run me downtown so I could have some official peace and quiet in order to put in two additional calls: one to Logue, out of respect and also to ask him where his file on Picasso might be, and one to Inspector Neglio.

Neglio was the more difficult call.

Naturally, I rang Logue first. I reached him easily enough at his home in the Bronx. Much to my surprise, he said, "I'm glad you called me, Hock. I'll be right down there. Have the captain let you into my office, take a load off."

The night clerk in Neglio's office read me the inspector's

evening itinerary and if I did not know better, I might have thought the guy was running for public office. Neglio was scheduled for a Knights of Columbus spaghetti banquet at half-past six out in Bay Ridge, then a mid-evening drop-by back in Manhattan at some Park Avenue soiree to benefit the poor and downtrodden, then he had to make some after-dinner remarks at a session of the New York Press Club. I finally reached him up at Gracie Mansion, where the mayor and his wife were tossing a party for the U.N. crowd.

"What is it, Hock?" he barked when a butler on the city payroll handed him the telephone. I was fairly sure I heard a woman nuzzling his neck and ear. "And it better be damn good!"

"Have you heard any news broadcasts tonight?"

Neglio sighed. "By that, you mean have I heard about the homicide at Bellevue?"

"That news, yes."

"I knew I shouldn't have answered the phone!" Neglio sighed again, and then some baby-doll voice in the background on his end said, "Oh, you're no fun!" Then Neglio covered the telephone speaker with his hand and said to the baby doll, "Christ, I'm on the horn!"

"Inspector?"

"Okay, so I heard about that," he said to me. "In fact, they were asking my reaction at the press club and I said I deplored the senseless violence."

Baby doll muttered "Oh, pooh!" and Neglio sighed again and said, "All right, what is this, your latest nut job in action again, what's his name?"

"Picasso."

"Yeah, that one. We got an APB out on him, right? What's going now, a serial number?"

"No question about it. And you know how jumpy head-quarters gets about serial murder."

"Not to mention that the second hit takes down a doctor, right *in* Bellevue Hospital."

"Sorry to upset your evening, Inspector."

"Well, not as sorry as the doctor, I guess. Dr. what's-his-name."

"Reiser."

"Yeah, that doctor. Look, Hock, you got any kind of a line on this Picasso character?"

"There's not much to go on. I've got Logue on his way down here from the Bronx, and we're going to look over the record, such as it is. I do know one thing . . ."

"Which is what?"

"I'm going to need you to smooth the way for me on this one. You're good with the types likely to be getting in my way."

"Like the press, right? Yeah, I can see that coming."

"Also I can see City Hall wanting to get all over my case, along with the usual flock of free-lance justice seekers."

"I *knew* I shouldn't have answered the phone."

So Neglio hung up.

And that was when I started in on the doughnuts and coffee. The third coffee sent me to the men's room, which is where I bumped into Davy Mogaill.

I was standing at one of those big old-fashioned marble urinals enjoying my relief and a couple of graffiti just above eye-level: BE RIGHT BACK—GODOT and DYSLEXICS OF THE WORLD, UNTIE! Then in walked Davy Mogaill, whom I know from the very old days up in the Twenty-sixth Precinct in Morningside Heights. Mogaill was already a detective when I was a rookie, then he rose to a captaincy at Central Homicide.

Mogaill unzipped at a urinal one over from mine, recognized me, smiled and said, "Is this where the dicks hang out?" He had himself a husky laugh, after which he asked, "What brings you to the murder beat, Hock?"

I explained how I was doing an override on the Celia Furman case, a homicide in my own personal neighborhood, and how Logue was the detective of record. Mogaill rolled his head and sniffed, "Oh, yeah, that lovely one in the barroom—a nine-to-fiver." I further told him that the guy we wanted for questioning in the Celia Furman case was now also implicated in the day's sole murder. Which caused Mogaill to whistle admiringly. "Now that one," he said, "is going to be grabbing them headlines big and black."

We zipped up at the same time and moved to the sinks to wash our hands.

"I'm waiting for Logue now," I said.

"He's coming in after hours? I'm impressed."

"He told me to make myself at home in his office."

"His *office,* is it? That's a bit of a grand word for what he has. But come along with me."

Logue's office turned out to be a corner of the file room that nobody else wanted because it had no window. Logue had arranged a dozen or so cabinets at right angles to the walls to form an enclosed space, inside of which he had a standard-issue green steel desk spilling over with papers and also a credenza spilling over with papers. There was a lamp on his desk and a Norelco electric coffee maker on a stand next to it. "Welcome," Captain Mogaill said.

I picked up a pile of manila folders off a side chair, stacked them on the floor and sat down.

"How long's it been since you and me had a jar together, Hock?" Mogaill asked.

I thought back and said, "It had to have been at Nugent's, uptown in the Thirty-fourth."

"Jaysus, that long ago?"

"It was long ago, wasn't it?"

"I remember it being always so full of cops, along with writers and poets and such layabouts living there in Inwood on account of the cheap rents. And the juke—it was heavy on 'Ireland United,' and Bushmill's or Paddy's was a half-dollar the shot. Oh, I wonder what ever happened to the glorious place."

"I still go there sometimes."

Mogaill was amazed.

I said, "I remember the first time we met at Nugent's and I thought you were one of the house poets."

"I remember it, too. I was in my cups pretty good and thinking about the other side, trying to drive sweet memories away . . ."

"And what you said was, 'Ain't it loveliness to be here in a grand dark pub in New York, so bless't far removed from the bloody peat bogs and all them smelly farmers' tweeds?'"

"Yes . . ." Mogaill's eyes grew to their brightest blue. "And also I was thinking how Brendan put it on the topic of New York, and I stole his line: 'I feel I'm a lonely flea what finally found his dog.'"

"Naturally, I took you for a poet."

"You were a classy one that long-ago night, sending the barkeep over with the gift of whiskey and the thanks of a fellow admirer of the Borstal Boy. I saluted you then, and I salute you now, Hock. Even though you were so very wrong."

"About what?"

"Wrong about us. It turns out you're the poet."

"No, I'm a cop."

"That's so, but I know about cops like you, and cops like me. Which is why I rose to captain and why you never shall, my friend. It means you're the one cursed with being forever curious about what it is that people choose to hide from the world; it means you're a trespasser."

He added, "Did you never hear it told, Detective Hockaday, of the poet's natural right of trespass?"

"I—"

Mogaill interrupted. "See them manila folders on the floor, Hock? And all them folders on that credenza back of the desk?"

"Yes."

"Come here a moment." I followed him out of Logue's makeshift office to the wider space of the file room. Mogaill stepped to a long wall filled with steel shelves and he ran his hand along the bindings of big books that bulged with more manila folders, and perforated computer print-out sheets. He said, "And see all this here?"

"Yes."

"This here's an office full of names that belong to people who don't talk too much because they're dead. At first, I tried like hell to remember the names, even if they were only John Doe or Mary Roe.

"But, Hock, they started gaining on me. And every year, I forgot more and more names. Then I went mostly by the numbers. Then guess what happened?"

"I don't want to guess."

"Then I'll tell you. They made me captain."

"And then?"

"Then I even started forgetting the numbers. One day I realized that everybody was zero to me, and that so far as I'm concerned, zero isn't a real number. So now you see what kind of a cop I have become, Hock—the guy in charge of homicide in a homicidal town, the guy in charge of all the zeroes."

"Which does not strike you as poetical?"

"Not bloody particularly."

Mogaill turned heavily to leave. "For old days' sake, we should have a jar together sometime."

"I wish you good luck, Davy."

"The same for yourself, Hock."

I returned to Logue's tiny office and sat down to think, but I did not progress too far. Five minutes later, there was Logue seated at his desk opposite me and riffling through the clutter of paper and telling me the reason why he was so happy to be with me at Central Homicide instead of in his warm house in the Bronx. The reason was not poetical.

"My wife, she's got it in her bonnet that we got to improve ourselves by listening to opera on the radio when we sit down to eat dinner," Logue said.

"That's rough."

"You're telling me. I am trying to enjoy my pork chops and hot applesauce and scalloped potatoes and, my wife, she's explaining to me how this unlucky gang of Ethiopian prisoners on a forced march in front of this Pharaoh; then about this babe called Aïda, who is a slave girl but actually she's the Ethiopians' princess. . . .Oh, and it just goes on and on like that forever, Hock. And everybody's singing in dago. Like the wife, she suddenly understands dago, right?"

I pictured Ruby and me at a table with pork chops for dinner and opera on the radio. This picture did not look so bad to me, even though I do not understand Italian.

"Well, I'm sorry for your troubles," I said.

"Thanks." Logue finally came up with the papers he was looking for. "Okay, so what's new with our boy Charlie Furman, Picasso?"

I quickly filled in Logue about the murder of Dr. Reiser, and the relationship between Picasso and the psychiatrist. Also I showed Logue the Polaroid that Picasso had sent me.

"Holy flying crap!" Logue said. "Old Charlie's really branched out from knocking off his wife, hey?"

"It looks that way."

"Anything else I should know, in case somebody asks me?"

Since he asked, I told Logue how it all began for me, about the picture, the dark maze, Coney Island. I told Logue all this mostly so I could say it to myself all over again.

"The Fire and Brimstone," I said, "you would have to see to believe."

"I seen that Coney Island stuff before. I don't know from art, but I know a bugged artist. They sure went and hired some beauts to paint up Coney, didn't they?"

"Yeah, they sure did." I do not know why, but I left out my encounter with Johnny Halo and Big Stuff at the Neptune and the transparency of their lies when I asked them if they knew Charlie or Celia Furman. Neither did I tell Logue about the old black-and-white snapshot of Celia when she was young and beautiful and high-spirited, and walking the Coney Island boardwalk back in '54 on the arms of two men.

"So you're out chasing a bugged artist, Hock. You're going to need help. I don't mind helping."

I was surprised. "You told me yourself this was strictly nine-to-five, Logue. Besides which, the word on you is that you're putting in for pension any day now."

"Hey, you never changed your mind? And who says I'm strapping on the parachute anyways?"

"What does it matter?"

Logue pulled on his square chin. "The way it looks to me, retirement's going to mean hanging around the house trying to survive the wife's ideas on how we got to enrich our lives—like her freaking opera. I am therefore seeing retirement in a whole new light."

I am fond of honestly stated motives, and I could use extra legs. "All right, Logue. Here's what I need: I want you to run down everything you can on Celia Furman, her life and her loves and all like that. It ought to be easier getting a profile on her than on Charlie."

Logue started making notes on a pad.

"Remember back at the Ebb Tide the other day, you said you thought Celia was off-balance?" I asked him.

"Yeah, off-balance from the gambling rackets, which is where Angelo says she came out of."

"There's also the IRS business."

"Oh, yeah, them government accountants keep very good tabs I can check out."

"That's the idea," I said. "Something to give us a hook. I didn't find any hooks or much of anything else on her husband."

"You think I did?"

"I was hoping."

Logue picked up a piece of paper on which he had earlier scratched some notes.

"I wish I could say I found out a whole lot," he said. "But, really, to judge him by the record, the life of Picasso don't add up to much."

"It ain't your fault you don't know me. I ain't made much of a mark in this life."

"Just tell me what you have."

Logue put on a pair of half-frame reading glasses and consulted his notes. "There's a birth certificate from a small town in Kentucky called Payne, which figures. And then Pfc. Charles Bernard Furman got an honorable discharge from the Army in September of 1945. Sometime right after that, he winds up in Detroit."

Logue looked at me over the tops of his glasses and said, "Detroit is where I'm getting this stuff, by the way. There's nothing on him here in New York."

"Yeah, I know."

"Anyhow," Logue said, continuing, "the local V.A. hospital out in Detroit says Charlie had ringing in his ears and came in for treatment a few times, but they couldn't do nothing to help him."

Logue read a little further. "Oh, and there's papers at the welfare department that says once he needed help feeding his family, which was him and his pregnant wife, Celia."

"What about work?"

"The guy never had a payroll job. Can you believe it? And Detroit being a boom town after the war and all? Anyhow, the welfare office out there says he used to sell little pictures he painted, at fairs and such. That's all anybody knows about a job. Charlie was not a big provider."

". . . As a husband and a papa, I was a lousy flop."

Logue dropped the notes from his hands and said, "So that gets us to Charlie Furman in the year 1950."

"And then?"

"End of story."

"That's it?"

"Unless you know something I don't know."

"No," I said. Not about Charlie Furman's life anyway.

"Strange, ain't it? I never ran across anybody who dropped clear off the page like this guy did. It's like one year in the prime of his life, the record just stopped on Charlie Furman."

"Like he stopped living."

"That's it, like he just stopped."

And at that moment, I did what I do every day. Which is to have a passing thought of a man I never met. He is a photograph in a picture frame on top of the dresser in my bedroom. I have had dreams about him all my life. But in the dreams, he never makes it out of that picture frame; in my dreams, the frame sometimes has two legs and soldier's boots, and the photograph is marching through a battlefield.

"I know a guy like that," I said.

"Who?"

"My old man."

TEN

Logue yawned, loud and wet. "Fathers and sons, now there's a long freaking story. I lay you ten to one, somebody's already made an opera out of it."

I appreciated now my instinct to hold back on Logue. Maybe I was right; maybe he was one of those steak-and-potatoes detectives, best left unburdened by the idea of the big picture of a case. Give the man a specific investigative task—his own personal meat—and he becomes a competent bloodhound. So okay. Logue would handle the ancient history part of Celia Furman's life. The rest of it was mine, including all surrealistic thoughts of pictures coming to life.

"I think we're finished here," I said.

Logue yawned again. "Great. Me, I'm for the sack and watching Johnny between my toes. How about yourself?"

Logue had his own Buick parked outside and said he would not mind giving me a lift home.

I looked at my watch.

"It's not so late," I said. "I can still check out a couple of things."

"Like what?"

"Two places where Charlie Furman had jobs—I mean besides the artwork out in Coney Island, which can wait until tomorrow."

"And here I thought you had zip on him."

"I remember him telling me about these jobs he sometimes does. Chump jobs, nothing payroll."

"Oh, of course not. This guy he don't put nothing down on paper but paint."

"Seems that way."

"What're these little jobs of work anyways?"

We got up to leave Central Homicide and as we walked the corridor I told Logue, "Picasso does windows for this bodega in my neighborhood. You know, advertisements in calcimine paint on the window glass? Also he passes out palm cards for a strip joint in Times Square called the Horny Poodle."

"Well, hey, a guy's got to eat," Logue said, laughing. "So, where to first?"

"I guess the bodega. You can leave me there and I'll go on to the Horny Poodle. Hell's Kitchen—Tenth Avenue and Forty-fifth."

We were out the front door and down the stoop and almost inside of Logue's Buick when I heard my name called. I turned and saw Captain Mogaill's sturdy silhouette in the door at the top of the stoop.

"Yeah, you, Hockaday. Come on up here, I got something for you," Mogaill yelled down to us at the curb.

"Suppose I ought to wait?" Logue asked me.

Mogaill answered before I could. "Logue, you can go on home."

"Okay, captain." Logue shrugged, got into his car and drove off. I walked up the steps to Mogaill.

"I got a message," Mogaill said. Then he shook his hand like it was burning and added, "Here comes those big black headlines."

"What are you trying to say, Davy?"

"I just got done talking to your boss and he's on his way down here now—from Gracie Mansion, where he's been having a little chat with the mayor."

"I'm supposed to hang tight for Inspector Neglio?"

"Exactly so. And by the by, guess who also had a small word with me?"

"I said, I don't like to guess."

"Oh yeah, that's right. So there was I, having a talk with the inspector when himself the lord mayor comes on the blower. The mayor informs me that Central Homicide is now at your disposal in this Bellevue matter. It seems the inspector has sold you to Hizzonor as the department's leading expert on footloose maniacs."

"I wonder if I should be flattered."

"Wonder as you will, Hock. Me, I'm wondering about packing it in right here and tonight. I could file the resignation form and in three short weeks be collecting half my captain's pay for all the rest of my days, please God, right and regular, in the mail."

I commiserated, and honestly so. "I think about that myself."

"I am not so old I cannot take a proper order, you understand."

"No, I know . . ."

"It's the bloody arrogance, and the presumption, and the flamin' politics!" Mogaill laced his fingers behind his neck and cracked his knuckles. This relaxed him some. "You'd best cut me off, or else I'll be going on about these stinking politics."

"If it makes you feel any better, I think the situation stinks, too."

"Thank you for that, Hock. Jaysus but I could use a drink! We should have that jar together this very night. But you've got your orders, haven't you now? And I mine."

"Tonight, yes."

"Pity on us."

"Another time, Davy. And soon if you like. We'll make it Nugent's, for auld lang syne."

"Nugent's—God, yes, that's the place for us."

"For now then, Captain, sleep easy. I won't be pushing it."

"No, you won't. Not even you, my friend. The mayor and all of them be fooked. I'll see to it there's fair play!"

"Right enough. I'll only work through Logue for now, to keep the waves low."

"All right, then. I'll be saying good night to you, and safe home."

He turned, leaving me to wait for Inspector Neglio.

I watched the broad back of Davy Mogaill as he plodded through his fiefdom of zeroes, toward his hard-won command office, and his bottle.

"Do you suppose this psycho actually expected to sell the painting?" Neglio stared at the Polaroid I had given him. "I mean, what in hell's the chance of this kind of garbage ever hanging up over somebody's sofa?"

We were riding uptown in the back of Neglio's armored black Chrysler sedan, a car from the headquarters brass fleet. Up front at the wheel there was a beefy young cop with oiled red hair packed into a shiny suit. A thin shaft of light from the rear seat limousine lamp poured over Neglio's satin lapels. He looked even slimmer than usual in his tuxedo. I noticed a button missing on my shirt cuff. It had begun to rain.

"He's not making a living off his paintings," I said. Neglio kept staring at the Polaroid. "But it's no hobby either."

"Oh? No shit, Sherlock." Neglio laughed at his joke. The shiny suit laughed, too. "But you know what I see in this?"

"What?"

"Opportunity."

"You sound like you've been watching those insomniac shows on cable where you send in for the tapes and booklets so you can wind up a millionaire and you don't have to spend your nights in front of a TV set worrying about the bills you can't pay." I laughed at my joke. Neglio and the shiny suit did not.

"Let's just say that here we have in our hands a class-A psycho on his warpath. *Plus* we have got ourselves a brand-new mayor, right? And you know how brand-new mayors are."

"No, how are they, Inspector?"

"Still full of themselves and their campaign slogans. Just for one thing, they're still believing all that tough-talking crap on the subject of crime in the streets."

"Our new mayor, he's against crime?"

This won a tight smile from Neglio, and: "Come, come, Detective Hockaday. We must all do our bit in trying to take these people in high office seriously. Next you'll be telling me you don't vote."

"Most of us got the message a long time ago. Which is why we would never spoil a perfectly good election day by going out to the polls."

"How old are you now, Hock?"

"Somewhere in the middle."

"And looking every day of it, too."

"I don't mind," I lied.

"No, not now you don't. But then, you're not the thrifty type. So you'd better listen: my advice to a man of your age and ability who is stuck at the rank where you have been stuck for so many years is that one day you ought to get smart—"

I interrupted, with the truth this time. "I don't mind being stuck."

Neglio was exasperated. "One day, you maybe should warm up to the people who can do you some good in the end."

"That sounds painful."

He told me to shut up.

Which I gratefully did since I get irritable when Neglio's conversation veers toward his confidentialities with people in high office. I do not like hearing him on the topic of how he leans on such people, no more than he might enjoy learning how I sometimes lean on my lowly snitches. To my way of thinking, shutting up sometimes is a good thing; this is how cops from two different worlds may live in friendship and relative respect.

Neglio handed back the Polaroid and I put it away in my jacket. He switched off the limousine lamp. The young cop up front switched on the radio to all-news WINS and, among other current events of note, we heard the latest on the "Bellevue Slasher," who murdered a prominent shrink right on the rooftop of the city's best-known hospital. We also heard a tandem item on the "Happy Hour Shooter," who the other day had snuffed an obscure lady barfly on an unfashionable block of Ninth Avenue.

The public intelligence was not much beyond clever taglines and an echo-chamber hype of the plain and lurid facts of the cases, each labeled as bold and chilling and, of course, senseless. But there was no real connection made between the two homicides; not yet, anyway. In a day or two at most, the important people would get edgy, and they would lean on those for whom they had done so much good.

We passed the old West Side piers in the lower Village where transvestite pross go to entice middle-aged sports out in their station wagons looking for a good time. We passed the Holland Tunnel approaches where teenagers from Jersey come cruising for roxie and China white. We passed the joints along Twelfth Avenue, nameless save for white X's painted on dingy doors, where the bored and the depraved come in search of one another.

It was a few blocks past the ghostly pale night-lights of the glass-walled Javits Convention Center when Neglio finally broke our suffocating silence.

"All I am saying," he said, cupping his mouth confidentially with a hand, "is that under the political circumstances it would not hurt either of us if a brand-new mayor, you know, sort of had a hand in this investigation. Follow me?"

I looked at Neglio's well-cut tuxedo. "Go back to your party. Tell the mayor I'll be chasing this killer as fast as I can."

"There's a drift here, Hock. But you don't seem to be catching it."

Oh, but I caught it indeed. *Political circumstances.* I thought then of Davy Mogaill and how heavily he walked these days; how he missed Nugent's so badly, how I was still free to drink at that dear old dive. And so I did not care to leap into Neglio's drift.

Neglio sighed, impatient with me. "You know I would bang all the right drums for you, Hock. You know that! How does a post at headquarters strike you, at the rank of detective-sergeant? Your own secretary, maybe."

"It strikes me I'd be in line for more money. So what, I should hire a butler out of my pay raise?"

"Don't be a hard-ass. I'm trying to help you."

"I see. You're trying to help me see my very big opportunity."

"That's it!"

"For which I have got to do exactly what?"

"Use your imagination a little. That's all I ask."

"At my age, maybe the imagination is not all that dependable anymore. Maybe you'll have to spell this one for me, Inspector."

Neglio was pimping and he knew it, and he knew that I knew it. We have tapped this bogus dance many a time before. Now came the part where I wanted to make him sweat because, as I say, I can be irritable. But Neglio kept cool. He adjusted the peaks of the nonfunctional white satin handkerchief poking out from the breast pocket of his jacket.

"Think what a nice TV picture it would make if the mayor

was actually right on the scene, right there when you bust your boy," he said. "You know how gentle it usually goes down when you finally make the collar, especially when it's some poor crazed sod of a serial killer."

I know that, generally speaking, a murder is more evil than the murderer. There is a famous story that detectives all over the world tell about a German killer named Joachim Kroll, who was thought to be evil incarnate since he had murdered and raped a dozen or so schoolgirls and carried off bits of their little bodies. He turned out to be a quite pleasant, quite absentminded character who could not remember most of his crimes. He worked as a public-toilet attendant. It was hardly necessary, but the German cops used a battering ram to get the drop on the evil one. The monster was in the kitchen of his modest flat, cooking his evening stew—the left hand of his latest victim, a pretty five year old with brown eyes and blonde braids, boiling it in chicken stock with some carrots and noodles. Kroll acknowledged that his taste was somewhat uncommon, but he honestly never knew that eating children for supper was illegal, let alone morally repugnant. He went along quietly with the cops, certain that after medical treatment, they would return him to his flat.

"True enough, most killers are regular sweethearts when it comes to being arrested," I said. "I know it, you know it, and the showboat candidates for mayor, they know. Or else somebody clues them in.

"But the voters don't know it, do they? They see the mayor on the nightly news clamping the bracelets and leg irons on some sorry psycho after all is said and done by some hard-working cop such as myself and, by God, the leader of our great metropolis is a fearless crime fighter! Now, would that be the nice picture you're talking about?"

"If it was good enough for LaGuardia, it's good enough for this mayor," Neglio said.

"Fiorello never had TV around to make himself look as

cheap as the blow-drys in blue suits we've got now. Besides which, LaGuardia was a hero. We don't have heroes today. We have celebrities, on television."

Our driver had pulled off the highway, and we were now cutting across West Thirty-sixth toward Tenth Avenue. About midway down the darkened block of squat, grimy tenements and loft buildings, I spotted a street snitch of mine who calls himself Rat. He was standing in the foggy yellow light of a doorway, pushing a needle into his arm. I would have to look up Rat sometime soon, maybe tomorrow; he might know something about Picasso.

Neglio also spotted Rat, and the general decrepitude of the lower end of my neighborhood. Neglio can also be irritating when the unfortunate differences between us show. He passed a remark up to the driver: "Isn't it lovely here in Hell's Kitchen where the high-minded Detective Neil Hockaday lives?"

The driver looked back at me in the rearview mirror. He gave me a nose laugh.

I leaned forward and tapped his sharkskin shoulder and said, "Just be a good errand boy now and drop me at Forty-fifth and Tenth, near-left corner. And stop at a drug-store, get something for your nose."

"Hey," he squawked to Neglio, "I don't got to take that, do I?"

I said, "Officer Flunky, he speaks!"

Neglio told us both to shut up. And so I enjoyed nine blocks of peace and quiet.

As we passed my apartment house at Forty-third, I saw that Ruby had put on the light by the window. I imagined her sitting on the couch with a book, her smooth brown legs curled up under her hips.

When we finally got to the bodega, Neglio touched my arm before I could leave the car. "Try to understand one little thing, if nothing else. My world's just as real as yours, Hock. Okay?"

I was certainly willing to concede him the point. "Yeah, okay."

"So try thinking my way. This new mayor of ours— whether or not you even voted—you remember how he damn near lost the election to that Italian twerp of a federal D.A., right? The one with the really bad comb-over? The one with all those cockamamie law-and-order speeches?"

"Come, come, Tomassino Neglio. Such talk about a *paisano.*"

"Never mind that. The thing is, you think cops have interference from City Hall now? Can you imagine what it would be from an ex-D.A.?"

Again I conceded.

"So you see how there's no harm in helping our guy's image? Which is all it is—image. We help the mayor, the mayor stays off our backs when it really counts."

There was a certain attractive logic to what Neglio was saying. But I kept my doubts firmly in mind, which is something that only comes natural after a few years in my trade.

"Let's get this straight," I said. "Supposing our boy keeps going off his nut like he is, and he wipes out a few more solid citizens, and the tabloids put two and two together and have a field day . . ."

"Oh, they will. Unless you think you can poke your boy tonight and be done with it."

"Well, probably not."

"No."

"So down the line, when I'm ready to take down my man, you want me to wait for the camera crew and the mayor's limo?"

"Crudely put, but that's more or less it."

"And if I do this, you're going to set me up downtown? And see me to a pay bump?" It occurred to me that I might talk this over with Ruby.

"See? Not so bad, right?"

"What's in it for you? Are you gunning for Senior Inspector? Or Super Chief so you can get a bigger car and a brighter flunky?"

The driver squawked again. Neither one of us paid him any attention.

Neglio said to me, "Could it happen to two nicer guys?"

"What are you, lonely down there at headquarters? Is that why you'd want me around, to share the misery?"

"It's a reward—"

"Try thinking my way," I interrupted. "Taking some desk job down there with you would be like retirement for me. Only you probably wouldn't allow me to go to the ball park every day."

"Christ, Hock! With all due respect . . ."

"Yeah, let's keep this respectful. Which means I do want my pension one fine day, but I also want to be the one who says when I'm ready to collect. It also means I get to make my own goddamn collars my own goddamn way!"

I stepped out of the car as a fine flourish to dressing down the boss. The bodega did not have any customers inside, but the gates were not down yet and the place looked open still. Picasso's terrified pig was gone from the window, but there was something else in its place, something in calcimine.

Neglio rolled down a window of the car and barked, "Hock, get over here, and that's a goddamn order!"

So I walked on over, but I took my time. Neglio leaned out the window with his wing-collar shirt and black bow tie and his teeth were clenched and he said, "I could have you up on insubordination charges first thing in the morning, Hock. Remember that. You push me, and you'll learn how there's good opportunities in life—and then there are bad ones."

"I'm on furlough, remember that? And you're way out of bounds interfering with an officer. So maybe this insubordinate conversation never happened. So don't bust my chops, I've got work to do."

Neglio made some growling noises.

"Besides which, I'm only handling this job because you and your buddy the mayor have decided I'm the only cop you got who might clear it before we get some real serious panic going in this town," I said. "Which, by the way, reminds me, I'm working on my own clock—your words."

"Well, just what can we do about that?" Neglio said, smiling.

"I'll make you one little deal tonight, just so you can keep your buddy happy. You shuffle the paper and get me back on the city's clock, and I'll think about it."

"About the mayor?"

"I'll think, I won't promise."

"Deal."

Neglio rolled up his window, a happy man for effecting a minor corruption. He waved, then his car lurched off the curb and crossed the avenue and turned east up at Forty-ninth Street and then out of sight.

Behind me, a woman screamed in Spanish.

ELEVEN

Han matado a mi esposo!"

The screams came from inside the bodega. They grew louder and louder, piercing through all other sounds of a Hell's Kitchen night until only the widow's cry was heard: *"Han matado a mi esposo!"* They killed my husband!

A gang of teenagers loitering outside a video store at the corner heard her. They started toward me, en masse.

A woman appeared on the fire escape outside an apartment directly over the bodega's door. She leaned over the edge of the black wrought-iron railing and called, "Carolena, Carolena?"

I crouched, pulled the .38 revolver from my shoulder holster and scuttled toward the doorway. I shielded myself behind a steel corner plate that connected the long curved glass display window and the entrance.

The woman up on the fire escape spotted the gun in my hand and shrieked.

"Carolena! Benito!"

The gang of teens, maybe a dozen boys and three or four

girls, had become silent. They moved toward me, but more slowly now.

I pulled back the firing hammer of the revolver, gripped the hand stock and tucked the barrel close against my chest. I had only seconds to get a fix on whatever lay waiting inside the bodega.

There was a small sales floor with a couple of dividers that made aisles of canned goods, cellophane-wrapped snack foods, infant formula and diapers, six-packs of beer, soda, mousetraps, cockroach bombs. Noisy cooling cabinets held milk, cheese and fresh meats. Cigarettes, coffee, candy and sandwiches were sold at the counter. There was a curtained door in the back that probably led to an illegal apartment.

A woman about fifty years old sat squat-legged on the floor in front of the counter, with a man's bloody head flopped in her lap. *"Han matado a mi esposo!"* She looked directly at me, seeing nothing but her own fear and loss.

She raised her head to the ceiling. Her body rocked back and forth. Blood sloshed across her large bosoms, and trickled down her arms and elbows into the dusty cracks of the wooden floor. Her screams turned to desperate prayer: *"Dios, guardar mi esposo!"* God, save my husband!

The teenagers had stopped about thirty feet from me, afraid to come farther and startled by the sight of my gun.

I pulled my gold shield from a side pocket of my jacket and held it up high, so the woman on the fire escape could see it as well as the teenagers. I said in Spanish, then English, *"Llamar por teléfono las policía."* Call the police.

The woman on the fire escape disappeared into her apartment.

One of the teenaged boys stepped forward. I knew the kid, thank God.

"Luis, I need your help," I said to him.

"What's going on here, Hock?"

"Listen to me carefully. There's been a murder. People

are afraid. *I'm* afraid, Luis. The killer might still be inside there."

I jerked my head around and looked at the widow again. She kept on screaming and rocking. The huge gash across her husband's neck kept spewing blood.

"You understand it's dangerous?"

Luis turned to the others and said something that persuaded them to take several steps back and out of harm's way. My own Spanish was nowhere near fluent enough to handle a crowd. And so Luis, the busboy at my regular neighborhood spoon, had become my deputy.

He turned back to me now, eyes hot and excited. "What do you need, Hock?"

"A police backup squad. Somebody should call up 911. Say an officer's in trouble, got it?"

"Yeah." He turned and said all this in Spanish to the girl just behind him. She ran to the public phone at the corner.

"Okay, I'm counting on you, Luis. On you and your friends. You all have to stay cool, and you have to help me by keeping the area clear, understand? I don't want anybody in the neighborhood getting hurt."

Already there were separate streams of curious forming crowds. There was a knot of them across the street, another at the opposite corner.

"You got it, friend."

"Great. Thanks, Luis."

Luis and the rest formed a line between me and the people starting to get closer and closer to the widow's screams.

And then I heard the comforting sound of approaching sirens. Soon I would have plenty of help. I looked back inside the bodega.

So far as I could tell, the killer had already left. And only moments ago, just moments before Neglio's car had delivered me to another murder in my own backyard.

The killer could be hiding yet in the back room, but that

was unlikely. The way things looked, the wife—Carolena, going by the upstairs neighbor—had come out from behind the curtained back door to find her husband dead out in the store. And certainly from the look of the gash that halved Benito's neck, the killer had been ever as swift and sure with this deadly job as with the two before.

How did I know it was my killer who had now struck three times?

I knew.

I turned and looked through the crowd of frightened faces held off by Luis and his friends, to the darkened park on the other side of Tenth Avenue, the park where I had met him, and listened. "... *this is mainly how I now have the artistic thrill of being a painter these days. . . . I wish you would cross over there to the bodega sometime before next week's special —so you can see up close how I captured the essential terror . . ."*

I knew. The proof was there. But I did not have to look at it right away. It would wait.

Just now, the widow inside screamed her loudest. And prayed. And six squad cars roared up the avenue and dispersed the crowd, and the streets and sidewalk became brilliant with flashing blue, red and white light. And more cars came, blockading the avenue and the side streets.

I held up my gold shield as uniformed cops swarmed at me. I called out my identification: "Detective Neil Hockaday—Street Crimes Unit, Manhattan!"

Now I was surrounded by uniforms, at either side of the doorway. Somebody said, "We've got a team on the roof and a couple of teams around back. If he's in there, we got him." Somebody else called something to the widow in Spanish; she did not respond. She kept rocking and screaming and praying. The blood kept flowing.

"Han matado a mi esposo . . . Dios, guardar mi esposo!"

"I'm going in . . ." I said.

"You wearing a vest?" somebody asked me.

DARK MAZE

"I'm going in!"

There is nothing like murder to calm a room. Outside the bodega, the lights were flashing and the people were shouting and the terrible screams of the widow Carolena floating out the door quickened the night. Inside, the screams seemed somehow quieter with every step I took toward her. When I passed very near, on my way to the curtained door, they seemed no more than wind in trees.

I stood very still near the counter. Nothing in the bodega moved besides the gently screaming widow, and there was no other sound. I saw a seven-inch box cutter lying on the floor near the dead man's feet. Muggers who cannot afford guns use these weapons, known as shanks.

It was an ugly, efficient knife—and sticky with blood. The tip of the retractable blade was still pushed up through the smooth steel handle. That blade, so capable of slashing open the strongest packing box with a single swipe, so capable of laying raw a man's windpipe and vocal cords.

The curtain over the back door did not move.

The widow, in the trance of her shock, paid no mind as I moved past her.

I looked at the floor as I advanced toward the back room, careful not to step into the streams of blood filling wood grooves. At the edge of one small pool of blood was something green: a feather. I bent and picked it up, and slipped it into my shirt pocket.

I touched the curtain over the passage to the next room. Then I pulled it open.

On the other side was an extension of the store space fashioned into a one-room apartment with a separate alcove at the front containing a sink and toilet and makeshift stall shower. The place was empty.

The bodega owner's wife had probably been sitting in a rocking chair with her sewing, judging from the kit of needles and thread and a button jar sitting on the seat, and some shirts and a pair of trousers slung over an arm. Up front, her husband was tending the store. Maybe she thought it had grown too quiet, maybe she called his name and he failed to answer; then maybe she got up from her rocking chair, put down her sewing things and shut off the television set to listen; then she bustled out the curtained door and found her husband fatally wounded.

That was how it played.

I returned to the other room. The cop who had asked about a vest was standing just inside the door, and I saw by the stripes on his shoulder patch that he was a squad leader from Midtown North. His name tag said Sergeant Walsh.

Beyond the sergeant, out in the street, I saw a new kind of blue-white light. They were kleigs, the kind of lights used by television camera crews at night.

I walked up to Sergeant Walsh and said, "Easy in, easy out."

Walsh nodded. "That's the way it is these days, hey? These freaking kids, they walk up and down around here robbin' stores like they got the right to help themselves to whatever they want. Like they think they're all freaking Congressmen or something."

I laughed. "But I don't think it's robbery."

"How come? You looked in the till already?"

"No. Just a guess."

Walsh stared at my clothes and said, "You look too good to be working SCUM patrol tonight."

"I'm not, exactly."

"Exactly how does it happen you're here and guessing about goings-on in this godforsaken neighborhood?"

I took the sergeant by the elbow and steered him closer to the front door, out of respect for the screaming widow. I did not bother telling him that it happens I live only a few blocks away. I am the only New York cop I know who lives in a crime-ridden neighborhood of New York City, which was not a distinction that I cared to discuss just then with the likes of Sergeant Walsh. Instead, I briefly told him that I was investigating two linked homicides, which had led me to the bodega to question the owner about a possible suspect. I also told him that Inspector Neglio and the mayor were especially interested in any progress I might make.

Walsh whistled appreciatively. "So, your suspect went and whacked another guy, and now you really got yourself a serial case?"

"It looks that way."

"So how do you want the cleanup assigned?"

"I'll put in a call to Central Homicide, so you don't have to bother your own PDU."

"That's okay by me." Walsh looked back over his shoulder at the widow. "You think she's approachable yet?"

"Give her a minute," I said. "Then have a couple of your good men pry her off and get her to a hospital."

I left Walsh and stepped outside into a sudden flood of harsh television lights. They beamed in on me since I was so far the only cop around without a uniform.

Cameras were restricted to the street, behind a wall of blue uniforms and sawhorses that had been set up along the curb. Reporters barked questions that I decided not to hear. I covered my eyes against the glare of the lights and looked for Luis. I spotted him back behind the line of cameras and waved him over.

Luis walked self-importantly through a trail of kleigs to my side. We stood in front of the bodega window. Finally, I turned to look at it, knowing what I was to see.

There, in neatly brushed calcimine paint, was the picture of a sprawled man with a gaping hole in his throat. And despite the simple, blunt lines, there was an essential fear in the wounded man's eyes.

"Who painted this?" I asked.

"I guess the usual guy."

"The funny-looking old guy in the beret?"

"Yeah, him."

I touched a stroke of the calcimine paint. It was still tacky. "Did you see him do this?"

"I seen him maybe an hour ago, hanging around here like he does. You know, painting."

"And he was with somebody, right?"

"No, man. He was alone. He's always alone."

"You know where he lives?"

Luis' eyes grew big. "Hey, that old geek, he iced Benito?"

"I don't know, but I want to talk to him." I pointed to Picasso's latest work. "What do you make of this, Luis?"

"Looks spooked to me, man. Don't look like the usual shit he paints, you know? Chickens and pigs and shit like that's his usual thing."

"Have you been hanging out at the video store all night?"

"Yeah, pretty much. We drank some beer over there in the park," Luis said, pointing across the avenue, "but the girls they don't like it there. So we hang out at the V-store with them. You know."

"Who went into Benito's store, say in the last hour or two?"

"Oh, I don't know, lots of people."

"Did you see the funny old guy in the beret go in there?"

"Yeah, but he come back out with Benito. Then Benito he goes back in, then the old geek he starts painting on the window—real fast."

"Then what?"

"Then he goes away."

"Did he come back?"

"No, I don't think so."

"Who went in after he went?"

Luis thought for a second. "I don't know, really. Maybe ten different people, you know?"

"Who was the last person you saw go in?"

Luis thought. "I don't know, Hock. I was just hanging out

on the corner and I wasn't really paying much attention, you know? People I might of seen going in and out of Benito's, they was like just shapes to me."

"Did you see anything unusual?"

"No, man." Then Luis smiled. "Except when you come up in that fine black car. That I seen. And then Carolena she starts screaming and everything."

The lady upstairs made another appearance on the fire escape. She looked down at me looking up at her, then she looked at Luis. And then she shrieked and ran back inside her apartment.

"Who's that?" I asked Luis.

"My mother, man. I live up there, right over Benito and Carolena's store. My mother, she don't speak no English."

"Your friends, and your mother—could you ask them who went into the bodega tonight? I need a list of names, as best as I can get. And information on anybody who looked like they don't belong around here. You know what I mean?"

"Sure," Luis said, nodding. "I can ask."

I had every confidence that Luis would ask the right questions, and every confidence that any answers would not be particularly helpful. When a killer has an easy job of it—easy in, easy out—the cop's job is harder at least by half. Nobody notices the easygoing killer; he is invisible, like the public-toilet attendant back in Germany.

"Luis, do you know the old guy in the beret?"

"Like, do I know his name?"

"Yes."

"Well, I know Benito used to call him Picasso, like the artist Picasso, you know? Benito, he liked the old guy, he tried to help him. But me, I never talked to him."

"So, this Picasso, he never gave Benito any trouble?"

"No, there wasn't no trouble. I never heard of trouble."

"How long had Picasso been painting the windows?"

Luis thought. "I guess about a year. He just showed up, you know? He wasn't no skell, but he wasn't right in the head neither."

About a year, I thought. Right about the time I myself moved back to Hell's Kitchen, the neighborhood of my youth.

I asked, "Did Picasso ever talk to you?"

"Well, I used to come downstairs and he'd be painting his chickens and cows and shit on the window. And he'd start saying something. I thought he was talking to me, but then I seen he's a guy who jabbers to himself, like he thinks there's somebody right next to him."

There was probably nothing more that Luis or anybody else on the scene could tell me so I thanked Luis for his help and said I would look him up in a day or so. He got a little shirty about the anticlimax.

"Say, what, you got nothing more for me, man?" he asked indignantly. "Helpful types like me, we ought to get rewarded, you know?"

I looked over in the direction of the barricaded television crews. A boisterous and jostling crowd that I noticed had been swelled by the arrival of newspaper writers and photographers. At front and center of the press mob, I recognized Bill Slattery from the *New York Post*, and I figured if I ever got to sleep that night I would dream about streamer headlines and cards in hat-bands.

"You know, Luis, you're right," I said. "You really deserve something. Something even better than money."

"What?"

"Your very own fifteen minutes of fame, Luis."

Then I clamped a hold on his shoulder and said, "Come on," yanking him along with me toward the milling press corps. The kleigs fired up and bathed us in mazda light. Trench coats with microphones and notebooks lunged at us. Slattery hollered, "How about a statement!" and then everybody else started yapping for the same until they all looked and sounded like so many hungry, croaking seals at the zoo. So I fed them Luis.

"This young man has your story," I said to the press, holding up my hands for a little order and quiet. I said to Luis, "Just tell them what you told me. Here's your reward, kid, you're going to be on TV."

Then Luis nervously stood there in the television lights in front of all his friends from the neighborhood and told what he knew of the murder in the shop below his own apartment. As I walked away, I could hear the zoom lenses whirring to get their close-ups for tomorrow's news thrills.

And I also heard Dr. Reiser's voice: "... *Picasso, my pixilated friend, what makes you the loon you are is that you're the worst kind of artist there is, the kind that gets ignored.*"

Picasso would be ignored no longer. In the morning, he would be the tabloid toast of the town.

TWELVE

Back in the bodega, the widow Carolena had been success-fully removed from the body of her husband; a cop was holding her, smoothing her hair and saying, "Take it easy now," as if he was stroking his own mother's head at a funeral.

Sergeant Walsh tapped my shoulder. "I seen you had your hands full out there with the press and all, so I went ahead and called out Central Homicide for you."

"Thanks," I said. Then I went into the back room and out into the courtyard and through an adjoining tenement building to the side street.

I found a telephone out of sight of the press conference and called Mogaill.

"Jaysus, Hock," he said, "but you've got yourself an industrious murderer, hey?"

"Easy goes it this time."

"How so?"

"No signs of resistance, and it's a slow night. The killer walks in, whacks the victim with a shank, and walks out."

"Nobody sees nothing, am I right?"

It was like the others, like Celia Furman and Dr. Reiser. Easy going. "There was nothing to see," I said.

"In other words, another zero for my vast files."

"Well, your guys will be wanting to ask their questions even so, and I've got mine, and maybe this time there'll be answers that add up past zero." I heard the sound of a bottle clinking glass on Mogaill's end of the line. "I'll check with Logue tomorrow to see what comes of the team report."

"If anything, hey?" Mogaill said. I rang off with him and crossed Tenth Avenue walking quickly, heading east toward Times Square and the Horny Poodle where I could buy myself a badly needed Scotch and maybe turn up a link in the chain of events that had embezzled my furlough.

I glanced over my shoulder. Luis was still performing for the reporters and his friends.

Times Square on a clement April midnight usually gives me a fair idea of the tone of summer to come. Early April is that time of year when an army of grifters, pross, dips, beggars, cons, muggers, pushers, lunatics and religionists begin to establish their territories in anticipation of summer's high season at the crossroads of the world.

I spend a lot of duty hours in Times Square during the summer, which if my mother were alive would fill her not with pride for the many crimes I prevent but with sorrow for the fact that I have not traveled far in life.

When I was a kid growing up in Hell's Kitchen with my mother because it was one place where our kind of Irish were welcome to live, the nearby streets of Times Square were genteel by today's scabid standards. Yet still they were a forbidden world to the parochial likes of me, who wore his knickers and neckties to school every day and recited his catechism without needing the old nuns' sweet-voiced threats of eternal damnation and who sang soprano in the

Holy Cross boys' choir during all three masses each Sunday morning. Naturally, I spent all free hours possible exactly where I would most greatly disappoint my mother.

In those days, heaven was located at the corner of Forty-second and Eighth and it was contained in the fabulous walls of Hubert's Museum and Flea Circus. With money I made shining shoes outside the library over on Fifth Avenue, I played Skee-Ball and pinball at Hubert's, and shot war-surplus .22 rifles at wooden ducks in a gallery and marveled at the Great Waldo, who ate live mice. I felt sorry for the retired sports heroes reduced to talking to children for their dimes. And I wondered mightily at the knowledge that would one day be mine, when I was old enough to buy a ticket to the special show on the side stage, where I could learn with the sailors the hidden secrets of sex, right there at Hubert's courtesy of the "French Academy of Medicine, Paris, France."

There were dance halls like the Varsity and the Satin Ballroom and the Tango Palace, where meek little guys in suits met would-be actresses and danced with them to the music of six-piece bands. The Tango was where Barbara Stanwyck and Joan Crawford started out in New York.

Mobsters hung out at the Royal Roost and Zanzibar's and some, like my favorite, Frank Costello, still wore spats. Other customers came to gawk at the hoods. My friends and I used to watch them coming and going in their big cars.

And there was Birdland, where Charlie Parker played until he died from too much heroin and not enough understanding. There were all-night movies, too, at the Forty-second Street houses where they had premiered, with the stars rolling up in their limousines in front of newsreel cameras.

Somehow the lights were brighter, the neon signs bigger and more robust. The Camel smoker blew perfect rings high above the unruly intersection of Broadway and Seventh, one ring a minute thanks to the trusty Con Ed steam pipes.

Maxwell House coffee dripped long past its last drop, on into a seeming infinity. A ten-thousand-gallon Pepsi-Cola waterfall stretched a full block over the roofs of the Bond menswear store and the old Criterion, the real one. Little Lulu skipped eight stories up the side of a building to pluck Kleenex from a box.

Everybody dressed up in evening jackets and gowns to go to the Strand or the Capitol or the Roxy or the Paramount, where the great Frank Sinatra would sing. Broadway actors ate spaghetti suppers at Romeo's after their shows. The cops were on foot post all night long, and you walked where you pleased.

That was the Great White Way.

Those were the days before people had surrendered their sense of wonder to television, when popular music still soothed the savage breast and musicians had not yet lost their jobs to soulless synthesizer machines. It was a time when everybody wore hats and pressed their clothes, the time before all the neon read Japanese, when the idea of commercial sex was to allure, not to assault. That was the way it was.

In my seven-block hike over to the Horny Poodle, I witnessed the following: a buxom pre-op transsexual hooker voguing on a well-lit corner in red-sequined halter top and matching hot-pants, his johnson lolling out of her fly; two swishes debating the relative orgasm-enhancing merits of Rush and Quicksilver outside a grubby candy shop run by a dour giant in a turban; a loud-faced skell spitting and howling like a rabid dog, dodging cars in the middle of Eighth Avenue; a bag lady hunkered down under a tent of rags and papers, sharing a can of something with a half-bald cat; four teenage chicken fags huddled in a doorway with a crack pipe; a brain-damaged evangelist screeching about Jesus through an electric bullhorn; and a short, muscular drunk with two tall cans of Ballantine in his paws loping after a married couple from Nebraska or someplace like that and snarling, "What's-a-maddah, you doan like Spanish people?"

I did what I could.

I dialed 911 from a pay phone and reported the cursing dog-man, I tossed a dollar into the bag lady's tent, and I was glad to see the tourists duck into a hotel lobby. If anybody wanted to take up with the tranny or the chickens or the Jesus jumper, that was between them and their demons.

As for me, I had to get to the corner of Fiftieth and Seventh Avenue and the Horny Poodle. I crossed by the TKTS booth on Forty-ninth, where half-price leftovers to the Broadway shows are peddled. There used to be a statue there called "Virtue." This was a forty-foot replica of Miss Liberty down in the harbor, erected by a committee of do-gooders from yesteryear to challenge the great American pastime of disparaging New York City. Miss Virtue's bronze shield read OUR CITY and the poor thing was covered from crown to sandals with big dark stains, symbolizing the out-of-towner mudslinging she suffered; her plaque urged all good New Yorkers to DEFEAT SLANDER.

A block up the avenue from Virtue's last stand was the Horny Poodle, the last mastodon of the area's once-ubiquitous topless bars. Its wide double glass doors were frosted with the images of leering white French poodles dressed in cutaway coats and top hats; these portals were illuminated from above by a pair of stupendous pink neon breasts with blinkering puce nipples. The joint sparkled in an otherwise drab strip of changing Times Square real estate, nestled between a gay cinema that night showing "Foaming Fannies" and an all-American newsstand where the reader can buy everything from *USA Today* to the latest number of *Nuns & Nazis* magazine.

Strolling through all of this today makes me a little tired, and more than a little sad in my middle-aged heart. But I suddenly realized that since I was officially back on the clock, I could put my Johnnie Walker reds and Molson chasers on my investigative expense account somehow or other and this gave me a small lift.

Then I entered through the double glass doors. Inside the Horny Poodle, the atmosphere was something less than the tit-man's paradise it was cracked up to be.

A couple of million palm cards passed out in the streets over the last few decades by the likes of Picasso promised a lonesome guy in an adolescent mood the prospect of being surrounded by an adoring, laughing bevy of bare-chested serving wenches. The truth of the matter was that none of the wenches were laughing and the way they slammed down the beers and shots at the little tables clustered around a stage was not adorable to behold. They had slug-eyed expressions, most of them, and poor posture. The ones with acne on their backs and shoulders did not bother to cover up their zits with pancake and body powder. The last thing you noticed about this sullen fleet was that between the chin and the belt each happened to be naked; from the general pall of the place, I was by no means the only customer who felt deflated.

Up on stage was a tall waxy-faced gray-haired guy in a tux trying his best to amuse the disillusioned with a magic act. His strawberry-blonde assistant wore silicone breasts that were too high and one of those topless bathing suits from the Sixties that helped usher in the sexual revolution that I myself missed. Several old revolutionaries in the audience had lain their sleepy heads down amid the empty beer bottles on their tables.

I took a stool at the bar, which was only sparsely populated. One of the glum B-girls scuffed my way on her platform shoes. Her chest looked cold.

"What'll you have, Clyde?" she said lazily, her voice full of cigarettes.

I could not entirely blame her for this insolence. She had

no doubt lived a life requiring her to know far too many men far too well. Still, I do not personally enjoy being called a clyde. And after all, I was still a little tender from recently having seen a fresh murder. I was not in a trifling mood.

So I looked her up and down, thinking uncharitably of what I saw. "You know, you remind me of somebody," I said.

"Yeah, and who's that, Clyde?"

"My great-aunt out in Canarsie, the one with the boils and the bad knees."

"Whatta you, a homo got loose outta the movies next door?"

"You got me wrong, sister. I am in show business, though. In fact, would you be willing to star in my next picture?"

"Oh, we got a smart guy." She turned and screeched at the bartender. "Benny, come on over here and take care of this homo smart mouth we got with us tonight."

Then she flipped her head like maybe she had done when she was a miffed little girl and Harry Truman was the president. She scuffed along over to some other clyde down at the end of the bar.

Benny had a hairless head shaped like a kidney bean and he wore black horn-rimmed glasses. He was very apologetic.

"It's real hard to get the good help nowadays, what can I tell you?" he said. "These babes we gotta hire, they think just because they flash hooters they're all some kinda divas.

"But I'll tell you what, buy yourself a nice drink and the second's on me. How about it?"

I said all was forgiven. Then in a minute there were two nice reds and rocks sitting in front of me, along with a pair of Molsons in sweaty green bottles. And Benny standing by, in the mood to chat.

Naturally, I was anxious to ask Benny all about Picasso. But I have now been at the detective trade long enough to listen closely whenever certain bells go off. This time, the bell was the memory of Inspector Neglio on the day he promoted me to gold shield rank and gave me his standard lecture for the occasion:

"Today, Neil Hockaday, you are a detective. Which means you're an artist among cops. An artist is somebody who knows how to get function by going with form, you follow? In other words, he's got finesse. From now on, you're an artist, Hock. In other words, you should try going sideways after what you want, which in this business is answers to questions. Going sideways, you'll be very surprised how much you can learn."

So I took the oblique route with Benny.

"Sort of slow tonight, isn't it?" I asked.

"Yeah, well, your fleshpots ain't quite what they used to be."

"What is?"

"Ain't that the sorry truth?"

I gazed past Benny through a haze of smoke and fixed on the magician up on stage. His assistant with the silicone shelf was tying a black blindfold over his face. There was a hinged wooden sign off to the side with the magician's name painted in blue circus letters, but I could not make it out.

"My eyes don't work like they used to, that's for damn sure," I said.

Benny tapped his horn-rims. "You and me both, pal. That's how come I wear these bifocals. Couple of years back, it was just killing me to read and also the stuff in the distance was sort of fuzzy. So, I go to the eye doctor. He don't even give me the chance to first read him the letters off the wall; he right away asks how old I am. I tell him. Then he smiles this big irritating smile and guess what he says?"

"I don't like to guess."

"He says, 'I've been waiting for you!' "

I shook my head and put back half a red. I squinted and tried reading the wooden sign again, but my luck was no

better. I looked at the magician and somehow he was
familiar. I hoped when my time came, I did not have to draw
Benny's eye doctor.

"Who's the magician?" I asked.

Benny groaned.

"My genius partner," he said. "The Great Morris."

"Your partner?"

"Sure. Me and the prestidigitator, we own this dive. But
like I say, it ain't what it used to be. I mean, look around.
You think this raggedy old clip joint still has the draw to
shell out for a floor show?"

"I guess not."

"You guessed correct. Around here, we even sweat the
juice it takes to keep running them neon boobs over the
door. We gotta cut corners someplace, so I run the bar and
my partner Moe Stein's the entertainment, such as it is."

"Who's the charming assistant?"

"Oh, that's a lovely old broad who used to strip here and
some other places, too. Called herself Delilah in her prime.
Maybe you won't believe it, but next year she starts collecting on her Social Security."

"Well, I don't know . . . my eyes." I squinted at Delilah
and could just make out that her bathing suit, such as it was,
was tight around the beam. I looked at Benny's partner, too.
Where had I seen this guy?

"Peeling's not your big draw no more," Benny was saying,
"and it's very labor intensive like the economists say. So we
had to fire everybody, except for Delilah. Hell, everybody
who wants to watch puss all night sits at home these days
with a six-pack in front of a goddamn VCR, you know?"

"Is he any good?" I asked. "The Great Morris, I mean."

"As you can tell, he tries. He's doing this mentalist act he
done back when Hector was a pup. Somebody told him
mentalist acts was all the thing with the Jap tourists like we
got throwing money all over town nowadays. So, Moe trots

out his old schtick. He even talks me into stocking saki and plum wine. But so far, no Japs. My genius partner."

The Great Morris' blindfold was now firmly in place. Delilah flounced herself out into the audience, which inspired some of her customers to sit up straight and pay attention. She picked on one lonesome clyde in the thin crowd and wiggled at him to make him laugh. Then she bent over and picked up a dollar bill from his table, then led him back up on stage and had him hold the dollar. Some of the other clydes clapped and whistled.

I watched intently.

Benny groaned again and said, "Here's where he gets mental."

The Great Morris raised a hand and set it dramatically against his forehead. There should have been a drum roll, but I suppose the cost of that was prohibitive. Clyde grinned at the audience while The Great Morris issued instructions, which I could not quite hear.

"What's he going to do?" I asked Benny.

"He's going to do a number so old it's got arthritis," Benny said. He pronounced it *arthur-itis*. "See the dollar bill the goof is holding?"

I said yes.

Benny stepped to the cash register and picked up something and returned to me. He was holding a red grease pencil.

"See this?" he asked. "The deal of this number is, you wind up making a shill out of some unsuspecting dork in the audience. And how do you do this? You take a dollar, any dollar, and before the show you give it to The Great Morris, and he memorizes the serial number. Then, you make two little red spots on corners of the bill with the pencil—one spot on a side and a little different from each other, so it ain't too overly obvious. You get the drift?"

I said, "Then you make sure the marked bill eventually

winds up as change on somebody's table and all Delilah has to do is look around until she finds the perfect volunteer."

"And shazzam! The Great Morris, even though he's blindfolded, can read off the serial numbers from the bill the schmuck on the stage is concentrating on with all his mind, such as it is."

Up on the stage, this looked to be exactly what was happening. Every so often, the clydes would *ooh* or *aah*.

"He'll toss a rib once in a while," Benny said. "He'll say something like, 'Well the number I'm seeing seems to be upside-down, and I can't tell whether it's a six or a nine. Now really, sir, you've got to do your part! Concentrate, man! Don't let Delilah get you all hot and bothered standing there wiggling her booty like she's probably doing, and hey, get that number sixty-nine off your mind! I can see it, you know.' That rib, it usually gets a yuk out of them."

Sure enough, the clydes all laughed.

"See what I mean?" Benny said. "Why, sometimes he'll even blow a number on purpose. Them sapheads, they see Moe make one boner and they'll buy everything else he tosses at them."

I put back the rest of the first red, then I took a long swallow on the first Molson. I asked Benny, "Any special reason why you're giving away trade secrets to me?"

My great-aunt from Carnarsie clomped up to the bar just then and she slammed a tray down and said she needed two drafts of Rolling Rock. She curled a lip at me and said, "You still here, Lance?" I blew her a kiss. Benny got her the drafts, and she scuffed away on her platforms, which I noticed were made from some kind of a lizard.

"No special reason," Benny finally answered me. "I'm just trying to somehow make it up to a nice customer like yourself for the way that goddamn old harpy rides you."

"Thanks, but you don't have to worry about me. My friend warned me all about her. But I came in anyhow."

"Oh yeah? Who's your friend?"

I moved in sideways on Benny. "Well, he works around here sometimes. Free-lance he says."

Benny scratched the skin on his head. "If he works here, I'd know him. Who is he?"

"I guess you'd know him, all right, you being the owner and all. Only thing is, I just know him by his street name. Picasso, like the painter."

Benny's face and kidney-bean head darkened. He said, "Funny little guy? Wears whiskers and one of them French hats? That's your friend?"

"Yeah." I thought about singing soprano in the Holy Cross choir and blinked innocently.

"Pal, that guy is hinkier than Hallowe'en."

"Aw, maybe he's a little nutso, but . . ."

Benny interrupted. "Hey, the Ayatollah was a little nutso, too, wasn't he? I'm telling you, I think your boyfriend's dangerous."

"What makes you say that? I mean, he works here, doesn't he? You hired him—and he's not my *boyfriend.*"

Benny started rubbing his scalp in a very aggravated way. I put some money on the bar and said he should have a drink on me, which he did—a Bushmill's, neat. He said he was sorry about the boyfriend crack, that he never meant it the way it sounded.

He put back his whiskey. I started in on my second red.

"If you're a smart guy like I think maybe you are," Benny said, wiping his lips, "you'll take what I say as a friendly warn-off. This Picasso, he's a time bomb. One day— BOOM! And down goes anybody fool enough to be caught near him."

"There's something I don't understand," I said. "If you think Picasso's about to blow, how come you have him around here?"

Benny rapped the bar with his knuckles. "Knock on wood, he ain't never coming back."

"He isn't working here?"

"It wasn't like he was ever on the payroll or like that. We just had him passing out palm cards. You know, you probably seen our cards if you ever walked through Times Square in your life. Well, Picasso shows up at the door one day when we had a want ad running in the paper for palm-card men and at first he seemed okay," Benny said. "He says he's no bum or nothing, that he's got his own room out in Brooklyn and all."

"Coney Island?" I asked, innocence itself.

"That's right, the Seashore Hotel. How'd you know?"

"He said something about how he used to paint for the carny attractions out there, at Astroland."

"Sure, that's how come they call him Picasso. Some joke, hey?"

"Not the way you're telling it," I said. "But, go on. What did he do to you?"

"At first, nothing. He tells us about the painting dodge, and how it ain't what it used to be out at Coney Island and how he needs some work, and also that he's a little hungry and thirsty. Okay, I figure, the guy is obviously no lousy skell from the neighborhood around here so maybe he's halfway dependable. So we feed him and give him a tryout."

"How did that go?"

"Okay. We posted him right outside the joint and had him palming to the after-five bunch. That way we could watch him, see."

"And?"

"He was kind of lazy, I'd say. But he didn't go and toss the cards in the garbage like a lot of these guys do, so you could see the guy was at least honest. But also you could see the guy was definitely a head case by the way he was all the time jabbering with some imaginary friend, like a goofball little kid does."

"I saw him do that, too!" I said, giving Benny the wide eyes.

"Yah, well then you know how it ain't doing us no good

when we pay a guy to palm, and he's out there acting so schitzy all he does is scare away half the potential customers."

"So you canned him?"

"Hey! If I'd of had it all my way, the little psycho and his French beanie would've been heaved out into the ambulance lane of Seventh Avenue at rush hour. But, oh no! My genius partner, he feels sorry for the old coot. Like he feels sorry for old Delilah and for that goddamn harpy. Honest to god, sometimes I don't know whether I'm running a bar here or some kind of freaking house of charity."

"I take it things got worse with Picasso?"

"Get this," Benny said. "One day we get these new palm cards printed up. It's my idea. I want to see if we can scare up some more daytime business from the suits, you know? Guess what the new cards say?"

"Just tell me, Benny."

"Oh yeah, you don't guess. The cards, they say 'Sex for Lunch.'"

I laughed. "Not bad."

"Yeah, well, I thought it was a pretty cute idea," Benny said. "Moe thought it was a ripper, too. Anybody in his right mind'd think it's funny. Guess who don't think it's funny?"

"No guess there."

"Right. So, next thing we know after we give Picasso the new cards is there's so much goddamn noise outside the door you'd of thought it was World War III. Moe and me, we go rushing out and there's Picasso, screaming at everybody. He's throwing all my new palm cards at people in the street and screaming, 'Filth! Philistine filth!' over and over. And he's kicking and punching people, too, and some of them's falling down on their keisters. He takes one look at Moe and me and he starts screaming 'Whoremonger!' over and over, then he pops us both pretty good. He knocks my upper plate out of my mouth and mashes my nose and clouts Moe so bad he can't hear right for a whole week. And then the cops come running up and they drag him off to I-don't-know-where, Bellevue, I guess."

Benny caught his breath and poured himself another drink. I sipped at my second beer.

"The guy's little," Benny said, "but he's piss-willy mean and a lot stronger than he looks. It took a half-dozen big cops to take him down that day."

"When was that?"

Benny scratched his chin. "Just shy of a year ago."

"Did he ever come back?"

Benny rapped the bar again. "Nope. I told the cop in charge we don't want no trouble on account of him. I told him how we paid him off the books and all, and how I didn't want him around except my bleeding-heart partner did and look where it got us. I gave the cop a twenty for his troubles, and he said, Well maybe we can just forget all about it. So that was that."

But Benny added, "You know, though, afterwards he started creeping my dreams, you know? I'd see him sitting at the bar, eating the food we'd give him as a favor because of Moe and his goddamn charitable weakness. I'd see them eyes of his, crazy big eyes following me while he sat there munching. You ever take a good look at that bird, I mean close up?"

"Now that you mention it," I said, "he does look a little hinky."

"A little! Adolf Hitler was a little hinky, too."

"I see what you mean."

I wanted to get out of there fast to call in a Brooklyn squad to roust Picasso from the Seashore Hotel in the unlikely event he was there; I wanted to tell Benny I was a cop. I wanted to have him take precautions in light of what happened to Celia Furman and Dr. Ronald Reiser and now Benito. But some instinct told me to keep quiet, at least for a while; a halfway competent cop, which is what I enjoy thinking I am, learns to trust his instincts.

DARK MAZE

"But tell me this," I said, "what's going to happen if Picasso ever turns up here again?"

Benny smiled. No good could come of such a smile.

He leaned down under the bar. When he stood up again he held a .44 revolver, as big and as ugly as the Charter Arms I own and every bit as capable of blowing a hole in a man's chest the size of a baseball.

Benny stroked the heavy gun lovingly with his free hand. He smiled and said, "Next time you see your friend Picasso, tell him me and my friend are ready and waiting for him."

A man who has got my powers of observation, he naturally learns faster than the ordinary sucker. That's a fact of life. Ain't I right?

Damn straight I am.

Your peasant, he's got that dumb flat face of his until he's about fifty freaking years old. This is because it takes the sucker half a century to wise up to the fact that the rules of the game are crooked, which is way too late.

So you would think the guy who learns fast like me would stand a much better chance at getting his share, right?

Wrong, sucker!

God is a goddamn ironist. He gave the powers of observation to broken-down artists and other kinds of odd socks of the world, then he went and put blinders on everybody else so they could just stupidly concentrate on making themselves happy ever after.

You ask me, it's screwy. But since it's all God's fault they say it's divine.

Well, okay.

I learned a long time ago I should just bide my time. And I learned how lessons have a way of sneaking up on everybody.

And here's one of the biggest lessons I ever learned: no good deed goes unpunished. . . .

THIRTEEN

I found a pay phone out on the street that was not broken and rang up Central Homicide. It was ten past one and Mogaill had gone home. The desk sergeant referred me to a detective on the overnight shift who was working up the preliminaries on the murder scene at Bellevue.

"This is Neil Hockaday. I'm catching on the Reiser homicide."

"Yeah, I heard. I just typed your name. I'm Hooper. The captain says for me to leave this stuff with Logue for you."

"Thanks. I want you to do something else for me, Hooper."

"What's that?"

"Call up the Coney Island station house in Brooklyn and have them arrange a stake on the Seashore Hotel, on Surf Avenue. All entrances and exits covered, okay? Better watch the roof, too." I finished with a description of Picasso and what he had been wearing in the park. "The name is Charlie Furman, also known as Picasso."

Hooper whistled. "Yeah, Picasso—that's the guy all over

the radio news. I hear he clipped two tonight—the doc at Bellevue and a bodega owner on the West Side. Making it a total of three so far, counting the barfly the other day."

So it was out and connected, I thought. "Tell Brooklyn I don't think our boy's going to be there, but I want a round-the-clock watch until I say otherwise. It's the best we can do so far with a location fix. Anybody in Brooklyn has a problem with this, tell them to check it out with Inspector Neglio."

"Okay," Hooper said. "That's it?"

"Give Brooklyn my home telephone." I gave the number to Hooper. "I want to be called right away if he shows. I think I can prevent a lot of damage if I'm there for the takedown."

And then because I was so tired and, truth to tell, so fuzzy from two murders and four drinks, I flagged a taxi and rode the few blocks home to Forty-third and Tenth. But not before being accosted by an ancient mariner shaking his cup on Broadway; Times Square would not relinquish me so easily that night.

He was tall and gaunt, with a face that had clearly been handsome in better times; a face that looked like the one in the frame on the dresser in my bedroom, my father's confident soldier face. The clothes he wore—two checkered shirts, a greasy bush jacket, corduroy trousers frayed at the cuffs, shoes with the heels broken off—were lifeless, as if they had been stripped off dead men. His hair was brown and matted and his eyes were green, one of them rheumy.

"Young sir," he said as I stepped away from the pay phone, "you see my predicament." He shook a paper coffee cup at me and coins clunked inside.

I reached in my pocket for a quarter.

"Oh, it's not your money I want," he said.

"What do you want?"

"I'd like your opinion."

"On what?"

There was a crack of lightning and the air was soon heavy and moist. Then the first drops of a fine spring rain fell.

"You see before you a beggar man," he said, rainwater streaking his lined and yellowing face. "Please, young sir, look into my cup and tell me, do you see the beggar's cup half-empty, or half-full?"

I gave him the quarter I held, and a five-dollar bill besides. "Sorry, old man. I've got nothing I can tell you but God bless."

Then I climbed into the back of a yellow cab and rode through the thundery light. The cheap flashing of Times Square shone outside my spattered window. For a few moments in the private darkness of a taxi, I mourned old lost men.

Ruby was asleep in my bed.

Out in the parlor, she had set out a plate for me: a doughnut, two aspirins and a glass of warming milk. There was also a spray of daisies in a glass of water.

I took a towel from the bathroom and dried my head and face from the rain while I sat in the green chair. I dialed information and asked for the number of the Seashore Hotel.

After nine rings, a voice from Brooklyn rasped, "Seashoa."

"Charlie Furman's room, please."

"Who?"

"Picasso."

"What's this, some kind of a gag?"

"No—don't hang up."

There was a pause. "Who the hell is this calling anyways?"

"Detective Neil Hockaday, New York Police. I'm looking for a guest there by the name of Charles Furman, alias Picasso."

"If you mean that old carny painter, you're way too late, mister. He ain't been here for all of a year."

That was about what I expected.

The voice from Brooklyn added, "We had to put him out after he wouldn't pay his rent no more."

"Do you know where he went?"

"You kidding? People here don't leave no forwarding addresses. Besides which, we looked all over Coney for the bastard since he burnt up his room before he went. I like to burnt *him* up if I ever catch him!"

"All right, thanks anyway," I said. I decided for the time being to keep the surveillance detail on the Seashore.

That final bit of the day's business completed, I undressed and climbed into bed with Ruby. Which seemed as right and natural as if my nights had been thus complete for many years. She awoke, only just slightly startled by the new surroundings; she nestled against me and said thickly, "I'm glad you're finally home, Hock. Let's hear all about it tomorrow."

So warm she was beside me, making her soft slumbering sounds. I touched her bare shoulder and it occurred to me that even Picasso had once in his life known such goodness, and that maybe I was merely a luckier man than he. I draped an arm over Ruby's slender waist and lay restless for an hour, waiting for my cop dreams to come. The visions of the day's blood faded, and I felt myself drifting finally into the safe harbor of sleep in my own house.

Then I fell.

And that night, Picasso and the beggar man and a card in a hatband creeped my dreams.

We occupied the last booth of the window side of the spoon across the way, Pete Pitsikoulis' All-Night Eats & World's Best Coffee. Pete himself was in the kitchen cooking our breakfast.

147

Wanda the waitress had brought black coffee for me, which truthfully was not the world's best, and herbal tea for Ruby, along with ice water and good, fresh country-style orange juice for two—the kind of honest orange juice that has been muscled clean out of America's countryside by the Tropicana cartel. Spread across our formica-top table were the late morning finals of the *Post* and *Daily News*. I had not bothered picking up *Newsday* or the *Times*, which in their different ways are practically out-of-town papers. There was also the notebook I had finally remembered to begin.

We sipped, and read for a while. I, the *Daily News* and Ruby the *Post*.

When Ruby finished, she said, "Now, isn't this very instructive for me? An actor will sit up at Sardi's after the big show waiting for reviews of the play, whereas a cop hangs out in a Greek coffee shop to study how tabloids play the big murder case."

I suggested, "It's theatre all the same, isn't it? A good reporter knows that New York crime has what it takes to charm an audience: comedy, drama and tragedy—all without rehearsals."

"And the play's the thing?"

"Sure, so long as the terrible story up on the stage has no real effect on the storyteller."

"How cynical," Ruby said.

"Not at all. It's the way the newspaper business has of encouraging exceptional reporters to quit scribbling facts and eventually move on to the truth of fiction."

We traded papers.

The *Daily News* account of New York City's latest multiple murder spree had been suitably punchy and mostly accurate, so far as it went. But as usual, the paper founded in 1801 by the aristocrat Alexander Hamilton had gone over the top.

DARK MAZE

Inky block lettering and a grainy photograph packed with gore and misery covered the front page of the *Post* like a fat man's body splattered face down on Thirty-fourth Street after a long tumble down the Empire State Building. "Maniac in Manhattan" was the pithy title riding over a picture of poor bloody Benito being transported by stretcher from his bodega to a morgue truck, with the sobbing Carolena huddled in a cop's arms and wide-eyed Luis pointing to where the victim's shop window had been weirdly defiled. The bottom of the page promised all the ghastly details inside: "Horror by Day & Night, Full Coverage and More Pix, Pages 2–3."

I opened the paper in a hurry.

There was an old newswire photo of Celia Furman, and a new picture of Angelo's Ebb Tide taken from the street. The caption under these read, "Woman Gambler from Detroit Is First Victim, Gunned Down in Hell's Kitchen Bar." A Bachrach portrait of Dr. Reiser appeared alongside a *Post* file photo of Bellevue Hospital, with an airbrushed arrow indicating the rooftop where Reiser died: "Top Psychiatrist Knifed to Death by Crazed Intruder." An enlarged close-up section of the cover photo zeroed in on Picasso's grotesque drawing of the throatless man, which begged the question, "Brand of a Killer?" I supposed the question mark was published on the advice and counsel of the newspaper's lawyer. There was also a two-column cut of a now-grinning Luis—"Witness Describes Prime Police Suspect for *Post* Artist"—with an accompanying sketch of Picasso that I thought was an excellent likeness. I wondered what Picasso thought, and where he might be reading his press notices that morning.

The story's bulky headlines were a stream of black, spread over two full pages. Nobody plays crime better than the New York *Post,* and nobody writes about it with more comprehensive flair than my friend Slats:

Thomas Adcock

Major Manhunt Is On—Serial Killer Slays 3

Cops Search for Street Artist Called "Picasso"

By William T. Slattery

The murderous rampage of a brutal serial killer began in broad daylight, with a shooting in a Ninth Avenue bar. Two days later, in the dead of night, the killer struck down two more victims, first evading Bellevue Hospital security staffers to plunge a butcher knife into the back of a prominent psychiatrist, then calmly walking into a Hell's Kitchen bodega where he slashed open the neck of a hard-working shopkeeper with a box-cutter blade.

Sources tell the *Post* that homicide detectives are engaged in a desperate manhunt for a homeless artist known only as Picasso. Officially, the police would only say that Picasso is wanted for "simple questioning." But the *Post* has learned that Picasso may have a history of violence and mental illness, and that he has direct personal links with at least two of the three recent murder victims. Those victims, in order of their deaths, are:

• Celia Furman, 59, of Detroit. Gunned down in a noisy crowd at Angelo's Ebb Tide bar on Ninth Avenue at West 44th Street at about 5 P.M. Monday by an unknown assailant dubbed by some in the media as the "Happy Hour Shooter." The unrecovered weapon used was a small-caliber pistol, according to police, who believe the killer fired at close range as Ms. Furman sat on a barstool, then left without notice. The owner of the bar, Angelo Cifelli, said in a brief telephone interview: "She was an old pal from Motown and I'm upset, okay? This is a friendly neighborhood-type place. Nobody saw anything, nobody heard shots, and that's all I got to say." A Detroit newspaper, which supplied the *Post* with an exclusive photo of Ms. Furman, reports that she had an extensive criminal record for gambling violations in that city.

• Dr. Ronald I. Reiser, 48, of Manhattan, an innovative psychiatrist well respected by his Bellevue Hospital colleagues. Stabbed to death yesterday by the so-called "Bellevue Slasher" sometime during early evening hours while tending an open-air garden he maintained on the roof of the hospital's psychiatric ward. The killer left an eight-inch household butcher knife buried in the doctor's back. Bellevue's public relations office would issue only this statement: "A person or persons unknown apparently gained access to Dr. Reiser's unauthorized roof garden, then assaulted the doctor with a knife, resulting in his tragic death. Hospital security officers are cooperating with the police department in a thorough investigation of this matter." Others on the Bellevue staff, who asked to remain anonymous, said Dr. Reiser was a "selfless humanitarian" who had been treating Picasso unofficially for several years—up until eight months ago when Picasso physically attacked him, for reasons Reiser did not discuss. Picasso was at that time restrained by orderlies and then evicted from the hospital, according to these sources. It is believed that Picasso had not recently seen Dr. Reiser for his usual treatments, described by the sources as "psychiatric counseling in connection with habitual and potentially violent hallucinogenic episodes."

• Benito Molevo Reyes, 40, of Manhattan, owner of the B&C Superette, Tenth Avenue near West Forty-fifth Street. Knifed in the throat last night as he tended his store alone, between the hours of 11:00 and 11:30. The killer, unnoticed by neighborhood residents upon entry or exit from Reyes' bodega, left behind a blood-soaked box-cutter knife. Police said there were no signs of struggle and that Reyes' widow, Carolena, discovered the body after failing to get an answer from her husband when she called him from a back room of the shop. About an hour prior to the murder, Picasso allegedly used white paint to draw the figure of a man dying from a knife wound in the neck on the window of Reyes' bodega. According to Luis Riestra, 16, who lives with his mother in an apartment directly over the bodega, Picasso was informally employed by Reyes to paint advertisements on the shop window. But Riestra told the *Post* last night, "It was strange, because Picasso usually painted in the daytime. Last night I was on the corner with my friends and I saw Picasso come by and go into Benito's place, then Benito came outside and they talked and Benito went back inside." The two men did not argue, Riestra said. "Then I noticed Picasso was painting the window real fast, then he took off. I didn't notice anybody else go in the store after that, but somebody sure did."

Riestra added that a police officer of his acquaintance who lives in the Hell's Kitchen neighborhood— Detective Neil Hockaday of the Street Crimes Unit, Manhattan—had arrived at the bodega in a large black car minutes before Reyes' body was discovered. He said Detective Hockaday, whom he referred to as Hock, got out from the back of the car and spoke to someone else in the backseat for a while before the car drove off.

"Then when the black car left, Benito's wife started screaming," Riestra said. "Me and my friends ran to the store and Hock was at the door with a gun and he said to call 911, which my mother did and also one of my friends. Then there were cops all over the place."

Riestra also said that Detective Hockaday questioned him about Picasso. "I didn't bring up Picasso, Hock did," Riestra said. "He asked me a whole lot of questions about Picasso, like where he lived and how long he's been around the neighborhood. But nobody knows about Picasso, except he's a very strange dude."

Detective Hockaday was seen by reporters at the scene of last night's bodega murder, but he declined to speak about the case. He did, however, present Riestra to reporters by saying, "This young man has your story."

Other officers on scene at the Tenth Avenue slaying, including commanders from the Midtown North station house, were also unusually reluctant to answer questions. At *Post* press time, the only official statement came from the Public Information Office of police headquarters: "The department has taken special steps to ensure the expeditious apprehension of a perpetrator in what may be a series of related homicides. Inspector Tomassino Neglio has temporarily reassigned Detective Neil Hockaday of Street Crimes Unit, Manhattan to lead a team from the Central Homicide Squad in the investigation of the deaths of Celia Furman, Dr. Ronald Reiser and Benito Molevo Reyes."

Meanwhile, a number of New York political leaders joined the mayor in issuing a statement from City Hall expressing their anger. . . .

There was not much more to Slattery's story, but I stopped there because I could see that breakfast was coming and there is no sense in spoiling good food with mealy quotations from New York political leaders. Wanda was carrying our plates in her ample arms and Pete trotted after her in his white chef's clothes with black hairs curling out from his collar and cuffs.

"Hey, you see the picture of Luis in the paper, eh, Hock?" Pete said, as he reached our table. Wanda set down the plates with her customary groans, then she waddled off to another booth. "My own busboy—his picture in the newspaper! Oh, he got something on his ball! Like you, Hock, when you was a boy around here, remember? Hey, maybe Luis got so much on his ball he buy me out some day."

"You without a coffee shop?" I said. "Where would you spend all your time, Pete?"

"I give up this city with the criminals! I leave all to you. Old Pete retire in nice sunny Florida."

Not having the heart to tell him about nice sunny Florida these days, I asked, "Where is our bright young man of the hour this morning?"

"Luis? He work late today. Night shift."

It finally occurred to me by the way Pete was talking to me while he was mostly looking at Ruby that maybe I was not the main reason he had come by. I took a bite of my eggs on a slice of toast. Pete stared at Ruby and smiled. I said, "Pete, I'd like you to meet Ruby Flagg."

Pete took her hand and kissed it and said, "I don't like I see Hock alone by himself so much."

"Neither do I," Ruby said.

Pete said to me, "She is such a pretty plum. You don't do nothing to make her run away, you hear?"

Ruby said, "Don't worry, Pete, he's still got a lot on his ball."

"This one I like her okay, Hock," Pete said, beaming at me and then Ruby. "But she don't eat so good like you. Bring your Ruby here, I feed your jewel right."

"I will," I said.

Pete slapped my shoulder with one of his big hammer hands. "You are lucky man!" he said. Then he returned to his kitchen, trailing behind him the aromatic wake of fried onions.

"I'm glad he approves," Ruby said.

"So am I. He's important to me. I've known Pete just about forever," I said. "Sooner or later, he'll tell you my biggest secret, which he's already told everybody else in the neighborhood."

"And, the secret is?"

"Pete claims I'm his long-lost son. From the days he was a young cook in the Greek navy, and he jumped ship at Dublin one fateful day, then took up with a colleen who only broke his heart by stealing away to America with his baby boy. Which brought him here, of course, in search of myself."

Ruby laughed, and so did I. Then she spooned up a small bit of her peach-colored melon. I watched it slide between her lips. And for a wonderful second or two, I shared Pete's myth of carefree days in the sun, Ruby and I, somewhere far beyond New York.

"No wonder you eventually came home to Hell's Kitchen," Ruby said. "Your heart always lived here, didn't it? The wonder is you ever left."

Yes, that was true. Then why had I never uttered, even to myself, this obvious truth of me? And how had I lived so many faithful years with the likes of Judy McKelvey, with whom I could never share a proper shame for our common childhood streets, no matter how I tried?

"I remember the first time I was ever in this very place," I said.

"Tell me."

"My mother took me to the doctor that day. It wasn't pleasant, but I was brave. Afterward she brought me here to

Pete's, for a reward—a Coca-Cola and an egg-salad sandwich. And that was the finest meal I've ever had. Thinking about it now, I can still taste it."

"Some day I want to hear all about your mother and the two of you living here. And your father, too . . ."

Ruby struck my hollow place.

". . . I mean your real father, Hock. The handsome soldier in the picture frame, who looks so much like you. What about him?"

My mother's words were ever the same—repeated exactly so—when I was brave enough to ask about a man she would never mention; whenever I would simply ask, "What about Papa?"

"Your papa went off in a mist, that's all there is to it; it hurts too much to speak of him as if he was ever flesh and blood and bone to me." That much, and little more, until her boy's bravery faded. She died when I was a full-grown man, in my first week of being a cop. Among other things, my mother left me the picture of a young soldier never returned from his war, and my own hollow place.

I told Ruby all of this while she stared quietly at me.

Then she said, "I'm sorry, Hock, but shame on your mother."

Had I not said this same secret thing to myself?

"Your father should never have been allowed to die that way, with nobody to give you his memory," she said. "Nobody survives without memories."

And was that not the very thing I would begin to discover that day in Coney Island?

They think they're closing in on me, hey? So let them think I'm just another dumb maniac. I tried to tell them, didn't I? Didn't I go turn my old sick soul inside out so everybody could see me die?

Didn't I?

DARK MAZE

Damn straight I did.

But they don't want to see!

Okay, so I'll show them some more. Knife, gun—those I already done. Something a little more interesting for next time, hey?

Sure, and why not? Variety is the spice of death.

FOURTEEN

Naturally, I was very anxious to see Johnny Halo and Big Stuff again at the Neptune Bar. Which I would—eventually.

Right now, though, they were the last I had to consult. First things first. That meant a long day of leg work, talking to lots of other characters out in Coney Island; that way, maybe I could get an angle on riddle number one in my notebook: Why had Halo and the dwarf denied knowing Picasso?

"You had a hunch those two were lying the other day, didn't you?" Ruby asked me.

"Of course I did."

After all, we had gone to Coney Island for the express purpose of seeing Picasso's "masterpiece" at the Fire and Brimstone, which the once-living, breathing Dr. Ronald Reiser had urged me to behold when he handed over the disturbing Polaroid mailed to him by an equally disturbing ex-patient. On top of that, Benny from the Horny Poodle told me that Picasso kept a room at the Seashore Hotel. That was easily confirmed by the desk clerk who, during our telephone conversation, let drop the arresting item about

Picasso torching said room in response to his being dispossessed.

To say the least, Picasso was a known quantity on the boardwalk at Coney Island. Especially to somebody like Johnny Halo, who proudly hailed himself as so Coney he knew from Archie Leach on stilts and Abie Relis falling out a window of the Half-Moon Hotel accidentally on purpose; to Big Stuff, too (". . . *him and the woman, they as't about Fire and Brimstone"*).

And, there was that very first thread to Picasso's Coney Island fabric: an old black-and-white snapshot in Celia's handbag, the picture of a bathing beauty with her two attentive escorts, one of them wearing glasses with whiskers on his chin and a beret on his head; the writing in fountain-pen ink—*Coney I., summer '54.*

I tapped my shirt pocket. Inside was the old snapshot. And Ruby and I were on our way to the boardwalk again.

"You knew right off that Halo and the little fellow were lying, so how come you didn't call them on it?" Ruby asked.

"Because that serves no purpose," I said with great patience. "Whenever I am given bald lies—what my Uncle Liam on the other side would call 'a fine load of codswallop'—I am thankful for the gift."

"The gift?"

"Eight times out of ten, a liar presents me with a helpful shortcut. Here's how it works being a cop: Most of the time, I spend my days stumbling around and around for what I'm supposed to be after. You've got no idea how tiring this is. But when somebody kindly lies to me, there's my breather. A lie allows me to slow down, get off the track and just look, because it's likely there's something useful behind a lie."

There was a bright dawning in Ruby's face. She said, "And when people tell the truth . . ."

"The truth is the long way around," I said, finishing her thought. "I'm a detective; the truth doesn't hold the same value for me as it does for other people, not that I'm knocking it. Lies, though—now, that's my bread and butter."

"Well then," Ruby said, "we're professional cousins."

I was now the naïf. "We are?"

"Certainly. You're the detective, so you look for useful lies. I'm the actor. I get up on a stage full of wooden scenery, I wear costumes instead of just plain clothes, and I deliver made-up lines that ring true only when I've rehearsed the playwright's script." Ruby smiled. "So, you see? I give the audience the gift of lies."

"In your case, that's art." And as soon as this had escaped my lips, there was Neglio at my ear: *"You're an artist among cops . . ."*

We had been riding the F train and now we sat for several minutes without speaking, listening to the subway sounds and to our separate thoughts. The train pulled into East Broadway station, doors opened and closed; people got off and people got on, as if walking in their sleep. We rolled on through the tunnel beneath the East River, Brooklyn-bound; lights clicked off and the car went momentarily black and when it grew bright again the passengers had not moved, their heads still drooping and lolling above their newspapers and open books.

I thought of coming home last night, of milk and cookies left out for me. Imagine—milk and cookies. I thought of Ruby in my bed, and me with my troubled dreams.

I thought about revealing lies and artless truth. And the hidden work of uneventful days. About Picasso, and murder.

Ruby's thoughts were far more immediate.

"Would you mind telling me, by the way, exactly why are we traveling by subway all the way out to Coney Island?" she asked. "The police department can't spare a car for the guy in charge of catching the Manhattan maniac who's selling so many papers today?"

DARK MAZE

It had not occurred to me to sign out for a car, actually. nd until Ruby asked, the reason behind this failure lay ɛep and unspoken in my Manhattan soul (my Uncle Liam ould call such a person as me a "city hike").

And so, I offered my confession to Ruby: "I don't know ɪe way by car."

She laughed in my face. But the way she did it made me ɛr willing clown.

"Just look at my man. He'll have a dinner of chicken and ɔrnbread at Princess Pamela's, or else that chili mess I ɔticed last night all over the stove. He has breakfast every ay with Pete and Wanda. He lives in a Hell's Kitchen ump, he gets around by subway—when he gets around— ɪd the way he dresses is never going to get him in the *GQ* agues. He doesn't put on too much of a front for a girl, ɔes he? Are you thoroughly incorruptible, Detective ɔckaday?"

What she said about my clothes struck a deadened nerve. was wearing a pair of nice soft tan corduroys I found for ve dollars one day at the Salvation Army, a two-dollar ɛen jersey from the same haberdashery, a perfectly good avy blue windbreaker I found on a park bench and a pair of eebok tennis sneakers bought at full retail.

"I wouldn't know any better," I said, "if that's what you ɪean."

"Yes, I think so. Don't change."

"Don't worry. It's too late for me."

She laughed again, caramel lips taut over rows of perfect hite teeth. "When I was coming up in New Orleans," she ɪid, "all the boys at my school ever talked about was riving around in big cars someday."

"I don't like to drive," I said. "It only gets me out of ɔwn."

"Where you don't belong?"

"That, and where I never understand the layout."

161

"How so? Aren't there plenty of cops commuting into the city every day?"

"Sadly so, the department is turning into a regular suburban occupation force," I said. "We've now got thousands of young cops living out on the Island, in their cheesy cop towns—Massapequa and Bethpage, places like that."

"You've seen these awful places?"

"I have, and it's just what I mean by strange layouts. People living in neighborhoods where some developer came in and ripped down most of the trees, then named streets after them."

"Even so, I'll bet everybody in those neighborhoods will swear they live where they live for the pleasure of seeing nature right in their own backyards."

"Well, nature is also a crowded street. I am saying hello to dear Mother Nature every day myself, and from the things she has said back to me over the years, I am beginning to suspect she's not a fine lady."

We were nearing the end of the line.

The train moved slowly along elevated tracks, over Brooklyn slums filled with sagging windows and sooty life down on the streets. It was raining now, the kind of gray rain that falls on funerals. Soon the sweep of the Atlantic would come into view beyond the tarred rooftops. I touched the pocket of my windbreaker, to be sure again; there was my wallet, where I carried the snapshot of Celia Furman and her beaux from one sunny day in the carefree year of 1954.

Ruby slid closer to me on the vinyl subway seat. I felt the heat of her leg against mine.

She put a hand on my arm and asked, "Hock, do you promise you won't change?"

By the secret code of irony in which women so often speak of and to their men, I understood this question to actually mean that Ruby Flagg had decided right then and there—on the F train to Coney Island—that she wanted both of us

hanged, until death us do part. And now she stared at me, earching my face as I thought carefully of how to answer.
"I do," I said.

We walked along the fenced vacancy that once had been teeplechase Park, where once there was a graceful glass and ast-iron dome that contained a world of wonders a boy aturally believed would live forever.

We walked some more, past the last remaining wall of teeplechase. The rain had softened now to little more than nist.

Ruby spotted a mural on the low wall, recently put up by n outfit called the Coney Island Hysterical Society. There /as the familiar logo of the Steeplechase man, with slick lack ringlets on his forehead and a black moustache curled p over his full-face, toothy smile. And a drawing of the old lass and cast-iron dome. And the legend:

> Steeplechase Park . . .
> Come Back . . .
> Come Back . . .

We cut along the back end of Nathan's Famous. A rostitute lazed in a doorway, lit a cigarette and sized me up s a no-sale. Bowery Avenue was steely wet. In the distance, oward the water, was the rubble of giant spokes from the /heel of an abandoned carnival ride; it lay in the sand ooking like wreckage from a battle to the death with 5odzilla.

Then a sound came through the clammy air of the Bowery nd cleansed it like sunlight, a sound I knew from so many ears ago; so real a sound as my mother's voice, as if it were eally possible for a world to come back.

"Where is it coming from?" Ruby asked.

The softly booming sound, the clatter and whine and

thump of a carousel. Bellows pushing air through rolls of perforated paper, brass pipes tooting, felt-covered wood mallets pounding out a dozen different tones. And with the music, the painted horses would be lifting and falling, lifting and falling . . .

It was from another life, I thought. "It's from the carousel over on Surf Avenue," I said.

"It's a pretty sound," Ruby said. "Maybe we can take a ride before we go back?"

"I don't know, maybe."

We moved on, past the lane to Picasso's masterpiece, then up the stairs over the sand and onto the boardwalk, where I would spend the afternoon in and around the concession booths gathering information on the Furmans—Charlie and Celia, in the snapshot with the unidentified man. And, just maybe, some reason behind the lies of Johnny Halo and Big Stuff.

Rain threatened again, this time a real storm. Black clouds formed low over the ocean and there were distant thunderclaps.

A boardwalk barker took advantage of the turn in the weather: "Hurry, hurry, hurry! You'll want to get in here quick; you'll want to stay dry. The show's almost over, folks, but I'll tell you what—pay me half price now, and a new show begins in thirty minutes and you're welcome to stay. Now, how can you do better than that? Hurry, hurry, hurry! We've got nature's oddities on parade today! You'll see them all, at half the price! You'll see them high and dry. Hurry, hurry, hurry!"

Ruby grabbed my arm and pulled me toward the barker. He stood on a riser outside a large rickety shed, flagged with huge canvas posters of sideshow performers. A small crowd was circled around him, mostly old gents with nothing to do anymore and teenage mothers from the nearby housing projects.

"Look at the posters," Ruby said.

I looked, and saw what she meant. "It's Picasso's style," I said.

"Nature's oddities, folks!" the barker cried. "Yes, we got them right here. We got them just the way you like them! And right now, so long as the rain holds off, you got them for free! That's right, free! Keep that money in your pants, folks. This little show's on me!"

A skinny young woman draped provocatively in black lace stepped from behind a curtain at the barker's side, then took her place below a canvas poster that bore only a vague resemblance. She had long black hair that cascaded down her back and past her waist, olive skin and black Arab eyes. She wore a speckled python wrapped twice around her shoulders, once across her bare belly. The cool sea breeze made the fine hairs on her arms rise. She held the serpent's bony head in her hands, pointing its leathery eyes and its darting tongue at the crowd.

"Now, ain't she beauty-ful?" the barker said.

The old gents returned a mumble.

"Meet Sparkle the snake charmer, di-rect from Damascus, in faraway Syria!" The barker leered. "Don't you men out there wish you had a nice big snake for beauty-ful Sparkle tonight?"

The old gents had a throaty laugh. The teenage mothers watched, blank-faced, staring at Sparkle as if she were a goddess. I looked at the canvas poster of a dark-haired and full-bodied woman, with snakes choking the life from her body; I saw an essential fear in the eyes of the painted poster lady.

Sparkle's python arched and hissed as she squeezed its neck. Then it slithered into a new position, revealing one of her lace-covered breasts. Sparkle blew kisses to the crowd, turned daintily on her scuffed high heels and returned inside to her snakes.

And the barker said, "You want to see Sparkle shake her snakes, she's all yours at just half the price—today only!

Just one single dollar gets you in! A dollar gets you dry, folks. Rain's coming!"

Then a man stepped from behind the curtain and positioned himself below the poster of a big red-faced fellow with his hands planted on his knees, his mouth opened wide, and spewing out frightened mice. The man in front of us on the riser was not nearly so rotund as the image on the poster, but was indeed large, and his cheeks and nose were ruddy. He stood with his arms crossed over his wide chest, looking like he very much wanted a drink.

"Say hello to Waldo, folks!" the barker cried. "Waldo, the professional regurgitator!"

The crowd was not enthusiastic.

"What's that?" the barker said. "You say you'd like a little demonstration? All right, I promised a free show, and I'm a man of my word. Who's got a small object they don't mind getting a little gooey?"

Ruby poked me in the ribs. "Go on, give him something, Hock."

"No!"

The barker squawked, "Somebody out there got a silver dollar? Somebody got half of that?"

Ruby opened her purse and went into her wallet. "I've got a quarter," she called out.

"Well, hand it on up, little lady, and for being a sport, I'm going to let you into the show completely free of charge!" the barker said.

One of the teenage mothers said to a friend, "Shit, I wish't I'da had a quarter."

Ruby's quarter floated on hands up to the barker, who in turn gave it to Waldo, who promptly swallowed it. Then he leaned off the edge of the riser and opened his mouth so that people in the front of the crowd could be sure the coin had gone all the way down.

"Satisfied?" the barker asked.

Then Waldo stood back up. His face reddened and

contorted. He stroked his heavy neck with both hands as the barker intoned, "It's coming . . . it's coming . . . it's . . ."

Waldo spat up Ruby's quarter. It glistened in the palm of his hand.

The crowd offered a modest cheer. Ruby called out, "He can keep it."

Waldo pocketed the quarter and nodded his head toward Ruby. Then he returned inside the shed.

"Now, folks—how'd you like to see Waldo do that little number with a live mouse?" the barker said.

The old gents started clapping, and the little mothers came alive.

And then the rain pelted the boardwalk, the thunder broke and the barker popped open an umbrella and motioned toward the shed's door and turnstile and said, "One dollar, folks, and you're high and dry and highly entertained. How about it?"

Ruby and I hurried inside to escape the storm, as did twenty or so of the crowd. We sat in the lower tier of bleachers set up around a large, brightly lit stage. There was room enough for an audience of two hundred, but the bleachers held less than half of that, even with us newcomers.

A huge blonde woman, easily three hundred pounds of femininity, was at stage center. She wore a gauzy, red ballerina's outfit and was busy pulling a sword from her mouth. The crowd applauded listlessly.

The barker bounded up on stage to pick up the pace. He used a microphone and wore a top hat.

"Folks, let's have a great big hand for the lovely Estelline, the hungriest little gal in all Coney Island!" His amplified voice was far louder than necessary.

There was slightly more applause.

"And now, a little something to tide her over until dinnertime. Mr. Drummer, if you please!"

Seated at a drum at the rear of the stage, in the shadows,

was a man about one-third the heft of Estelline. His sticks beat out an energetic snare roll. Estelline picked up a pair of thick swords and carefully lined up the blades as the drum roll continued. Then she tilted her big yellow head back and shoved the steel wad straight down her gullet.

"How about that, folks? A double-decker sword sandwich!"

The applause was now more to the barker's liking. Estelline curtsied with the swords still rammed down her windpipe. The applause crested, Estelline removed the swords, and then took her bows and exit.

Then the drummer got up and started pushing a wheelchair onto the stage. In the chair was what appeared to be one-half of a red-headed man smoking a cigarette. The barker announced, "Say hello to Sealo, the man with flippers instead of arms and legs!"

The drummer shoved the chair to a table at the side of the stage and stopped. Then he picked up Sealo's torso and set it on the tabletop. Short, finlike limbs poked out from shirtsleeves and through small holes cut from the pockets of trousers that were pinned in the shape of a diaper.

Sealo used his dexterous lips to shove his cigarette over into the corner of his mouth. He looked over the audience and coughed.

Then he dropped his head forward and spat out his cigarette. It landed on the stage floor, and the barker picked it up. Sealo stuck out his agile lips and used them to reach into his shirt pocket for another cigarette and a wooden kitchen match.

He maneuvered the cigarette over to the left side of his mouth, the match to his right. Then with his tongue, he pushed the match upward and struck the tip against one of his upper teeth. The match flared.

Sealo's tongue worked the match flame close to the end of the half-swallowed cigarette. The cigarette took and Sealo dropped the match, then returned the cigarette to the center of his lips, fully extended. He took several long drags and the audience applauded wildly.

Ruby and I applauded politely. Sealo was about to do an encore when I felt somebody tap my shoulder.

I turned sharply. So did Ruby.

A baby-faced man about four feet high said to me, "You come out to Coney Island again to enjoy the day with your girly, buddy?"

It was just about the same way he said it the other day when he also wore a white jumpsuit and white sailor cap. He also carried the same newspaper bag, slung over one of his misshapen shoulders.

"As a matter of fact, yes," I said.

Big Stuff passed some handbills to the people sitting near us:

> HOW SWEET IT WAS!
> WE CAN BRING IT ALL BACK!
> LEGALIZE CASINOS!
> IT'S OUR BOARDWALK!
> LET'S GET INVOLVED!

"I see you're still spreading the good word," Ruby said.

Big Stuff eyed her suspiciously. "Yeah, that's right. I see you're still hanging around with your cop friend."

"Right," she said. "I enjoy my friends. I like talking about my friends. Do you like talking about your friends?"

Big Stuff ignored her. He looked at me and said, "I seen you're in the *Post* today."

"It was a long article and I was mentioned near the end," I said. "Most of the rest was about a guy you never heard of—Charlie Furman, better known as Picasso. Like the artist. Of course, my man's an artist, too. He painted Fire and Brimstone, which you *have* heard of, and the posters outside of this place. Quite a fellow. I talked to him once, you know."

This surprised Big Stuff. "You did?"

"Oh sure. And to his wife, Celia, poor thing."

"Yeah, poor thing." It did not seem to surprise Big Stuff that Charlie and Celia were connected by marriage.

"I'd give anything to talk to him again," I said.

Big Stuff thought for a second and said, "Well, what if I said I maybe did know one or two things about the guy?"

"I'd say we should talk about that."

"Talk's cheap."

"In this case, not necessarily."

Big Stuff caught on quick.

I kept a poker face. I wanted Big Stuff to beg me for it, which I have found to be sound policy when I am dealing with a would-be informer who is unknown to me; a little begging instills in the snitch the need to please.

"So maybe we got a little something for each other?" Big Stuff said.

"That's not going to cut it. I want a lot, for which I'll pay a lot."

I pulled out my wallet and opened it so Big Stuff could see all the currency I was going to charge back to the city. I took out a fifty and offered it to him.

Big Stuff licked his lips. But he would not take the money, not yet.

"You say you talked to him?" he said.

"Picasso, you mean. Yes."

"What did you think of him?"

"Picasso ought to hear my answer himself. Tell him I think it would be too bad if all anybody ever said about him was, 'He came and he went and who cares?' Tell him I care."

Big Stuff took a pencil out from under his sailor cap and a handbill from his bag. He wrote down an address on the back of the handbill.

"Let's see that fifty bucks again," he said.

I gave him the fifty and he gave me the handbill.

"You come by there at seven," he said. "There ain't any

name on the door. But when somebody answers, say you're looking for the Carny Club. I'll be waiting."

"I'll be there," I said.

Big Stuff left us. He crossed in front of the stage on his stumpy legs, shifted his newspaper bag to his other shoulder and then walked out the door, back to the boardwalk and the gray rain.

Waldo took his place on stage.

He held up a mouse by its tail—a quivering, red-eyed white mouse who did not look to be a willing trouper.

The drummer in the shadows went into a roll.

And Waldo brought down the house.

There was no question Waldo swallowed the mouse. We saw it go down, we heard the mouse complain, then we saw its damp and frenzied reentry.

FIFTEEN

For the next few hours, Ruby and I hiked up and down the boardwalk. The storm had rolled safely by and the sun was making a comeback, but the air was still wet. Rainbow arcs shimmered around stone seawalls down on the rain-streaked beach. As the day progressed, the boardwalk filled with neighborhood people. Young couples speaking Spanish or Russian pushed baby strollers; widow ladies still bundled in winter woolens gathering on benches in the sun to gossip and smoke; teenagers returning home from school.

I asked concessionaires and anybody else who looked local if they knew Charlie Furman, a/k/a/ Picasso. Everybody looked at me like I was a cop. Mainly, I learned that in Coney Island a question from an outsider is usually answered with another question: usually, "So who wants to know?"

When I did manage to get actual answers, they only confirmed what I already knew or could easily deduce: Picasso was an itinerant carny painter with a murky past, at best. He left Coney about a year ago when times went so bad he was put out of his room at the Seashore. He was an elusive, troublesome, quarrelsome sort who had no friends anybody could recall, save an imaginary sidekick he was forever chattering to. He was a brooder who had some intelligent observations to make if you cared to listen between the screeds, and he probably took his art too seriously.

The locals knew far less about Picasso than I did, and they knew him as a far simpler quantity. At least from Logue I knew some of Picasso's complexities: I knew he had served his country in war and that he had ringing in his ears as the result of action he saw; I knew about his five failed years in Detroit after the war; I knew that his wife, Celia, had known trouble with the IRS.

But what of it?

I showed around the snapshot, too. Nobody could identify anyone in it but Picasso himself.

For all the information I was unearthing, I told Ruby, I might as well have relied on some leg cops from Central Homicide to canvass the boardwalk. The reason I was doing my own routine nosing around, I told her, was because what few things I might absorb from this trip to Coney Island were bound to be more useful than the turgid facts accumulating for me back in Manhattan, thanks to Logue and Mogaill and company: the forensics reports, the weapons checks, the rap sheet backgrounds.

So here was I in the thick of it, the place I had claimed as rightly mine. Neil Hockaday on the case, the cop who had nobly sacrificed his own furlough and become the specially appointed hope of fear-plagued New York City, birthplace of the killing spree. Here was I, getting nowhere slow.

"In a word, I'm discouraged," I complained to Ruby, who was not sympathetically moved.

"My feet are pooped," she declared.

Ruby treated for vinegar-soaked French fries in paper

cones, a can of Molson for me and Barq's vanilla cream soda for herself. We sat on a bench facing the sea and watched the ocean churn up the sand.

"Not so long ago, I was a skinny sunburnt kid out there on that beach," I said. "The priests would bring us choirboys out here for a day of fresh salt air, and we'd always have a contest to see who could snatch the brightest shells that washed up on shore."

"Did you win?" Ruby asked.

"If there was ever a day I won, I don't remember it now. I was a hopeless case. The shells would come flying up to shore in the breakers and I could see the bright ones dancing in the foam, but I never was much good at grabbing fast enough or holding on tight enough to save them from the undertow."

"Who is?" Ruby said.

"Nobody, really. It's a stacked contest. The ocean always beats you. When you do snatch a bright shell, the ocean has another that's even brighter coming in on the next wave."

"It's like Princess Pamela said, Hock—you're no easy man."

"I wish I was."

"And I hope you'll never be. I've known my share of easy men. I've forgotten all their names."

"You're a good one, Ruby."

"Yes, I am." She finished her Barq's and handed me the French fries she did not want anymore. Then she reminded me, "There's lots more ground to cover, and time's wasting. There are lies yet to hear, there's the hotel to check, there's Johnny Halo to pressure, and who knows what might turn up tonight when I'm out of your hair and you drop by this Carny Club place?"

"When you're where?"

"Oh, I didn't tell you? We've got something on at the theatre tonight. A staged reading of a new play, for the potential angels, you know?" Ruby looked at her wrist-watch. "I've got to be heading back pretty soon."

This was very surprising. I was getting so used to the two of us, on the case and otherwise. Ruby was smart and fast and when I am around somebody like her I naturally get a little faster and smarter myself.

"Hock, you'll come by the theatre tonight, won't you?" she asked. "Everybody'll be there late."

"I should come by for a lot of white wine and cheese and the sort of people who actually like that stuff?" I said, with more surliness than I meant. "I thought you were riding with me today."

"Gear down, boy. I've got a life, too. I'm just the girl friend here, remember?"

There was no recovering from what I had stupidly said, but I did not want Ruby to leave me yet. "What about the Neptune? Do you still have time?"

She looked at her wristwatch again. "Okay, Hock. But you have to promise me a ride on the carousel after."

Johnny Halo was thumbing through the *Post* and sipping a short glass of beer at the far end of the bar where his sole customer had lain his head on a damp rag and fallen fast asleep. Halo looked up as we walked in off the boardwalk; he did not seem appropriately pleased by the new business.

"You two again?" he said. "Officer Frick and Officer Frack."

We took stools at the middle of the bar. Halo closed his newspaper and walked over to us without the slightest enthusiasm.

Ruby said to him, "That's Detective Frick and Frack."

Halo rolled his eyes. "What'll it be this time?"

I told him Molson, Ruby said club soda with a lime twist. Halo said, "Give me a freaking break with the twist bit, lady." He poured us our drinks, minus Ruby's lime, and set them down, obviously waiting for me to continue.

I sipped my beer and ignored him.

When the beer was half-gone, Halo lost it. He said to me, "You better not be on the job now, pal, or else maybe some concerned citizen might call up the department to report how there's a cop in my bar who's drinking on duty."

"Well, I guess you got me, Johnny. I am on duty." I drained my glass. "Just like I was on duty the last time I drank here. You remember that, Johnny?"

Halo's expression was malevolent. He looked like he might bite. He said nothing.

"Remember when you told me that big fat lie about how you never heard of a Coney Island character called Picasso? And how you never noticed your pay phone over on the wall was tied up with all kinds of calls from Celia Furman on the day she was killed?"

"When a cop waltzes into here asking about customers of mine, the house policy is see no evil, hear no evil."

"Nothing personal," I said. "But I am now going to have to place you under arrest."

"What the holy hell?"

"The charge is impeding an officer in the course of a police investigation. Which under certain circumstances— like a murder investigation—is a felony in the State of New York."

I got up off my stool and unbuttoned my windbreaker and Halo caught an eyeful of shoulder holster. I took a small card from my shirt pocket since it happens I sometimes forget the lines the Supreme Court gave me. I decided maybe I did need bifocals like Benny suggested because now I was squinting at the close-up words as I read them: "You have the right to remain silent, anything you say may be used against . . ."

Halo interrupted with a wounded, "Aw, come on! Give me a freaking break here!"

Ruby calmly opened her purse. She took out a quarter and

eld it in her fingertips for Halo to take. She said, "The call's
n me, Johnny. Go ahead and ring up the department. Tell
hem Detective Neil Hockaday's having a beer on duty."

"Hold the phone, lady. I wasn't never going to really do
hat!" Halo pushed Ruby's hand away. He was now leaking
weat like an open hydrant in August. "House policy's see
o evil, hear no evil, remember?"

Ruby sighed, turned to me and said, "Gee, I sure don't
ke the way this concerned citizen goes all hot and cold on
s. I think he's way too slippery to fool with."

She turned to the very damp, pale Halo and said, "You
now all about the murders, right, Johnny?"

"I read in the paper where some people got killed," he
aid weakly.

Ruby said to me, "Notice how strange Johnny looks when
e talks about people getting killed? Maybe you better read
im again, Hock, from the top."

I shrugged and said to Halo, "You have the right to
emain silent, anything you say may be used against you in a
ourt of law . . ."

And poor Johnny Halo looked at me, then at Ruby, then
t me.

"You have the right to have an attorney present during all
uestioning. If you cannot afford an attorney . . ."

Halo made a sharp noise that reminded me of the mouse
oing down Waldo's insides.

"What's that, Johnny?" Ruby asked.

"I was trying to say . . ." Halo choked and went into a
oughing spasm. He got himself some water, recovered, and
aid, "What do you's want anyway?"

Ruby answered, "Well, maybe we want to give you a
reak, Johnny. You think about it and we'll talk it over,
kay? Meantime, give us another round—a Molson for
)etective Hockaday and another soda for me—this time
/ith a lime twist and a nice big smile."

"Yes, ma'am." Halo smiled, but he had teeth like a tobacco-chewing baseball player, and so this was not a pleasant sight to behold.

Ruby laid out a five-dollar bill on the bar. Halo pushed it back at her and said, "This one'll be on the house."

"That's real friendly of you," Ruby said.

Then Halo turned to get our drinks.

I said to Ruby, "That was quite a performance."

"Of course. I'm good at what I do."

"I never doubted it for a minute. What do actors call that anyway, improv?"

"Well, well, Detective Hockaday. So you know some stage lingo. Didn't I tell you cops and actors are cousins?"

"That you did."

"The good-cop, bad-cop routine, it's the oldest improv in the business, isn't it?"

"And just now done to a classic turn."

"Admit it," Ruby said. "I'm the best partner you'll ever have."

"I would kiss you, but I'm on duty."

Johnny Halo returned to us. He set down the fresh drinks, this time complete with lime. "Okay," he said, "so I know Picasso."

I waited, but he was no more forthcoming than this.

Ruby gave him a bit of the bad cop. "We're going to need lots more spill than that, Johnny. And in a real big hurry."

"Nothing personal," I added, "but we're running out of time for informality. If you want formal, you'll have to close up the bar and come along with us to Central Booking in Manhattan."

"Aw, I don't want no trouble," Halo said.

The guy dozing down at the end of the bar belched in his sleep. His head popped up and he looked around, then he dropped back to his rag pillow.

"Where's Picasso?" I asked.

"Hell if I know," Halo said. "And right now, after what I

ead about him in the paper, I'd tell you! But I ain't seen the lump in I don't know, maybe a year or better."

"He was a customer here?"

"Yeah, I said that. A good steady customer, too, when he vas flush. Which in the better days around here in Coney he isually was. The guy was a great artist, I'll give him that."

I told Halo there was no disputing taste.

He said, "Yeah, that's true. But here's one thing nobody'd irgue about: The big trouble with old Picasso is, whenever ie ain't painting the guy is hell on wheels."

"Like when he was evicted from the Seashore?"

Halo looked at me with surprise and respect, and a trace)f impudence that showed me his starch was coming back. 'You're good, Hockaday," he said. "Real, real good. Where'd you hear he used to live there?"

I asked myself why a liar like Johnny Halo would need to <now. Having no good and immediate answer, I decided for he moment to keep him and Benny at the Horny Poodle itrictly separate sources. So I lied, naturally.

"Medical records," I said. "Picasso's address was in the iiles at Bellevue, in his doctor's office. The doctor who was nurdered."

"Oh, yeah," he said, seemingly satisfied.

"Exactly what kind of hell did Picasso raise here at the Neptune?"

"None, really," Halo said. "He'd be in your occasional ihoving match, something like that, but he never pulled ione of that wild-man act like he done in so many other)laces."

I asked Halo why.

"I guess we understood each other," he said. And then his vatery eyes warmed and saddened, until they turned the :olor of an old frayed blue collar. "We had lots of talks, him ind me. I always knew he was crazy, and I always knew iome day he'd go off his nut, but I'm telling you, the guy had i way of seeing things real straight and he talked straight, too. There ain't been a day gone by when I don't miss the old loon."

I stopped Halo. "Did you ever hear him threaten to kill somebody specific?"

"No, not in so many words. Picasso'd maybe pop some barfly in his puss and there'd be some blood, or else it was the other way around; but that'd be the end of it, so far as I ever seen around here. I ain't saying Picasso wouldn't of whacked somebody if he had the chance, I'm only telling you I never personally seen him boil up to that kind of a heat."

I said, "He burned down a room over at the hotel, so we know the guy can boil."

"Yeah, well, I ain't defending that or nothing else violent he might of done according to the newspaper," Halo said. He nodded toward Ruby. "I am only trying to explain how Picasso has unfortunately got one of these pathetic artist's souls, like she as't me to."

Ruby said, "And you're doing a fine job of it, Johnny."

. Johnny said, "In my book, the man was a great artist and it don't matter he was nutso."

He stopped then. He said he suddenly needed another Dewar's for one thing. For another, two likewise needy regulars I recognized from my earlier visit came in from the boardwalk—a pair of matted survivors with nowhere else to spend a weekday afternoon besides the Neptune.

Halo drew them drafts of beer and I heard him say the drinks were courtesy of the house. "Much obliged, Johnny, much obliged," they said.

Ruby stared at her drink. I stared at mine, too, and tried to think of something to say. But the pictures in my mind thickened my tongue.

I saw Picasso's terrible masterpiece, his Fire and Brimstone tableau of suffering and drowning and waste.

"Ruby," I said, taking her arm urgently, "let's go ride that carousel."

"What, now you mean?" She was puzzled by my haste. "Don't you have more questions here?"

I had many. Too many for now.

I looked down the bar and caught Halo's attention, which was not difficult since he was keeping half an eye on us. I waved him over.

He walked back to us like a cop walks when he enters a strange room for the first time, body and eyes wary. He said, "So what more can I tell you's about old Picasso?"

"Since you don't know where he is, nothing that's going to help the cause right now," I said.

Then I pulled out the snapshot and put it down on the bar for Halo to see.

"I would like you to tell me who these people are, Johnny. And it's only fair I should remind you about how it's a shame and a sin to tell a lie."

He reached into his shirt pocket for a pair of those half-frame glasses that sell for around twelve bucks at pharmacy counters. He slipped them over his ears and glared at me over the tops of the magnifying lenses as he picked up the picture. He put his thumb on Celia's thighs.

Halo had turned cocky now. "I will do my best to do my duty and be a good citizen, okay?"

"It's good we can depend on public-spirited New Yorkers like you," I said.

Halo mumbled and looked down at the snapshot. He turned it a bit and read the blue fountain-pen lettering along one of the crinkled edges: *Coney I., summer, '54.*

"I see here this is a very old pitcher," he said. "Where'd you get it anyways?"

Again I asked myself, Why would Johnny Halo need to know this?

"Let's go, Johnny," Ruby told him. "Just give with the names of the happy trio there."

"Well, there's Picasso, of course," he said, fingering the image of Charlie Furman. "I guess he must of been born with that goofy beret. This other guy here and the broad in the Esther Williams tank suit—well, you sure got me in the dark on them two."

Halo looked up. He wore an expression intended to be as innocent as a bare-bottomed child, which fit badly on a guy with Halo's creases and yellow-brown teeth. He tried giving back the snapshot but I was not up to taking.

Ruby was not buying his face, either. She turned to me and tossed a cue: "Detective Hockaday, if you please?"

I dragged out my card, squinted, and took it from the top: "You have the right to remain silent . . ."

Halo cut me off with a nice forthright lie for a refreshing change. "Aw, c'mon! Let's wait just one freaking minute while I take another look at your old goddamn antique pitcher, okay? Can't a guy change his freaking mind?"

"We haven't got a whole minute to spare," Ruby said. "The best we can offer is five seconds, starting now."

Halo looked at the snapshot again, but it was half-hearted and really quite unnecessary. He said, in well under his allotted time, "Okay, so I notice the broad is Celia Furman, who I knew from gambling one hell of a long time ago, and which I don't want to say nothing more on the subject on the grounds of it might tend to incriminate me."

Ruby said, "That's a boy, Johnny. Two more seconds to go! So, who's the guy in the pretty picture? Tell us quick and we won't put you up in a cell tonight with a big guy who wants to get married."

Halo blanched. "C'mon, Hockaday, get her the hell off my neck, will you?"

"Time's up," I announced grimly.

Halo became so loud and agitated that he woke up the dozer at the far end of the bar, who was none too pleased about being disturbed. The survivors, on the other hand, were a perfect pair of lumps who did not want to get involved in anything that was not their business. They ipped their thinned beers and remained unfazed by all the noise their host was making.

"Jesus, Mary and Joseph!" Halo shouted. "I don't know he other guy, the one who ain't Picasso, okay? That's the traight truth, so help me Christ!"

"For the love of God, how come a guy can't have peace ind quiet around this dump?" the dozer hollered.

"Shut up, old man!"

"Go blow it out your hole!" the dozer snarled in return. \fter which, he lay his head back down on his rag pillow and esumed snoring.

I started writing in my notebook.

Halo said to me, "What's that? What're you writing down n there?"

"You're way too curious, you know that, Johnny?" I said.

"Look, I don't want no trouble, like I said. I'm telling you traight, I know Celia and I know Picasso. And I even know hey was married once-upon-a-time and that she jugged him n the ha-ha house. See, that's stuff that wasn't in the iewspaper." Halo picked up a terrycloth bar towel and)atted his wet forehead. "But Hockaday, honest to Christ, I lon't know who the other guy in that pitcher is."

"Johnny, my partner and I have come in here like nice)eople and we have asked you to do the right thing and we iave witnessed your various conniptions just because well-)ehaved cops want to ask you some things that connect to nurder."

I took a breath, made another note and said, "Now ohnny, I can't pretend I understand your hesitancy. That's vhy I am writing down my impressions of today, and also a iote to remind me to kind of check out your references, you :now?"

Halo slowly reached his hands down toward his pants)ockets.

I dropped my Bic and opened up my windbreaker and)eat him to the draw, so to speak.

"In here, I've got two things," I said, wrapping my fingers around the trigger of my .38. "My service revolver and a pair of NYPD bracelets. I figure you've got one of two things in those pockets you're trying to get into, Johnny."

"Look, I . . ."

"It's either money, or a gun," I said. "I'll make you two promises: if you pull a gun on me, you're going to get real hurt; if you offer me money I'm putting the bracelets on you and we go visit the rubber room at the Coney Island station house, and you get real hurt."

Ruby said, "What'll it be, Johnny?"

Halo raised up his hands.

"That's right," Ruby said. "Nice and slow."

"Christ, I wasn't going to do one freaking thing that'd make any trouble," Halo said. His voice sounded leaky, as if he were losing all his air. He looked at Ruby. "C'mon, check out my pants."

"No, thanks," Ruby said.

"All right, Johnny," I said. "Now I'm going to ask you some questions nice and easy, to which I want your fullest answers until I tell you to shut up. But since I can't exactly trust you, and since my partner declines your offer to drop them for her, and since I've got no way of knowing who's coming in here and when, I'm going to keep my piece handy like this."

"You don't got to . . ."

"Zip it, Johnny. You make me very nervous if you speak when you're not spoken to."

Halo's face went blank. He nodded slowly, a sick smile played on his dry lips.

"Much better," I said. "Now, I want to know the nature of Celia Furman's telephone calls on the day she was murdered."

"Like I said, she's a gambler," Halo said.

"I'd heard that," I said. "She was a big whale in her day."

"Yeah, but times are—times *were* hard for her, and she

couldn't get the action for years on account of her being some kind of a federal snitch. But she was looking for action anyhow, all the time."

"So she was calling you for action?"

"No, Hockaday, it wasn't like that. I been out of it for years, not as long as Celia but for a long time. I only got the bar and real estate now, okay? Look—I don't want to get into something where I'm exposing myself to any kind of trouble at all. You got to promise me: no trouble."

"Johnny, I can tell you I'm not real interested in your sins with the dice or blackjack or whatever the hell," I said. "You want absolution for that, go see a priest. Otherwise, listen to your better angels and also to me."

Halo nodded yes.

"On the other hand, I will be all over your ass if I find out your sins had anything to do with murder."

Halo shok his head no.

"Okay, then. Why was Celia Furman calling you up for action?"

"There's all kinds of rumors about gambling coming to Coney Island. Well hell, Hock, you seen Big Stuff and his freaking handbills for that outfit wants to legalize casinos here."

"I've seen the handbills. What's back of them?"

"Ever hear of Wendell Prescott, the big real estate hog?"

"I heard of a *Daniel* Prescott, the real estate hog."

Halo said, "Wendell's his brother, the Prescott you don't hear about too much because The Dan—people call him that, The Dan—is also one of the biggest press hogs of all time."

"I'm not getting it yet, Johnny."

"Okay—you know The Dan's casinos down in Atlantic City?"

"I read the papers," I said. "One of his brand-new ones is going bankrupt, which makes The Dan look like the jackass he is, and so suddenly he got rid of his press agent?"

"That's right. So brother Wendell—dig this, Wendell's the *older* brother—figures now's his chance to go for the glory that The Dan's been hogging all these years."

Ruby interrupted, "Wendell wants to one-up his brother by building casinos right in New York? Here, in Coney Island?"

Halo said, "Right on the money."

"So Wendell Prescott's doing what, the political ground-work now?" I said.

"Yeah," Halo answered. "He's got this cockamamie handbilling going on out here and meanwhile he's greasing palms up in Albany so the politicians can change the law and we get casinos out here in little old broken-down Coney Island."

"Has he got a chance?"

"Over my dead body!" Halo said.

"What have you got to say about it, and why would you want to say anything?"

"I got three personal reasons. First off, I was a gambler like I say. I wasn't no big whale like Celia, but I sure done my share. I got out because I finally decided one day I didn't want to be sick in the head no more from the gambling disease, which is stupid games of fantasy up against house odds which ain't stupid at all. Not to mention I don't want to have to go through the rest of my days watching my back and I really ain't saying no more about that aspect of the gambling disease on account of no matter what you say, me definitely may tend to incriminate me if I talk."

"All right, all right."

"Okay. Second, I am deep-dyed Coney like I already told you. I love this place. Maybe it don't look so good like it did in the old days, but it's still a damn sight better off than the sinkhole they made out of freaking Atlantic City once Prescott and the other hogs took over the boardwalk down there.

"So I want to protect my turf. What's more natural and patriotic than that I ask you?"

"Natural, patriotic," I said.

"I got a little money here and I borrow some more there and I even got this here bar in hock to the bank. Anyway, I'm picking up parcels all up and down the boardwalk and I ain't going to sell off to no Prescott creeps, and also I ain't afraid of any hoods he might be connected up with since—well, that'll be off the record also, okay?"

"For now, all right," I said. "But where does Celia come into all this?"

"Word's out all over town that somebody fronting for Prescott's trying to get the casinos started up out here early. You know, sort of to lay the groundwork for a convincing load of bullshit to lay on the politicians up in Albany that gambling's good economics for a rag-tag old seaside slum and so why not do it legal and get the tax revenues."

"And Celia was looking for this action?" I asked.

"Yeah, she was bugging me day and night, her and me being one-time acquaintances in the old rackets and being that she's so out of it she don't even know there's no way I can steer to nothing since I am death on gambling, especially in this place I love and am going to protect."

I thought about all the notes I would now have to make and my head started aching.

"There's just one more question, Johnny," I said. "You mentioned three personal reasons. You only told me two of them."

"Well, third, I told you how I personally think Picasso is a great artist. You know what Prescott would do if he put up casinos here?"

Ruby turned to me and said, "Hock, don't you see? They'd tear down Picasso's masterpiece."

SIXTEEN

She said she was scared to death.

"You sure fooled me," I said.

"That's because I'm a professional. It's supposed to look easy when I put on an act."

"It was more than easy for you, it was natural."

"No," she said. "I almost fell off my barstool when you went for your gun, and at that moment all I wanted in the whole world was just to duck into the ladies' and throw up."

"Well it's all over. So what do you want now?"

"I want to get back to Manhattan, I want to sit down in my own place, I want to try and recover before the reading tonight."

"But what about the carousel?"

"God, Hock, I don't think so! How can you want to go do something . . . something *fun* and *romantic* at a time like this? Three people have been murdered."

"I'm well aware of that."

"You're dealing with God-knows-what kind of deranged killer . . ."

She stopped and looked as if she might start crying. I put

my arm around her shoulders, and we walked along Surf Avenue, toward the B&B Carousell (that is how carousel happens to be misspelled there, the fault of the original owner from way back when, and the wish of present management to respect a Coney Island tradition).

The sky grew close and gray again. Rain started spotting our clothes just as we reached the B&B.

"Step right up here, Ruby. Pick any horse you want," I said, holding Ruby's hand and urging her up onto the idled circular platform full of wooden horses. "They're all brave steeds and they'll treat you well, and I'll be right here with you."

The carousel was empty. But the evocative sounds of the organ were there—bellows pushing air through rolls of perforated paper, brass pipes, felt-covered wood mallets—music from another life.

So real a sound as my mother's voice. . . .

The carousel operator, a small dark man about Picasso's age with a toothy smile, stood by the organ. He waited patiently as we walked the plank floor of the carousel, looking over our exclusive selection.

Ruby finally made her choice: a huge calico stallion with a wide black saddle, hooves reared and nostrils flared and mane flying. She put her foot into the stirrup and I boosted her up onto his back.

"You picked the horse I favored when I was a kid and the B&B was always crowded," I told her.

"I did? You're kidding!"

"No, really."

"Why this one?"

"Look here," I said, pointing to the back of the saddle.

Ruby found the hidden carving, the skinny black cat with green eyes coiled behind the saddle. She was charmed.

"You're feeling better now?" I asked.

"I am, but I don't know why."

"What does it matter?"

I mounted the palomino behind Ruby. The carousel operator called out, "All aboard?" I nodded to him, he smiled and clanked a bell and slowly we began to turn.

Protected from the rain, we moved with the sweep of handsome wood horses, hand-carved by great artisans long since dead and gone—and forgotten by most. Our horses galloped as if soldiers' spurs were dug into their flanks, as if in battle against new marauders who had come to destroy Coney Island.

They galloped and galloped, round and around, carrying only Ruby and me. And turn after turn, there was the patient carousel operator and his smile. He nodded at me, turn after turn, as if he knew me.

The latest downpour of rain had finally cleared the streets. Nobody was willing to cope with this day, with the chancey April weather.

But we kept galloping, Ruby and I and our painted horses.

The organ played "By the Sea" and the horses lifted and fell.

And lifted and fell.

So, what's this Sweet Land of Liberty going to give to the next generation?

A dream? A promise?

That's what we got, ain't that right?

Damn straight.

But I ask you. What about the next generation? Ho, ho, they got some kind of a new deal creeping up on them, hey?

Used to be, work made money. Now it's only money that makes money. You want to know what I say about that? I say it's un-freaking-American!

It's killing us!

Ain't that what I been warning them all of these long goddamn years I have sacrificed myself to observing what I seen here in the Land of Our Pilgrims' Pride? Ain't it?

Ain't a guy with true love in his heart got the responsibility to observe like I have done? And make the people see what I seen?

Don't that at least deserve some respect?

Oh, but they don't see. No! They don't want to see. Consequently, this is how so many great artists ain't so respectable.

And where's that leave me?

Well, sir, you know the old saw: you always kill the ones you love. . . .

After I put Ruby on the Manhattan-bound train, I waited out what I hoped was the last of the unrelenting rain in a little bar on Surf Avenue that did not have a single drop of Johnnie Walker red for sale. I drank coffee and ate a cheese sandwich with a pickle, which I suppose would have made Ruby happy.

I also spent some money on the juke, which was good and heavy on Billie Holiday tunes like "My Sweet Hunk of Trash," "Do Your Duty," "In My Solitude," and "Gimmee a Pigfoot and a Bottle of Beer."

Dusk came early, and with it a swirling front of cold wet ocean wind. I walked briskly along Surf Avenue in the direction of the Seashore Hotel, but a quick step did not prevent my shivering in the damp evening breezes blowing up off the beach.

As I had requested, the Coney Island precinct station house had the hotel staked. A blue-and-white Brooklyn cruiser was parked in the west alley alongside the hotel; two uniforms sat inside, with a stained paper bag from Dunkin' Donuts propped open on the dashboard between them. Over on the east end, across the street, was a black unmarked car with exhaust smoke pluming out from the tailpipe. I assumed there was a cop or two on footpost out back and somebody up on the roof.

I stepped into the lobby, which was smaller than my apartment. It looked bigger, though, because there was only one chair in the place. A prostitute in a red wig sat there smoking with her skirt hiked up almost to her waist. The ceiling was low and full of buzzing fluorescent lights that bathed everything in a harsh shade of white that reminded me of refrigerator frost. There was a sour smell of dirty laundry that seemed more or less permanent. And a teller's cage against the back wall, near the stairway. Over the cage was a white steel sign with a bullet hole and brown lettering: IF YOU LIVED HERE, YOU'D BE HOME NOW.

The pross looked me over as I crossed through the lobby toward the cage. There was a young fat guy wedged inside with a till, a radio and a board full of mail and key slots. He had pale waxy skin, curly orange hair and a thick wart on his lower lip. He was listening intently to Dr. Ruth Westheimer's call-in show.

He switched off the radio and said to me in a tired-out tone, "Rates are twenty-two fifty a night plus tax—or by the week starting out at a hundred, plus your linen charges. Cash only, in advance."

I took out my wallet and showed him the NYPD gold shield.

"I guess you don't want a room?" he said.

"Tonight, no. I just want some information."

"Like I told all the other cops crawling around here, the Seashore Hotel doesn't give out personal information on our guests. It's a violation of privacy and nobody's got any search warrants out or anything like that. I know my rights."

"I can tell that you do," I said. My wallet was still out. I opened it so that the clerk could see the money inside. "But I'm special."

The clerk looked past me, over to the pross. Then he whispered, "How much you want to know?"

"That depends."

"On what I could tell you about this Picasso guy everybody's looking for?"

"That and whatever else it might occur to me to ask. Start talking and we'll see if we've got business to conduct."

I took out a twenty-dollar bill and crackled it. Then I heard the pross get up from the chair and head over my way.

"Well, let's see now, Picasso burnt up his room the day we had to have the marshall come put him out."

"That I already know, son. No sale. Tell me something original."

"The guy was a real loner type."

"You're not even trying."

The clerk thought, which brought pain to his broad face. Then he brightened and said, "Once he had a visitor—I was on duty! This was a very big deal because it was the only visitor the guy ever had in all the time he'd been here."

"First, how long did he live here?"

"Say, man, you ever going to let loose of that money?"

I crackled the bill and turned around. The pross smiled at me, and I counted three gold caps on her teeth. I asked her, "You ever visit Picasso, darlin'?"

"Hey!" The clerk complained so loudly there was an echo in the lobby. *"I'm going to tell you!"*

I said to the pross, "Ignore Fats back there in the cage, darlin'. Here's for *your* conversation." I handed her the twenty. She stuffed it in her bra.

"Hey, the name's Jerry!" the fleshy clerk complained.

I looked back and told him, "Okay, Jerry, now keep quiet so I can hear the lady. You just be thinking all about that visitor, and watch how easy it could be for you to make some money."

The pross asked me, "What're you, with the cops?"

I introduced myself, then asked, "What's your name, darlin'?"

"Chastity."

"That's a pretty name," I told her. She flashed gold teeth. "Did you ever visit Picasso?"

"Well, I been up to his room, oh, maybe six, seven times. No big deal. Mostly he'd pay five bucks for me to kneel down and pray with him."

I commiserated with her. "A lot of these johns nowadays, they're only looking for Mary Magdalene."

"Yeah, tell me about it."

"Did Picasso ever do anything else?"

"Naw, but once or twice he paid double when he wanted me to see him play with Madam Thumb and her four lovely daughters, you know?"

"You earn every penny you make, don't you, Chastity?" I gave her another twenty. I heard Jerry sighing behind me.

"Did you ever see Picasso with anybody, up in his room, I mean?"

"No," she said. "I only would see him going through the lobby here, then up in his room when he'd ask. I never saw him even out in the street or the boardwalk."

"Can you tell me anything else about him?"

Chastity shrugged and said, "People said he was hot-tempered, but I never saw that. I know he was a painter over at Astroland. That's it, I guess, unless you want a date tonight."

"No, but thanks, Chastity. I'm sort of going steady. She's a real nice lady."

"That's good," Chastity said. She went back to her chair.

"Hey, you!" Jerry bellowed.

"You just cost yourself a ten-dollar penalty," I said, turning to him. "Now, quietly, tell me how long he lived here."

"Five years, thereabouts."

"Where'd he live before?"

"Nobody knows, honest."

"When did he have this one visitor of his?"

"Just before we had to call the marshall to come put him out."

"What was the visitor's name?"

"Hey, man—the names you get around here! I mean, give me a break—Picasso and Chastity? We don't even bother asking anymore. Somebody gives us a funny name for their convenience, we use it and that's it."

"Let's keep it short and to the point, Jerry."

"Okay, but how about—you know?" Jerry stuck a soft hand out from the cage.

I gave him a ten. "Let's try for the twenty this time around. Did you personally see the visitor? What did he—or she—look like?"

"It was a he, about the same age as Picasso, I'd say. He came in right about this time of night and I was on the desk here."

Jerry earned a twenty. I crackled another one at him. "What do you suppose the visit was about?"

"Well, we don't know," Jerry said. "But I'd guess the subject was money. Picasso was really under the gun since he was owing us six months rent or so and he was owing everybody else up and down the boardwalk, too."

"He didn't have any work?"

"No. They're not painting anything at Astroland anymore, not even maintenance painting. It's all just going to pot."

"Have you ever seen this visitor around here before?"

"Nobody's seen him before or since."

"How long was the meeting?"

"How long've I got to keep answering questions with no more revenues?"

"Don't be greedy, Jerry. Did you see Chastity over there being greedy? If I think you deserve it, I'll take care of you."

Jerry sighed and said, "Okay. They were up there about an hour. On my break, I went up and sort of listened outside the door."

"I figured you were the type," I said, handing over another twenty. "What did you hear?"

"An argument, but not anything real bad as far as they go.

See, I've heard Picasso carry on pretty good all by himself. Everybody has. He talks to himself, you know, usually after he's been drinking pretty good over at the Neptune where he hangs. You'd swear sometimes there was two people up in his room."

"This little argument, what was it about?"

"Oh, that I don't remember—honest. I think maybe it might've been about a woman. But you know, over the years you hear guys having so much grief over women it all sort of runs together until you don't pay attention anymore."

I took the snapshot out of my wallet and showed it to Jerry.

"Who are the people in this picture?" I asked.

"That's really old, right?"

"Never mind that. Just tell me what I want to know."

"I'll try." Jerry took the snapshot and studied it. He pointed to Picasso and said, "That's your boy, Picasso. He's younger in this picture, of course."

"Who's the other man?"

"He kind of looks like he might've been that visitor we're talking about. I can't be real sure, though."

"And the woman?"

"Sorry. I got no idea about her."

I looked at my wristwatch. It was closing in on seven, and I was due at the Carny Club in a few minutes.

"You've been a real brick," I told Jerry. "I'll probably be back sometime soon, but until then, do you want to tell me anything else you think is worth my while?"

Jerry looked up. His lips moved in thought and he drummed his heavy fingers. "Nope. Can't think of anything right now. I'll make a list for the next time, though. Don't forget to bring your wallet."

He switched on the radio again. Somebody was telling Dr. Ruth about rubber suits and purple whips.

It was time to leave the Seashore Hotel lobby for the relative comfort of the dank breezes of Surf Avenue, and I was thinking how I had no time to spare. Not if I wanted to be prompt about meeting Big Stuff over at the Carny Club.

Then Chastity threw me off schedule. She got up out of her chair, smoothed down her skirt in a semblance of modesty, and planted herself between me and the front door.

"I got to ask you something, Detective Hockaday," she said sternly.

"Go ahead."

"How long before them lousy newspapers hang poor old Picasso for murder?" There was a sharp accusatory tone in her voice. I thought we had got along well before; now it was as if she had consigned me to the familiar category of big dumb heartless cop.

"I don't write newspaper stories," I said. "I'm only trying to find Picasso in a hurry. You want to help the cause, there's some fast money in it for you."

"I don't want more money. I just want to tell you, for whatever it's worth, I think Picasso's got royally jerked around his whole life."

"Maybe so. What do you know about it?"

"Nothing you could go to court with. It's just something I feel, all right. Don't laugh, even a girl like me's got some women's intuition."

"I never laugh at a woman's intuition."

"Men never should. But most do. It's because men naturally hate women."

"Oh, why?"

Chastity looked at me with great pity, as if my head was full of dents. "It's because of our women's intuition," she explained. "You hate us because we always know where things are."

"I see."

"That's what you all say."

Maybe so, I said to myself. "Let me ask *you* something now."

"Sure."

"Do you like the life?"

"If you mean hooking, honey, it's like sweet old Coney Island itself. I don't like it and I don't dislike it, I'm just used to it."

I hurried along to my appointment.

Naturally, I wondered what lay ahead at the Carny Club. But I was not so preoccupied by this that I could not appreciate the richness of Chastity's intriguing logic, Jerry's minor revelations, Johnny Halo's major evasions and Ruby's inarguable conclusions about the chances of Picasso's posterity if the artless fangs of the Prescott organization were to start chewing up Coney Island real estate.

I was glad, finally, that I had trusted Ruby and myself to this long day's leg work, that I had not sloughed it off to Logue or anybody else at Central Homicide. I was relieved that I had not wasted my time after all. In a word, I was no longer discouraged.

Here I had reached that interesting and delicate point in a criminal investigation—the intuitive point—where a detective may rightly feel possessed of all the main elements of a solution, in the legal if not moral sense. All that was needed to be known was there. The facts may not have been fully visible, but they were available just below the surface.

All that was needed now was time and opportunity to compute dozens of naked, fugitive facts. A good night's sleep might do this detective's trick. And I am a believer in dreams that forge sense from senselessness.

But for one weakness, I was confident as I moved through dark wet streets toward the Carny Club. All my satisfaction in a day's work well done was based merely on a man's intuition.

West Fifth Street, where I walked now, was once backstage to Coney Island.

DARK MAZE

Here I remembered seeing machine shops and studios and hangars, and hearing their noises, day and night. Giant roller coasters were fabricated and assembled here on West Fifth. Carousel horses were carved from tree trunks by proud craftsmen who added conceits to their work such as a black cat coiled beneath a saddle. Great chains of light bulbs were strung together on this street, sketching a summer's boardwalk night in electric flame, such as I will never forget from my childhood.

Here, flats were painted for Astroland attractions. Here was where Charlie Furman began to nurse his grudges. And rightly so.

Now the street was devoid of light and sound. The buildings were black from fire or else abandoned, the dwelling places of squatters and vermin.

In the lanes off West Fifth were clapboard tenements and low cramped row houses where hundreds of Brooklyn workers had once lived and raised families. Now they were warrens for classes of the unemployed who did not burden the government so long as the government did not burden them.

I looked at the handbill that Big Stuff had given me, checked the West Fifth Street address he had written out on the back. Two more doors, then I was there.

My spirits lifted again when I heard a bit of music floating out the door of a low, boarded-up shop. It was the unlikely sound of the Benny Goodman orchestra, swinging with "Mama, That Man Is Here Again" as I knocked and waited.

Then the music died.

"What is it?" a woman's voice said from the other side of the door.

"I'm looking for the Carny Club," I said.

"Who's looking?"

"The name is Neil Hockaday."

I heard feet shuffling, then excited voices. Then the door opened a crack.

There appeared in the crack the heavyset face of a young woman vaguely familiar to me. She might have been thirty or thirty-two, thereabouts, but excess weight aged her. She had pink skin, a wide nose over a small mouth wet with red lipstick and a pile of curly hair the color of scrambled eggs. Her eyes were brown, embellished with so much liner and mascara it appeared she might have mashed two chocolate cupcakes in her face.

She looked me up and down in a matter-of-fact way and asked, "You the cop?"

I showed her my shield.

Most people do not actually look closely at a police shield. They notice the shape of it, whether it is a star or not; they see the beveled outline of it; they see that it is either silver or gold, but never ask the difference. This one with the cupcake eyes was different; she inspected my gold shield closely, so closely she read off the name and badge number.

"Detective Hockaday, 4321," she said. "Okay, Hockaday, let's see your guns."

"I don't—"

She interrupted with, "If you want in, you have to check the hardware. Nothing personal, just house rules."

"I'm looking for a dwarf named Big Stuff," I said. "Tell him to come here."

"Let's see the guns."

"I can get a warrant."

"You do that." She started to close the door.

"All right, all right," I said. "I'll take your drill. Let me in."

A man's voice behind her said, "Go on. He can show us once he's through the door."

The music started up again and I stepped into a foyer fashioned out of plywood walls. The man behind her turned out to be Waldo, the professional regurgitator. He was holding a drink that looked to be rum and coke.

"I seen you earlier, out on the boardwalk," Waldo said pleasantly. "You was with that very good-looking black lady. Where'd she go?"

"She went home."

"Tough luck," Waldo said. He pointed a thumb at cupcake eyes and said, "This here's Evie. You got to show her what you're carrying."

I opened my windbreaker and pulled the .38 out from the holster and emptied the magazine, then gave it to Evie after putting the bullets in my pants pocket. "Where are you going to check it?" I asked.

There was a cabinet on one of the plywood walls and Evie opened up its padlock and put it on a shelf. She said, "You carrying anything else?"

I had a .22 Beretta pistol strapped on my ankle and debated with myself over the pros and cons of an honest response. Noticing that the cabinet was full of sidearms, my decision tilted toward honesty. I unstrapped the Beretta and gave it to Evie. She put it up on the shelf with my .38, closed the cabinet and locked it.

"Okay, come on in," Waldo said.

I followed Waldo and Evie through the foyer into a single large room full of chairs and low tables with dim lights on top, and drinks and ashtrays. I saw the boardwalk barker at one of the tables. He had his hand on the nice-looking knee of Sparkle the snake charmer and she was laughing. I did not see her python.

The Benny Goodman tunes were coming from a big floor model Atwater-Kent radio like my mother used to have. This was next to a bar along the back wall, tended by the small dark man from the B&B Carousell; when I recognized him, he nodded at me the way he had when Ruby and I passed him all those times going round and around.

Four guys were playing cards at a large table in the corner. There were poker chips piled up in front of them and they all smoked cigars. A couple of women played mah-jongg in another corner table. Everybody else was scattered around drinking and talking.

I felt something on my leg.

"Welcome to the Carny Club."

The voice belonged to Big Stuff, who had come up behind me and pulled my pant leg. He had changed out of his white jumpsuit and now wore a blue blazer and a purple necktie. I noticed how everybody else was dressed for a nightclub and felt suddenly a little sloppy.

"You have quite a way of sneaking up on a guy," I said to Big Stuff, looking down at him.

"I'm not walking around at your eye level," he said. Then, "You're a little late, but I guess prob'ly you had trouble finding us."

"All the street lamps are out," I said.

Waldo explained, "The crews that push all the crack around this neighborhood, they shoot them out. The city's about given up trying to replace the lights."

"Say, you want a drink?" Big Stuff asked.

I asked for a Johnnie Walker red in a big glass with a few ice cubes, and Evie went off to the bar to get it.

"Come on over here and we'll start talking," said Big Stuff.

Waldo and Big Stuff and I sat on three chairs out of four that were circled around a beat-up coffee table. The other chair was for Evie.

"First I should tell you, Hockaday, that this here's an unlicensed social club which I am going to assume you don't care nothing about seeing as how you're after bigger crimes," Big Stuff said. "So, that's right, ain't it?"

"That's right."

"Okay, good. Now, you're after Picasso, right?"

"I want to talk to him."

"And you're paying for information as to his whereabouts, right?"

"Right."

"See, Waldo," Big Stuff said, "I told you."

Evie handed me the Johnnie Walker and sat down.

"You didn't miss nothing yet," Big Stuff told her.

"Supposing we get down to it, whatever it is?" I said. "I've got a long ride back into the city ahead of me."

"This afternoon, what you said about Picasso—I liked it," Big Stuff said.

"What?"

"You said you thought it would be too bad if all people said about him was he came, he went and who cares. I told Waldo here, and he told Evie."

"Do you know where Picasso is?"

"We think Picasso is a great artist," Evie said, "the best painter on the boardwalk. He's had a lot of trouble the past year, and now the cops and the newspapers are after him."

"And we're not saying he's your chamber of commerce type of guy," Waldo said, taking over from Evie. "But we're saying he's got rights, like even the big shots. Which includes the fact that since nobody's got any proof he's guilty he's still an innocent man."

Big Stuff asked me, "You think he done those murders?"

What I thought was, these three were coming at me sideways for reasons of their own that I would probably not determine tonight. I figured the best way of getting anything at all useful to me was to move sideways myself.

So I ignored Big Stuff like he had ignored me when I asked him if he knew where Picasso was. I asked Waldo, "How do you do that swallowing number with the mouse?"

"I pull out the claws and the teeth and then I soak him in a little butter and olive oil and he goes down easier than anything," Waldo said. "Also he comes up real easy since he's so anxious to get air he's helping me and I don't have to use half the muscles I got to use with coins or like that."

Big Stuff said, "You didn't answer me, Hockaday."

"You didn't answer *me,*" I said.

"We don't know where Picasso is," Evie said. "None of us has seen him since he left Coney. You heard about how they put him out over at the Seashore?"

"I did."

"Well, that was better than a year ago," Evie said, "and then Picasso disappeared off the face of the earth. All we know is there's all this stuff about him in the newspapers and on the TV and radio, with the murders and all . . ."

Waldo broke in. "And then Big Stuff tells us that you were saying to him this afternoon how you recently talked to him."

"Is he all right?" Evie asked.

It suddenly came to me where I had seen her before.

"You run that candy stand at the subway station, right?" I asked her.

"Yeah. Philips Salt Water Taffee and Ka-Ra-Me-La," she said. "I remember you from a few days ago. You and the black lady. She's pretty. She ain't a cop, is she?"

"No."

"What is she, an actress?"

"Yes."

"I thought so. Didn't I tell you, Waldo?"

Big Stuff cut in. "What'd you talk about with Picasso?" he asked me.

Figuring they might possibly be shocked into revealing something about their motives in inviting me to have a free drink at the Carny Club, I said, "Oh, he was telling me how he wanted to kill somebody."

"How come you didn't just put him in the trap right when he told you that?" Big Stuff asked.

Evie answered for me. "Because, you little stupe, if the cops went and jailed everybody who says they're in the mood to murder, they'd never have any room in the jug for the serious criminals. Like for instance the ones trying to make Coney into some kind of a new Las Vegas."

"Real funny," Big Stuff said. He did not laugh.

I asked Evie, "I take it the membership here is slightly divided on the question of casino gambling on the boardwalk?"

"How come you think we got the house policy of locking up the guns?" she asked.

Waldo said, "Look, it's obvious you don't trust us carnies. Okay. You don't have to tell us what you and Picasso talked about exactly. We only want to know if he's okay, that's all. And we just wanted to take a look at you and see if you're an all-right guy—which I think you probably are."

Big Stuff said, "The membership's divided on that one, too."

Evie asked again, "Is he okay?"

I said nothing.

Waldo said, "Detective Hockaday, we just want you to know that no matter what you or anybody else thinks of us carnies, we're like anybody else would be when they got trouble in the family. Which is what we are here, family. We all got individual differences, and we take care of different business. But we also take care of each other, you see that?"

"Let's say Picasso done them murders," Big Stuff said. "Sooner or later, you're going to catch him someplace, which ain't going to be far since he ain't got the wherewithal to travel nowhere, and even the Foreign Legion don't take old guys with bad eyes.

"The thing is, though, we'd like it if you didn't go shooting him down like a dog. If you give him a little dignity when you find him, on account of his art. Well, that's all we're asking."

Waldo said, "All of us have been pushed around here, and Picasso got pushed right up to the edge. Look around this room, look around the boardwalk, and Coney's side streets. We're all looking right into the gutter. When we fall, the smell of that gutter's going to come as no big surprise. We're doing the best we can, which includes throwing each other on the mercy of cops that seem like they might be all right."

"See, we love him," Evie added.

"There isn't a man or woman here who's missed out on a bad run-in with Picasso," Waldo said. "But there's nobody here in Coney who hasn't got great respect for him as a carny and as a great artist."

"You love him, too, Waldo?" I asked.

"Yeah, I do."

"All day out here, people have been telling me in different ways they love and admire Picasso," I said. "I was at the Neptune, and Johnny Halo goes on and on about him, actually *quoting* the guy."

Evie narrowed her cupcake eyes and asked, "Johnny Halo told you he loves Picasso like we do?"

"In a manner of speaking, yes."

I had drunk half my Scotch. Now I put back the rest of it and looked at my wristwatch.

"Johnny Halo has warm eyes and a cold mouth," Evie said. "You follow?"

"You mean you don't trust him?"

"No, I don't."

"I'll tell you who else never trusted Johnny Halo," Waldo said. "And that's Picasso himself. Him and Johnny, they were enemies."

"Since when?"

"Well, after Picasso was kicked out of the Seashore, he was staying down under the boardwalk like folks do when they're between places or hiding out," Waldo said. "Two or three days after Picasso's down there hiding, Johnny Halo's suddenly got money, all kinds of money. So much money he buys out the Seashore Hotel from the landlord.

"Which is very strange since Halo's been living there himself paying rent on a room, way longer than Picasso lived there. Sometimes Halo's had his troubles paying on the first of the month, too, even though he always had that ratty bar of his."

"Where does Halo live now?" I asked.

Waldo said, "Oh, he's still at the Seashore. He took over three rooms on the top floor and connected them up. He's real proud of his place. He calls it the presidential suite."

"Don't tell him no more about nothing," Big Stuff said to Waldo. "I can't stand listening to you; you sound like a gossipy old magpie."

"I don't have time to listen anyway," I said, standing up. I took three twenties out from my wallet and dropped them on the coffee table. "That's so you can all have a drink for yourselves, all right?"

I headed for the foyer, and Evie followed me. Sealo was on his way in. Estelline the sword swallower was pushing him in his wheelchair.

"My guns," I told Evie.

She unlocked the cabinet and gave me the .38 and the Beretta .22. She looked in back of her, then at me and she said, "When you see Picasso, tell him God bless."

Then I walked back along West Fifth to Surf Avenue. But before I got on the subway, I cut over to the boardwalk and dropped in at the Neptune for a word with Halo.

But Halo was not there.

The bartender on duty was named Mike. I identified myself and asked where Johnny Halo was.

"He decided to take the night off," Mike said. "So he called me up to fill in."

"Did he say why he wasn't working tonight?"

"Well, he just said he had a little business over in Manhattan."

SEVENTEEN

I was making good progress with my notebook until the woman with the rhinestone sunglasses and the cotton wads in her ears boarded my Manhattan-bound F train at Brooklyn's York Street station.

There were lots of seats available since the car was less than half-filled. But she stood at the door looking everything over carefully, then chose to camp next to me.

She was maybe ten or twelve years older than me, which I realized was an age when people begin looking a little battered unless they take extra time with their grooming. She did not.

Her hair was dull yellow with white streaks in it that made her look youthful, oddly enough. But her skin was doughy and wrinkled, especially around the mouth and neck. She smelled of strong soap.

"What're you writing in that book there if you don't mind my asking?" she asked.

This could have been worse, I told myself. I could be on an airplane, trapped for hours with a chatty seatmate. But this was only the subway and I could get off at the first stop over on the Manhattan side, at Essex Street. It would not be long.

"Just notes," I told her. "To remind myself of what I've got to do tomorrow."

"Oh, well that's okay."

She had a big leather bag with her which she now spread out across her lap. She rooted through it, elbowing me in the process. She pulled out a silver flask and a small plastic bottle.

"Here's to you," she said, unscrewing the top of the flask and then slugging back a drink. She capped the flask and returned it to her bag.

I said nothing, hoping to discourage conversation.

"I don't much like traveling these trains when I'm by myself at night," she said. Then she let out a long sigh. "But let's face it, I'm alone day and night now since my Henry's been gone."

"I'm sorry, ma'am."

"How come?"

"I'm sorry your husband's gone."

"Husband? Don't make me laugh. Christ, I never married him!"

"Well, anyway, I'm sorry he died."

"Oh, that's okay. Henry was a shit." She took the flask out from her purse, unscrewed it and slugged back some more. "You're a married guy, right?"

"I used to be."

"Yeah, you got the face of a married guy."

"Is that good?"

"That's the best. That's how come I sat down here beside you."

"I see."

"Henry was a hotshot business executive down in Wall Street. What's your racket?"

"Cop."

"Yeah, well it don't surprise me." She opened up the plastic bottle and took out a white wafer and put it in her mouth. "So you prob'ly busted lots of robbers in your time?"

"A few."

"So now when you retire you can look back on your brilliant career in law enforcement and claim you did your part to vouchsafe the city for truth, justice and the American way. Right?"

"I don't know about that . . ."

"Well I do, boy. You never touched my Henry, so in my personal book you're a big flop as a cop."

"What did Henry do?"

"I told you, he was in Wall Street."

"What was his crime, I mean?"

"I just told you!"

"Working in Wall Street's not a crime."

"Oh really, Snow White?" She took out her flask again and drank it dry. "Shit, it's empty."

"It's just as well," I said. "It's against the law to drink in the subway."

"Yeah, and it's also against the law for the poor to beg. So you know what you can do with your law, right?"

"Lady, are you all right?"

"Of course not. I get on this train expecting that if I sit down next to a good-looking man, I'll be safe out by myself. So you turn out to be a cop with this goddamn overexaggerated respect for the law—which by the way is an ass. How safe do you think you're making me feel right now?" She took another wafer from her bottle and started chewing it slowly.

"You want to tell me exactly what it was your Henry did when he worked in Wall Street?"

"Ever read the business page, Snow White?"

"Sometimes."

"You ought to be reading it every day. It's a police blotter. Ever hear of junk bonds?"

"Yes."

"Ever buy one?"

"No."

"What a dope! You own any life insurance, you have a bank account?"

"Yeah."

"Then you bought junk bonds, chump. Who do you think my Henry sold that crap to? Grads from Harvard and Wharton? No way. He peddled them to the savings and loan crooks and the insurance dorks and the bankers who are already pretty notorious about making dumb loans. He collected five percent of the action he peddled; his lawyer pals got four hundred an hour easy for drawing up the indentures, then kicked over some to Henry for tipping them business; and Henry's other cronies at the banks and thrifts got promotions for these really shrewd deals he conned them into, and they kicked back on their Christmas bonuses.

"And here's the part where the law is an ass: just about nobody goes to jail when the whole house of cards falls down! Nobody gets rubbed out in a clam bar in Little Italy over this kind of a swindle, right? Hah! Instead, the president of the United States of America and all his flunkies in the Congress sucker the taxpayers out of money to cover up what Henry did!"

The train slowed. Soon we would be at Essex Street.

"I got to get off, lady," I said.

She popped another wafer and chewed furiously. Then white foam started trickling out from her lips.

"What's the matter with you? What is that stuff, lady?"

"Alka-Seltzer," she said. "I chew it up when I'm on the trains and you see what happens. People see me like this, they stay away from me."

The train stopped.

"Good night, lady."

"So long, sucker." Some of the foam flew out of her mouth. "Have a buttercup day."

I walked up the stairs from the subway platform and out to the corner of Essex and Delancey Streets where I flagged a taxi cruising east on Delancey. I gave the driver Ruby's address and we were off.

My bad luck, the cabby was the chatty type.

I asked him please, for the love of God, to give me a break.

Ruby's theatre is called the Downtown Playhouse. It is located on the third floor of a two-hundred-year-old skinny brick federal-style building on South Street, in the shadow of the Brooklyn Bridge.

There is a decent bar and grill at the street level, Vern's, and a barber shop on the second floor. Ruby lives in a studio at the back of the fourth floor, which is the top of the building; she has a large terrace that looks toward the graceful old iron suspension bridge spanning the East River. Most of the rest of the top floor is given over to a reception room for theatre functions, and Ruby's office.

My clever girl friend owns the deed to the whole works.

All her savings and everything she could borrow while she was still making her brisk Madison Avenue salary got her the place. The day she closed on the deal was the same day she blew off the uptown life, causing most of her friends and colleagues to pass the word that Ruby Flagg was ungrateful and unhinged.

"Actually," Ruby told me that first night we met, "I'm only one of those."

I naturally wondered, "Which one?"

"That, sir, I leave to you."

Then she asked impulsively, "So, let me find out about you. Are you the kind of man who knows the difference between a smart person and a genius?"

"I only know that nobody's ever called me either one of those."

Ruby laughed. It was the first time I had made her laugh and so I decided to remember that, no matter what might happen with us.

"My friends and colleagues used to say I'd started out a regulation smart person, but that I reached the genius ranks in record time," Ruby said. "They taught me that a smart person knows what smart people want and a genius knows what stupid people want."

"Could that be why the advertising business is so full of geniuses?"

She laughed again and put a hand on my arm and said, "Why, Mr. Hockaday, we're two of a kind, aren't we?"

I agreed. And Ruby and I have been together ever since.

But tonight was the night we would become an item, as Walter Winchell used to put it in the *Mirror*. Tonight I would learn that the big answers to my life—as a man, as a cop—would begin to come by way of Ruby Flagg.

It was a quarter-past ten when I finally made it to the Downtown Playhouse. Which turned out to be just in time to catch the start of the second of two one-acts that Ruby was auditioning for potential backers.

She was happy and relieved to see me. But also rushed and nervous and preoccupied, with only a minute or two for me before the program began.

I asked her about the crowd of eight up front, four suits and their wives. Ruby's spare, brick-walled theatre far from the precincts of expense-account dining was not the sort of place I expected to see suits and wing tips.

"They're friends from the old life," Ruby explained. "Reasonably good guys, still doing the dance but looking for ways to spend money like the angels would. Which I'm hoping means me and this little old theatre."

"I thought you never saw geniuses anymore."

"What do you think, I'm unhinged?"

"Break a leg, Ruby."

"Thanks, sweet. I'm going to scoot away now. The wine and cheese act is upstairs, right after this; I want to clear everybody out early, though, and then you can stay at my place for a change."

"I don't mind if I do. The inspector's probably been telephoning my apartment every hour on the hour. I could live without that for a night."

"Thanks, Hock. You really know how to make a girl feel convenient."

I kissed her cheek. "Sorry, you know I don't mean it that way. Go on, get your show on the road."

Ruby went up front to sit with the geniuses and I settled down by myself in the back row of the theatre, a small house of ninety-nine seats. Tonight there were maybe thirty people in the audience—the suits, their wives and a scattering of Ruby's show-business friends.

Up on stage was a bare-bones set and scene. Actors sat in folding chairs around an open casket, mourners at a wake. The coffin was tipped upward at the head so that we saw the actor inside, in the role of the deceased.

The stage lights went up and the house lights dimmed. Then one of the actors in the folding chairs stood up and faced us. He crossed himself in the Catholic manner, and spoke:

"The man in the coffin is named Arthur Colfax. We all used to call him The Mister. He was my father. The color of that necktie he's wearing is the same shade of blue as The Mister's eyes. Which, since they're closed in death, I thought you would be interested to know."

The actor paused, then turned to the other mourners and pointed to a man. "Over there's Mr. Lyle Grant."

The actor playing Grant rose from his folding chair and nodded at the audience. Then he sat down again.

DARK MAZE

The opening monologue resumed:

"Now, Mr. Grant did a fine job of making The Mister look good for his wake. I'd have to admit, my father had an evil look in life. He had a dirty black and gray fringe of hair on his head that was always wild with peaks, like his head was full of horns. And his lips stuck out and they usually turned down, like he was forever perched in a stadium seat shouting boo at the teams.

"So Mr. Grant worked oil into his hair and smoothed down the horns, and now his hair's nice and silvery. Kind of distinguished, don't you think? And also Mr. Grant forced the lips back and pulled them straight. And besides that, Mr. Grant clipped away most of the stiff little black hairs that snaked out from my father's nose and ears.

"Like I say, The Mister looks real good tonight. Better than I've ever seen him look, truth to tell. I'd say downright well groomed.

"But I can't believe The Mister's dead. What I mean to say is, I can't *trust* the old man's dead, and even though I can turn around right now and see for myself he's gone, which ought to satisfy me that everything's going to be all right now. . . . Well, I'm still afraid . . ."

And then, to everybody's complete astonishment—the actors playing the mourners and everybody in the audience practically jumped out of their skins—The Mister bolted upright in his coffin. His eyelids popped open, his bright blue eyes blazed. With his hands folded tightly over his chest, he said:

"Oh yeah, I'm dead, all right! But you people out there, I suppose you're the type who believe dead men tell no tales?

"Hah! That's nothing but an old movie line. It's a crock, just like a thousand other lines you've heard all your lives about people who can't speak up for themselves."

The Mister wiped his mouth, the way a drunk does.

"I expect from now on that most everybody's going to say

215

nasty things about the kind of man I've been in life—things they never had the balls to say to my face.

"Hah! There's another crock for you: Never speak ill of the dead."

I had sneaked out of the third-floor theatre and down the stairs. Now I stood at the bar in Vern's, with a double of Johnnie Walker red, believing that this might help me escape the overlapping waves—the undertow—of memory and coincidence that had dogged this day and every day since Picasso in the park.

If nothing more, the Scotch helped soothe the still-prickly shock of seeing that actor upstairs bolt open his eyes and speak from the beyond; hammering back into my head the always-hovering image of my own soldier father. A father I never knew or saw, save in old photographs of made-up poses; he, too, had been a blue-eyed man, so my mother once told me in a rare and womanly reminiscence of the man she married.

But never before tonight had I realized this: my father's image in my mind was black and white; the color of the man was only now beginning to take shape.

Often lately, this happens. I am stopped in the midst of what I am doing by my father's image. I am more and more struck by the notion that my job is only rehearsal for a greater detective case, namely the mystery of my hollow place. As a detective and a drinker, I am also lately asking myself: Do I go about solving the mysteries of others for their sake, or do I see their mysteries as clues to my own story?

Just before taking up with Ruby Flagg, I had been thinking seriously and soberly about booking an appointment with a doctor. By which I mean a shrink. But not the department psychiatrist, for I have my vanities; I did not want to risk that sort of thing getting around, which it does.

I wanted somebody on the outside; somebody like Dr. Reiser would have been ideal.

But then my thought broke. For suddenly, there was Ruby's voice at my back.

"I see you're missing something, Hock." She seemed very irritated.

"What?" I spun around.

"Was the play really all that bad?"

"No, that's not it."

"All right, so the play didn't stink. So you were overcome by a sudden, terrible thirst, is that it?"

"Ruby, I'm awful sorry."

She said angrily, "There are people upstairs waiting for me, Hock. Waiting for *us!*"

"I said I was sorry. It's the case, Ruby. Can you understand? And, it's my father."

Forgiveness softened her face. She placed a hand on my forehead, as if checking for fever.

"Can you remember what you said at breakfast?" I asked.

"What, about your father?"

"Yes."

"Not exactly. Can you?"

"Yes, I can."

I pulled out my notebook and found the page where I had jotted down a list of impressions and dissonant things people had said, things I would try to organize into some possible meaning. Later, maybe as I slept.

"Your exact words: 'I'm sorry, Hock, but shame on your mother. Your father should never have been allowed to die that way, with nobody to give you his memory.'"

Ruby said, "You wrote that down?"

They say, "You're a great artist!"
Can you beat it? Fat lot of good that does me.
They say, "What you paint, it's the truth!"

Ho, ho, ain't that the truth?

Damn straight, so far as it goes.

But actually, they ain't got a clue how truly great I am. They think I don't know exactly what I'm doing.

Ho, ho, but I do!

It's what the holy goddamn bible says I got to do, "Be sure your sin will find you out."

EIGHTEEN

I woke up in Ruby's place at the crack of noon.

The bed I was in was one of those big regal numbers, the kind that go with country inns in New England—high off the floor and full of pillows and chintz covers, with four tall mahogany posters and curtains that drew closed by day. It was a bed straight out of a photo layout in one of those magazines for people who live in Manhattan studio apartments, people lacking space but not style.

Ruby walked by, on her way to the terrace with coffee and newspapers. She said, "Aren't you going to open it up, Hock?"

She meant the rectangular box on the bed next to me. It was wrapped in gift paper and ribbons, with a card attached that said it was for me.

Inside was a terrycloth robe from Saks. It was blue with handsome pinstripes of purple and red.

"I told the clerk blue because my guy's a cop," Ruby said. She sounded almost like a high-school girl, her voice young and weightless. "Do you like it?"

"What, are you kidding? I love it!"

I got up from the bed and put my arms through the sleeves and wrapped the robe around me and knotted the belt loosely. Then I followed Ruby to the terrace. There was a table set with cups and saucers and fruit and rolls. Ruby poured us coffee from the pot she had brought from the kitchen. We sat down, looking out toward the Brooklyn Bridge with the sun straight overhead, glinting off the silvery gray towers spanning the water.

This was the first day of the new spring when the breeze did not chill the skin. The clouds were high and milky, a sign of clear weather for the next several days. Seagulls streaked lazily through webs of steel cable up on the bridge decks. Tugboats went about their slow, quiet business of shoving barges and tankers up and down the river. And there sat I, a soundly slept prince of New York in his royal blue robe that smelled of newness, steam blowing off my coffee cup in the open air and Ruby Flagg beside me, a slice of orange touched to her tongue.

"Thanks, for everything," I said to Ruby. "Really, thanks."

I must have sounded a little overwhelmed by my thoughts. Ruby looked at me and asked, "Are you all right?"

"Sure I am. Just, thanks for the coffee, and for last night. And for all your help on the case."

"You're welcome."

"And thanks for the robe. It must have cost a fortune."

"It did."

"So it's pricey gifts now. We're getting in deep, Ruby."

"You bet your life."

I sipped my coffee and looked at the bridge and asked, "If we could do exactly as we pleased, how should we spend this gorgeous spring day?"

Ruby did not now sound at all like some innocent schoolgirl. "We'd stay in."

"What's this, a randy streak?"

"A criminal streak, that's more like it. I think you and me

together in the sack is still against the law in four or five southern states."

"Is it now? And here I'm always saying how civil disobedience has its honored place."

"And time, which is what you haven't got this afternoon, Detective Hockaday." She held out the *Daily News* and the *Post.* "I hate to remind you, but there's still a killer out there."

I took the papers and scanned the contrasting methods employed in the exercise of that hallowed tabloid principle of presumed guilt. And I could easily see how these tabloids would not bring cheer today to the mayor or the commissioner or Inspector Neglio, and certainly not to the poor hounded Picasso.

The *Daily News* now had its own artist's sketch of Picasso, thus playing catch-up with the *Post* on graphics. Over Picasso's likeness was the streamer, "Dragnet For a Loser." The story accompanying this was an imagination of Picasso's down-and-out life in the streets of Hell's Kitchen, almost entirely based on quotations from Luis Riestra. It read to me like Luis had goofed on the press after a night full of funny cigarettes.

But the *Post* once again had the journalistic leg up with its streamer, "Secret Plan To Nab Psycho Killer Revealed To *Post* Reporter, See Page 3." Slattery was at it again.

I sighed and turned to page 3.

There was my photograph, and the *Post* drawing of Picasso from the other day. And Slattery unthrottled:

EXCLUSIVE!

Solo Detective Stalks Mad-Dog Slayer
"Terror Is a One-Man Job"

By William T. Slattery

The hope of a city seized by the bloody nightmare of serial murder rides on the shoulders of a single, highly unorthodox cop—Detective Neil Hockaday of the Street Crimes Unit, Manhattan, popularly known in police and criminal circles as the SCUM patrol.

Detective Hockaday is virtually alone in stalking a homeless artist called Picasso, wanted for questioning in connection with three stunningly brutal murders in recent days.

"We got a suspect, but routine investigation has come up with just about zip on him, so it all comes down to one guy—Hockaday," said Hockaday's superior officer, Inspector Tomassino Neglio, in an exclusive interview with this reporter. "That's some hell of a secret plan if you want to know the truth, but there you go."

With unusual candor for a top-echelon police commander, Neglio added, "You ask how we're going to find some mad dog who's out terrorizing this town. I'm squaring with you. Not with some huge gang of cops. Terror is a one-man job, and Hock drew it."

"Hock," as the SCUM-patrol detective is widely known, has investigated many of New York's most baffling homicides. Only recently, he was credited with solving the murder of flamboyant radio preacher "Father Love," the long-time pastor of Harlem's Healing Stream Deliverance Temple.

In referring to that case, Inspector Neglio said, "In the whole department, Hock's the only cop who could have dug up the crazy bedbug who did that preacher. He's not the easiest cop I ever knew, and he's got his own quirky ways of working, but Hock brings them in, boy! I don't know what it is about the guy, but when a bedbug starts scratching Hock starts itching."

Neglio added, "Right now, we've got a bedbug someplace out there with a head full of hate. So we put Hock on the trail. God bless us all."

Detective Hockaday himself was unavailable for comment.

I skimmed the rest of the story, which mostly only recapped the murders of Celia Furman, Dr. Reiser and Benito Molevo Reyes. Even the great Slattery had not made the Celia-Picasso marriage connection, nor Picasso's connection with Coney Island.

I examined my photograph. It did not reveal much, which pleased me. A grainy head-and-shoulders shot of a guy somewhere way past his rookie days who had not shaved in a few days, wearing a Yankees cap and sunglasses. The point to publishing this escaped me.

"What do you think?" I asked Ruby, holding up the picture for her to see.

"So, that's supposedly *my* Neil Hockaday?" She laughed softly. "No, I don't think so. That guy looks like some ball-park lout, from the cheap seats."

"Thanks, it's how I look about half the time. You really know how to make a guy feel adored."

Ruby laughed again and the lightness of her voice floated in the clean April breeze like a paper kite; she turned, as if watching the last easy moment of our day rise up and up until it faded from sight. Then she turned back to me, her mood grown heavy.

"I wasn't thinking about newspapers, actually," she said. "I was thinking about something important."

"Like what?"

"Like the dream I had last night."

There—it went through me again: the prickling shock of some odd recognition. Last night, the shock of the blue-eyed man rising from a coffin in Ruby's play. Now the shock of a terrible closeness between us; knowing that Ruby could now take my place at dreaming.

"What did you see?" I asked her.

"Picasso, at his easel painting."

"What did he say?"

"Nothing, it was nothing direct. But he gave me an idea."

"What?"

"To try looking at this murder case by Picasso's lights. Try it, Hock. Shut your eyes. What do you see?"

I closed my eyes. I saw Picasso's masterpiece, the montage of demons and drowning mortals. I heard the music from the Unicef Pavilion, the children's sweet voices singing, *"It's a small world after all . . ."*

Ruby asked again, "What do you see?"

"Picasso's mural at the Fire and Brimstone."

"That's it, exactly! That's the idea."

"But Ruby, I don't *get* this idea."

"You imagine yourself thinking like Picasso would think," she said slowly, allowing me time to catch up to her vision. "The idea is, you imagine you're Picasso looking at the bodies dropping dead. Celia, Dr. Reiser, Benito. But you see how it's not murder."

"Not murder?" I stopped myself, and then I began to see.

"By Picasso's lights, no," Ruby said. "What you see is an artist painting about death."

I said, "Not murdering, painting . . ."

I finished my coffee, hung my new robe in Ruby's closet, dressed and then left her place for my own. At home I would change into some fresh clothes, make some telephone calls and try to spend the rest of the day thinking like Picasso would think.

All the way up the staircase to my apartment, I heard the telephone ringing.

I sank down into my green chair, picked up my telephone and said, "Hello there, Inspector old sock. Nice of you to call."

There was a voice on the line that did not belong to Neglio. It was one of his two secretaries, the brunette who did not know how to type.

She said, "Is this Detective Hockaday to whom I am speaking?"

"Yes, dear, it is."

"Hold the line, please. I'm supposed to go get the inspector wherever he is."

I heard tiny heels click away across a tile floor. Then about a minute later the sound of a man's size-tens came into range. Knowing what was likely to come next, I held the phone receiver several inches away from my ear.

Then, Neglio's bark: "Hock, where in the fuck have you been?"

"Oh, just down at the newsstand buying extra copies of today's *Post*. I want all my relatives to read my boss's lovely sentiments on the topic of me."

"You haven't got relatives, you hump. Except that screwy uncle of yours over on the other side."

I ignored the family slander. "That was a real load of crap you dumped on Slattery, Inspector."

"Hey, I don't know what happened. The guy provoked me into a talky mood. You know how irritating he is. Slattery won't ever get the hell away from me unless I give him something nobody else's got."

"Come off it. I'm no super-cop. We both know what that was all about in the paper."

Like a rosy-cheeked old nun Neglio said, "Whatever do you mean?"

"You're putting this all on me. You're busy making nice with the new mayor and along comes the first crime wave on his watch, so you want to be sure he gets the message there's nothing you can do about it. Not *you!* Nobody in the department ever got in trouble by doing nothing, right?

"Which is where I come in, the cop with his picture in the *Post* when he never asked for the publicity, the guy who always brings them in, boy! And if I don't—or if I can't make the bust quick enough—then how can that be the fault of somebody who does nothing?"

"Didn't I promise you a promotion out of all this?"

"The promotion I'll take. But the promise I made about having your pal the mayor tag along on my collar, forget it."

"I don't have to take this, Hock."

"Sure you do. Slattery provokes me into a talky mood, too. You know how irritating he can be."

"It's breaking my heart to see how you're becoming more and more of a cynic every day."

"Eat a fig newton, then take a nice long nap," I said. "You'll get over it."

Neglio said nothing, but I knew he was steaming. I had called him on one of the small treacheries that emerge from time to time in our unspoken pact: I will use him, he will use me, back and forth and et cetera. Small treacheries, like the minor sins of marriage.

"I have been calling you day and night, Hock, but you're not answering, let alone reporting in. So I'm asking now, what the fuck is your progress on the case?"

"With one or two more breaks, I think I'm close." And I was actually beginning to imagine that was true. "Would you like to do something to help the cause?"

"Well, I . . ."

"I knew you would. Take down this name—Johnny Halo, just like it sounds. So far as I know, he's got no aliases. He says he's an Army veteran, second war. He owns a bar in Coney Island called the Neptune. Also the Seashore Hotel in Coney, which he recently took over and where he's lived for a long time. I want the deep check on this guy."

"All right, Hock."

"I want to know what the guy eats for breakfast, who he sleeps with, what he's got in his family—especially the family part. I want to know if he's in bed with any mafiosi."

"I'll have it inside of twenty-four hours," Neglio said. "Meanwhile, I want you to keep in touch with me, you hear, Hock?"

DARK MAZE

"I will. But don't call me, I'll call you."

"You fucking hump, you! What am I supposed to say to the mayor?"

"Tell him to have a buttercup day."

I took a look at the mail I had brought upstairs with me. There was no plain envelope with an upside-down flag stamp today, so I hoped Picasso was lying low. Con Edison sent me a second notice on my bill, which I immediately tossed since I have never seen the point of rushing these things. A magazine subscription service informed me that I might soon become a millionaire, and this I reluctantly tossed. There was finally the air letter from Ireland, postmarked Dún Laoghaire, but not addressed in my Uncle Liam's familiar hand. I opened it and read:

Dear Mr. Hockaday:

I write on behalf of your dear uncle, Liam Hockaday, who has fallen ill. As you know, he suffers from a poor heart. The doctor has now confined him to bed and I have been engaged to look after your uncle's needs and attend to any business that needs conducting.

This letter, then, does the duty of informing you of unpleasant news. As a loyal friend of your uncle, I am, of course, terribly sorry for your troubles.

I might add, however, that the doctor feels Liam's life expectancy is relatively long as these things go—perhaps a year or better. And I can assure you, his only discomfort in these days is in the forced physical idleness.

Should you wish further details, or the arrangement of a visit, I shall be only too happy to oblige at this end. I am currently in residence at your uncle's home, here in Dún Laoghaire.

Yrs faithfully, in the name of X,
Patrick Snoody.

How long had it been since I had seen my Uncle Liam, the man whose monthly checks, drawn on the Bank of Ireland, kept my mother and myself well and fed during my early years when father was gone off in the mists? Liam, who would come stay with us, and have whispered conversations with my mother in the kitchen after I had gone to bed.

Only twice had I seen him since my boyhood. Once when he came to New York and we buried my mother in Woodlawn, up in the Irish section of the Bronx; once more when he came to the city on business he said was of no importance compared to the time we two would spend together again.

That, in fact, was the last time. And I have never, to my regret, been to Ireland in return.

Did I once take the chance of asking Liam about his brother—my father? No information was volunteered. And now Liam was dying.

I took my personal directory out of the drawer below the telephone stand and looked up Liam's number in Ireland, dialed it direct and waited.

Five rings later and there was a "Hallo" on the line.

I asked, "Is this Patrick Snoody?"

There were crackling sounds, then an echo of my question, then, "Yes, yes. Snoody here."

"I received your letter today," I said. "This is Neil Hockaday, in America."

Snoody spoke excitedly over my echo and so I missed much of what he said, hearing only, ". . . resting now, musn't be disturbed now. . . . Sorry."

"Can you give Uncle a message for me?"

"Yes, yes."

I waited for Snoody's echo to clear. "Tell him, I'll try coming for a visit soon. Tell him I've got pressing business to clear, but that I'll be there. Tell him to wait for me."

"Yes, yes—wait for you."

"Mr. Snoody, thank you for your letter. I'll call when I'm able to come."

"Yes, yes. We'll be waiting."

Then I rang off, with the guilt in my heart that is deserved by all ungrateful relations of the old and alone. I told myself I would really make the trip. Then I cursed Picasso. I could get on a plane right there and then if not for him.

I dialed Central Homicide. Logue was out in the field, but Captain Mogaill was on hand. He said, "That's quite a trumpet blowing your tune in the *Post,* I see."

"It only sounds that way now," I said.

"That's possibly so. The press has a way of setting you up as a fair-haired boy today, expressly so they'll have something pretty to knock about tomorrow, when it is hoped you'll fall from the weight of your own swollen head."

"My thoughts exactly," I said. Then I asked, "Has Logue come up with anything useful, do you know?"

"He has, and he's dying to tell you direct but since there's no love lost between us, I don't mind bursting his bubble."

"Tell me," I said.

"First, he says that Celia Furman had very serious troubles with the lads at the IRS."

"That I know."

"But did you know the extent of her trouble? Did you know that the feds even impounded the lady's car, which is what she was sleeping in?"

"I didn't know that," I said. "But it sounds like something the IRS would do."

"So Logue says by this that the lady was especially desperate for money, you see."

"Yes. Anything else?"

"One more thing," Mogaill said. "Logue himself was nosing it up and down Forty-second Street yesterday, asking after Picasso of every skell and con who'd talk to him, and every shopkeeper likewise. He took along four dicks for help, and between them they combed the Deuce close as an egg to his chicken."

"Did they find anything?"

"Who knows what this means, Hock, but the owner of one of them perpetual going-out-of-business electronics joints for the tourists, he remembers dealing with a geeky little guy in a beret. This was only about a week ago."

"Dealing how?"

"The shopkeeper, he says your boyo was in the market for a good tape recorder. Which he did buy, with cash. Plus plenty of batteries. The shopkeeper remembers this particular transaction because of what the guy in the beret keeps saying, mostly to himself."

"What was that?"

"Picasso keeps saying, 'I got to get down this autobiography of myself, ain't that right?' He keeps saying this to somebody like somebody's standing beside him. Anyway, business is business and the shopkeeper takes the wacko's money and off goes Picasso with his tape recorder."

I thanked Mogaill for the information and told him to tell Logue I would speak to him soon. I entered these items in my notebook, adding to the list of unrelated items to be sorted out as I slept.

Then I rang up the Neptune Bar in Brooklyn.

Johnny Halo was not on the job.

"We ain't even open today," a janitor told me. "I come around this morning since it's payday, but Johnny wasn't here. So I let myself in and I been waiting ever since. I'm still waiting, and helping myself to a few drinks."

I rang the Seashore Hotel and asked for Halo's room.

"He ain't up there," the desk clerk said. "He never come back last night."

"Ring the room anyway," I said.

There was no answer.

* * *

DARK MAZE

They'll never get rid of the hate in my head.

I'm the only bedbug who can do that, which I will in the sweet by-and-by.

But I got miles to go before I sleep.

Ho, ho, ain't that the truth?

Miles to go!

Meantime, wait'll the little lady gets a load of what's coming to her!

NINETEEN

I made one last telephone call.

Neglio did not seem pleased to hear from me so soon after our last conversation. He said, "Christ Almighty, Hock, what do you want out of me now?"

"I need you to run a rapid warrant."

"Search?"

"Yes. I'll be on the F train out to Coney Island in about fifteen minutes, it'll take me forty-five minutes to get to the Stillwell Avenue station and five minutes more to walk from the station to the Seashore Hotel on Surf Avenue. Which is already under police guard. I'd like the warrant to be in the hands of the cops at the hotel by the time I arrive."

"You're taking the *subway* out to Coney Island?"

"And I'll be putting the out-of-pocket for tokens on my expense report."

"Hock, there are faster ways of getting around town, you know. Not to mention safer."

"You're saying you want to loan me that armored black Chrysler of yours with Officer Flunky at the wheel?"

"I don't think . . ."

"Neither do I." I could hear steaming noises from Neglio's end of the line.

"Total time for me to get from my place out to the Seashore Hotel is one hour and five minutes, okay? I'm asking you to run a search warrant through the Brooklyn D.A.'s office during lunchtime, *plus* have a police courier deliver the paper for me all the way out to Coney inside of that time. Now that's a very rapid warrant. Which is how come I need you. Or I could call up your pal the mayor if you don't think you can handle it yourself."

Neglio made a few more steaming noises. "In case anybody should ask, Hock, what's the purpose here?"

"I want to search the business and residential premises of Johnny Halo. Make the warrant out for the Seashore and his bar, the Neptune. And make it for forty-eight hours in case I have to make two visits."

"Johnny Halo? This is the same guy you've already got me doing the nine yarder on? If you go turning over his place, Hock, you might wind up crumbing the play."

"Read the *Post.* Right there, black on white, it says I've got my own quirky ways of doing things, but that I always bring them in, boy."

"Cut it, Hock. That's an order. And so's this: spill."

"All right," I said. "The thing is, Halo's been missing since last night."

"Johnny Halo. He ties up to Charlie Furman, alias our man Picasso?"

"Yes, he does. Only I don't know exactly how. I can't read between the lies yet."

"But what do you figure right now?"

"Today, I figure there's a percentage in taking Halo off the tilt. He's an easier guy to find than Charlie Furman. And I figure if I find Halo, then I'm closing in on Picasso."

Neglio paused, thinking over the percentages. Then he

said, "Okay, Hock. The warrant will be there. Go catch your cockamamie train."

True to his word, the warrant was waiting for me an hour and change later with a cop at the wheel of a squad car on surveillance duty outside the Seashore Hotel. The name tag on his blue twill shirt said he was Patrolman Harold Gotha.

I showed him my gold shield.

Gotha looked it over, then he flicked off a transistor tape player on the dashboard. I had recognized "Tangerine," somewhere halfway through the piece and nearing the end of the lengthy middle-saxophone solo.

He turned the warrant over to me. I slipped it into a pocket of my windbreaker and asked, "That's Dexter Gordon you're playing?"

Gotha's voice was loose and smoky, like a jazz musician's. "Long Tall, the one and only."

"From 'Nights at the Keystone,' right?"

He gave me an approving lopsided smile and said, "You're all right. I've been reading about you today, Superman. The story didn't say anything about you knowing your bebop, though. By the way, you take a lousy picture."

"It only shows you how it wasn't my idea to get in the newspaper."

"Yeah, I guess. You need any help up there in the hotel, detective?"

"Not for what I'm after now, but maybe later. How long are you on this detail?"

"I started at noon, I'll be here awhile."

"Good. I'll see you when I come down."

"I ain't going anywhere." Gotha flicked on the tape player and Long Tall played on, from beyond his grave.

The lobby was almost the same as it had been the evening before: coldly lit, sour-smelling and with Chastity the red-wigged pross smoking a cigarette and sprawled in the only chair, the same skirt hiked up over her nylon-encased thighs. Two things, though, were markedly different: Jerry, the night clerk, had been spelled by a beagle-faced old fellow drinking beer from a can and today Chastity sported something new and intriguing—a lady's green felt hat, with a broken feather on the side.

Chastity turned as I walked in, the feather shaking with the motion of her head. She stood up and opened her arms wide and said, "Well if it ain't my favorite cop, Officer Hockaday. Here I was, like to die of boredom and you walk in to save the day. Long time no see, baby!"

The old fellow in the clerk's cage dribbled beer and said sleepily, "Cops. What?"

I could not take my eyes off Chastity's hat. She seemed completely innocent in the wearing of it, unaware of its former owner.

She felt me staring at her head, of course, and said, "You like the chapeau, honey buns?"

"Yeah, Chastity, I do," I said. "It goes real good with your auburn hair. Real pretty."

I took a twenty from my pocket and gave it to her and said, "Come on, let's talk upstairs."

"Sugar, you just made my day."

We walked to the clerk's cage and the beagle said to me, "It's seven bucks an hour, pal, three-hour minimum, plus a dollar for the towel deposit. Chastity, she knows the room you should go to."

I took the search warrant from my pocket and showed it, along with my shield. I said, "How about just for today I'll take the key to your presidential suite, free of charge, okay?"

The old fellow took the warrant and held it up close to his face and sniffed at it after he read it. He curled a lip and gave it back to me, along with a room key, and said, "Well, I guess it's no hair off'a my butt."

Then with Chastity hugging my arm, I headed for the

staircase. We passed under the bullet-scarred sign—IF YOU LIVED HERE, YOU'D BE HOME NOW—and walked up four flights to Halo's lair.

A presidential suite it was not, certainly not in these modern times when presidents cost so much. Abraham Lincoln's mud-chinked log cabin back on the Illinois prairie probably had more luxe than Johnny Halo's digs—three tiny, hot, airless rooms covering half the top floor from front to back and connected by arches cut through flimsy plaster-board walls by somebody who had no business calling himself a carpenter.

The window of the back room had a view of the blue-gray ocean, and around this window Halo had fashioned a parlor. Chastity said he had used all the lobby furnishings, with the exception of her chair. "I'm an institution down in that lobby," she said, "which means I have earned reserved seating for my behind for all the times I sold it upstairs." The front room had two skinny windows that looked out over Surf Avenue. There was a hot plate and a sink against one wall and a desk and chair against the other; the desk top was cluttered with papers and magazines and I started leafing through the mess.

Nothing looked particularly important, or even mildly significant. Nothing anywhere in Halo's seedy quarters looked important even to him, as if the man did all his living somewhere else. And it struck me for one unsteady moment that somebody looking through my own apartment back in Hell's Kitchen might draw this same sad conclusion about me. I quickly consoled myself with the thought that my place at least had plenty of booze and books on hand, and an old photograph of a soldier.

Chastity, meanwhile, had parked herself on the edge of Halo's freshly made-up bed in the middle room. "Hockaday," she called. "Come on in here, it's time to play cops and robbers."

I opened up all the desk drawers. They were empty, save

for one pencil stub, three ball-point pens and a family of startled cockroaches. I checked the tiny bathroom and found it was used as a clothes closet, with most of Halo's wardrobe piled on the floor or slung over the shower rail.

Then I stepped into the middle room. Chastity sat there on the bed unbuttoning herself. I checked the bathroom here, which turned out to be the one that Halo actually used. There were clean towels on a rack, a new cake of soap in a dish on the sink and not much evidence that Halo was a man who took lots of showers.

I looked out the window of the middle room. Down in the alleyway I could see Patrolman Gotha's hand sticking out from the squad car, tapping to the tempo of some Dexter Gordon riff against the chrome side-view mirror.

"Pay attention to me!" Chastity demanded.

I turned and looked again at Chastity perched on the old sagging bed, smiling. Despite the fact that she held in her hands a pair of pink and surprisingly comely bare breasts, my eyes were mainly fixed on the green hat. I said without much expression, "Where did you get that thing?"

She looked now to be either angry or on the verge of tears. Men have a hard time knowing which way a woman might go when they get that kind of look.

"You're talking about my hat?"

"Yes."

"Here I pegged you for this nice straight kind of a john, a traditionalist, you know?" Chastity shook her head slowly back and forth and dropped her hands to her sides. Her breasts dropped, too, but not much. "So tell me, Officer Hockaday, what's your brand? I heard of lots of different wankers in my time—shoe freaks, stocking freaks, panty freaks—but a *hat* freak?"

"You really don't know what this is, do you?"

"Nope, you just stumped this old hooker."

I took another twenty from my wallet and tried to give it to Chastity, but she would not take it. I said, "I want to know about the hat because it's police business. The last time I saw that hat, it belonged to a woman named Celia Furman who a couple of hours after I saw her in it got herself murdered."

Chastity took off the hat and threw it at me. Then she buttoned her blouse.

"What the hell do I care, she's only somebody in the newspapers to me." She stood up and smoothed her wig. "Go ahead and keep my hat. Use it for evidence to fry poor old Picasso."

"Look, I came up here on a warrant to search Johnny Halo's rooms because I think he's part of my case and now suddenly he's missing. So I come here to the hotel and the first thing I see is you in the lobby wearing a hat that's missing off a dead lady."

"You saying I had something to do with that?"

"No, I'm not. I want to know where you got the hat, though, and so I invited you up here with me so we could talk someplace in private. That's it. Get it?"

"Sure, Hockaday. I get it. Do you?"

I did not, and it showed.

"There's an awful lot of men I've had to kiss in my time, but I still own my heart," she said. "That means I'm not ready to be thrown away, see."

She took my hands and pulled me, made me look into her uptilted face. Maybe because I have been a cop so long I felt like laughing at her; maybe because I have not been a cop long enough I then felt ashamed.

Chastity could see my thoughts. She looked down at the cracked floor between us. A tear fell, one of thousands to be shed that day in Coney Island.

All I managed was, "I'm glad we're friends, Chastity. I mean that." She looked up and there was generosity in her damp eyes, even after hearing my inadequate words. In her time, she had come to know all of men's inadequacies.

Chastity broke away. She said, "That's swell, we're

friends. But only so long as you keep handing out those tips, okay?"

"You want to help me?"

"I might."

This time she took the twenty.

"Johnny Halo's missing. Do you happen to know why, or where he is?"

"I know a lot of things."

Chastity accepted another bill.

"Let's take a little look-see around this dump before I answer any of that," she said. I followed Chastity into the back third of Halo's suite, the parlor room with the window out to the sea. "Here's where Mister Big Shot does his living, such as it is. Seek, and maybe ye shall find."

The bathroom was empty here, except for some dirty low-ball glasses in a sink full of greasy water and a wastepaper basket that yielded nothing but an empty pint bottle of bourbon. Besides the lobby chairs, the furniture in the parlor consisted of a battered television set under the window and a round coffee table in front of a vinyl couch. The table was a jumble of newspapers, some yellowed with age; odds and ends that can wind up in a man's pockets; mail, mostly overdue bills of the sort familiar to me; ashtrays, and a hotel phone. Several pairs of soiled socks lay under the couch, some of them hardened with age.

One of the ashtrays had a crumpled book of matches in it. I picked this up because the matchbook cover had drawing on it, a drawing of a recently familiar sight in Times Square: double glass doors frosted with the images of leering white French poodles dressed in cutaway coats and top hats.

I put the matches in my shirt pocket.

"Well now, see how we're getting somewhere?" Chastity said. There was a lot in her voice that told me the city's money had been well invested. "Let's seek some more, shall we?"

There was nothing interesting about the mail, or the

newspapers. So I picked through Halo's odds and ends while
Chastity watched, bemused. I pored through old lottery
tickets, OTB slips, laundry receipts, dimes and nickels and
blackened pennies, empty twisted cigarette packs, loose
sticks of brittled chewing gum. And then something interesting: a miniature bible with a pebbled black leatherette
cover and red-tipped pages, about one-by-two inches.

"Well here's a real surprise," I said, picking up the bible.
"Would you have figured Johnny Halo to be a religious
man?"

Chastity had no comment. But she smiled when I opened
the bible and found tiny letters stamped on the inside cover.
My eyes strained as I read:

Crown of Thorns Holy Tabernacle
—A Refuge from Sin in Times Square—
—Friendly & Clean—

384 W. 41st St.
New York City

Nightly Vespers
Sunday Services 10 A.M.

"He's not only a religious man; he's a real thumper, I see."
I leafed through the miniature pages, something that Halo
had never done from the feel of the stiff paper. I asked
Chastity, "And what do you know about this?"

"Only what they say."

"What do they say?"

"Oh, that old one about still waters running deep, that's
all." And there was that tight smile of hers again, the one
that said: this avenue of inquiry is temporarily closed.

"Have it your way," I said.

Chastity gazed around the sparse parlor with the cheesy
furniture, then out the window, and then toward the arch-
ways leading off to the other rooms. She said, "You know,

Johnny's finally got himself a halfway decent setup and here he don't have a clue about making it look nice like a regular home. I should be sitting so pretty like this; I'd know what to do with the place."

I allowed Chastity a few seconds of her *House Beautiful* dreams, then I brought her back around to business. "Maybe we could please pick up on my earlier questions?" I asked.

"Sure, let's do. I couldn't live with myself if I thought your tips were going for nothing, Hockaday."

"Where's Halo, and why is he missing?"

"I honestly don't know. And I honestly don't give a rat's fanny."

"You don't like the guy?"

"It shows?"

"So what's he done to you, Chastity?"

"I don't remember you asking that earlier."

"You only had a hundred forty bucks earlier," I said, reaching for my wallet.

"Save it," Chastity said. "Like I told you, I got a heart. Which means I realize the city's not what you'd call flush right now. Besides which, you'd find out somewhere else anyways."

"Find out what?"

"That everybody around here pretty much equally despises Johnny Halo for the simple fact that everybody's usually into him for at least a yard. It's not hard to hate a guy's guts when you're owing him money all the time."

"What kind of a scam does he run?"

"The straight six-for-five rip. Anything higher, he knows he'd never live to spend his profits."

"You borrow five bucks, you pay back six at the end of the week?"

"That's it. One hundred bucks is the minimum hook. So at six-for-five, that counts up to twenty percent worth of vigorish on the unpaid balance—a week."

"Very sweet," I said.

I decided to let this particular detail of Johnny Halo's précis alone for a while.

"Just one more question," I said. "Where did you get the hat?"

"There's a private dive around here by the name of the Carny Club," Chastity said. "Ever hear of it?"

I said I had.

"Last night I dropped by late. When I was finally going home, there was this nice green-feathered hat hanging on a peg in the foyer, just waiting to get pinched."

"So you pinched."

There was that tight smile again.

Down in the alley, Patrolman Gotha was tapping in time to "Sophisticated Lady." He waved when he saw me come out the hotel door.

"Find out what you're after?" he asked.

"Some, not all," I said. "Do you have a crowbar in the trunk of this car?"

"Sure."

"Good." I crossed in front of the car and then got in on the passenger side. "Drive us up to the boardwalk. We're going to open up the Neptune bar."

"I can't leave my post."

"I'm the guy in charge of your post."

"That's true." Gotha started the car, put it into gear and we turned west onto Surf Avenue, then south on a sand and blacktop drive that led to the boardwalk. "The warrant covers the Neptune, too?"

"Yes."

"How come the place needs a forced entry?"

"Because the owner's been missing since last night. That would be Johnny Halo. His place never opened up this morning."

"Wait. I thought we were looking for this Picasso guy who used to live at the Seashore."

"We're looking for both of them now," I said. "Pass the word along when we're all done here, okay?"

"Sure I will."

Gotha parked the car and took the crowbar out from the trunk and we headed up the boardwalk for the Neptune.

As I figured, the janitor had given up and left. And locked the door again.

Gotha put the crowbar to it and snapped it open. We walked in and turned on the lights and heard the sound of scurrying mouse feet.

I looked around for something in the way of an office and records. The nearest I came was a storeroom full of empty deposit bottles and a broom closet.

I checked behind the bar. Nothing.

My work here was through, at least for now.

I ought to give titles out of the holy goddamn bible for some of these paintings. How about that? Ain't that just the thing for my reputation?

Damn straight.

Haw! Maybe I should apply for one of them grants! Hoo-boy, that'd be something, hey?

Let's see. How about, "Ye lust and have not, ye kill and desire to have and cannot obtain"? Yeah, some of that New Testament crapola!

Or how about, "If a man know not how to rule his own house, how will he take care of the church of God?"

Now you're talking!

Damn straight.

TWENTY

I was surprised it was only four o'clock. Time always seems so much longer in Coney Island than it does back in Manhattan; the tides and the rolling ocean sounds of Coney are never in a hurry.

There was no point now in my dropping by the Carny Club to nose around. Nobody would be there until at least seven. Besides, it might prove well to let a day lapse; nobody in that crowd was in a hurry to help me find Picasso, or Johnny Halo for that matter. I could make far better use of this afternoon working some other angle of the case. And dreaming up some sideways approach to all the questions popping in my mind about Celia Furman's traveling green hat.

I left Patrolman Gotha and walked aimlessly through Astroland until I came on the Fire and Brimstone. And just as those few days ago when Ruby and I stood here together in shock before Picasso's ruthless masterpiece, I again remembered my many years' indifference to the bloody cruel knowledge in Charlie Furman's vision of the world.

DARK MAZE

A glimpse of someone else's nightmare, and then a round of brave laughs. What reason had we to wonder about an artist's mind?

I turned away and walked back through the lane to Bowery Street and up to Nathan's Famous. For the next fifteen minutes I stood at the open-air counter on the Surf Avenue side, nursing a short beer. I bought another beer when the organ at the B&B Carousell just across the way started up with "By the Sea," turning I watched the wooden horses lift and fall and also the small dark man who ran the organ pumps and the carousel motor.

He clanked a bell and waved in my direction. Even in the deep shade where he stood, I saw his smile. I waved back.

A red-and-yellow taxicab pulled up in front of the B&B and stopped at the curb, blocking my view. The driver got out and helped his passengers with the back door, a rare sight in New York nowadays. Sparkle the snake charmer stepped from the taxi, her long black hair rising in puffs with the street breeze. She and the taxi driver leaned together into the cab and brought out a wheelchair, then Sealo.

Sparkle paid the driver and then wheeled Sealo across the avenue. I watched as the two of them cut through the gaudy aisles of Astroland—just a pair of nature's oddities, reporting for duty on the boardwalk at Coney Island.

I paid for my beer and crossed the avenue to the subway station.

It occurred to me that I should probably drop by Central Homicide on the chance that Logue had returned from the field with something useful, something that would help compute. If not, there was always the entertaining possibility that Captain Davy Mogaill would be in a mood to dragoon me off to a sentimental journey up Inwood way— to Nugent's bar, where a lonely flea might find his dog.

Or, I could drop by the Horny Poodle to see if I might get

a sideways answer from Benny at the bar on the matter of a customer called Johnny Halo. Or maybe I should take in vespers this day at the Crown of Thorns Holy Tabernacle. I could call up Ruby, to see if she was a game girl and willing to be my beard again in the cause of law and order.

I entered the business about the Crown of Thorns in my notebook, and the matter of Halo's trip—or trips—to the Horny Poodle. And the business of Halo's six-for-five scam, no doubt the principal source of revenue at the Neptune bar; of Chastity finding Celia's lost green hat where she had; of finding that Johnny Halo was not much of a one for bookkeeping.

I read over these new items after I had them all written down. Then I flipped through the pages of my notebook and read all the old items, hoping a few things might begin to relate. Which they did not.

How in the world had I managed such cockiness when Neglio asked about the progress of the case? *"With one or two more breaks, I think I'm close."* A detective is nothing but a sloppy cop when he depends on luck, which is hoping a display of confidence will bump things along; I have never known of a fastidious detective outside of a detective novel.

The subway pulled into the Seventh Avenue station in Brooklyn's Park Slope district. Twenty minutes more, I thought, and I would be back in Manhattan, where I would have to decide on someplace to go to display some confidence.

But I did not go directly to Manhattan.

Instead, I got off four stops later, at the Bergen Street station in South Brooklyn, and walked a few blocks up to the Atlantic Avenue offices of Wendell Prescott Real Estate Development Company, Inc., having no notion of what I might do or say should I find the man in.

But I suddenly did feel important purpose in being there on Atlantic Avenue that afternoon, relating to the fate of

DARK MAZE

Coney Island and art and murder, and Johnny Halo's question, *"You know what Prescott would do if he put up casinos here?"*

Ruby had answered, *"Hock, don't you see? They'd tear down Picasso's masterpiece."*

On the outside, Wendell Prescott's base of operations bore little more resemblance to his brother Daniel's glitzy Manhattan skyscraper headquarters than my own tenement in Hell's Kitchen. The company was located on the second floor of a two-storey brick and stucco loft building. The ground floor was called OK All-America Tile & Carpet Center.

The inside was not much to speak of. I climbed a flight of rubber-padded stairs and found a large room at the top, full of desks and some drafting tables and guys walking around with white shirts rolled up at the sleeves and bad neckties. A lot of them smoked, some pushed pencils around on paper, some talked loudly on the telephone; they all drank coffee out of styrofoam cups. The place reminded me of a detective squad room on a quiet day.

I asked one of the white shirts where Wendell Prescott kept himself. He pointed his thumb toward a glass doorway in back of him and said, "His secretary sits in there." So I pushed through the glass door and found myself face-to-face with Eileen Cream, according to a plastic nameplate on the edge of her crowded desk.

"Who are you?" she asked.

Her voice was thick from eating something, which I guessed was chocolates from an open Russell Stover box.

"My name is Neil Hockaday," I said. I showed her my gold shield. "I'd like to see Mr. Prescott."

"You don't look like a cop. Where's your uniform?"

"I'm plainclothes."

"How come you're not wearing a suit and tie?"

"I'm very plainclothes. Could I see Mr. Prescott now?"

She put on a pair of glasses and looked me up and down. "Hey, don't I know you?" she said. "Aren't you that cop in the newspaper? The one in charge of the big murder thing with the maniac running loose and all?"

"That's right. Now, I'd like to see Mr. Prescott."

"What for?"

Inspiration finally came. "Because I've got good reason to believe the maniac is gunning for Prescott next," I said. "Would you like to see your boss's dead body all over page one of tomorrow's *Post?*"

"Do I get a choice?" She popped a chocolate into her mouth and chewed it lustily.

I walked on past her toward the great man's office and she did not seem to mind. But Prescott did.

"Just who the hell do you think . . ."

Wendell Prescott stood up from behind his desk as he said this. Except for their different haircuts, Wendell and his brother Daniel—The Dan—were twins. They both had puffy faces as white as Maine potatoes, small feminine lips, high-pitched nasal voices, and pointy little muskrat teeth.

"Detective Hockaday," I said, walking to him. I showed him my shield. He glanced at it the way most people do and then took a look at my clothes; he did not seem to approve. "Sir, I think we need to talk."

"I doubt if my lawyer would think the same," he said.

"Your *lawyer?* I come up here to warn you about a crazed murderer who's probably after you right now, and what you do is you tell me about your *lawyer?*"

Prescott's puffy white face went even whiter. "Look, I . . ."

"You want to call up your lawyer, that's okay," I said. "Maybe I should just forget about you. Do I look like I care if a rich real estate guy gets popped by some maniac?"

By this time I was making a big impression on Prescott's sense of self-preservation. He relented and allowed, "Well, maybe it'd be okay," and he sank back into his seat and waved his hand around saying, "Make yourself comfortable."

Wendell's private office was small but poshy. There was an Oriental rug on the floor, dark red with blues and beiges in it. And a large desk with a green leather top, some lithographs of old New York street scenes on one wall, a sofa and matching wing chair upholstered in soft navy blue corduroy and even a mahogany liquor cabinet. It was a room I would have liked for myself, except for a framed photograph on the other wall of a grinning George Bush dressed up in his inauguration tux and flanked by the Prescott twins.

I walked up to the photo and said, "It's really hard to tell you guys apart. I mean you and your brother."

"My brother and I are very different men," Prescott said. There was a catch in his voice that reminded me of what Johnny Halo had said about the rivalry between Daniel and Wendell.

"Well, you've got different hairdos," I said.

"Dan's hair is too long and it's all feathery, like he's some heartthrob on a soap opera," Prescott said, the catch rising. His own hair was cut in a standard corporate style. "And that's the least of our differences."

"I like that one over there," I said, pointing to the navy blue wing chair. "Would you mind if we sat down now, sir? And would you have something to drink?"

Prescott looked at his wristwatch, so I looked at my own. His was a silver Cartier tank model. My brand ended in the letters *ex,* but not like in Rolex.

To help him make up his mind, I said, "Have a heart, Mr. Prescott. It's almost five and time for cocktails and I've been on my feet for hours out in Coney Island. I met a lot of people out there who don't much like the idea of your tearing everything down in Astroland and shoving them aside just to maybe put up casinos. You might say they're violently opposed to the idea."

I was then invited to sit in the blue chair. Prescott opened the liquor cabinet and asked if I might want a taste of his twenty-one-year-old Macallan's single-malt Scotch whiskey.

"Is the Pope Catholic?" I answered. He poured us each a jar and then sat down across from me on the blue sofa and regarded me with his cool, watery eyes as if considering me for a major role in the cement foundation of his next building project.

"A lot of those people out in Coney Island," Prescott said, "would like nothing better than for me to improve the neighborhood with casino gambling."

"What people? You mean that dwarf they call Big Stuff? What do you pay him to peddle your propaganda anyway?"

"I don't know if I like the turn this chat of ours is taking. Maybe I should call in my lawyer, Detective . . . Hockaday, is it?"

But Prescott made no move for his telephone.

"You know the name and you know exactly who I am," I said. "But go call your lawyer. I'm not the one who'll get his bill in the mail. Maybe the counselor can help us figure out our problem."

Prescott put back his drink and grinned at me. It looked as sincere as George Bush's grin. As sincere as a cheap toupee.

"It strikes me you're the only one with a problem here, Hockaday. Which I think you've already solved, all by yourself. After all, here you sit drinking my whiskey and pumping me for God-only-knows-what on the pretext that I'm somehow on line to be the next tabloid murder sensation."

"Oh, that's no pretext," I said. "Murder and real estate have a way of finding each other in New York."

"Would you take another drink?" Prescott asked me. "Never mind, I know about the Pope."

He got up and fixed us two more. And when he sat down again, he looked ten years older. He shook his head and drank half his whiskey.

"Hockaday, don't confuse me with my brother, Dan. You and I have got no quarrel at all about him, ethically or aesthetically. I know that flashy operation of his over there in Manhattan never got started up by virgin birth, all right? But like I told you, we're different men. I run a clean shop here. Just look around, man. Do I look like the kind of a guy they call The Wendell?"

"You've got me on that, sir." I tipped my glass to him and then sipped.

Prescott shook his head sadly again. "There's no way I'm winding up like The Dan. No way. First, you see, there's no bimbo in my life like he's got and *my* wife isn't hiring any press agents or divorce lawyers. Second, you can see for yourself I'm not in any danger of going bankrupt like my brother from carrying too much expensive overhead. I do indulge myself in the very best whiskey, however."

"Indulgences must never be hesitant," I said.

Prescott now tipped his glass to me. Then said, "You know, Dan's not actually a bad guy. At least he never was when we were growing up together, here in Brooklyn. He's just stupid. You'd be surprised how many rich people are stupid. The world listens to them, though. Why, I don't know."

I thought about that a minute and said, "In many cases, that's how the rich get richer. Take that wife of your brother's. How smart is she?"

"Dumb as a hydrant."

"I read in the paper just the other day how some publisher is forking over a million dollars to put her name on a ghost-written novel all about the glamorous world of the rich and foolish."

"Well, there you are, and I expect the peasants will lap it up," Prescott said. "Here's to business in a rich and foolish country, long may her banner wave."

"I'll drink to that."

"Maybe you understand why I want to invest in gambling

casinos," Prescott said. "It's one of the first places fools go
to part with their money."

There was a knock at the door, and Eileen Cream stepped
in. "If you don't need anything else today, I'm going home
now, Mr. P." Then she looked at me and asked, "So, the
boss going to get hacked to death tonight, or what?"

Prescott answered, "For heaven's sake, Eileen, I'm going
to be just fine. Detective Hockaday had his fun. Now run
along home and try to save some of the gossip for the
newspapers."

When she left, Prescott looked a little whiter in the face
than usual. He asked me, "Well, what about it?"

"Have you heard the news about the homeless artist the
police are looking for in connection with all the murders
lately?"

"Of course I have. They call him Picasso."

"There's a painting of his at Astroland."

Prescott cut me off. "I know all about that. When my
office was out recruiting people in Coney Island to pass out
handbills for casino gambling, this dwarf you're talking
about . . ."

"Big Stuff."

"That's him. Anyway, he came by here one day asking a
lot of questions. And telling us all about Coney Island and
what a great artist this guy called Picasso was. And I mean
was, as in has-been."

"What kind of questions did he ask?"

This put a little color into Prescott's potato face. He said,
"Oh, just a lot of things that weren't any of his damn
business. Which is exactly what I told him."

"Have you ever been out there to see Picasso's painting?
It's on the front of a spook house called Fire and Brimstone."

"Sounds real scary, Hockaday. But the answer is no, I
haven't been out to see the great has-been artist's handi-

work. Why should I? I don't own the Fire and Brimstone, or anything else in Astroland." Then Prescott grinned like the president and added, "Not yet, anyway."

"I guess not. I hear you've got a competitor out there in Coney for the carnival property along the boardwalk. A guy called Johnny Halo."

Prescott laughed at that. Then he got up, poured himself another drink and offered one to me. I declined. He walked unsteadily back to the sofa and sat down heavily.

He grinned again and told me something he might never have said if his lawyer had been with us, or if the whiskey were not so good. Or maybe he wanted me to know, maybe he was afraid. He said, "I know Johnny Halo. Halo's no trouble to me, or my plans."

And I congratulated myself. I had come here on instinct and I had played Wendell Prescott by instinct, and with a little good luck and good whiskey I had now penetrated one of the important lies.

"May I use your telephone, sir?" I asked.

"So long as it's local," Prescott said, slurring his words.

"Oh it's local, all right."

I got up from my chair and stepped over to Prescott and said, "Maybe you ought to lie down. You look a little rocky."

"I don't mind if I do."

He lay down and shut his eyes and by the time I was across the room to his desk he was snoring.

I dialed Central Homicide in Manhattan. Captain Mogaill was still there. I asked him to arrange an immediate round-the-clock police guard for Wendell Prescott, both at his business premises on Atlantic Avenue and his home on Montague Street.

Then I stepped out into Eileen Cream's empty office. There was no shortage of records in the file cabinets off to the side of her desk. I looked through them long enough to confirm the lie.

And then I sat tight for about fifteen minutes. A pair of Brooklyn uniforms arrived and took over custody of Sleeping Beauty on the blue sofa.

Back at the Bergen Street subway station, I telephoned Ruby at the theatre while I waited on the platform for the Manhattan-bound F train.

She was frantic.

"Hock, this is too much!" Her voice was high, and on its way to a screech. "I've never . . ."

"Take a breath, Ruby. Then tell me slow. What's the matter?"

I heard her trying to catch her breath.

"Something came in the mail this afternoon," she said.

"And?"

"Addressed to *me,* at the *theatre!"*

"What?"

"It's a plain white envelope, Hock, with an upside-down flag stamp! Just like the one that came to your apartment the other day, the one with that Polaroid of a painting by Picasso."

"The painting of Dr. Reiser?"

"Yes."

I heard Ruby crying now. And I started to think of the people who knew we were close, and who among them might have passed this knowledge on to Picasso; who among them knew where Picasso was.

I asked Ruby, "Did you open it yet?"

"No," she said. "I was waiting for you to call."

"Open it."

Ruby put down the telephone. I heard her footsteps fade out, then fade back in.

Then the sound of ripping paper.

And Ruby, crying. "Hock! Oh my God, Hock! This is just horrible, horrible . . ."

"Ruby, what is it? Take it slow and easy. Just tell me."

"It's another Polaroid . . . horrible!"

"A photo of another painting?"

"Yes . . ." Her voice trailed off in tears.

"Who's in the painting, Ruby?"

"I can't tell exactly. There's a naked man . . . with something like spikes in his head, and there's blood running down his face and his chest. . . . The blood, all the blood!"

"Easy, Ruby."

She took a deep breath and said, "He's hanging, from a wooden cross . . ."

And I knew.

"All right. That's enough, Ruby. You can put the picture down, you don't have to look at it anymore."

My train pulled into the station. I would have to board it, it was the quickest way to get where I now had to be. There were only seconds.

"Listen carefully, Ruby," I said. I gave her the number at Central Homicide, along with the address of the Crown of Thorns Holy Tabernacle in Times Square. "Talk to Captain Mogaill for me, tell him I'm on my way to the church. Tell him I'll need a murder scene investigation unit to meet me here."

Ruby said, "Got it. And please, Hock, promise you'll call me later."

"I will. I'm going to need you."

TWENTY-ONE

A police photographer was snapping off shots of the blasphemy behind the altar. Logue was there with a small swarm of detectives, uniforms, and forensics officers. He was smoking a cigar. So was everybody else, except for a pale young fat guy sitting next to Logue in a red plush chair.

The fat guy was dressed in a shiny black suit and string tie. His sandy hair was piled up in a double pompadour and hardened with spray. He held a white leather-bound bible in his lap and every so often he lunged forward and shouted, "Flaming fire shall taketh vengeance on them that knoweth not our Lord Jesus Christ!"

One of the uniforms tapped Logue's shoulder when he saw me come steaming in. Logue turned and waved.

I was sweaty and breathless after running four blocks from the subway station at Sixth and Forty-second. Now the sight behind the altar—and the stink—was making me dizzy. Logue knew just what to do.

"Here you go, Hock—you're going to need one of these babies," he said. He pulled a Dutch Masters panatella from the breast pocket of his suit coat and then lit it for me with a

256

Zippo. "That poor sod hanging on the big stick there, he went and crapped himself up pretty good when he got the business."

The guy in the chair had himself another outburst. This time it was, "The sword of our almighty Lord shall striketh down all apostates!"

Logue looked down at him and snarled, "Jesus H. Christ, can't you never shut the hell up?" Then he flicked some hot cigar ash on his wrist.

"Ouch!" the guy hollered, rubbing himself. "Ouch, God damn it!"

Logue said to me, "Sounds like the Rev is finally coming around, don't it? When we first come in, he was talking in tongues."

The cigar was making me feel better. I could have used another taste of Prescott's Scotch, though.

I looked at Logue, then at the Rev rubbing himself, then at the blasphemy. I crossed myself and asked Logue, "How do you think this one plays?"

"You tell me, Hock. We ain't touched nothing here yet, on account of my orders are to wait for you to join the party." Logue leaned over and jabbed the young guy's collarbone. "What do you say, Rev? This what you'd call a case of all hell breaking loose?"

Logue laughed at this and so did a couple of the uniforms standing near us. The butt of the joke only rocked back and forth in his chair, poker-faced.

I looked at him fondling his white bible, then I asked Logue, "Who is he?"

"Say hello to the Most Reverend Billy-Boy Miracle, Hock. Believe it or not, that's what it says on his driver's license from Arkansas." Then Logue said to Miracle, "Rev, this here is Detective Neil Hockaday. He's the one I told you about with the rubber hose."

"Thanks," I said to Logue, who shrugged. Then, to the reverend, "Reverend Miracle?"

He looked up at me with his sallow poker face and said solemnly, "Are you written in the book of life, Detective Hockaday?"

"Quit busting our chops, padre," Logue said. "Detective Hockaday and me, we're a couple of regular shamrock Catholics, okay? We belong to the biggest show in town. So we won't be needing your little tent."

I took Logue by the arm and pulled him off to the side of the altar. A uniform moved in close to the Most Reverend Miracle.

"So what do you have, Logue?"

"A perp is what."

"That cracker?"

"Look, he'll do. You got Slattery at the *Post* and everybody else up your back. Maybe a nice loony perp from Arkansas can take some pressure off?"

"How about you just tell me what happened?"

"Fifteen minutes ago, we get here. The door's open and we figure somebody's inside, so we slip in quiet. Right away we seen what you see, and smell what you smell. Also, there's Billy-Boy standing right about where we're standing, beholding this sick thing. He turns around and notices all us cops. Then Billy-Boy gets the very bright idea to flop down on the floor and have himself one lovely holy-rolling spastic screaming fit. Too bad you missed out on that, Hock."

"Did you read him yet?"

"Well, we put him in the chair and we tried. But he don't say he understands his rights, he don't say he wants a lawyer. All he does is start spieling the scriptures, which you heard yourself."

I looked over at the glassy-eyed Miracle. I puffed my cigar. "Maybe he looks good," I said, "but I don't think that's our maniac."

"To tell you the truth, me neither." Logue shrugged.

"He might've been innocently standing here drooling over a bare-assed dead guy, then in waltzes a gang of cops and Billy-Boy is suddenly mortified so he goes into his act," Logue said. "He wouldn't be the first Jesus jumper who's a homo and a pervo, right? Besides which, there's eight million stories in the naked city."

"You've got a very prurient imagination, Logue."

"I think it's on account of all the freaking opera my old lady plays on the radio."

"Could be," I said. "Come on, let's take a look up there."

Logue followed me to the altar, then around behind it to where the naked corpse was lashed at the wrists, waist and ankles to a tall wooden crucifix.

Dark brown blood streaked his face. There was a knife stuck in the left breast, the blade sunk into his heart. The smell was overpowering now.

I scraped a patch of blood that had dripped down from his chest to his toes. "It's not sticky anymore," I said.

"Yeah, he's been hanging a while," Logue said.

I would not have recognized him by looking at his face. Not with all that blood and the agony that had twisted the features.

But I knew.

And there was no mistaking the meaning behind the words penned on a plain white envelope stuffed between the dead man's blood-caked ankles: WHAT HAPPENS TO HALOS.

Logue was looking at me. He said, "A penny for your thoughts."

I was about to answer when I heard Inspector Neglio call my name. He stood in the aisle, holding a handkerchief to his nose. A uniform gave him a cigar.

"Save your money," I said to Logue.

I walked down from the altar and stepped over to Billy-Boy Miracle. I looked at his pale clean hands folded on top of his bible and said, "Son, I know you didn't have anything to do with this. Your hands are spotless."

Miracle looked up at me. His eyes were red and wet.

"Reverend Miracle, can you help me on this? Anything you might know?"

He lunged forward in his chair and shouted, "Whosoever obeyeth not the gospel of our Lord Jesus Christ shall be punished with everlasting damnation! Whosoever is not found written in the book of life shall be cast into the boiling lake of fire!"

I left him shouting in his chair and walked over to where Neglio stood. I said, "Let's get some air."

"Yeah, Hock, let's."

I left Logue to supervise the scene. Neglio and I went out to the street where his black Chrysler waited, along with a couple of television camera crews—so far—and the ever-dependable Slattery yelling after us about a statement.

A half-dozen uniforms formed a walking circle around Neglio and me, leading us toward the Chrysler. The air on the street was hot with strobe lights. We slid into the backseat of the Chrysler; the driver gunned the engine. And the car sped west across the sealed-off block of Forty-first Street, then turned downtown onto Ninth Avenue.

I leaned forward and told the driver, "Go to Thirty-fourth, pal, then take a right. Right again on Tenth and crawl slow along the east side of the avenue, real slow so I can check the side streets."

When I sat back, Neglio said quietly, "Question time, Hock."

"Ask away. You've got until I get to my stop."

"Let's start with the corncob in the chair back there at the church," Neglio said. "Who is he and why was he yelling from the bible?"

"I guess he's the pastor of the cracker box," I said. "He discovered the murder you saw and smelled. I think he's a young, frightened thumper and that's about it. If he's got any ulterior motive for the theatrics, it's only publicity."

"Publicity for what?"

"Logue's holding him as a perp. Talk it over with him.

Logue seems to think maybe we'd all get a little more breathing space if the press bought it that we had a major break in the case."

"What's the thumper's name?"

"Get this: the Most Reverend Billy-Boy Miracle, direct from Arkansas."

"Beautiful," Neglio said. He thought for a second, and we stopped for the light at Thirty-fourth Street. "But you're thinking it's only a cheap turnaround collar?"

"Yeah, I am. I don't see guys like Slattery buying the Reverend Miracle as our real McCoy maniac. So, I don't see the percentage of even holding Billy-Boy. Besides, if he is spouting off just to get his name in the papers, what do you suppose happens?"

"What else?" Neglio said. "Billy-Boy winds up with more sheep to fleece, which means he gets richer."

"It's sweet if you look at it his way."

Neglio nodded and the light changed. Then he said, "Next question: who's the dead guy on that cross?"

"Johnny Halo."

"What?"

"The one and only," I said. "What did you dig up on him so far?"

Neglio groaned. "He's connected, all right. But sometimes that's all they need to know."

"They?"

"Know-nothing reporters who think every guinea in New York who maybe once got a favor from the outfit is some kind of a major hood. The Mafia Writers of America."

"Don't take it so personal, Inspector. Just tell me how Halo was connected."

"Strictly errand-boy, that's all the guy ever was, Hock. The biggest thing he ever did was run cash through his bar once in a while that a friend maybe didn't want to put in the bank. He's forever a small-time wise-guy. He never had the *cojones* to make the big score."

Neglio paused. Then he asked, "Or was that about to change?"

"Yeah, I think it was."

Neglio waited for me to say something, but I did not feel like elaborating since we were now headed up Tenth Avenue and I was intent on looking east down the side streets.

Finally, Neglio said, "You're just going to leave it like that?"

"For now," I said.

At the corner of Thirty-eighth Street, I saw what I had hoped to see. I had the driver stop. "Here's where I get out," I said.

Neglio took a long look down the black street full of dark shapes and said, "So it's back to your briar patch, Hock? Lots of luck."

"Go tell the mayor he shouldn't worry, that I'm closing in," I said, starting out the door. "Meanwhile, Inspector, with all due respect, if I were you I would get myself and my big black car out of this part of Hell's Kitchen."

I walked slowly down Thirty-eighth, stepping over and around broken glass and used condoms and bullet casings and smashed syringes toward the gang of junkies I had seen from the corner. They were lounging in the same doorway where I saw my snitch, Rat, only the other night, the night Benito Reyes was killed, seven blocks up Tenth Avenue.

Once again, here was I—a perfect slob of a detective. Once again trusting in the uncertain rhythms of luck and instinct. Because I am an artist among cops, not a scientist.

It turned out to be my night.

There was Rat himself, nestled contentedly in a tangle of ten or so ragged men and women nodding off to communal oblivion that had come from what the heroin mainliners in my neighborhood call "passing the prick"—the needle.

Rat is the ultimate fatalist of his breed; even worse, he is out of fashion. Today's politicians and journalists are appalled by crack cocaine, and something called "ice" looks to be next season's dread. But old-fashioned dopers like Rat have never gone away, and old-fashioned cops see that their ranks are hardly thinning. They are still out there injecting every day, seeking the rush of yesterday's horror; they stare at their own blood filling a syringe, mixing with silvery junk. And thousands and thousands of Rats do not give a drug czar's damn whether they live or die after pushing the plunger down.

I stood across the street from the doorway where Rat and his gang lay like dying horses in their wary junkie sleep: eyelids at half-mast, hands clutching valuables and tucked into armpits, knees loose and feet ready to run. I made a smacking sound with my lips. Heads rose in response, sniffing the air.

"Rat!" I called.

I saw him put his hands on his chest, as if saying, Who, me? He looked my way. Again I called, "Rat!"

Then he picked himself up and stepped away from the pack, rubbing his nose with a sleeve. He did not look as he crossed the street. A taxi nearly struck him down; the driver shouted a curse at his dark shape.

"Hello, my friend," I said, taking his thin, cold fists into my hands. I opened the fingers of one fist and laid a crisp twenty-dollar bill across the palm. "I need your help tonight."

It had grown chilly and my words were followed by puffs of frosted air. Rat looked at these puffs with his liquid eyes, black and dilated. Then he looked up at me, trying to understand this reversal of our custom; it was usually he who came to me.

Rat was a head shorter than me and only a few years younger. His hair was black and gray, tied back in a ponytail. His rough and reddened face was high-boned, spotted by grime that had worn into the creases of his skin over the years. His thin brown lips puckered over parts of his mouth where teeth were missing.

Rat bent at the waist, as if he had suddenly broken. He slipped the twenty into his shoe and stood back up again.

"I am already fixed for the night, Hock," he said in his soft, slurry voice. "But I thank you for tomorrow's stake. I'll think of you in my technicolor dreams."

He gave me a mock salute.

"I'm looking for somebody in the cracks," I said. "It's what the twenty is for."

"Somebody I know?"

"A squatter," I said. "I think he's right here in the neighborhood. Have you heard of a man called Picasso?"

"Every serious person has."

"I don't mean the painter. Well, he's a painter. But I mean the guy in the newspapers, the guy the police are hunting in connection with the murders."

"I don't read newspapers, Hock. I've got enough vulgarity in my life."

"Please," I said. Then I described Charlie Furman to Rat. And then I got lucky.

"Yes, I've seen the man," Rat said.

"When?"

"Last fall, thereabouts."

"Where?"

"In this very street, Hock. But only once. And I only remember it now because of the beret you mentioned and because he carried something large and bulky under his arm. You say he's a painter?"

"Yes."

"Well, now that I think of it, it could have been an easel."

"Did you see where he went?"

"I had no reason for that," Rat said. "But I can tell you this about him: he was walking along talking in the fiercest way to somebody."

"That's Picasso, he does that," I said. "He's got some imaginary friend he's always talking to, or arguing with."

"No, this was nothing imaginary."

I thought, Of course not! There was Ruby's dream: *"What you see is an artist painting about death—not murdering, painting."* Picasso would have to know one real friend, at least one real and murderous friend.

I said, "Who was he with, Rat?"

"She wasn't much to look at. So in fact, I didn't."

"A woman?"

"She wore a coat, a big coat. I can't tell you what she looked like, I can't tell you anything about her."

I could see that Rat was honestly straining his memory. I believed him.

And I knew what I might do next to best puzzle this out.

I gave Rat another twenty and said good bye, then walked back to Tenth Avenue and up to my building at Forty-third. I checked the mailbox. Nothing but bills to ignore.

I climbed the stairs to my apartment where I put the newly gathered bills on the sideboard at the top of a mounting stack of other such appeals. Beside this lay Patrick Snoody's letter about my dying Uncle Liam.

Then I telephoned Ruby. "Remember how I said I'd be needing you?"

She said she would meet me in an hour.

I took a hot shower. Then I hauled out my best suit and tie and put them on.

Too bad about Celia, and I really mean that. But she went rotten on me, didn't she? Ho, ho, didn't she, though!

Damn straight.

And ain't I always said nobody beats the odds?

Damn straight I said that!

And who needs another one of them shrinkers with only questions and no answers? Ain't I always said fuck Dr. Freud? Ain't I?

But you think they'll listen, even now?

Hey, how do you like the balls on that Puerto Rican? I do my very best for him, I put my best observations on his windows. Like that pig I showed you that day—the essential fear I captured in that pig's eyes, remember?

How does he pay me off? In crummy sandwiches! Can you beat that? Not cash money like an honest hard-working artist deserves, sandwiches! You call that respect?

So, I don't respect him back. Him, I don't give the respect of oil on canvas. I give him calcimine on glass, the Puerto Rican bastard!

Johnny Halo! They ought to give me a medal for painting Johnny Halo like I done!

Damn straight.

Oh, this is some lovely bunch of coconuts I got in my broken-down life, hey?

Ain't it the truth?

Ain't I got the rest of my work cut out for me?

Ho, ho! One potato, two potato, three potato, four!

Five potato, six potato, seven potato, more!

TWENTY-TWO

I got over to Angelo's Ebb Tide before Ruby.

The dining room in back was filled with generally the same types who were inconvenienced the other night when Celia Furman took it in the neck and upset everybody's happy hour by being dead on her barstool. The crowd around the bar looked much the same as then, too—mostly the types that annoy Angelo so much. Which is maybe why he took the dim view of my good suit.

"Who went and died, Hock?"

"That is all too painfully obvious if you read the newspapers. What I want to know is, who went and killed everybody?"

"I didn't mean it like that."

"Yeah, I know."

"It's awful good to see you," Angelo said, rolling his eyes in disgust at the rest of the crowd. "How about the usual? The first round's on me."

"Thanks," I said. "I'll just have a red, before she gets here."

"Oh, so that's what's got you dressed to the nines tonight—a *she,* is it?"

"I forgot. You haven't met Ruby yet."

"Ruby's her name, is it?"

"You'll be seeing a lot of her."

"What, you're getting married again, Hock?"

"I didn't say that."

"And did I say anything against it? I happen to believe marriage is a fine institution. After all, it's a friendship recognized by the police."

I changed the subject by looking up at Charlie Furman's painting of his late wife Celia chatting with Angelo. I was surprised to see it still hanging up behind the bar. Angelo followed my gaze with his own as he turned and poured out my drink.

"Me, I would have thought that picture was bad luck," I said. "But I notice it hasn't scared off any business at all."

"Every night we got a full house since the murder," Angelo said. "The ones who were here that night, they come back the very next night. And the next. And they brought more of their friends with them. I don't know if I can take it much more."

"You can't take what, success? Stop complaining. The Ebb Tide's a hit."

"With this kind of bad crowd, sure. But you know how come?"

"No, I don't."

"They're packing my place because there was a splashy murder of a lady that made all the papers and the TV. So now they all got something to talk about besides real estate and what other joints they go to."

My stomach rumbled.

"You say something?"

"I said I haven't eaten anything since this morning." I looked at my watch. Ruby was late. Which was good. I had begun suspecting her of perfection. "How about getting me a table, Angelo."

"Stay up front here with me, so I can see the missus. You can take the table over there by the phone booth." Angelo signaled a busboy. "There's two guys there now waiting to pay their check."

"I'm really hungry, I want to order before she even gets here."

"What'll it be? I'll tell the kitchen myself."

"The hamburger platter."

"I'll have them toss on lots of extra stuff."

I finished my drink and thanked Angelo for the treat. Then when the table was clear, I sat down by the phone booth.

Which was when Ruby arrived.

I can say with confidence that every man in the place agreed with me at that moment: Ruby Flagg knows how to make an entrance. She was dressed all in black. Black dancer's slippers, black tights, black skirt, black blouse that dipped nicely in front, even a black raincoat. She stopped just inside the door, took off a pair of Ray-Bans, and smiled when she spotted me.

Ruby crossed through the bar, looking at nobody but me. She sat down and stretched her arms over the table and I touched her fingertips. I said, "Mind if I say wow?"

"You'd better," Ruby said. "I just showed all your pals in here that you have got your sorry self a sweetie."

"You think anybody's looking?"

"Take a look at that one."

Ruby pointed to Angelo standing behind the bar with his mouth open. When he saw me, Angelo made a circle with his thumb and forefinger and said, "You get one of these, Hock." We could hear him perfectly well since everybody at the bar had pretty much stopped talking to look at my sweetie and sorry old me.

"That's Angelo Cifelli, the best bartender in New York City," I told Ruby. "He owns the place. Also, he's something of a mother-man tonight."

"A what?"

"He thinks I ought to get married."

"Oh, then he's seen your apartment?"

"What's that supposed to mean?"

"Bachelors live like bears with furniture."

A waiter stopped by our table. Ruby ordered a *salade Niçoise* and a glass of red wine. I impressed her by ordering a seltzer.

"But right now, Hock, you don't look like a bear at all," Ruby said. "What's with the suit? I thought you said it was casual tonight."

"Casual for you. I've got someplace to go later."

"I thought as much. The Johnny Halo murder is all over the news already. Did you know?"

"I thought as much."

"Which is why I'm trying to get your mind off the case. You should have two or three minutes of every day when you don't think of dead bodies and paintings and psycho artists who send out Polaroids of their latest works. That would be healthy."

"Healthy is when you eat what you don't want, drink what you don't like and do what you'd rather not."

"Very funny, Hock." But Ruby only sighed. She opened her purse and took out the picture that Picasso had sent to her at the theatre and gave it to me. "By the way, where are you going later?"

"That's what I need to talk about."

The waiter returned with the wine and the seltzer and Ruby's miniature meal. And also the hamburger platter I had ordered earlier. This featured red-skin potatoes in sour cream and chives, three nice big shiny herrings, a hard-boiled egg, a dab of grilled mushrooms, two kosher pickles and a steaming medium-rare burger on an open kaiser roll.

Ruby looked at my platter and said, "You're going to eat that?"

"What can I tell you? I'm not a salad man."

"You don't know from health, but you know baseball," he said. "Didn't you ever hear of Satchel Paige's first rule of longevity?"

My mouth was full of what I liked, so Ruby did not wait for me to reply.

"He said, 'Avoid fried meats, which angry the blood.' "

"I'll try to remember that when I think something might be gaining on me."

Ruby sighed again. "Hock, what is it you need from me tonight?"

"For right now tonight, I want to talk out the case the way I see it playing. The lies and the motivations. And I'd like you to help me think it through, inside-out."

"Okay, but I'm no cop."

"I don't want a cop. I want a different kind of imagination."

"All right, where do we start?"

"Well there's four bodies . . ."

"Unless, of course," Ruby cut in, "there was news in *your* mailbox today."

"No, nothing like that. Bad news, though."

"What's wrong, Hock?"

"There was a letter this morning from Dún Laoghaire. My uncle is dying."

"Oh. I'm sorry. When are you flying over?"

"With this case?"

"Then let's get it solved quick," Ruby said. "Four bodies. All right, besides Picasso, what do Celia Furman, Dr. Reiser, Benito Reyes and Johnny Halo have in common?"

"All were significant to Picasso's suffering," I said. "But what's important here are money and lies. The money part's easy, it involves gambling. Celia was a gambler, and so was Halo."

Ruby said, "Then there's the little matter of this Wendell Prescott and his grand designs for casino gambling in Coney Island, Picasso's masterpiece be damned." She paused, then added, "Of course, Johnny Halo said that would only happen over his dead body."

"Famous last words. I remember thinking that at the time," I said. "Which is why I went out to Brooklyn today and paid a couple of very interesting visits."

I quickly filled Ruby in on my talks with Chastity at the Seashore Hotel and with Wendell Prescott at his real estate office. I also told her what Inspector Neglio had dug up on Halo. And I mentioned Chastity's intriguing green hat, and the intriguing lie I found while snooping through Eileen Cream's files.

"What do you make of the lie?" Ruby asked.

"It didn't surprise me that Halo was fronting for Prescott on all those property acquisitions in Coney. I halfway figured that out when I didn't find any deeds or title papers at Halo's bar or at his suite at the Seashore. And then, bingo, there was everything at Prescott's place filed under Johnny Halo Enterprises, which is owned by guess who."

"So Prescott just bought Halo's name?" Ruby said.

"Something like that. Prescott needed a real deep-dyed Coney type for his silent partner. Too many people out there had respect for Picasso's work, which casinos threatened. But it was more than that. Too many people out there would hate to see what little is left of the whole carny culture get wiped out by Prescott and his dreams of boardwalk glitz."

"And so Johnny Halo became the perfect cover for Wendell Prescott, the cover of perfect irony," Ruby said, smiling as she realized the ripeness of Halo's lie.

Picking up on her ironic thread, I said, "On the one hand, here's the neighborhood loan shark everybody loves to hate; on the other hand, here's this guy wearing his heart on his sleeve for poor old Coney Island."

"Reminds you of Nixon, doesn't it?" Ruby said. "The

voters hated Nixon's cheating guts on instinct, but they oved it when he waved that flag."

"So the boardwalk locals believed Halo because they oved his flag-waving, because why would such a creep lie about loving his dear old Coney?" I said. "And property owners just hanging on by their fingernails to money-losers n Astroland—owners with nothing left but pride and a sense of tradition—they sell out to Johnny Halo Enterprises."

"Naturally believing that means Johnny Halo himself," Ruby said, finishing my thought.

"Sure. They know Halo's a creep, but he happens to have money and, as lousy as he is, he's at least willing to be the keeper of the carny flame."

Ruby added, "And they figure sometimes in this world you have to deal with the devil—especially to keep the Prescott types from stealing your soul."

"And so that was Halo's lie."

"That's some convincing act," Ruby said.

"Not everybody bought it, remember."

"Well, no. Certainly not whoever killed him."

"And certainly not the other liar."

"The *other?*" Ruby stopped herself then and, judging by the earnest set to her face, she started thinking fast about all the crazy angles to the messy story I had been feeding her, one bite at a time. Finally she said, "You're talking about the dwarf?"

"What makes you think that?" But my expression told her she had guessed right.

She said, "Because the irony fits, I guess. Why should Halo be taking the only pose in all this? Here's Big Stuff the dwarf with his handbills, shilling for Wendell Prescott's dreams of casino glitz and outdoing his little brother Daniel and all. So, you're saying Big Stuff is a liar, too?"

"It's what I'm thinking," I said. "What I'm saying is, there's more than irony behind it."

"Like what more?"

"One day, Big Stuff went down to Prescott's place and asked lots of questions that Prescott didn't want answered."

"How do you know that?"

"While I was rattling Prescott, he let it slip between a few drinks," I said. "I really didn't think too much about it until just now."

Ruby waved for the waiter. She said, "Think about this: how hard would it have been for Big Stuff to find out exactly what you did about Halo being Prescott's front man?"

"Not especially hard, I imagine. Big Stuff is short on stature, but not brains."

"And something else," Ruby said. "What's the chance of Big Stuff being in touch with Picasso, despite what he says to the contrary?"

"The chances are good. He's a liar, after all."

"Sure he is. Then he's also maybe the one guy in this whole cast of characters who could lead you straight to Picasso, wherever he is."

"Could be," I said. "But then, there could be others in the cast who know . . ."

The waiter arrived. He cleared away our dishes and made so much noise about it there was no sense to us talking. When he was through, Ruby ordered another wine and I another seltzer.

"Chastity!" Ruby suddenly said. She looked up at the painting behind the bar—of Angelo in his white shirt and black vest, of Celia in green. "Chastity's got Celia's hat. She had to get it from the killer, or from Picasso. Or Chastity's the killer!"

"Nobody knows about the missing green hat, except the killer," I said. "And the killer wouldn't be wearing it. That would be nuts."

"And you think Chastity the whore is sane?"

"I don't know." I thought about Chastity's tight smile, the

one that came to her when I had questioned her at the Seashore. "But I do think she knows or suspects lots more than she's saying."

We were silent for a couple of long minutes, both trying hard to break through the haze of so many unsettled and incoherent facts. "You know," Ruby said finally, "you're back at square one. You've still got to find out where Picasso is squatting. That's the meaning of this whole thing."

"Don't I know it."

"I have this terrible feeling he's right under your nose somewhere, right here in Hell's Kitchen," Ruby said. "I mean, didn't Picasso tell you outright that he'd been following you around here for months?"

"Yes."

"Well! Then he's got to be here in the neighborhood."

"Of course he is. That's easy. But take a look around here someday—look at the vacant tenements and warehouses, blocks and blocks of them. It's not like it was when I was a kid here, that's for sure. It's all different, all empty. It would take months to search all the empty places in Hell's Kitchen."

Months and maybe years to search the empty places of my youth in Hell's Kitchen; months and years to search the hollow places in my life.

"I see your problem. It's like trying to find somebody from an old picture."

An old picture.

Did I have my wallet? I reached into my suit coat, past my shoulder holster to the inside pocket. And there it was.

I took it out. Inside was the black-and-white snapshot from a long-ago summer. There was Celia Furman when she was young and beautiful and high-spirited, on the board-walk at Coney Island with two young men; one of them her troubled husband Charlie, the other unknown.

But now I knew.

I did not tell Ruby about the book of matches I had found in Johnny Halo's room. Or about why I wanted to look the way I did. Or about the time last fall, when Rat saw Picasso walking Thirty-eighth Street with an unknown woman.

There was no time for all that.

TWENTY-THREE

She scuffed up to me on her lizard-skin platform shoes and banged her tray down on the bar next to where I sat looking over the smoke-filled scene. I was busy noticing what I had failed to notice before: the staircase way off in the back of the place, back behind the now-empty stage. I thought as much.

What *she* now noticed was my nice suit. And the fact of where I was looking with great interest. Apparently deciding this time that I was no clyde, she asked in her husky cigarette voice, "Feeling active tonight? Maybe I can help."

I smiled at her and looked at her bare chest, which made me feel cold. Then I reached into my suit coat for my wallet and took out a hundred dollars of the city's hard-earned money and asked, "What's your name, doll?"

"Candi," she said.

"Candy's nice."

"It's with an *i.*"

"Well I don't think I'll be needing to write you a love letter, doll."

She had not taken her eyes off the cash in my hand. She said, "So tell me what you do need."

"Friends of mine out in Vegas, they say it's a good square room you've got upstairs here. They say I should ask around for Moe Stein when I'm in town and, like you say, feeling active."

She plucked the hundred from my fingers and said, "So maybe I could go find him for you."

"Good idea."

She scuffed down a few spaces along the brass rail to where the bartender with the kidney bean head was pouring a martini for some guy dressed in a lime-colored, double-knit jacket and a flower-pattern shirt with a big collar. The clyde in lime was chatting up one of Candi's topless comrades, who looked like she had heard his story a few thousand times before.

Candi tapped the bartender's shoulder and pointed down my way. I heard her say, "Benny, the guy over there in the suit, he's from Vegas and he's asking after Moe and he sounds like he swims with the whales."

Benny put on his bifocals and looked over at me, and so I snapped off a salute. This did not make him look any more pleased to be seeing me again, even if maybe I actually was a big swimmer.

He wiped his hands with a towel and reached under the bar and picked up his .44 and tucked it into his belt. Then he came over to where I sat.

"I remember you, you're buddies with that psycho from Coney Island," he said. "What's with this I'm hearing you're from out West?"

"Everybody's got to be from someplace," I said.

"Yeah, only you don't look like somebody who ever even seen the other side of the freaking Hudson."

"Benny, you're making me feel bad. I don't like this suspicious mood you're in."

"I don't like reading this scary stuff I see in the papers about your boyfriend Picasso."

"Listen, you think all this bad publicity doesn't make me nervous, too, not to mention chagrined?" I opened up my suit coat so that Benny could see the butt of my .38 sticking out from its holster. I will do this under certain circumstances and everybody has always assumed what I want them to assume, that I am anything but a cop.

Benny patted the grip of the .44 sticking out from the top of his belt and said, "Well, you can't never be too careful when you're in the middle of one of these New York crime waves."

"That's so true," I said, closing my suit coat.

Benny was now at ease with me. He said, "It's the Johnnie Walker red for you, am I not wrong?"

I laid out a hundred-dollar bill on the bar—more from the crime-wave fund—and kept my hand over it. I said, "You're right."

"I never forgot a man's drink yet." Benny built me a double red, neat as I like it.

"Neither do I; you're a Bushmill's man," I said, pushing the hundred towards him. "Go ahead and have one for yourself."

"Thanks, I don't mind."

He poured himself the Irish and said, "Candi tells me you want to see Moe. How come?"

"I'm in the active mood."

Benny looked at me now without a trace of the old suspicion and I smiled at him pleasantly. Then he looked at his wristwatch. I looked past him, toward the staircase way in the back of the place where I now noticed some fellow suits were walking up and down, coming and going.

He finally said, "Well, I don't see why not. Moe's in his dressing room, probably *schtupping* old Delilah before he has to get up on stage with his act. You remember Moe's mentalist act?"

"I remember."

Benny called Candi over and gave her a key on a big ring and informed her that I was an "all-right guy," and that she should escort me to Moe's dressing room and tell him so. Candi crooked a finger at me and said, "Okay, you, c'mon. It's this way."

I followed her as she scuffed around the bar, then past banquettes with moony clydes making time with bored topless B-girls drinking phony champagne in the flattering low light, then past candle-topped tables circling the stage and filling up with customers since it was now nearing show time, then finally to a door behind the back staircase. The door had a gold star painted on it, and there were blue circus letters that spelled out, THE GREAT MORRIS—MENTALIST EXTRAORDINARY.

Candi slipped the key into the lock and opened the door to a narrow front waiting area where there was nobody waiting. Mismatched chairs and end tables with ashtrays lined knotty-pine walls decorated with yellowing posters of a tuxedo-clad Great Morris in his salad days. The young Morris had dazzling white teeth and brilliantined hair and was posed waving a wand over rabbits leaping out of his magician's top hat. And below his picture were the particulars of long-ago gigs in clubs and carnival midways all over Michigan, Ohio, Pennsylvania, and New Jersey.

"Hey, Moe, you got a visitor out here!" Candi hollered this in the general direction of beads hanging in an open passage to the actual dressing room. Delilah stepped out from behind the beads. I do not think I would have recognized her except for the vintage chestless bathing suit and her two big, rigid silicone breasts, which she covered up with her arms when she saw me through her thick black horn-rimmed spectacles. Candi asked her, "Is Moe back in there with you, honey?"

Delilah standing there in the harsh fluorescence of a bare

ceiling light looked every bit a woman on the verge of
collecting her Social Security. She was only halfway caked
and powdered and lipsticked for the show, revealing a face
and throat full of lacy wrinkles, and her thin white hair was
matted down under a nylon mesh cap; the puffy blond coif I
remembered from a few nights ago was no doubt taking five
on a wigstand until its stage call.

"He's taking a catnap," Delilah said. Then she pointed
my way and asked Candi, "Who's that?"

But before Candi could answer, there was Moe Stein's
gravelly voice from behind the beads: "What's going on out
there?" Then the sound of his shuffling feet, then Moe Stein
in mules and boxer shorts and a sleeveless undershirt with
different colored food stains standing next to Delilah and
looking me up and down. Then he said to Candi, "You going
to introduce me to this here visitor in the nice suit, or
what?"

Candi said, "Benny says I should bring you this guy here
from Vegas, he says he's an all-right guy."

"Oh he is, is he?" Moe gave Delilah a light pinch on her
rump and said to her and Candi both, "How about you's
two ladies getting lost out of here for a while?"

Delilah went back through the beads and made some
rummaging sounds, then emerged wearing sunglasses and a
man's fedora and a long coat. Then she and Candi left me
with The Great Morris in his underwear, which highlighted
the sagging physique of a man in his early sixties: pot belly,
skinny-bird legs with liver-spotted knees and bony, rounded
shoulders.

The Great Morris said in a friendly way, "You, come on
inside and let's have a talk." He turned and swept the beads
open with one hand and motioned me through with the
other.

His inner room was about twice the size of the waiting
area. The walls were cinder block—painted creamy white—
but the room seemed warm with its green and beige rug and
softly lit floor lamps. At one end there were twin dressing

tables with tiny light bulbs arcing over mirrors, a nearby sink and a clothes rack that held a top hat and a tuxedo and some women's things on hangers. The other end of the room held a couple of cozy-looking easy chairs and an old velvet sofa with tassels and fringe. There was a small refrigerator and a table that held liquor and glasses, cigars and cigarettes and ashtrays, a black rotary telephone and newspapers from the last several days. I sat down in one of the chairs and Moe Stein settled into a corner of the sofa, lifted up his bird legs and stretched them out.

He said, "So welcome to the Horny Poodle. What can we do for you, Mister . . . What's your name, anyways?"

"Hockaday."

"Mr. Hockaday." He licked his lips like he could taste the name, then he gazed up at the ceiling as if in deep contemplation. "The name sounds sort of familiar. Ain't I seen you someplace before?"

"I doubt it," I said. "But the other night I caught your mentalist act. Funny, I thought you looked like somebody I'd seen a long time ago."

"Oh, is that right?" Stein put his feet on the floor, leaned forward to the table and poured himself two fingers of bourbon and splashed it with water. He asked me, "Drink?"

I passed.

Stein sipped his bourbon and said, "Well, Mr. Hockaday, it's a small world, ain't it? Maybe we got some of the same kind of friends out in Vegas—the active kind?"

"Or maybe the kind who aren't so active anymore."

Stein gave me a suspicious look now, like Benny had looked at me earlier. He said, "How come my genius partner sent you back here to me? You want my autograph or what?" He laughed a snorty laugh.

"Maybe later." I did not laugh, which made Stein uncomfortable. "I'm here tonight to catch your show upstairs, which I guess means you're going to have to decide if you want to clear me for the action."

Stein was coy. "What's this action you're talking about."

"Well, for one thing, Celia Furman tells me you run a pretty square craps table."

The glass of bourbon slipped from Stein's hand and landed in his lap, spilling all over the fly in his boxers. He stood up and brushed himself and pointed to the newspapers on the table and sputtered, "Hey! I know who in hell you are, you're that cop they're writing about!"

I said calmly, "That's correct."

"We got nothing going upstairs," Stein said.

"You're operating a casino right in the middle of Times Square, which takes some real balls."

"Look . . ."

"Cut it," I said. "If I wanted, I could get a warrant in about ten minutes flat and close you down and bundle you and Benny off to Riker's Island for the night. But maybe I want something else."

"What's that?" Stein sat down. He poured himself more bourbon. I let him drink it down before answering him.

Then I told him a couple of lies, which is kosher since the law only requires me to tell the truth when I am under oath in court. "I know all about your casino, from the late Johnny Halo. Even old Charlie Furman mentioned it once or twice, the crazy bastard."

He reacted to these names like they were stones being thrown at him. "Charlie! Oh God, Charlie!"

And Stein now looked like something far more painful than a little bourbon and water had caught him in the crotch. His eyes darted around the room, like he was measuring off the distance between where he sat shaking and where he might go stick his head in case he had to heave. He said weakly, "I don't understand . . ."

I took out my wallet and showed him the snapshot from the happy, carefree summer of '54.

Stein's eyes filled with tears, and then the tears overflowed. He did not bother wiping them away, and the tears ran down his chest over his undershirt and collected in splotches on top of his pot belly. I let him hold the old snapshot. He looked at it for several seconds before handing it back to me and asking, "Where'd you get that?"

"Off the late Celia Furman."

"Celia . . . Oh God, my sweet, sweet Celia!"

I poured another two fingers of bourbon and water and gave it to Stein and he took it back in one swallow. He waited until he was calm again, or as calm as he would get that night. Then he said, "What do you want out of me, Hockaday?"

"I want you to tell me a story."

"What makes you think I got a story to tell?"

"Like I said, I think I can get a warrant in about ten minutes, and then you and Benny will be sleeping on steel cots up at Riker's."

"That don't faze me now." Stein said this like he meant it, and I believed he certainly did.

"No?" I decided to lie again, bald-faced and sideways or any other way that would rattle Moe Stein. "Then how about if I just walk out of here now and let Picasso come after you tonight like he's already gone after Johnny Halo and your own sweet Celia?"

Stein paled and said, "Picasso . . . " And that showed me he not only knew Charlie Furman, but that he knew Furman was also Picasso.

"You read the newspapers," I said to him. "Let's not forget how Picasso went after the guy in the bodega over in Hell's Kitchen, or the shrink at Bellevue. And here's a news flash, Moe: I've ordered a police guard out for Wendell Prescott—you know, the big real estate developer who wants to bring your kind of casino action to Coney Island?"

"Ain't I got the right to police protection, too?"

"It doesn't work that way, Moe. First you help me like Prescott did, then I decide if I feel like helping you.

Otherwise, I let the chips fall any old way. Which in your case, I would hate to imagine."

Stein began dribbling. His hands shook and he again dropped his drink, and I again had learned something useful: Moe Stein saw reason for Wendell Prescott to fear the wrath of Picasso.

"You want me to fix you another one?" I asked.

He ignored me and he ignored his wet lap. He managed to say, "What's the story you want to hear?"

I held up the snapshot and said, "Way back in 1954, here we see the three musketeers. And now today I see before me one of you going to pieces whenever I mention the names of the other two. I naturally ask myself, What's wrong with this picture?"

Stein recovered enough of his composure for a last stand at belligerence. "You sound like a cop who's got all the answers, Hockaday. So what do you need with me?"

"Let's just say I've got suspicious questions. That's not near as interesting as answers."

"Maybe you should answer me this: if I tell you a story, do I get police protection like Prescott got?"

"Depending on the story, I'll consider it."

Now Stein had nothing to lose and everything to gain. "Let me have that drink," he said. I fixed it for him because he was still too shaky. He drank down half.

"You hear the phone ringing in here?" he asked.

"No."

"I got telephones in all my rooms—this one, my apartment, and everywhere I go. None of them ring. Back in my prime, I was known to be good for taking ten grand on a number, personal. Now I can't get a jingle out of all my phones. Guys used to call me up from all over the world for odds, or point spreads. Now, zip.

"So get a load of me now and ask yourself, Ain't I paid?" Stein started blubbering again and this time it was because of fear. "Look at me sitting here in this cheap hi ya sailor dump trying to jolly up the clydes with shows I done when I was a good-looking kid with teeth and a flat stomach back in the midwest. Ain't I paid?"

"Paid for what?" I asked.

"You want a story, you have to listen to it the way I tell it," Stein said.

"Okay."

"I was working the Bob-Lo boat out of Belle Isle in Detroit this one year, right after the war. Sleight of hand stuff, close-ups and like that. This guy likes the way I'm doing the act and says he'd like to book me for a club he's starting up on the East Side—which, believe me, beats working on a boat every night. So okay, I sign up.

"Turns out, this club is a casino that does pretty good since the cops and the politicians are kept happy. The owner, he gets a big kick out of my act and me; I get a big kick of the gambling action. One thing leads to another and I've got this second career since I take to the croupier's stick like a baby takes to a rattle. Also I work the craps tables, the card games and my personal favorite, the board of horse-race results.

"Pretty soon I'm the big-shot manager and I'm bringing in all kinds of new business and so I got to hire more help. So I got this kid brother who's home from the war and he can't hold down a job because of the ringing in his ears, and the Veterans Hospital can't seem to do nothing about it and meanwhile he's got a wife to feed . . ."

Stein could see I was making connections. "Charlie Furman is your brother?"

"That's right," he said. "I was born Morris Furman, I changed the name to Stein when . . . Well, that gets us ahead of things."

"Go on with your story," I said.

"I start by putting Charlie 'on the fence,' what we call it. This is where he's hanging around certain blocks of East

Jefferson Boulevard with a flashlight, waiting for the right kind of cars to come by so he can guide them into the driveway to the mansion where the owner has his casino. It's easy work and the tips are great, but Charlie he can't hack it.

"Then I put him on a job stocking the bar and he can't hack that. And eventually I have him washing dishes, and even that he don't do right. The one thing he done right at the casino was one day he brings his wife in—"

"That would be Celia," I said.

"—Celia, that's right. I see right away how little brother's wife is the show-girl type, so I put her to work in the coat-check room. She then graduates to cigarette girl and I see her gliding around the place in her fishnet stockings under a little skirt and she's wearing this low-cut top that shows off plenty of curves when she leans over with her tray, you know?"

I said, "I guess you had to be there."

Stein said, "You should of seen her in them days, she'd make your heart stop."

"I've seen the type," I said. "Young and beautiful and high-spirited. Very often they wind up coming between the best of friends. In your case, even brothers."

"You get the picture."

"So Charlie doesn't work out, but Celia does," I said. "And you and Celia naturally wind up spending more and more time together."

"Charlie's off doing his painting, and also getting more and more churchy and nuts," Stein said. "But Celia, she's like me—taking to the gambling business like a baby takes to a rattle."

"So you naturally teach her everything you know."

"Naturally."

"And of course the day comes when Charlie is only getting in the way, so far as you see it," I said. "Not to mention the fact that you're pressing Celia to make up her mind between the two of you?"

"You make it sound simple, Hockaday."

"It's only simple when you say it."

"Yeah, nothing's really simple when it takes so many hard years before it's settled. And then you only *think* you got things settled."

"How do you think it settled for the three musketeers?"

"Well, Celia chose me. Only, there were these complications."

"The kind that take nine months to start throwing everybody off balance?"

"That's it."

"Who was the father? No, let me guess. Nobody knows, right?"

"You're good, Hockaday."

"So what did you do with the baby, and the little matter of Mr. and Mrs. Charlie Furman?"

"Celia and I, we had the club to run. We didn't have no time for divorces and remarriage and that kind of stuff. And we definitely didn't have no time for a baby."

"So you left baby with Charlie and took care of business."

"Yeah, and we took care of Charlie, too. I ain't saying it was right or we were proud of what we done, Celia and me, but we tried to make the most of it. We even traveled around together, the three of us, including to New York in '54, when we went out to Coney Island one day. Once Charlie saw that boardwalk, boy, he never wanted to leave."

"So he stayed?"

"Pretty much. Celia and me, we started off on our own about then, building up a string of sawdust houses from Detroit through Toledo and Cleveland and on into Pennsylvania. Places where I knew a lot of people. Oh, do you know what a sawdust house is?"

"I know."

"Celia was the one who really built the business. I concentrated on making new acquaintances, and then pretty soon we had regular casinos going. Which I then started running while Celia picked up on gambling herself."

"And got so good at it she became a big whale."

"Like I say, you're good."

I said, "And then there's some more complications in your life—the kind that involve the IRS."

"You got the answers to those kind of complications, do you, Hockaday?"

"Nobody does."

"Maybe you know the rest of the story anyhow."

"I know that the feds pressured Celia into grand jury testimony, and that nobody trusted her after that."

"That's putting it mild," Stein said. "Celia couldn't scare up a monopoly game. She never snitched once on nobody and it would have been easy, but she didn't. Out of professional honor, which is a laugh if you ask me. Anyhow, that's when even me and Celia had our complications and it's when I changed over to Stein, since Furman wasn't such a hot name to have in the gambling business no more. I had to start lying real low and go back to the magic routines, you know?"

"Until you found this place, of course," I said.

"Well, running one kind of a clip joint's pretty much like running any other kind. Only if I had my choice between a straight-out casino like upstairs and a hi ya sailor joint like I got downstairs here, hell, I'd take the casino every time, on account of that way you don't have so much female trouble."

Speaking of which, Delilah had now returned.

"Thanks a bloody hell of a lot!" she sniffed. She looked at Moe, who was still shaking a little and whose undershirt was damp with his tears and she said, "Moe, you're a goddamn mess! You ain't even dressed up in the monkey suit, and we're on in five minutes. What's been going on in here anyways?"

Stein looked at me like he wished I could somehow rescue him from Delilah, but I only said, "You hear the lady, Moe. The show must go on."

He said, "You sit here telling me that old gag? Give me a freaking break!"

I stood up.

Stein got panicky and asked, "Where do you think you're going? I thought I was getting some protection."

"What's he talking about?" Deliiah asked, wandering over to her dressing table where her blond wig waited.

Stein ignored her.

I said to Stein quietly, "Don't worry, I'll be out watching. I'm going to get a drink at the bar."

I left his dressing room then, thinking about a couple of things that Stein had failed to mention in his story. One thing I could clear up by talking with Benny. The other thing was the name of Celia's baby.

But I had already made that connection.

Hock, you got to see things my way!

I done what I done because I think everybody's got to pay to play. Ain't that right?

Damn straight!

Like it says right in the holy goddamn bible, "He that loveth not his brother abideth in death."

TWENTY-FOUR

Benny was surprised to see me back at the bar. Surprised and suspicious once again.

I ordered a red.

"I thought you was wanting to get in on the action upstairs," Benny said when he put my drink down on the bar.

"You mean the casino?"

"Yeah . . . " Benny sounded like he was sorry to have answered me so openly.

I started to say something, but I was interrupted by some loud recorded music that announced the start of The Great Morris' first set that night. I turned toward the stage and saw Delilah all dolled up in her blonde finery, and The Great Morris in his tux and top hat. Moe looked a little wobbly.

"I'm just crazy about mentalist acts," I said. Benny looked relieved the subject had changed. Which made me go right back to it. "So, you're running a gambling operation here on the premises?"

"This don't sound right," Benny said.

I reached into my suit coat and pulled out my gold shield

and dropped it on the bar. I sipped my Scotch and looked over at the stage, where The Great Morris was starting a run of card tricks and the lovely Delilah was picking out audience participants.

"What the . . ."

I introduced myself. "Detective Neil Hockaday."

"I see you ain't from Vegas after all," Benny said.

"No, you were right all along."

"What is this?"

"Oh, I was just telling your partner all about myself, how I'm a cop, what I'm working on nowadays, that sort of thing. Moe was telling me quite a bit about himself, too. And this place the two of you have got here, upstairs and downstairs."

"Why'd Moe go blabbing that to you?"

"Because I need to know if I'm going to catch his brother Charlie before Charlie comes and kills him," I said in my best deadpan. "Aren't you afraid Charlie might come kill you, too, Benny?"

"Picasso!" And now Benny had lost some of his bravado. He went a little blue and shivery, like he had been standing in a meat locker for an hour or two.

"I had a hunch you knew the connection."

Benny fingered the gun in his belt and looked around the room. "You're the cop who's hunting down that freaking lunatic?"

"Correct."

Benny turned and poured himself a Bushmill's, drank it down and asked, "Is Picasso—is Charlie Furman after Moe and me now?"

"I wouldn't be at all surprised if he's got the two of you on his list."

"That son of a bitch!"

"That's no way to talk about your partner."

"I meant Charlie, not Moe."

"You want to help Moe, and yourself?"

"Of course I do. What do you think?"

"Then you have to answer my questions, like Moe did. Otherwise, just like I told Moe, I see to it that Picasso knows the coast is clear here."

Benny drew out his .44 revolver. "He'll have one hell of an argument on his hands!"

I laughed at him. "Do you really think Picasso cares about getting shot? Picasso's all about taking certain people down in flames. People like you, Benny. Get it? You shoot him, it'll be the last thing you do in this life."

This held a certain logic for Benny, who slowly put his revolver back in his belt. Candi came by with a drink order and winked at me. Benny filled the order and I glanced over at the stage. The Great Morris was blindfolded and guessing at objects volunteers from the audience held up in their hands. Every so often, laughter would break out.

I asked Benny, "How's he do that?"

"You mean Moe?"

"Yeah. How's he get the right object?"

"Delilah gives him the clue. She puts a little emphasis on a certain word, which will have a letter beginning with what the object in question is. There ain't too much variation to the play. Guys only have a certain few things they carry around in their pockets, you know."

"Well, that's simple."

"It all is," Benny said. "Including the saps in the audience."

"Interesting."

"Mind if I ask you something?" Benny said.

"What?"

"How come you ain't calling in the paddy wagons to bust up our action here?"

"It's a matter of priorities, Benny. First things first, you know? The first thing I'm trying to do is prevent you or

Moe—or both of you—from being pictures of dead meat on the front page of the *Post.*"

"That's the kind of priorities I like."

"Enlightened self-interest, your partner's sentiments exactly," I said. "That's why we were having such a productive heart-to-heart back in Moe's dressing room—up until show time anyway. Unfortunately, we got cut off just when I needed to know something real important. Which is where you're going to chime in, Benny. Okay?"

"I don't know."

"Oh, I'm sure you do. After all, you know all of The Great Morris' trade secrets and you don't mind giving them away to me. Seems the least you can do to help me catch the lunatic Picasso and keep your own ass alive is to break a few more minor confidences."

"Well, when you put it like that."

I asked him straight out, "How come you and Moe opened the casino upstairs?"

Benny sighed. "It ain't none of my bright idea, I can tell you that. Remember how I told you my genius partner's all the time feeling sorry for certain ones?"

"Yes. Delilah, and Candi . . ."

"Yeah, and his brother's old lady, too."

"Celia."

"I suppose you know her whole story?"

"Enough of it."

"Well, then maybe you know how she needed big money pretty bad?"

"That, and a way to get it in a hurry."

"Did you also hear how she got blacklisted from the gambling circuit, where she was a big whale and all?"

"I heard."

"Well, so there's the answer. Don't you see?"

"I guess I don't."

"Moe talked me into opening a place here so Celia could

inally shoot craps again after all the years she had to lay low ıerself. I mean, where else's she going to get action in the vhole freaking world but here in a joint where her ever-oving old softhearted brother-in-law's in charge?"

"She could have gone to Vegas," I said. "Or Atlantic City, ır Amsterdam."

"Don't be such a hayseed, Hockaday. You think them ılaces is democracies?"

Benny held up the bottle of Johnnie Walker and I nodded ınd he poured me another red. He watched The Great Morris perform while I sipped my drink and thought about he simple reason he had just given me for laying the Horny ʾoodle open to all the risk—and expense—that came with :asino gambling.

The music got frantic up on stage and I turned to see)elilah blindfolding Moe. Then Benny reached into his ıocket for his bifocals and said, "Well, there's my cue for vloe's piece-a-resistence."

I could see Delilah handing The Great Morris one of two ıig writing pads, and then one of two felt markers. Then I :aw her take the other pad and marker and wander out into he crowd.

Benny explained, "Some sap in the audience's going to lraw a picture of something and then Delilah'll hold it up ʾor everybody to see. And then, presto! The Great Morris, nentalist extraordinary, will draw the same thing."

"Pretty slick."

"Aw, it's a real crowd pleaser."

"How's he do it?"

"Simple technology," Benny said. He reached into his ;hirt pocket and pulled out an electronic voice transmitter he size and shape of a cigarette lighter. "See this?"

"And Moe's got a receiver?"

"Sure. It's a little bean in his ear."

"And so you just stand back here at the bar . . ."

"Watching what Delilah holds up, that's right."

"And then you describe it," I said. "Very, very slick—and simple."

"Simple as pie."

I saw now that Delilah was holding up a pad, and walking back toward the lighted stage to display it to the crowd. And to Benny and his bifocals. I could not make out the drawing myself.

"What is it?" I asked Benny.

Benny did not answer. I turned to him and asked again, "What's the picture?"

He said, "This don't seem right."

I grabbed his arm. "What's wrong?"

"It's a picture of this guy . . . in a top hat and a tuxedo like Moe . . . and his face, it's shot full of bullets, I guess."

I grabbed Benny's transmitter from his hand and said to him, "This is it!"

"Oh shit! What'll we do?"

"You call 911 and tell them we've got assault with a deadly weapon in progress; tell them you're calling for Hockaday. You got that?"

"Yeah, okay." Benny ran for the telephone.

Then I headed across the room toward the stage. I did not run. I looked over the crowd at the tables ringing the stage. I did not see a gun barrel anywhere.

I flipped the transmitter switch to open mic and whispered into it, "Moe, this is Hockaday speaking. Listen very carefully to me. When I tell you, I want you to drop down flat on the stage. Just drop flat. He's after you, Moe. Do what I say. Now!"

Stein dropped.

A gun fired.

There was a howling mix of male and female screams. Chairs and tables scraped the floor, falling over with thuds. Screaming men ran.

Another shot.

The sound of police sirens in the street.

Now the panicking customers were gone from the tables
that ringed the stage, leaving in that clearing a small and
unsuspecting—and familiar—figure. I saw him raise a
pistol in two hands and take aim at Moe, sprawled on the
stage, blindfolded and screaming. Delilah backed away from
Stein, holding two hands over her mouth.

I called to the man with the gun, "Big Stuff!"

The dwarf reeled, and spotted me.

I pulled out my .38 and bulled my way through a line of
screaming customers, toward the dwarf. I called his name
again, "Big Stuff!"

He saw my gun now, his eyes went wild. He tucked his
head and ran at a right angle from me, toward the bar. I
shouted, "Halt!" But he kept running, with the pistol in his
hands.

I turned and chased him and called out, over and over,
"Halt! Police!"

I tried, but I could not get a clear shot at him. The crowd
was too thick and Big Stuff was too low to the floor.

Cops were pouring into the place now. Customers started
freezing in place.

I got nearer to Big Stuff.

He turned and saw me. His face was twisted in shock and
fear.

He raised the pistol at me.

"Don't do it!" I shouted.

But I could see he meant to surrender his weapon, that he
had no intention of shooting me.

But Benny did not see it that way. He fired one shot of his
.44 revolver.

Big Stuff crumpled at the waist, stumbled forward a few
steps toward me. Then he fell facedown on the floor.

I ran to him and stood over his misshapen body, my legs
straddling his back. I held my gold shield high above my
head so the uniforms could easily make me. About ten of

them formed a circle around Big Stuff and me. I saw the others fanning out through the club.

I grabbed the shoulder of a sergeant and pointed him in the direction of the stage, where Delilah stood trembling. "Put the collar on her," I told him. "She's in on this."

Then I knelt to the floor. I saw that Big Stuff had taken the shot in his lower back, and I saw the blood flowing freely from his mouth and nose.

I touched his face.

Big Stuff turned his head and looked up at me with one eye, knowing that he would soon shut it forever. I said, "Don't move."

One of the uniforms put in a call for paramedics on his point-to-point hip radio.

Big Stuff hissed at me, "Lean down here."

I put my face down near his and said, "Go ahead, tell me."

His words came in sprays of blood. "We had reasons for what we done. Coney Island reasons, you understand?"

I lied to the dying man. "I understand."

Big Stuff smiled a bloody smile. "It's all we have anymore. We're trying to hang on. See? Coney Island reasons." He was slipping fast.

Quickly, I lied again. "I should go tell her it's all over now."

He said, "Yes . . . over . . ."

"Where is she, Big Stuff?"

He said, "Want a laugh? I loved her. I'd do anything for that crazy woman."

"Where is she, Big Stuff? Tell me."

The dwarf's last words were, "With him, in the old slaughterhouse. Where else?"

TWENTY-FIVE

I had a squad car run me over to my apartment.

Ruby was there, reading a book.

I kissed her, then I telephoned Neglio at his home. I was happy to get his answering machine. I said, "I'm going in after Picasso."

Then I changed out of my suit into jeans, boots, a sweatshirt and a jacket. I strapped on a second shoulder holster for my .44 and I filled my pockets with three sets of bracelets and extra bullets for both the .38 and the .44.

Ruby stared at me.

"It looks worse than it is," I said.

"That's a damn lie," she said.

"When I come back, we'll talk about taking a trip, all right?"

"I'll be waiting."

Did she know how good those words sounded? Does anybody besides a cop know?

I picked up a flashlight from out of a drawer in the sideboard and left.

* * *

Standing in front of it now, I could only think how I should have known. I should have known from the day Picasso told me about the bodega windows, and the fear he had so proudly captured in the pig's eye. If not then, I should surely have known after the murder in that bodega.

Like Ruby said, *"Right under your nose—right here in Hell's Kitchen."*

Like Big Stuff said, *"Where else?"*

Where else but the old kosher slaughterhouse hugging a desolate stretch of Eleventh Avenue, between Thirty-eighth and Thirty-seventh Streets?

I had walked all around the place, figuring where Picasso might have made his door and where in the big old hulk he had set up his studio. Probably somewhere on the north side, I told myself; artists like working in north light, the truest light. The door was probably a hole, covered by some salvaged piece.

I looked up now at the wide gateways that once were filled by wooden chutes and screams of dumb fear, now sealed with cement and cinder block; ten stout floors in all, windows shuttered over in tin; and the big terra-cotta busts of ring-muzzled hogs and lambs and steers set high along the old red-brick walls. And all of it coated gray from the perpetual swirl of exhaust grime from the Lincoln Tunnel traffic.

There was a steel trash bin set against the limestone base of the rear wall. I pushed past it to find the opening, a small triangular gap punched between two sections of crumbled brick. I bent, flashed light inside, and startled a rat. Then I hunched my shoulders and exhaled, and squeezed my way into the black insides.

I stood in heavy darkness and waited for my eyes to adjust, and my ears.

Now came fading echoes. And furtive scratchings from interior walls alive with vermin. I drew out my big piece, the .44 Charter Arms Bulldog in my shoulder holster. This I held in my right hand. With my left, I swept my surroundings with the flashlight beam.

I had entered a wide corridor beneath an iron staircase. Down the corridor and beyond the stairs was a line of tall hollow spaces, each the size of a large door. A bank of elevators must have been there years ago.

I directed the flashlight beam up along the staircase rails and disturbed a nest of bats clinging upside-down to an asbestos-covered pipe. The animals dropped through the dank air in frenzied loops. I covered my head and moved forward, and headed up the stairs.

Near the top of the first flight, a rusted step gave way. My leg sank into a hole and pain filled my knee. From that point on, I tested each riser before putting down my full weight. And I walked along the edges of the steps, close against the wall, the way a good burglar will quietly stalk through an unfamiliar room.

At the fourth floor, there was the strong odor of cats—male cats who had sprayed urine to mark their territories. Anybody living in this place was sure to have cats about to control rodents.

I went up one more floor where the cat odor was strongest. Then I moved toward the north side of the building, through a hallway where there once might have been offices full of people with work to do. Emptiness and stillness now, and all the doors gone but one.

The single remaining door was closed. On it was written:

HOME IS WHERE
THE HATRED IS

I knocked. There was no answer. I kicked the door, and it fell open stiffly.

At least a dozen cats were in the big room beyond the door—backs arched, yellow-green eyes wide, fangs bared, throats hissing and growling.

Then, something cold and hard poked at my neck.

And a ragged whisper: "Hang onto your rosary beads and say good bye!"

I shot my hands up into the air. The flashlight fell to the floor, rolled around and settled against a stack of newspapers shaped like a chair.

I recognized the voice, of course. From the taffy stand on Stillwell Avenue, from the Carny Club. From the times she had said in parting, *"God bless."* I could see her puffy pink face and her hair the color of scrambled eggs, and her eyes done up like a pair of chocolate cupcakes.

"You don't want to shoot," I said. "Who would tell the world of your father's great works?"

"My father?"

"May I turn around now, Evie?"

She said, "So, you know?"

"I'm turning around now," I said, moving slowly. She withdrew the gun at my neck, but kept it pointed at my chest. I said to her, "I've got some bad news for you."

"You must be crazy. I'm standing here with a gun on you."

"Oh, but you won't shoot," I said. "Not me. Your father wants me to know; he *picked* me to know, didn't he?"

Evie lowered the gun, the second one I had faced in the last thirty minutes. I quickly said a silent prayer of thanks.

Evie said, "What bad news?"

"Big Stuff is dead."

She put a hand over her heart and her eyes welled up with tears.

I told her what had happened at the Horny Poodle, and I said I understood the Coney Island reasons behind all else that had happened. And it was the beginning of the truth I was speaking now.

"You tell me the reasons, Evie," I said. "Tell me you understand, too."

She said simply, "The paintings needed to come true.

verybody's going to know him now. They can't forget
bout him now."

"That's right," I said. "And now it's over, Evie."

"Yes."

"Are you glad?"

"Yes. I'll see the face of God now."

"Will you first hand me that gun?"

She turned it over to me and said, "See how nice I do what
ou say? I'm not some maniac like they say in the papers."
nd I offered up my second silent prayer, this one to the
atron saint of the mentally impaired.

I asked, "Is your father here somewhere?"

She looked up. "He's in his studio, praying."

"Why is he praying, Evie?"

"He's praying for the Lord my soul to take. You see, I told
im what I done . . ."

"He had no idea, did he?"

"Papa painted his pictures. I made them come true."

I took a pair of NYPD bracelets out from a pocket and
aid, "You probably know, I have to arrest you now."

"Yes," Evie said. And then there was a dream in her voice.
They knoweth not what they do, O Father . . ."

I cuffed Evie's plump hands behind her. Then I stepped
ver to where the flashlight had fallen, picked it up and
hined it on her.

"I'm going to read you your rights, Evie. Listen carefully
ow, okay?"

She nodded. I found my Miranda warning card in my
allet and put light on it and read her. After I had finished, I
aused. "You made the pictures come true, is that right?" I
sked finally.

"First, I killed *her.*"

"Celia, your mother?"

"Yes. She was a harlot from Hades."

"And then you killed Dr. Reiser?"

"I made Papa's picture come true."

"And Benito Reyes at the bodega?"

"I made Papa's picture come true."

"And then Johnny Halo?"

"Big Stuff helped me. He hated Johnny bad."

"Why?"

"He was jealous of Johnny and me."

"Jealous?"

"I was trying to save Johnny Halo's soul is all, trying to get him to give his life to God, like I give my life to God . . ."

"And so you'd sometimes go up to Halo's room at the Seashore, to try saving him?"

"That's right. Big Stuff, he took it all wrong."

"And Big Stuff was in love with you, wasn't he?"

Evie laughed at me. "Don't be so surprised. Maybe I ain't your type, Hockaday. It don't mean nobody else can love me."

"No, of course not."

I took a couple of seconds to think. "So you and Big Stuff took down Johnny Halo and put him on that cross, at the church?"

"We had to. Johnny wouldn't come home to God. Besides, Big Stuff found out he was nothing but a liar. And there was Papa's painting I had to make come true."

"How did you get into the church?"

"I got a key since I'm one of the big shots in the congregation."

"The Reverend Miracle?"

"Billy-Boy didn't have nothing to do with it, if that's what you're asking. Big Stuff and me, we did it to Halo one night on that dark block where the Horny Poodle is, then we carted him to the church, where he should of gone in the first place like I told him."

"And of course, you really needed Big Stuff's help when it came to doing Moe Stein," I said.

"I couldn't very well go into that Horny Poodle place

myself," Evie said. "I'm a Christian and a lady, I don't go into evil places full of harlots."

"You had a real problem on your hands."

"Yeah, but when I showed Papa's drawing of Moe Stein to Big Stuff he figured a plan. He goes to the club a few times and he seen his old pal from Coney, Delilah. He talks her into the big gag of picking him from the audience. She don't even know what's happening, Hockaday."

"I see."

Evie said, "But I guess it's like you say—all over now."

"Yes."

"I'm going to see the face of God."

"Let's go see your father first."

"Okay."

I followed Evie out the door and back to the staircase. She said, "It's all the way up to the top."

We climbed to the tenth floor. I steadied Evie by holding onto her arm since her hands were cuffed behind her. We walked past the row of hollow spaces where elevators used to be, then to a north room with a door. We could hear Picasso's voice on the other side.

"He's in there," Evie said. She started backing away from me.

"Stay here," I told her.

But she kept on walking, backward toward one of the tall hollow spaces.

I ran to her and reached to grab her in the dark, but felt nothing except a whoosh of air as Evie fell back into the hollow space, then down ten floors to her death. She made no sounds in her descent, only a thud at the end of her fall that echoed heavily upward through the dark maze of a deserted slaughterhouse.

My heart raced and I felt faint. I put my hand up against a wall and rested.

Then I went to Picasso's door and pushed it open.

There were candles burning everywhere—on the sills of the big windows, on the floor, on top of stacks of rubbish, on easels holding murder tableaux yet to come true: Wendell Prescott with a knife in his heart, Benny's severed kidney-bean head sitting on a bar.

On the far wall was a large canvas, about six-feet square. And there stood Picasso in front of it, a cassette tape recorder in his left hand and a .22-caliber revolver in his painting hand.

"I figured you'd find your way," Picasso said.

"Are you ready to come with me?" I asked him.

He said to an imaginary friend, "He says am I ready, can you beat it? Ho, ho, am I ready!"

Then to me, "She says if I paint it it's going to come true."

"I know. Evie told me all about it."

"So you two met. She's really nutso, ain't she?"

"Yes."

"The poor kid. I ain't nowhere near as nutso as poor Evie."

"No."

"She got things way out of hand, Hock. So I had to lay low here."

"I see. But I'm here and it's all over now."

He said to somebody who was not there, "Can you beat it, this one he says, *'It's all over now'!'*"

Then to me Picasso said, "The sins of the father are visited on the son, Hock. Ain't you never heard that one? Or maybe you never had a sinful father."

"I had a father," I said. "I never knew him."

"If he was anything like me, you're better off."

Then Picasso turned and pressed the left side of his head against the big blank canvas on the wall. He raised the revolver in his right hand, put the barrel into his ear and popped off three shots.

The cassette recorder fell from his hand and clattered

across the floor toward me. His body slumped, then slid down the canvas. His head oozed blood.

A few inches below the top edge of the canvas were the three tiny bullet holes. And an explosion of wet red and gray that streaked downward, dripping to the floor where the artist lay.

I shined my flashlight on black letters that were painted along the bottom of the canvas. Dry black lettering applied days ago to spell out the title of Picasso's last piece: SELF-PORTRAIT IN BRAINS.

EPILOGUE

*They say when you come to New York you ought to bring
your own body-outline chalk.*

*Also they say life's messy but death don't do nothing much
to tidy it up.*

That's two jokes I am floating around Hell.

Which is where I am, Hock. Home-sweet-Hell.

It's been nice chatting with you.

So long, suckers!

I switched off the tape recorder. It had taken me three full
days to go through all that Picasso had left behind in his
slaughterhouse studio, hours and hours of his general observations, his explanations, his Bible quotations.

This was the remaining quiet business of the case I had to
wrap up. Meanwhile, Inspector Neglio and the mayor and
the tabloids took care of the noisy business of claiming that
New York was back to normal. Slattery's assurances in the
Post came under the heading: "Maniac Duo Dies in Horror
Hole—Father-Daughter Reign of Terror Over!"

When I had finished with the tapes, I saw to it that Moe

and Benny were taken off in manacles for arraignment on illegal gaming charges. And then I dropped by to visit Wendell Prescott, just to tell him I was onto his connection with the late Johnny Halo and that if he did not care to do me two simple favors I would have a talk with Slattery about the mafia figure he kept for company in his Coney Island real estate deals.

"What do you want out of me, Hock?"

"I want you to very carefully dismantle Picasso's masterpiece at the Fire and Brimstone out in Coney, then I want you to truck it into Manhattan and put it all back together again, on display at the nicest Soho gallery you can find."

"Are you as crazy as him?"

"No, but you are, Prescott, if you don't take advantage of the tremendous price you could get for it, what with all the notoriety."

"Well, when you put it like that—"

"I thought that part would be easy for you," I said. "But there's something else."

"What?"

"There's a prostitute who works at the Seashore Hotel in Coney, another one of your properties. You'll find her in the lobby most times; her name is Chastity."

"Oh boy!"

"I want you to set her up in Johnny Halo's old rooms, rent free, for the rest of her life."

"I'm not going to do that."

"Should I call up Slattery now?"

"What's her name again?"

After I was through with the remaining police business, it was time to settle some personal accounts. So I first dropped by a travel agency in the McGraw-Hill building on Forty-second Street to book a pair of round-trip tickets aboard Aer Lingus, JFK to Dublin.

And then Ruby met me for dinner that night at Angelo's Ebb Tide.

"I want you to meet my Uncle Liam," I said, handing Ruby one of the tickets.

"I'll go with you, Hock," she said. "But tell me there's something else to it besides making the acquaintance of an old Irish gentleman."

"Maybe I wouldn't like it said that I live like a bear with furniture."

She kissed me. "Maybe that's a good enough answer for now."

But then a great serious concern spread over Ruby's face. She said, "I'd love to see where your people come from, where your father came from. Wouldn't you, Hock?"

I did not answer her for a while. I heard my mother's words, the only ones there in my hollow place. *"Your papa went off in a mist, that's all there is to it. It hurts too much to speak of him as if he was ever flesh and blood and bone to me."*

I only said to Ruby, "I think I would . . ."

She said, "That's a funny answer."

I said, "Isn't it, though?"